A Russian Mafia saga. Joe's Beginning.

Czarina

Eva

A

Novel

Mike Seigler

Copyright

Contents

Chapter 1

A dark cold night on the outskirts of Moscow, a BMW parks in front of a residential building. Two big men emerge from the car and approach the front doors. One has a key that he uses, and they enter. They walk across the old faded lobby to the elevators. They stop; one takes out a cell phone and speaks quickly in Russian. He closes the phone and nods to the other man. They use the elevator when it arrives.

On the tenth floor, they hear noises emitting from the apartments they walk past. At door number ten-twenty-nine, they stop and pause in front of it. Down the hallway, a door opens, and a woman looks out with wide eyes. One-man pulls out a gun and puts a finger to his lips. The woman nods quickly and closes her door. They turn their attention back to the door.

They look at each other and put on ski masks. They glance down the hallway in both direction as they screw silencers on their handguns and nod when finished. The man on the right takes a key out of his pocket; he insets it in the door lock and quietly turns it. He withdraws the key and puts it back in his pocket and nods. Then quickly, he opens the door; they enter guns forward. They stand, look and listen. The room is dark. They hear laughter coming from another room. They look and go toward the noise.

They stand on either side of the closed door. One-man counts to three with his fingers. At three, he opens the door and goes forward fast and off to the right side. The second man breaks to the left. They stop and quickly survey the room. Man and woman nude on a large bed with the TV on.

The couple immediately look up at both men. The man to the right puts a bullet in the women's head before she could scream. Her friend visibly shocked has blood splatter on his face. He pushes the women aside and looks from one masked man to another. The man on the left holds a finger to his lips and the man on the bed nods slowly. The right man picks up a pile of clothes and tosses them on the bed. He motions for the man to dress. Visibly shaking the man on the bed slowly obliges.

The men nod their heads in satisfaction. One takes out a cell phone and quickly presses a number and says something. They hold their weapons on the man getting dressed.

Chapter 2

A few hours later, a black SUV and a black BMW drove slowly along a darkened road. The two vehicles take a turn on another rough dirt road, then onto another. They stop in front of a large building the Soviet Army formerly used. It fell into disrepair as the old government ended and the new government did not need it. Ten buildings are in the complex. Now the ownership was a murky company that paid the right officials, and nobody cared.

The occupants exited the SUV with automatic weapons scanning the area, and then disappeared into the darkness to create a secure area around the building. They protected the larger perimeter.

A man and women then exited the BMW. They entered the building and walked down a hallway that emptied into a large area that used to be a mess hall. The man leads the way the lady right behind. They head to a well-lit area that had a man tied to a chair. He has a blindfold on and his head is hanging toward his chest.

The men standing guard all nod to the man and the lady. She slowly nods back, and then sets her eyes on the man tied to the chair. Everybody stopped and stared at him. The lady motions to the man. He steps over, grabs a handful of the man's hair and yanks his head then let it go. The man in the chair shook his head and yelled. "Fuck." He worked his tied hands and wiggled in the chair.

"Fuck!" He yelled again and moved his head around. The lady stepped into the lit area.

"Hi, Andre."

Andre stop moving his head after hearing the voice.

"Eva, what's going on here?" He asked with a shaky voice.

The man, Ivan, kept his eyes fixed on Andre.

He starts immediately. "It's not easy information to get. I do not want to get suspicious. It'll be bad for me if the others figure out you understand. A sure death for me."

His voice was pleading and that did not help him now to get his point across. The problems he was having did not influence Eva in the slightest. He showed weakness and that she did not like or the man himself.

"You're taking my money and living well. I ask for updates and I do not get any. I want meetings to keep me updated and you make excuses. I hear you're with women having fun; not a care for what you should be doing. Now you are afraid for your life with the Red Mob when you should dread me."

Eva steps closer to Andre pointing with a knife that appeared out of nowhere. A trademark of Eva's that surprises no one present.

Everybody locks eyes on the knife inches away from Andre's face. A collective thought to all present was that, blood is going to spill because Eva rarely pulls a knife without using it.

"I have tried to serve you well, Eva. I will accept whatever you decide. Please remember, I am one person between two enemies and it is a difficult task to please each." Andre said nervously.

"You owe me. You owe me. Money and I want it in cash or information or your blood, and, I'm not your enemy. You gave your loyalty to the Red Mob and now they are your enemy. You confuse me, Andre."

Andre nodded nervously.

"I want to know what Ureinchencko is doing." Eva shouted with the knife inches from his face. Andre did not see this.

"Yes, I will do that, and I don't see you as an enemy." Andre stammered.

Eva eased for a moment. She then did a pirouette as her arm with the knife darted forward then stopped. She stood looking down on Andre. A delayed response at first, and then he let out a scream. The slice across his chest went through his clothing and blood was starting to seep out. Andre screamed more as he looked down toward his chest. She continued to look down at him with an evil smile.

"I think you understand me now, Andre."

Andre nodded his head nervously and moaned with pain.

Eva turned and walked past everybody with Ivan behind her. She looked at the blade of her knife, no blood on it. She liked that, closed the blade, and slid it back into the secret pocket in her clothing.

They left the building and walked back to the waiting vehicles. She stopped as Ivan opened the BMW's back door.

"I hope he gets the point now," Eva said with a sly smirk. Ivan nodded. Giggling she climbed back into the car. Ivan closed the door.

The BMW took off and Eva tapped Ivan on the shoulder. He turned and looked at her. "Setup a meeting this week with the emissaries for Friday in New York."

Ivan stared for a moment, and then turned back forward. His phone was out, and he was talking fast. Eva now had the full import of the pills in her body and it felt good.

Chapter 3

Thousands of miles away in New Jersey the only call Joe Bergen wanted was from his wife. They been trying to have a child for five years. What with the tests and ovulation timing, he was tired. Carol mentioned adopting but Joe was not open to it. The mention of it a few years ago had put him in a depression. He did not want to feel a failure. He told her more than once. If this test came back negative, he would have to give adopting some thought he knew.

Joe pushed from his desk, got up and stood near the window of his corner office. He looked out at the view of New York City far in the distance. Then narrowed his view to the parking lot full of cars and the sign that read, Bergen Foods.

Joe had some down times in the business, recently a national food service company took away some of his best customers. Being a competitive business by nature that didn't bother him.

He reflected on the success of his business. He started in a small warehouse and five years later, he bought it, more than ten years ago. Today, Joe did not have to worry much about money. From five floors, up, he smiled down on his new Lexus.

The phone buzzed gently and that brought him back to his desk from his daydreaming. Maybe that was his wife with some good news.

"Yes Cheryl."

"I have a call from a Mr. Goldberg. He's from the law firm of Goldberg Steinhardt. He didn't state his business. Would you like to take this call?"

"A law firm, yes I'll take it. Thank you, Cheryl."

Joe sat behind his desk and lifted the receiver. "Hello, Joe Bergen here."

"A good morning sir. I'm Julius Goldberg from the firm of the same name. A client of mine is interested in buying your business. Sorry if I'm getting down to it fast." He chuckled, then stopped for a beat; Joe kept the phone to his ear and leaned forward resting each elbow on his desk. Julius continued. "I don't like talking on the phone with matters like these."

Joe decided to use that pause. "I don't know. My business is not for sale, though I will listen to your client's offer." Not what Joe wanted to say.

"Good. I'll take that as we can meet for a lunch."

Joe did not like being forced into situations, but he did have enough free time.

He supposed this would be fine. He won't be signing anything. Won't hurt to listen.

"I have noon tomorrow free."

"Excellent. I'm sure you know the Empire restaurant in Manhattan. They have fine food and private booths, so we can speak freely."

"Yes, they are a frequent customer."

"Excellent, say noon tomorrow. I'll have a table waiting."

"Okay, I want to repeat my business is not for sale, but I will listen."

"Yes, I understand and will not persuade you into anything you don't want. The client hired me to make an offer."

"Very good I'll see you tomorrow Mr. Goldberg."

"Yes, noon tomorrow."

A thought came to Joe. That national chain that took some of his customers?

"One question. Who is your client?"

"I will reveal that when we meet. As I said, I don't discuss details over the phone."

That put a hook into Joe. He was going tomorrow.

"Okay then Mr. Goldberg. See you tomorrow."

"Yes, and a pleasant day to you Mr. Bergen."

Joe placed the phone down slowly and leaned back in the chair. He sat staring for a moment at nothing. Unexpectedly somebody wants to buy my business. Is it another larger warehouse chain wanting to expand with his customer base? Of course, somebody larger. He knew he has customers that another wants. And, they be willing to pay?

Staring at the ceiling tiles he wondered what it would be like to retire at age thirty-five.

Chapter 4

A tap on the door brought Joe to reality. It was Thom Heller, Joe's CFO and next in command. He had been working for him since buying the business and knew he is a wizard in the finance department.

Seeing him, Joe felt a bit guilty. He paid Thom well over the years and he was a loyal employee. That unspoken loyalty promised him a job for life with a few others here. He knew he would not be here today without a few key employees.

Thom took a seat in a side chair and looked at Joe with big eyes. "I have some good news. That French place in the city has been paying on time so I decided to extend them a line of credit. It'll bring us more business."

Thom's look remained, Joe noted. Cheryl always kept the right people informed he knew.

"Thom, you told me this last week." Joe said smiling.

A slight sheepish look now appeared on

Thom's face. Joe continued. "I guess the rumors are starting."

"Joe, you know I would never stoop to listening to rumors."

Thom then put on an innocent look that made Joe laugh and sit up straight with elbows on his desk.

"All right, I guess you know a lawyer called. He's representing an unnamed client, who is interested in making an offer for my business. I'll find out more at lunch tomorrow."

Joe shrugged his shoulders then continued. "I've never thought about selling, but I'll listen. It'll tell me how valuable this place is." Joe smiled realizing that Carol had not called, the smile went away.

"Hey, I'll be coming to you tomorrow afternoon for advice as usual and we'll have a good laugh at the offer."

"Joe, your name is on the front of this building. Never feel you owe me or anyone else here an explanation. Now this Goldberg is a high-priced lawyer with prominent clients in the business world. I did a fast Bing. I would suggest you listen well and think. Someone big who will pay generously?"

"Thanks Thom, despite what you say there are a few of you here I owe big time."

Thom stared a moment then stood. "I got work to do if you are going to sit here and wallow in pity for us."

Thom stopped at the doorway and turned

around with a wide grin on his face. Joe seeing this gave him the five fingers off his nose, the Polish salute

Chapter 5

The next morning a private car and driver car sped along the New Jersey Turnpike heading to an exit for the Lincoln tunnel that goes to New York City. Joe did not see a need to bring any papers. It's an informal meeting to hear what the client intended to offer. He wanted to learn who the client was. Then present a bid of his own way too high, of course. He continued to look out at the New Jersey landscape passing by.

It will amount to an enjoyable and pleasant trip to New York City for the afternoon. When he returned later, he would play with the guessing game at first, lightly. He knew some were stressed. He depended on the warehouse running solid, so the employees can provide for their families.

Joe thought about his wife. Carol. She was depressed when he got home yesterday. It was the usual response when the pregnancy test results were negative. She went to bed early, which left him and the TV as friends. He needed to stop this up and down every few months and decide what would help Carol. The thought of adoption depressed him as much as her having a negative test. This routine cannot go on, he knew.

He was up early, and she was still asleep. She probably did not know where he was going today. It always takes a few days for her to recover; Joe knew that Carol is not a strong-willed person and hoped she could try a little bit longer. Adopting was the final choice he knew. Joe wanted more time to face that choice.

The car came out of the Lincoln tunnel and into daylight of New York City. The driver took the dense city traffic casually.

A while later the car parked in front of the Empire restaurant. A five-star. The price of a meal would make a typical wage earner gasp. A restaurant that only survives in New York City.

The restaurant was cozy, with a private feeling that Joe liked. Attention to every detail with professional service.

The maître d' immediately recognized Joe. The man's face brightened when he saw him. They shook hands.

"Lowe, how's business."

"Good. As you can see, Mr. Bergen."

Joe quickly glanced around the establishment and agreed. "Yes, I'm here to meet a Mr. Goldberg. Has he arrived yet?"

Lowe immediately looked at Joe seriously. He knew most people who dined at the restaurant and their livelihood. Joe interpreted the look to mean that Thom was correct. He is a high-powered corporate lawyer.

"Yes, he is, if you would follow me."

Joe followed Lowe through the maze of tables and private booths. Normally a waiter takes customers to their table, but in Joe's case the maître d', did this, and it showed respect.

They reached a private booth; Joe never sat in a private booth. He liked to be at an open table, so he could see the customers enjoying their meals. In a booth he felt hidden. Lowe nodded and left but Joe could see the wheels turning in his head.

An impeccably dressed man squeezed out of the booth. He towered a good foot over Joe. A bear of a hand extended toward him.

"Julius Goldberg, glad you came."

The man had a casual look about him with an aristocratic face.

"Joe Bergen glad to meet you."

"Excellent, let's talk, and see what happens."

They squeezed into the booth. Mr. Goldberg took a moment longer because of his size.

Julius began. "As I said on the phone an interested party wants to expand their market share in the food service business. Now, they are prepared to offer fifteen times your annual earnings." Julius paused. "They would also want you to stay on in your present position for an unspecified time that

I'm sure would be open for discussion."

Julius relaxed back when the waiter came to take orders for drinks. Each declined. Not now, Joe thought. He did take a gulp of water and tried to keep calm.

He quickly calculated millions, tens of millions. Joe absorbed the possible price and regrouped his thoughts.

"All right, that sounds good. Who's the interested party?"

"XO Food group," Julius said without hesitation then started looking casually around the restaurant.

He kept up with industry news and remembered hearing that name before.

"Sounds familiar." Joe asked.

Julius smiled. "They are a private company slowly expanding into the restaurant service, supply business. They are a division of a much larger global business enterprise."

Joe was somewhat overwhelmed as his brain worked in overtime. He entertained offers for one-third of what this outfit was offering. Why the great offer?

Joe watched Julius as he drank a sip of his water. He then casually looked around the restaurant and spoke. "Like I said, they are prepared to offer you fifteen times your annual earnings. If you need time to think, then please do. The money I am sure is a generous offer. That is what they hired me to say."

Joe looked at the carved wood that

bordered the booth. His thoughts were starting to wander. He did not know how to take this, the offer. Time to retire? He needed time to think.

"Well, I am interested and do have some questions." Joe said as his eyes came back to Julius.

"Okay. Now I will contact XO and let them know you are willing to talk. They will take over."

"All right, I will take the next step. Sounds good for now." Joe hesitated a beat. "I have loyal employees who helped put me where I am today. I do have concerns for their future."

Joe saw this did not faze Julius. The man continued looking around the restaurant.

"I do have many pampered clients; maybe that's what attracts this XO Company." Joe said absentmindedly.

Julius glanced at him and smiled. Then said. "They'll sell themselves on this deal. I do some of their business dealings. Now, if you need a good corporate lawyer to review the deal, I can recommend a few. Just give me a call." Julius reached into his jacket and pulled out a business card. Joe read then put it in his own jacket pocket.

"I do have one over in New Jersey for my corporate business. Thanks just the same."

Julius nodded. Not the least bothered. Joe supposed he made a handsome paycheck for a phone call and a meal.

Joe continued. "I need to think on this.

It's like a child that I raised and now I might let go. I don't know whether I should."

Julius moved in his seat and looked pleasantly bored. "I am sure they will let you stay with your child," he said kindheartedly.

"Yes, well, but the employees are a concern of mine. I hope this outfit does not cut costs too deeply to make their money-back." Joe noticed a move Julius made, as if to laugh. "They are good people. They helped me build what I have today."

"I suggest you take the money and have some fun. A house on a beach on a warm tropical island." Julius said with a laugh. Joe nodded and smiled.

"Time to order." Julius raised a hand and their waiter immediately appeared. Joe looked at an executive sitting in a booth direct from theirs. The man had his briefcase opened next to him and a cell phone in his ear. A meal was setting in front of him and his mouth did not stop talking in the cell phone.

Joe realized that retirement might not be half-bad. He and Carol would be fine on one-hundred fifty million. No children though? That thought started to take the high out of him.

Chapter 6

The nighttime illumination of the Kremlin was magical. Most people never see that view from a passing car or low-level building. Eva though had her private view of that scene every day. Her personal apartment was the top four floors of a residential building that sat closet to the Kremlin. There's been offers of outrageous money, but she would never sell her most cherished view eighty floors up. She had many properties globally but here she loved.

Eva sat on the white leather sofa with her legs up on the ottoman admiring the great view. She did this occasionally when needing to think through problems or just for the view itself. Tonight, though she waited word on a business deal before she could go make her usual journey to visit her Aunt Catherine. She needed confirmation that this deal would go through because she needed this information to tell her Aunt. Eva stood and walked to the wall of windows. She traced the onion tops of St. Basil's on the glass.

Aunt Catherine was the family patriarch and her word either completed or dissolved a deal. A shrewd woman who ran a global empire that consisted of laundering money. Illicit money needed to be back into the system legally. One mistake would raise questions. These days of terrorism have changed the rules. The illegal gains came from many sources, drugs, real estate, insurance, Internet frauds and on. Eva's latest idea was the food service business in America. Keep it discreet and do not grow too large then launder loads of money through the system. She was waiting confirmation on an outfit in New Jersey. The final piece.

At the far end of the room, a door opened and closed. Ivan her personal bodyguard and confidant entered. He has been with her for years and probably knows more about Eva than she cares to know. He has only a mother whom he visits quite often. The rest of his life is dedicated to Eva. Though they never had sexual contact, she always wondered what he would be like.

Ivan towers over Eva. He looks at Eva's tracing on the window, and then at Eva. She glanced over without saying a word then Ivan said. "He agreed to the offer and wants to hear more. He will have a meeting with your people."

She turned and walked direct up to Ivan and peered into his dark unemotional eyes. The look of arrogance that he always showed on his face would scare most people, but Eva is never frightened. A slight smile forms at the corners of her mouth.

"I hope he takes the offer." Eva said then turned and walked slowly away. She must decide whether she should go to Aunt Catherine now and say the pipeline is in place. She has never lied to her Aunt. It had to go smoothly to keep the money flowing.

Eva turned back to Ivan. "Let's go to Aunt Catherine."

Ivan nodded and backed away pulling out a cell phone. He spoke fast Russian. A house worker appeared having Eva's coat ready. A full-length black leather. It complemented the tightly fitting black outfit she is wearing. She and Ivan than get on her private elevator that gently whisked them down the eighty floors to the private garage.

A black BMW was warmed and waiting. Eva jumped in back and Ivan climbed in the front. An exact looking car was waiting to follow from behind. With a contingent of bodyguards, they leave the garage and follow an alleyway to the boulevard.

Eva glanced at the upscale stores that contrasted with what was there a few years ago when she first built her building. Her building doesn't exist, though. The old land records of the Soviet Union have not been updated so; buildings were going up all over with no government record of them existing. Money took care of any government inquiry.

The car entered onto the highway and

accelerated to a high rate of speed that made the darkened scenery fly by in a blur. Eva thought carefully on how to present this deal to her Aunt. A closed deal, almost. With the food service warehouse in New Jersey, a chain is complete. A chain they will use to launder money through that will go undetected. False sale receipts that nobody will care about.

Eva took comfort in the thought of the owner of the New Jersey warehouse. She had not seen him in years and doubted he would remember her. He made a wise decision years ago by keeping silent. Now, we will reward him.

Eva watched Joe over the years and had even sent business his way, quietly. The buy price is well over the value of it and she will have returned a favor he did years ago. A done deal. Now, Eva will not lie to Aunt Catherine.

Chapter 7

The road looked dark and evil with the low hung tree branches the BMW's sped under together. The gently rising and falling of the road and sweeping curves gave no challenge to the cars or the drivers. Eva knew this is a magnificent view of the countryside in daylight. The property belonged to the Russian Royal family for centuries. Then left for ruin in the Soviet Union days. Then bought by her Aunt Catherine in the first days of the new Russia and spending a royal sum to bring it back from the past.

The cars entered a well-lit gateway. Security men nodded as the cars sped by and up the winding road under the old trees that opened to a view of the castle aglow in lights. A summer palace for centuries the Czars and Czarinas had used leaving their mark on it. A Czarinas home again.

The cars stopped at the canopied front steps. The new owner had built a rain shelter that complemented the castle. Aunt

Catharine did not want to use a side entrance in inclement weather.

Eva stepped out the car before Ivan could open the door for her. She took the steps two at a time to the top where an oak doorway stood. As she reached the landing, the door began to open. A large man smiled gracefully at Eva. "I must be getting old these steps seem more a challenge every time I climb them."

The man continued to smile. "Hello, Miss Eva."

"Hi, Boris. Is my aunt in her room?"

"Yes, Miss Eva."

Eva made her way along the vast hallway of paintings and sculptures. She stopped outside a door and took a long breath, then gently opened and stepped into the library. She gently closed the door that did not give a hint of noise. Her Aunt had them all hinged and oiled, so she could open any door in her palace without an ounce of energy.

Sitting in a reclined leather chair was her Aunt Catherine. A soft light was burning nearby, and she was deep in a large book. So large and heavy that a small table cart was needed so she could read. Her red hair shone like fire that matched her personality. The blue eyes reading every word are ice-cold or like a warm summer. Eva always wondered why she had the same features of her Aunt but not her father.

Her Aunt spoke without looking up from the book. "Trying to sneak up on me little Eva."

Eva stood looking down at her Aunt with a warm smile. "No, you are too wise to let a tiny mouse sneak up on you."

Her Aunt looked up from her book and took off her glasses. "Who does the tiny mouse have loyalty to?"

"The Czarina."

Her Aunt smiled and slowly pushed the cart away. It easily rolled to one side. She placed her glasses on the table next to the recliner and rubbed her eyes gently.

"Still reading the books of the past Czar's." Eva asked.

"Yes, they had a wealth of knowledge in their libraries. They lent me that one. It's from a rare collection in Saint Petersburg."

Eva knew they were just being nice. Her Aunt controlled the whole collection of books in the Czar's libraries. She meticulously knew every book from all the palaces, and huge gifts from her keep them well-preserved.

Her Aunt continued, "That one is from Peter the Great's time. He had it transcribed into Russian. A good read on how to win battles and keep the population happy."

Eva nodded slowly. "I am sure it is not that simple as you say."

"No, it isn't.

Catherine touched a button on the control panel on the table and a large man entered pushing a serving cart that had a pot of tea and an assortment of pastries. He parked the cart in front of the women and left.

"I will have my tea plain and a sugar cookie, my dear." Catherine said to Eva. She was already in motion. Eva always liked the usual ritual. She liked to serve her Aunt.

They settled back for a few minutes of sipping tea and eating. Her Aunt had pressed another button that started music playing throughout the library. An old Russian tune brought up-to-date with a livelier beat. When they finished eating Eva put their plates back on the cart then Catherine began.

"I spoke with your father and he says all is going smoothly. He did have concerns about your food business venture. Tell me how this food venture and will help our businesses?" Her twinkling eyes were between a warm sunny day and ice.

"I bought fifteen around the U.S. next to every major city and I have placed trusted people in each as the presidents. It is what they call foodservice. They supply restaurants and any establishment that prepare and cook food. In addition, they are each in the twelve regions of the Federal Reserve Banks. They oversee the money supply so one in each district will keep the laundered money from notice. We can launder money through them without much concern of being caught. I am buying the last one this week, in New Jersey."

Eva stopped, and her Aunt was yet to make a facial thought. She watched her sip her tea and place the empty cup down. Her turn. "Yes, I know that business. I hear you have that pig in Minnesota a president of that warehouse. That is your choice, we owe him for the death of his father in the Ukraine, I guess. His father was no better, but he did help us in his way. Keep a watch on Minnesota. Now, this New Jersey warehouse, are you sure he will sell? There's others available?"

"I like the location and the accounts they have in the city. A perfect fit. It'll look questionable to have a group of restaurants leave one warehouse and go to another. I set this warehouse up to be bought by us. My years of hard work are going to pay off. And Minneapolis was dad's idea."

"Didn't the owner help you many years ago." Eva stopped short when she heard this. She was not aware that her Aunt knew of that. Eva was surprised but wasn't. Her Aunt did know what she needed to know. Never second-guess Aunt Catherine.

"He never spoke of that situation to anyone. I had him watched. That tells me he was probably frightened and if he had reported it that would have gone bad in his direction. He made a wise decision. I would like to feel him out for potential." Eva looked apprehensive at her Aunt. She knew how to bring out the truth. Never tell what you know until you need to tell. Then watch them sweat.

Catherine's ice-cold eyes looked at Eva.

"If he had spoken a word of that incident to anyone, I am certain you would have killed him. I won't doubt you on that. I know your loyalties, and, you know your job. Yes, I would say he was afraid at the time. We do not judge by that quality. Now, you have been grooming him without his knowledge by sending business his way, I would assume. That's good." Catherine hesitated a few moments giving careful thought to the next part. "I say that I see no potential that you see. Or you haven't described it well. Nevertheless, I respect your gut feelings, Eva. You have done well in the past and know how to go forward. Enough on that, and, your father I think made a bad decision in Minneapolis."

Eva nodded. "Thank you. Aunt Catherine."

Catherine put on a sly smile before asking. "When you feel him out, let me know whether he has a big one." Eva's eyes went wide for a moment then both had a hearty laugh.

"Speaking on that subject. Are you still seeing Leonid?" Eva asked.

"Why yes. I always have a good time with my special friend."

"And how is your love life?"

"Okay and getting."

"What happened to that attractive Italian fellow?" Her Aunt was questioning, and Eva was not sure what she knew and what she did not. That was Catherine's special way of reading the character of people.

"He had an upstanding family that did everything correctly. It did not feel right."

"I understand. Not much interest in the grape business or doing things proper."

Eva was right. Her Aunt knew.

"So, have you seen the latest movie Nick produced?"

"Yes. I received the DVD the other day. I haven't viewed it, myself and Leonid are going to."

"You will enjoy it."

"Yes. I always enjoy his movies. I wish he would take a more active role in the family business. But, it's just as well. Nick owning the chain of movie theaters."

"Yes, it is. Nick is a self-made man."

"Yes. Now the others? How are they doing?"

Eva cringed when her Aunt referred to her adopted brother and sisters that way. She would never tell them. They were family and played a big role in this empire.

"Great. Max's new device will detect cameras up to a mile away. Newspapers won't have any pictures of us. Olga and Mikal are busy with the fake loans to our businesses, and Uri is keeping our South American operations running smoothly. Now, Tatyana has finished making millions off the real-estate boom and is leaving that venture."

Her Aunt listened carefully. Eva knew she was comparing notes.

"Excellent. They are developing well." Her Aunt said slowly.

"Dad is doing fine. He has an enjoyable new yacht to relax on."

"Yes, he always did have time for fun. My brother. However, now, This Senator from New York, Wellington. He has ambitions to run for President there."

Catherine paused, and Eva was listening. Something new.

"He won't be voted in. His nephew has started too much trouble with that real estate deal." Her Aunt looked directly at Eva with ice-cold eyes and repeated. "He won't get voted in or even reach that time."

"I understand." Eva said.

"I'll take care of this myself."

Eva nodded. Something personal between her Aunt and Senator Wellington?

"Now, I want you to take care of this Red mob. That evil pig Ureinchencko is fooling with nuclear stuff. I want him finally done away with. It can't go on, it's bad for us. Just contact our friend in the government and they will clean up the mess and make it look good. They will just want that nuclear stuff and the contacts. He has stepped over the line this time."

"Yes, I agree." That fool is pressuring everybody, and no one needs that. Since, you mentioned it, last time; I have been gathering information on him and his operations."

"Yes, I know." Her Aunt said quietly and looked at Eva for a long moment. Then Eva continued.

"It is difficult getting inside that group and knowing the whereabouts for Ureinchencko. Even his trusted Andre is having a problem finding information."

"No, not difficult. I believe you will get the job done, Eva. Like you have in the past." Catherine paused for a moment. "You wouldn't be sitting with me if I didn't believe in you" The ice-cold eyes were speaking. One of those awkward moments that happens, and it didn't surprise Eva. Her Aunt continued.

"At the next meeting with the emissaries tell them the Czarina feels it is time to end the Red Mob. Tell them there is evidence of them stepping over the line into weapons. Tell them it's nuclear and selling to possible terrorists. They will understand and should agree. As an added incentive, they can divide the Red Mob's operations among them."

"Okay, they should agree. It's always good to remove some competition." Eva said and hoped they did.

"Now that takes care of business." Catherine said and stood, walked slowly, to Eva and looked down on her with warm blue eyes.

"You get orders accomplished. I do not mean to be ugly sometimes, but we are alike. You will take over this family someday.

I want to make sure you will accept it when the day comes. Remember this, because letting things go as they are is weak. Only make changes that help you and the family. The rest of the world is on their own"

"I understand. When I am Czarina, I will remember these times together and know how to move the family forward."

Her Aunt smiled lovingly and patted the side of her face.

"Yes, you will do well Eva."

Eva stood and gave her a hug. Eva did not like when she spoke this way. Eva wanted her to live forever.

Eva walked toward the door and looked back at her Aunt settling back in her chair and pulling back the cart with the big book. She looked up at Eva and said. "Remember, a wolf knows what it wants to eat and will do so with no concern of what others think." (Excerpt from a President/ Prime Minister Vladimir Putin speech)

Eva smiled, nodded then left the library. She had planned to meet the emissaries this week she knew, but, what evidence. Will they go along without evidence? She took a pill from her pocket and swallowed it. They help her stay calm and keep pace with life. She took another for good measure and did not need water.

Chapter 8

Joe was still feeling elated since the meeting with Goldberg one day ago. He had built up a small foodservice business into a more profitable one, and maybe time to let go and find something else, maybe consulting.

The money was blinding and Joe he knew it. Not many business owners at his age of thirty-five get one hundred fifty million dollars. At five percent interest, he and Carol can live comfortably. Then the question that Joe has been dodging in his mind came roaring back, children.

Joe glanced over at Carol; she was still quietly reading a romance novel, curled up on the far end of the couch. She paid no attention to the TV. A military channel that Joe liked to watch. He did not know why women read romance novels. Do they learn anything new or is it a dream they live through others? Joe enjoyed doing the act of romance instead of reading how others do it.

"Did, they start having sex yet?"

Carol looked up slightly and gave him a sour look.

"It's not a sex book. It's about two people in love. Certain social factors keep them from living a life together. It's a story of sacrifice and desire."

Carol remained staring at Joe with her innocent brown eyes.

Joe liked that look about her. It's attractive. Then she puckers her lips to add to it.

"We have those elements here, now, reality. Why read about it?"

"Reading about other people in love is interesting. You enjoy watching violence and military stuff. I enjoy reading about love and romance. Maybe it's why we love each other. I find you interesting."

Her answer threw Joe off. He was just joking with her and she noticed that and quickly put a smooth end to it. He finds her interesting also but rarely tells her. She probably knows this, Joe thought.

"Yes, opposites attract and do stay together." He smiled back.

Yes, Joe loved his wife. She has been good for him. She always lets him know that she loves him that keeps him always feeling secure.

Carol went back to her book. She then stopped, looked up and placed the book on the table. She then squinted her eyes at Joe.

"I want to talk to you about our situation. I know you are considering selling the business. Now, that will give us time to start a family. Maybe we look at this down different avenues."

Joe turned his whole body to face Carol. He knew this was going to be a serious moment. The leather chair made a sound.

"I know it has been rough on us." Joe hesitated a moment. "Medically the odds are in favor that we will conceive in time. That's what the Doctor said. So, let's go upstairs and try."

Carol's look did not change.

"Yes, we have been trying for years and we can probably try until we die. Look, how about we start thinking about adoption. There are countless children given up for adoption. Waiting for a family like us, who have the financial means to..."

Joe broke in.

"Look we talked about this before. I know you and your mother are desperate for a child, so am I. In a few weeks we are going to be multimillionaires. That puts a new emphasis on us having a child. A child that comes from us. Our DNA and intellect."

Joe took a sip of his drink then continued.

"Adopting, may give us a child with the mentality of a ..."

Carol broke in with a forward movement of her body.

"Hold it! You're getting ugly again. I just want a family and if we cannot do it between us naturally, then I want us to adopt. I did some checking. Now before any final deal happens, we will know the family history of the child, so we can make an educated decision."

Carol was sitting straight up looking at Joe.

"Do many well-educated people in this world put a child up for adoption? You see, we may have a child that has mental or physical problems. If that happens, we cannot return him or her like its Walmart."

Joe took another sip of his drink and added. "That's why I refuse to adopt."

Carol looked away and did not agree with Joe and he knew it.

"Maybe if you weren't getting drunk, we could have an intelligent conversation. Have you thought about my feelings? Do you wonder how I feel not being able to have my body transform your sperm and an egg into a baby? Have You?!"

Joe rested back in the chair. He felt weak, and Carol continued.

"Maybe it's not the drink in your hand, maybe it's just us. Why are we together if we can't agree on how to start a family? Why pretend we are going toward a goal when, we are not."

Tears were starting to well in Carol's eyes. She picked up her book and left the room. Joe listened as she went upstairs and slammed the bedroom door.

Joe let out a long breath. He felt weak. He didn't want to lose Carol. Losing her was not what he wanted.

Joe downed the rest of his drink. He shut the TV and lights off then sat in the darkness.

Chapter 9

Sitting behind his desk the next morning, Joe was still feeling weak. Carol did not wake him to go to bed and sleeping upright always left his neck muscles hurting. He did not have a refreshed feeling today; also, Joe did not wake Carol when he left for work. A repeat of last night was not what he needed before work.

Looking at his desk phone, he thought of happier days when Carol would call and tell him some good news. He knew that would not happen today and knew he could not change it, today.

He got up, left his office and headed for Thom's office. Approaching Joe heard Thom engaged in a conversation. He decided to, keep walking, farther down the hallway was Paul Letter's office the Human Resources dept. Joe entered the outer office and said hello to Paul's assistants, two women. Then looked in Paul's office.

He was looking intently at his computer screen. One hand covering his mouth as he read something of interest.

"Hi, Paul."

Joe stood inside the doorframe; Paul looked over a little surprised.

"Hey, what's up boss?"

"Nada, just wandering around."

Joe entered, took a seat. Paul closed out whatever he was reading.

"Sorry if I disturbed you. Was it a good porn site?"

Paul gave a sly smile.

"You know I do not do that on company time. I was just checking out a rumor."

Paul leaned back in his chair and waited for Joe.

"Well, I came to give you confirmation on a rumor I am certain you have heard. An outfit in New York has offered to buy the place. I have given it some thought and will decide after I meet with them tomorrow."

Joe knew his decision would be what he first felt he should do. But he didn't want anyone here to know just yet.

"Okay, I did hear the same rumor and so have the warehousemen. The union shop stewards have approached me already. I suggest a statement might be good now."

Joe thought, I haven't met anybody yet.

"No, keep it as a rumor. Shouldn't be a problem."

"Not at all. When you decide and have information then we'll all know."

Paul looked like he had a question and Joe didn't know how to ask, so, he decided to continue.

"I do not know much now but, I am sure they will need a good HR head."

"Joe, I am not that concerned with job security. I do float resumes from time to time and can move on. I stay here because you have a great place to work." Paul nodded in Joe's direction. Then started flipping a pen in his hand.

Joe had a moment of nervous guilt. He hoped this new outfit would keep it a great place to work. He stood to leave. Paul put the pen down and leaned forward. Joe waited.

"I heard a name of the possible new owner and ran a quick check, nothing. A private foodservice company that has bought a few choice warehouses around the country. They are quietly putting together a coast-to-coast chain. They are a division of an outfit called CZ Corp. CZ Corp., nothing. They've been around for years and nobody knows what they do. Now, if you approve, I can maybe get more information. It'll cost but, I can have it by morning, before you leave."

Joe thought for a moment. He knew Paul's skills for getting information were excellent, and what the hell. Won't hurt to learn who these people are.

"Alright, do a search, see who they are." Joe stopped at the doorway.

"Paul, thank you."

"Thank you, boss."

Joe left that office interested to see what Paul dredges up. They are starting a coast-to-coast operation. That did not thrill Joe, he decided to, take an early day and try to get around Carol and cheer her up.

Chapter 10

Joe and Carol ate dinner that night quietly. She made chicken as the main course that he did not like. Joe relaxed in the television room a while later. Watching the military channel, he wondered whether General MacArthur had problems with his wife and children. Probably not proper in those days.

Carol came into the room and took her usual seat on the couch. She had the same romance novel, Joe noted. She looked at the television and smirked.

"I have a decision to make tomorrow and I am going to want to call you and ask your opinion? I am going to be offered one hundred fifty million for the business and I want to decide with you."

Carol did not make the slightest facial movement at the money.

"I'll have my cell phone with me. I am not going to give you more advice than I can right now. I decided long ago not to get involved in your company. It's yours."

Joe did not have a good feeling from that

response.

"Well, I am responsible for people. They did help bring the business where it is. Do I just say thanks?"

Holding her book and thinking for a moment, Joe saw this as a good sign. He needed to keep her engaged in life. Carol looked at Joe.

"Why are you concerned for people with no incentive to accomplish anything? You took the risk, so you have the rewards. I don't have pity for people who hope the ones making a difference fail."

"Thank you for the vote of confidence. I feel the money is right. Their lawyer said they may ask me to stay on and run the place."

Carol looked at Joe with a sneer.

"Why do that? You said you wanted to retire, right." Joe nodded. "Why stay and help make money for someone else? That'll cause changes in you. You're the owner. Won't that be degrading to you? Being a paid employee? Be intelligent, invest the money and try something else. Leave a winner. I won't interfere. I want to see you succeed again."

Joe was stunned by her response.

"Yes, you are right. Thank you."

Joe sipped on his drink. Deep down he did like the encouragement Carol showed. He does owe her but, he is the one who will face all the employees and say thank you as he embarks on a dream life.

Joe pictured a yacht without a care in the world while the employees at Bergen Foods are getting pay cuts. Then he remembered that he knows nothing about yachts. What's the cost to operate one? He cleared those thoughts from his head and stretched his body.

"We can talk children when this business is over. I did some research today. A clinic in Boston is showing positive results with couples who have a difficult time conceiving."

Carol closed and slammed her book on the coffee table. Joe felt a knife go into his heart. He realized he said the wrong thing, again.

"I have a problem conceiving. We are never going to have children together. What the HELL you listening to at the doctor's office. My body keeps rejecting eggs. You understand. I cannot bear children. For us it is not going to happen, you have a damaged product, ME!"

Carol got up, grabbed her book and headed out of the room. She stopped short and turned to face Joe. "And, you can sleep in the chair again or leave." She then stormed out and up the stairs slamming the bedroom door.

Joe sat polarized; he did not have the energy to change the television or sip his drink. He felt as though he was spiraling downward.

Chapter 11

After a few stops in the Ukraine, Poland, Germany and France, Eva's personal Boeing 757 landed at JFK Airport in New York City. Ivan was on his cell phone keeping up-to-date. By the moment, if necessary. Who was where? Doing what? He never was short on information for Eva.

Most pressing was Andre. After Eva scared the shit out of him, they took him to a private doctor in Moscow to stitch him up. He then immediately took off for parts unknown. Probably much more focused on doing his job.

Eva tapped her fingers on the window of the jet as it taxied to a private hanger. She knew one of two situations was happening. Andre was plotting against her or he was doing as he was being paid to do. Yet, it did not surprise her if he were plotting against her. It is a common reality she accepts, a slight challenge to keep her alert.

Ivan sat near the door speaking quietly into his cell phone. The plane stopped, and he immediately stood and covered the exit door with his body.

Eva liked watching Ivan do his work. He protected her without thought of himself. She giggled quietly. A man giving his life for her and he was not her husband.

Ivan opened the door and the usual people from customs entered, looked around and checked passports then quickly left.

Eva's office assistants then came in, Mia and Mya. They are identical twins she met years ago in New York City and had worked for her since and would probably do it free. Both felt she is their third twin. They spend their days arranging Eva's appointments and keeping her best interests in mind. Ivan steps aside because he knows that she must be happy, and the twins keep it that way. They watch out for her when they are not in her presence.

A few years ago, a freelance business reporter tried to do an investigative report on Eva and CZ Corp. Not a complimentary article. The twins learning about this made sure the article was never finished or found. The man disappeared for a few months and returned one day addicted to heroin with a few warrants for his arrest. These days he is probably in prison or in a homeless shelter, he no longer can write anything good or bad about anyone.

"Hi, Eva." The twins said in harmony. Eva still had trouble distinguishing between the two.

"Hi, Mia and Mya. Now, who is who?"

"I'm Mia."

Said one.

"I'm Mya."

Said the other.

Ivan standing in back rolled his eyes.

Eva tried to isolate something in their dress to tell them apart today. However, their outfits were identical.

Eva hugged each and all left the plane. One of Eva's cars was waiting, a white BMW limo. The women got in back as Ivan took his position in front next to the driver. Another vehicle with darkened windows was waiting to follow.

The limo driver drove expertly toward Manhattan. Eva could have traveled by helicopter, but she wanted to be in traffic and see life happening around her. She always felt safe when traveling in New York City. Her eyes were taking in everything the limo passed.

One twin spoke. "The man from the New Jersey warehouse is going to meet with the XO people today."

Eva nodded. Then asked, hoping she knew the answer. "What's the likelihood he will sell?"

The other twin spoke. "He seems open to it according to Goldstein. Now, a minor problem came up last night. Paul Letter, a person from his warehouse made several calls and Internet searches on XO and CZ last night. Security told us this and Max will tell you the rest."

Eva nodded and assumed that this Paul Letter did a bad thing. She will decide how badly when she is briefed.

One twin spoke. "His chief of Finance seems a capable fellow to take over if this Bergen guy decides to sell and leave."

Eva thought a moment then spoke. "At first he will do if Bergen does not want to stay on. Then, we'll put one of our own in place."

The twins nodded. They needed to know the basic outline, so they can contact the right person when the time comes.

"Now tell me about Bergen." Eva asked.

One twin spoke. "He goes to work, well-liked by the employees. He occasionally goes to dinner with his wife Carol. For the most part, they are homebodies. Boring types."

"Any children."

"No. None."

Eva looked at them and they in turn looked at each other and shrugged.

Eva looked out at the sidewalk full of people. The buildings were getting larger the closer they approached hers. She knew Joe Bergen well enough. She's been watching him on and off starting that day many years ago to the present. That did not tell her what he thinks, though.

Her connections made it possible for him to buy that little warehouse and build it up. The pictures from his wedding day looked happy. She didn't care for his wife, but he's the one living with her. She knew she could only influence life to a point.

Eva liked the one trait he has carried throughout the years. He can keep a secret. She knows this well. Having seen him tested over the years with simple situations with the same results. He can probably fit in with the family. He has a clean record that is important. But, will he recognize her today, Eva will see by his first reaction. The limo entered a side street darkened from the tall buildings.

Chapter 12

The limo turned and went into a gated underground parking area. Inside it drove past employee's vehicles into another gated area for the family. There the limo stopped. A man waiting stepped over to open the back door. There was a private elevator opened and ready with another man waiting.

Eva and the twins got inside the elevator; Ivan did not join them. He stayed in the background in one the offices that security used.

On the top floor, the elevator door opened, and they stepped out into an office area that had some glassed walled offices and some without glass walls. Seemingly, happy men and women were going about the company's business in the executive office area. The ones that noticed Eva gave her a friendly heartfelt smile. They were happy to see her, and she knew that.

Eva's office area was the largest in the building. She had her own view of downtown Manhattan. Her secretary was the best she could hire. She employed a research staff to sort through news of the world whether it was business or criminal. She wanted to know what occurred everywhere in the world in the public news.

Eva and the twins entered the outer area of her office. Her secretary Natasha was busy on her PC when they entered. She looked up and gave a look of seeing her best friend in the world.

"Hi, Eva."

"Hi, Natasha."

Eva went into her office and stopped for a moment to take in the sweeping view. Her office faced the east because she liked the morning sun. It reminded her that every day was new and exciting. Also, it faced in her favorite direction, Russia.

The twins left Eva and went to their office that adjoined hers. They took care of business there and that business was Eva Bokanawski, of CZ Corporation.

Eva Bokanawski is CEO and President of CZ Corp. She controls a global empire that she helped build quietly. She only employed the most loyal of people who have clean records. They keep her informed about the businesses the company owns and explore new prospects along the way. Her employees work well on their own. They follow orders and maintain the flow.

Eva runs the business with some loans and credit from banks to make things look normal. Bankers and insurance companies were always begging for her business. She did not see a need for anyone looking at the company books too closely. They did not need the money. Few knew this so offers from banks are rarely taken.

The Co-Chairpersons are her father and aunt. The board of directors consist of her brothers and sisters. All of them adopted except Nicolas Jr. They run their respective businesses that connect to CZ Corp. and Eva.

She took a seat behind her desk and looked at the small pile of reading material. A daily briefing of what she wanted. That consisted of the company businesses then world events that may affect business or just plain interesting news. She flipped through the pages fast and comprehended even faster. When she finished, her phone gave a gentle buzz.

"Yes, Natasha."

"Al's here."

"Okay send him in."

A man of nondescript features entered, strolled over and took a seat in front of Eva's desk. His name was Al Stentski. A Polish born American who held degrees in physiology and human behavior sciences. He was the President of Human Resources for CZ Corp. The schooling and abilities have enabled him to hire the right people that Eva wants working for her company. She used to feel strange at first when she hired him. It was like he can get inside her brain or, so she thought. Until she realized that if he did get inside her brain, he would have been running away long ago.

Al can analyze people and know what they can do mentally. He can predict people to a degree and how much pressure they can probably handle. Eva also paid the man well, so he will never want to leave the company.

Eva looked at him brightly and he always stared back like a teacher looking at a student.

"How goes it Al?"

"Very well and how were your travels."

"Satisfying. There's no place like home."

They sat staring at each other for a moment then Eva continued

"I have a person coming today in about an hour. It involves a possible purchase of his warehouse." Al nodded, and Eva continued. "I want you to sit in and give me a thought on how he would be if I were to hire him. I want the best estimate of your skills."

"Okay, what am I looking for. In what capacity would you need him?"

Eva thought for a second. "A division CEO."

Al nodded and thought for a moment. "Okay."

"You are not going to ask."

"Ask what, Eva."

Eva sat back and laughed for a moment.

"I like you Al."

"And I like you Eva. My business is what people will do in this wonderful world; you on the other hand, make money with them."

"Yes, thank you Al. I am going to need a person to run the XO Food Service division. Do not tell a soul, and, your opinion will help greatly. I know this man from the past but, I need a gold medal seal from just you."

"I understand and will give you my best as always."

"Excellent. No mention of who I am. I'll be close by."

"I'm going to like this. Okay."

"Thanks Al."

Al left. His mind working as usual with a calm demeanor. Eva sat back and smiled. She knew she could trust his opinion on what to expect from Joe Bergen. He was a good prospect for the company and possibly attracted to him. That thought she quickly pushed aside. Married but not a problem if she didn't want it to be. Business keep the business first.

Mia and Mya came into her office and took seats in front of the desk.

Eva sat looking at them. She knew they did not miss anything. They knew she had a special interest in this food warehouse. Because they had recommended one, she could have bought inexpensively. Eva liked that they did not pry; they let things go, as Eva wished. They did though keep their ears open for an answer why.

"Well ladies, how about a bagel and coffee."

"Yucky." The twins said in harmony.

"That snot dripping old man who always takes our clothes off in his mind. He's a creep." Mia said.

"But if you're paying, we go." Mya said.

Eva got up from behind her desk and felt a little excited. She knew why but denied it.

Chapter 13

Down at sidewalk level the noise of cars and people walking was heard and seen. Eva and the twins absorbed this as they walked to the corner where a small lunch cart was. Keeping a safe distance but close, were three men who worked as security for CZ Corp. Dressed like any other in this lower Manhattan area, they were on their highest alert. Keeping Eva in view and ready to pounce on anyone.

The man working the lunch cart was a fixture on the corner. He has been there more than ten years and the longtime business residents liked him. He was going to close once a few years ago but the businesses in the area asked him to stay.

The three women looked like any other workers from the neighborhood. As they approached, the old man was giving change to a well-dressed executive.

"Hi, Poppy." Eva said.

Poppy turned to face her and opened his arms.

"Hi ladies. How are you today? I see that you're all pretty as ever."

The three giggled as the old man looked them up and down. Mia winked at Eva with a little extra laugh.

"Fine," they said in harmony.

"What'll it be today?"

Poppy waved his arm over his cart.

"Bagels and coffee around." Eva said.

"Good choice."

He expertly served the bagels and coffee in seconds. They exchanged money and thanked Poppy.

They started to walk slowly along the sidewalk back to the building. Nibbling, sipping and chatting.

"Did you see the boogers hanging off his nose?" Mia said.

"Ah come on. He's someone just trying to get by." Eva said lightly.

"Yea, him and his boogers."

The three laughed as they stopped by the front of their building. They stood looking at people and car traffic. A limo then pulled to the curb and two well-dressed men got out carrying briefcases. They paused and looked around then walked toward the building.

As the two men passed Eva and the twins, they gave business type nods then entered the building. The three watched until the two men faded from view inside. The twins then looked at Eva.

"He is handsome." Said Mia.

"I wouldn't kick him out of bed." Said

Mya.

"Who're we talking about?" Eva asked.

They looked at each other winking. They then also entered the building. They approached security where all visitors or unknowns had to sign in and go through a metal detector. As Eva and the twins approached, a big security person opened a side area without hesitation.

They got off the elevator on the eighteenth floor and casually walked through the office area nibbling on their bagels and sipping their cups of coffees. Eva stopped at random to talk with some people. She asked and knew personal things about most of them and, they talked like old friends.

They then came to an open lounge area that had a secretary happily working. Her name was Kim. The secretary for Rich Holbrook the interim Division CEO for XO Food Service. Rich was the top person for when the company entered a new field of business. He could grasp the fundamentals and organize the buyouts. He was excellent at doing the early work of building something. Then handed it off for someone else to run, whom Eva selected based on AI's examination.

A good system that worked for Eva and the family.

The women chatted with Kim lightly. Three men approached; two from the limo with a security escort.

Eva and the twins backed away to the

lounge area and took seats on the couches. They chatted lightly about fashion as they chewed on their bagels and sipped their coffees.

The two men came over and took seats on the opposite couch. They whispered, straightened their suits and prepared themselves. The three women watched this and ate. The men were whispering when they noticed the eyes looking at them. The two men smiled.

"Hi ladies." Joe said.

The three said hellos in harmony.

"There's beverages and doughnuts in the room." Mia said pointing to an open room off to one side.

"No thank you." Both said. The twins looked at Eva then at the two men.

"We have a few more minutes." Eva said.

"Well, let me introduce myself. I am Joe Bergen of Bergen food service and this is my CFO, Thom Heller."

"Hello." Mia said. Then continued. "I am Mia and she is Mya, and this is Eva."

"Twins." Joe said.

He noticed the redhead with sky blue eyes watching him. Her face had soft features that he found appealing and he felt as if he knew her or something, he could not explain it. She did not give him a feeling of intimidation being how beautiful she looked.

"Triplets." Eva said.

They both looked at the three smiling. Then Thom spoke.

"I do not see that as the case."

"No, it's not real; we can wish it, though." Eva said. Joe was watching every word she said and every movement of her face. Eva was absorbing his body language; it was better than she expected.

Joe broke from staring at Eva and casually looked around.

"A beautiful building. The owner must take great care in seeing the employees are in pleasant surroundings."

"Well, of course. If you give someone a positive environment to work in, they should excel. Unless of course they have emotional problems. Then there's no hope." Eva said.

Joe nodded yes. Then Thom broke in. "Well, if people want a position with benefits, they'll work in a rest room. It's about needs. Never let the employees dictate how to run a business."

Joe looked over at Thom. Then spoke. "You'll have to excuse my partner. He is strictly a numbers' man."

The women nodded. Eva and Joe regained eye contact and something more.

"I guess a woman is in charge here. The pleasant environment tells me that." Joe thought aloud.

"There is, a stern but personal touch helps productively and peoples' attitude. What else do you see?" Eva asked. They felt they were the only two there.

"The person in charge knows what employees she wants. I mean a software company will look for qualities in a prospective employee that will produce software. In contrast with an employer, that just hires anybody, feels, he can change that person to do the job, and wastes much time doing that. Everybody has certain qualities and motives that show whether they are going to be good workers. Now, in the short time we have been here I noticed that person sitting in the cube near the secretary hasn't stopped working. He has taken two phone calls, done work on the PC and looks happy."

Thom and the twin's heads turned to the cube. Eva kept eye contact with Joe. Then Thom broke in.

"Okay, I assume you ladies are secretaries or the like for the company. An employer shouldn't give special attention to employees and their surroundings, it is a waste of time. A desk and half-hour lunch will do."

All eyed Thom for a moment. Joe noticed a direct stare from Eva to Thom that he interpreted not as something good.

Eva weighed in. "Well, I like to see people who can handle their job and be proactive. That saves time for the boss. If the boss needs to wonder whether person A, did the task. He's then thinking, wondering and wasting time that could be useful else ware." Eva paused and realized she was speaking like a boss. Not the impression she wanted to give here. She continued. "As secretaries we appreciate that our employer goes out of the way here to preserve a pleasant atmosphere. We have a high productivity rate per employee. You can ask the Boss." Eva pointed up.

Joe moved forward and said.

"Okay, we have a difference of managing styles here, that's good and makes for a lively debate. But Thom is an excellent number's man for my company; he has helped the business immeasurably. He does not need any special atmosphere to keep the numbers rolling in."

Joe looked over at Thom with a smile hoping he would keep his mouth shut.

"I guess us secretaries will stay employed here." Mia said with a giggle.

The three women stood to leave. Joe and Thom got up, extended their hands and shook all three. Joe kept eye contact with Eva for an extra moment, which she did not mind.

They slowly left the area. Then the office door opened, and Rich came out, looked around and his face brightened. Eva and the twins stopped and looked back. Rich then said happily. "Hi Eva."

Eva gave him a little wave and, then she and the twins moved on. Joe got a good look at her lithe body that moved effortlessly. The red hair and those sky-blue eyes. He had met her before. The place and time he did not remember but he knew her. Or was it just a response to a gorgeous lady.

Rich walked to Joe and Thom with his

hand extended. They pressed palms.

"Good morning, I am Rich Holbrook."

"I am Joe Bergen and my CFO Thom Heller."

"You guys want any coffee, tea, pastries." Rich asked.

"No, I am fine." Joe said.

"I'm good." Thom said.

"Okay then." Rich extended his arm toward his office.

Joe stopped near the door looking back toward the red-haired one, Eva. She was a little way down the corridor talking with someone. Rich also stopped and looked.

"Beautiful, isn't she." Rich said.

"Yes, and intelligent." Joe added.

"She is the CEO and President. Eva Bokanawski. Her family owns all this."

Joe did not seem surprised at hearing this. A natural fit. He rather knew she was the boss and he knew her from somewhere.

Joe walked in the office. Thom was already sitting and pulling out papers. A man was also sitting at the small table who looked blankly at Joe. Mark introduced him as temporary help from the accounting dept. Joe let that pass and was feeling strangely happy. He knew he was about to sell his business for a small fortune, but his mind was somewhere else.

Chapter 14

The meeting finished with better than expected results. The sale of Bergen Foodservice Company is going to make Joe an instant multimillionaire. He wasn't dreaming of a yacht or a villa in the South of France. He was starting to wonder why they offered one-hundred-million plus for a business that they can have for half that. Joe did not understand that. He had some good customers but not the golden gooses of restaurants.

Thom's loud voice broke Joe's concentration.

"Well that's up to the boss. We're on the way."

Thom closed his cell phone and looked proudly out the car window. He glanced over at Joe.

"Paul. I guess him, and the others are curious. Maybe you should do a meeting. In fact, I am curious. What's my job going to be? Are these people going to keep me on?"

Joe remembered Paul wasn't at the office before he left today. He assumed Paul did not get any dirt on XO Foods groups or CZ Corp. and dodged him. Just as well Joe thought. The red-haired CEO was on his mind and he did not want to hear any bad news about her.

"Yes, I will have a meeting when my feet touch the ground. Not a good answer I guess but, I need to believe this myself."

"I understand if I were in your position, I would be on cloud nine myself."

Yes, Joe was on cloud nine. Not the money he was going to receive but this company CZ Corp. It put him on cloud nine. He saw happy people in control of their lives and the business, intoxicating. A new way of running a successful business. Joe just felt like he wasted ten years following textbook examples and only slightly successful. Compared with that corporation in just twenty years built-up one hundred-fold. A woman did it. Yes, Joe was on cloud nine. He saw something amazing, something fresh. A new way of doing things. Joe wondered, whether he really did employ the wrong people, but would he have broken the law if he did it the CZ Corp. way. He wondered now whether he really does owe anybody at Bergen foods.

Joe looked out of the limo and watched the roadway slip past. Thom blurted out.

"Oh, Paul also said he needs to see you when you get back. Something important. Maybe a warehouse guy broke the sexual harassment rules again." Joe nodded to him. Thom's belly was giggling from his laughter.

Joe also laughed though his heart was not enjoying the same joke. Because, he had seen a new level of doing business today.

Yes, sexual harassment. Joe thought. The alleged one incident was just the product of stupidity. If he did not employ the two people involved that would have never happened. Yes, as Eva said. He did waste much time with that incident. Who does he blame, Paul? His method of hiring people and evaluating them did fail most times. How does Eva Bokanawski do it? Joe was intrigued.

At the office everyone looked questioningly at Joe when he returned, and he still had nothing to say yet. Though he knew that he signed an agreement of purchase, it was just the first phase. Joe was looking at his business in a new perspective now. He half listened as Thom boldly told Paul of how he embarrassed himself in front of the owner. Then they chewed on some details like the price. That left Paul speechless for a few moments, Joe noticed. He also noticed that Paul was enjoying the conversation, but he seemed edgy.

When Thom finally left Joe decided to hear what Paul wanted to tell him.

"Be right back." Paul left out of Joe's office.

He returned and closed the office door. He pulled his chair closer to Joe's desk and laid out a stack of papers.

"What's this?" Joe asked. He hoped it was not some major recall news that may down his company like a recall or a lawsuit. He hoped he did not ship out any bad food product. Paul looked at him with a devilish smile then began.

"Okay, Eva Bokanawski is quite a shady person. She does run a large empire on both sides of the Atlantic." Joe was not impressed. He knew that by what he saw and heard today. Paul stared at Joe for a moment then continued.

"She was born in Brooklyn and I could not find any school records so, schooling is unknown. Now she's listed a CEO and President of CZ Corp. This company incorporated some thirty years ago but zoomed up in the 1990's. They bought the Clark pencil company and others along the way. They then sold it to a German company. This was leaked news." Joe was getting impatient. "Now this German outfit paid a hefty price and I guess had problems running it and closed it and sold pieces of it. Putting many people out of work. They had done other buys and sold to mainly foreign companies or investment companies. They seem to package things and sell them."

Joe was ready to say something sarcastic but decided not.

"This is not really interesting stuff. When flipping companies, it comes down to management skills. Now I guess she is building a food service chain and will sell it in time."

Paul nodded but seemed determined to make a point, Joe felt.

"There are some slight mentions of people

missing or unexplainable accidents. A little over a year ago they purchased a food service warehouse out in California. The owner rolled his car down a hill on the coast and died. The wife then sold the business to CZ Corp. A Minneapolis warehouse decided to vote out the labor union after CZ Corp. purchased it. The labor union's president is missing and hasn't been found."

Paul stopped and looked at Joe. Joe was tired and did not see the evidence that Paul was trying to present. He rubbed his chin then said.

"Paul, the California owner may have been drunk. The local labor union leader missing is no surprise. Maybe he's with Jim Hoffa. Now, a warehouse voting out a union is no surprise. That happens, some places unionize and some de unionize. I don't get what you're trying to sell me on here. I met Ms Bokanawski today and she's a capable CEO, shrewd." Paul looked away for a moment. Joe continued.

"Paul, you have been here almost five years and your work has been appreciated by me. I know some here don't want me to sell. But I've reached a peak and want to go on."

Paul nodded. Joe continued.

"Now I do plan on giving out some bonuses to show my appreciation to the valued employees here. Now, I suggest you destroy that pile and start thinking of how you will like working for them. I am going to give a high rating for the staff here, and with that I turn it over to CZ Corp."

Paul relaxed and thought for a moment then spoke.

"I should have just let it rest. I am sorry. May be a good time for Wendy and me to move on. We have an ample nest egg and have been looking for a country bed and breakfast to buy."

"Good to hear. XO foods may operate different. There'll be changes. I suggest those who stay, stay and see. If nobody likes the new regime, then move on."

Joe stood and stretched and as did Paul. He looked at the pile of papers then at Paul.

"If you gave me that this morning; I still would have not changed my mind."

Paul looked down at the pile of printouts.

"There's other stuff. Nothing that points to a bad business, I guess. I didn't have it this morning. I e-mailed this guy last night, he seems to have a grudge against the company. He sent me these links to this stuff. Some free-lance reporter; probably a nut case."

Joe shrugged. "People from XO food will show up probably next week for a look around. You'll be the man to show them around."

"Okay, I'll make sure to put dog food in the cafeteria for a buffet."

Joe snorted a laugh. Paul collected the pile of papers and gave Joe a salute then opened the door and left.

Joe slowly put on his suit jacket and thought about the redhead, Eva. Buy and sell for a little profit. Yes, the workers sometimes lose out. Maybe they refused to adapt to a new style of management. Maybe they did not have natural qualities that make them good workers. Eva must plan to a detail. Probably wants everything to fit a formula and if not, they won't work for her. Joe looked at his desk and would not mind if he never saw this office again.

Later when he pulled into the driveway, he sat in the car looking at the house he and Carol bought. With extra rooms for the children they hoped to have. At the time, the price seemed enormous and they struggled and saved. Joe remembered when he prayed, he would succeed and he did. Just a signature away was victory. He was sitting in his driveway looking at his house and a few days away from victory, alone.

Inside was quiet as he made his way to the den. He poured a whiskey and listened to the quiet of the night. He knew Carol was asleep and to wake her would be useless. He did want to talk and share what he was doing with her but, that was not going to happen.

Joe powered up his laptop, opened his briefcase and pulled out some papers from the days meeting. The cover sheet Joe had scribbled the purchase price and circled it. He would leave those papers on the desk and maybe Carol would look at them and see what he was getting for his years of work. Sometimes a passive touch would bring her around Joe knew.

He opened a website of general news to read what went on today while he was involved in his own life. Then remembered the end of the meeting when the temp guy from accounting, Al, gave him a tip. Thom was flapping his gums with Holbrook and he made his way over and said 'if you invest, try TWM for a few days it is going to move. Buy it today and sell no later than Friday. It'll be short and fast.'

Joe typed in the company stock symbol and the company information came up. A general house product company that had numerous products used in every home. Nothing explosive, not a tech stock. The latest news said that they were due to report their earnings in the morning and expected to beat the street estimates.

Joe took a sip of his whiskey and thought for a moment. Then went to his online trading account and logged in. He looked over his few stock holdings and mutual funds they were in the green. He typed in the company symbol and saw the same news that they were going to report and expected to outperform the estimates. He looked at his cash balance and decided to put in a buy and risk twenty thousand. A few days ago, he would not even have taken a risk like this.

He penned a note to sell in two days. He

posted the note to his laptop screen and shut it down. He sipped more whiskey and felt hurt or guilty that he was alone on this night. After the sale he needs to have Carol part of his business dealings. She needs to be involved and he needs to involve her in business. The whiskey was starting to take its effects as he left the den and climbed the stairs to go to bed.

Chapter 15

The beat of the music with rhythmic movement of bodies below on the dance floor created a world with no rules. Just move with the music, walk with the music and talk with the music.

The mezzanine level had private booths for the popular and wealthy people. They were singled out as they entered the club and asked whether they want a booth. And for people who wanted discretion there's a private entrance along a side alley. Politicians would lose a few votes if they saw their picture on page six of the New York Post going into a swank club. In the private booths they could hold court and watch the activity going on below.

The press was kept contained outside. Security and privacy are what people want in this dance world. Eva's dance world.

From one rhythmic beat to another the music changed, never ending. Eva watched the mass of bodies below and sipped her orange juice. The twins were dancing with what looked like a male model and enjoying. Eva knew he would be home with one of them in a few hours. She always enjoyed coming to this club. Her favorite of the ones she owned. She liked to see the rich and famous people that she knew and did not know and hoped to meet. They were like her in many respects. In that they worked hard and wanted to play harder with people of their same position in life. Nobody wants questions by strangers when enjoying a night out.

The rich and famous can feel secure at Eva's clubs. She looked and saw many the booths filled. Some had their privacy curtains closed for intimacy.

Ivan appeared and approached glancing over at Eva. Not known were the secret hallways for a quick escape. A few famous people had used them in the past when a situation called for a quick escape because of an unwanted friend or lover showing up.

Mia and Mya were making their way to the booth. They had a different blond-haired man in tow. Eva smiled as they sat in the overstuffed chairs. The security detail for Eva was closely watching the new arrival. The security they did not see was racing through the Internet to find the latest information on this individual while checking their own databases.

"Hi, Eva." Said the twins. The blond nodded and just stared lazily at Eva.

"Found a new dance partner I see.

Where's the model?" The blonde's sneer showed disdain for the comment.

"He had to go." Mia said.

"He's gay." The blond said. The twins did not like his answer, and Eva did not care for it either.

"I prefer to dance with you red." The blond said, and Eva smiled graciously. The twins looked at Eva with a subdued smile. Ivan stood behind the blond-haired man keeping eye contact with Eva.

"I choose mine when I am ready." Eva replied.

"Get a life red. You don't have that much game." The blond said. The twins leaned back out of his sight and covered their mouths to hide a laugh.

"Oh, I have choices everyday if I choose. What is your name blondie?"

Blondie put another sneer on his face.

"Hey red, be nice or I'll have you bounced out of this club. I do know the owner."

"Okay." Eva said with a smile.

"I know many people in this town. My dad is a powerful lawyer. The name is Eric Green."

He extended a hand. Eva just looked at it. He retracted his hand not looking satisfied. Behind Eric, Ivan waited for a nod and nobody would see this guy again but, Eva wanted to play yet.

"So, you aren't social, red."

"When the company is good, I can be very seductive."

Eric stared at her for just a moment.

"I bet you are red. Hey, you got a name red."

"The names red."

Both locked eyes.

"Sure, cool name. Okay big red wants some snort."

"No, I am not in the mood."

Eric laughed and pulled out a small vile of white powder. He poured and indulged himself. The twins did not want any. Eva knew they would in a better situation. She did not blame the twins and they knew this. It wasn't the first freak encounter.

"Well girls want to hit the dance floor. Your mom is boring me."

"Yea." The twins said in harmony.

The three took off to dance. Ivan approached Eva. She knew the look on his face and shook her head no. Then said. "Get Uri."

Ivan pulled out his cell phone and spoke rapidly in Russian. He closed the phone and nodded.

Eva looked down on the mass of people dancing. She saw the young Eric dancing with the twins. He did not have a care in the world tonight but, his dad is going to be awful angry in the morning.

A small entourage of people came walking by the booth. Eva saw somebody in the group she knew.

"Bob." Eva yelled.

A large well-groomed gray-haired man

looked around with a frightful look then he saw Eva and relaxed. The young lady on his arm wasn't his wife and the men with him, also, were not with their wives. So, the frightful look at first was real. Senator Bob Wellington of New York could not afford to have a picture taken now. Eva was walking to him.

"Hi, Eva."

"Bob."

"Good to see you, thanks again for the accommodations on my trip last month. It's a beautiful country, Russia."

"Bob you're always welcome. People there enjoyed seeing you."

"Yes, I saw and met some good people. My wife also enjoyed herself."

The Senator then glanced over at the young lady standing a few feet away. She had a sour look on her face.

"You are always welcome there, and I see you have a good time waiting for you. Do not let me hold you up."

The Senator smiled. He looked over at his friends then back at Eva.

"Yes, I don't want to be rude. You understand. But how about lunch Friday say noon time at my office."

"Sure, I'll be there Bob."

"Thank you, Eva." They shook hands lightly and parted. The Senator with his entourage headed to a private booth. Eva was at her seat thinking clearly even with the beat of the music. Why does her Aunt

Catherine want the man dead? Eva knew she must play along until she hears otherwise.

The dancers were in a frenzy now. Eva looked over at Ivan who just gave her a shrug of his shoulders. It meant he sent a message for Uri and he should be here soon. She sipped her orange juice and waited.

Eva looked over and saw the curtain closed partially to the Senators booth. The Senator from New York State. Raised in an exclusive neighborhood and groomed to do something in life. The Senator had helped Eva in the past with immigration. He never asked for anything in return but, she has donated to his campaign as required. Now, with his trip to some former Soviet republics some years earlier they have grown closer, professionally. Eva has helped him find some family history of his in Germany and he appreciated it. He had just won reelection to the Senate and took a first-class tour of Russia. He must have stepped on some toes or asked the wrong questions. His nephew did lose a few million of the family's money in real estate but, Eva knew that she and her family stood far from that deal. She did get her cut of the money, though.

A loud noise got her attention. It was Uri bear hugging with Ivan. He then came into the booth.

"Czarina."

Uri took Eva's right hand and kissed it. He then sat close to her, so their bodies touched. Their faces were inches apart.

"I am not the Czarina, my dear Uri."

Uri put a surprised look on his face.

"You will be my sister, I feel it."

"Yes, maybe, and have you been hiding from me Uri."

"No. Uri has been taking care of business."

"What can Uri tell me of this business."

"Uri reports that business is good. When the shortage ended people bought even more in Europe"

"Yes, the shortage was necessary. The police needed a bust. We sacrificed a pawn to save the dream. Oleg will be out of jail in time and live happily ever after."

"Yes, the things we must do," Uri said looking off for a moment then back at Eva. "The thing's people will do for us."

"Yea and all is good then."

"Yes." Uri answered seriously.

"Well the slow paces of your money coming in must be from the shortage needed in Europe to show that Oleg was the king pin."

"Yes, and for security reasons." Uri said.

"Okay Uri, if there are going to be more delays, let me know. I have people to answer to."

"Sure." Uri paused, and then said. "I think there's competition. Somebody is selling product in Europe for a low price and taking some of our business."

Eva looked at him for a moment, and then said. "I'll have Max look into that."

"And Nicolas, the hothead. He wanted product for his movie friends and wouldn't leave me alone until it got there." Uri looked at Eva pleading.

"Yes, I got word, and talked with him. People in that business are such addicts. Worse than the street people." Eva finished and giggled. She then squinted her eyes at Uri. "You had better not tell him I said that."

Uri put his head back and looked sternly at Eva. "I will never betray the future Czarina."

"Thank you, Uri."

"Okay, I have money ready. How would you like it, so I can tell my Jewish friends. Cash or diamonds?"

Eva thought for a moment. "Split it in threes. One third to Aunt Catherine and one third to dad. Diamonds for Aunt Catherine and cash for Dad."

"Done." Uri nodded.

Eva smiled warmly at him and knew he had the toughest job in the family. The drug business gave the best profits but much risk.

"Uri, I'm sorry for asking about the late transfer of money but, Aunt Catherine is the boss." Eva said kindly.

"My sister. You need never say sorry. You're my boss and I always tell you the truth." Uri said with his trademark sneer.

"Thank you, my brother."

Uri picked up Eva's hands and kissed them. Then up and gone with his bodyguard.

Eva smiled and watched as he left. She

loved her family and her brothers especially. They always showed their respect to her and she loved them.

Eva then looked at the dance floor and saw Eric Green with the twins and took out her cell phone. She called her brother, Max. After a few moments he answered.

"Maxi what's up."

"Oh, the usual. Watching over the world. Why, you need help?"

"I'm at my club in New York and on the dance floor with the twins is Eric Green. His dad is a powerful lawyer or, so he says. Probably the name sounds familiar. Now, he disrespected me earlier and I did not like that."

"That pig disrespected you. He will not live to see daylight."

"No Max. If his father is a famous man then he would not like to see his son, say, dating men."

A silence then a hearty laugh from Max.

"Yes, I can do that. He won't sit for weeks."

"Need pictures. You'll have to hurry the newspapers will start printing in a few hours. Use the usual connection, and yes, Internet it."

"I will do with pleasure. I will not let you down." Max said with a laugh.

"Bye Max and thank you."

Eva smiled to herself then looked at Ivan. The corners of his mouth were upturned, he knew something funny was going to happen.

Eva motioned for him to come sit by her. He took a seat close to her and waited as she thought something through.

"Contact Nicolas and tell him to be at dad's birthday party this weekend. Tell him I need to see him face to face."

Ivan nodded.

"And I am ready to leave."

Eva saw the twins coming up and toward the booth. They looked sad. Eva waited and stayed sitting. Ivan got up and went to the side talking on his cell phone.

"What's the matter?" Eva asked as the twins plopped on the seats.

"Oh, some blond bitch stole Eric from us." Mia said with a pout on her face.

"Yea, and she wasn't even a real blond." Mya said.

Eva could see Ivan hearing this and covering his mouth.

"You are two attractive ladies. Somebody will come-along. I am leaving now."

They put pouts on their faces. Eva got up and Ivan took the lead. She waved at the twins and they waved back.

Eva followed him into a hidden doorway that opened and closed fast. Inside the poorly lit hallway men were waiting with flashlights to guide them. Within moments the back door opened while Eva waited momentarily for the area to be checked.

An all clear and Ivan escorted her to the BMW. Few people knew of Eva in the normal world and a few in the abnormal world. One is never too sure.

Eva looked out at the passing buildings. Some windows lit up some not. She wondered what it would be like to live a normal life. Start a small business and have a few children and a husband. The same thing day after day. No, she thought. She was too advanced. She liked this life better.

She thought of Joe Bergen from earlier in the day. He was more handsome than she remembered and quite intelligent. Eva remembered what Al told her after the meeting. He's a person of loyalty to people above and below his standing. He is quick with figuring out complex things and will go the course even if he does not agree.' Al gave him a positive grade and feels he would be an asset to the company.

Eva thought back to that day many years ago when a lanky young man happened down the alley. He was cool under pressure and never reported what he saw. She liked that. She was ready to proceed to bring Joe Bergen into her world with or without his wife. Eva smiled.

Chapter 16

The morning sun shone through the kitchen windows. It was one hour later than Joe was usually home. Carol had made him breakfast more than usual. A plate over flowing with eggs and bacon.

Joe was going to enjoy early retirement. He already felt like slowing. He felt rested and in no rush to be anywhere. Might be okay, he thought.

"Thanks for the plate of food."

Without taking her eyes off the newspaper Carol said.

"I had to get rid of the eggs before they went bad."

Joe smiled but did not show the happiness that he felt by that answer. Her sarcasm was a sign of thawing.

"I still have time if you want to do anything."

Carol cleared her throat and turned the page of the newspaper.

"There's nothing I can possibly think of that we can do."

Good, Joe thought. The ice was melting. Maybe she saw the documents in the den he left out showing the purchase price.

Carol folded the paper and put it down. She got started clearing the table. Joe gathered the newspapers. The phone rang, and it sounded like an intrusion in the quiet morning. Carol answered it.

"Hello. Oh hi, Paul. Yes. Fine thank you."

Carol held the phone out to Joe.

"It's for you."

"Thanks."

Joe watched Carol pile the dishes into the sink. She looked good in the tight sweatpants.

"What's up, Paul?"

"Joe, I think you should get here. A group from XO food service has arrived. They're swarming all over the place. To say the least, they are taking over."

"Wait, who's there?"

"The new bosses I assume. Thom's with the leader. There's two in accounting and a few in the warehouse. They posted a bulletin that tells about the XO food group and the future of this warehouse. It's creating havoc with the warehousemen. The warehouse manager is trying to keep the guys calm but, he knows little about this himself."

"Okay." Joe let out a breath.

"There's murmuring of being left out to dry."

"Wait a minute. Paul, I haven't signed off on this deal yet. They have no right to do this. Who's in charge of the group that's there?

"I don't know. I tried talking to Thom but, they're not allowing us to have any privacy. All the one said is they're taking inventory and you already approved this."

"I approved it. I'll be there shortly."

Joe hung the phone and stood for a moment. He tried to understand what was happening. People show up at his business and are taking control. He did not sign over yet. He remembers signing a few documents but, why were they doing this like this. They have no right to do this.

Carol was making noise as she washed the dishes and ignored Joe.

Joe left the kitchen and went to change clothes and tried to keep calm.

Chapter 17

Joe pulled into the parking lot and checked the rear-view mirror to be sure the police were not chasing him for the red traffic lights he went through. He pulled next to his reserved parking spot and found another car parked there. A BMW with New York plates on it. Joe had to park a few spots away and felt his anger starting to grow. He needed to stay calm and find out what the hell was going on.

He entered the front doors and tried to smile to Erica the receptionist. She stood and started to say something, and Joe waved for her to sit. He took the steps two at a time to the upper management level. He stopped for a moment at the top to catch his breath and calm himself. He then walked to his office and heard voices coming from inside. Stopping in the doorway he saw Thom seated in front of his desk and a man he did not know sitting behind the desk in his seat, his chair.

The laughter stopped, and they looked at Joe. The smiles faded as they took in Joe's grim look. Thom started. "Hey, running a little late today."

Joe ignored Thom and walked to the front of his desk and extended his hand. "I'm Joe Bergen and you are?"

The man stood keeping eye contact with Joe. He was a little taller and heavier than Joe. A likelihood of fistfight wasn't going to happen. Maybe throw him down the front lobby stairs was not a far-off thought.

"I'm John Selvecki. In charge of the transition team. We're here to do a fast accounting of physical assets. We're here to match the numbers on paper. That was stated in the documents you signed yesterday. A site assessment will be done before the final signing. We also will need to look over your books."

Joe felt at a loss. Things happening too boldly. Did he sign an agreement to this?

"Right, how many with you?" Joe folded his arms across his chest.

"There's fifteen throughout the facility. The majority being in the warehouse checking physical equipment assets and will do a product inventory."

John fixed his suit jacket and came around from the desk. Joe then went around and sat behind his desk. He waved John to take a seat where he had been standing.

Thom broke the tension. "We were sharing a laugh about this just when you walked in." Thom tossed the New York Post Newspaper on Joe's desk. The front page pictured two young men arm in arm with briefs on. The second picture showed them kissing. 'A Butt Out.' Screamed the title with blurting under it reading. 'The eldest son of Eric Green Sr. the buyout lawyer/ Mongol has his own idea of a buyout.' Also, a regal picture of his father was inserted.

Joe stared at the picture for a few moments then looked at Thom then John. He knew the father was the owner of a big-time buyout firm that has made friends and enemies over the years. A public flogging maybe. It did catch Joe off guard and lighten his mood somewhat. He laughed and the other two continued their laughter.

Joe knew from news reports that old man Green was a tough old goat. He lived by the rule of God, country and family values. So today Mr. Green senior is probably ten shades of red. Joe pities anyone working at his offices today. He opened the page and saw another picture of Mr. Green and Senator Wellington together. Big connections there, Joe thought.

"Well, I guess one never knows." Thom blurted. "Junior won't be carrying-on the family name." He added.

The three laughed again. When that, settled down Joe tossed the paper back to Thom. Then he looked over at John.

"Okay, I was aware an on-site assessment was going to occur. I imagined it was weeks away with a schedule prepared."

John nodded slightly. "Before we begin, I

do have this for you."

John picked up his briefcase, opened it and took out two envelopes. He handed them to Joe. The first envelope was from Rich Holbrook and the second was from CZ Corp. Joe opened the one from Rich first. He glanced over it and saw it handwritten and signed by Rich. At first Joe thought it was a smoke screen. The letter said he directed the team to do an assessment. He hoped it would not interrupt his business today. Thank you and good-bye. And XO food service was looking forward to a great future with Bergen foods. He'd be in the office Monday if there's questions. He wanted to crush and throw it but, a done deal. Not the way he wanted it done but, that's the way it goes sometimes.

Joe handed the letter to Thom who quickly read it and looked back at Joe with a look. A bunch of crap.

Thom then put the letter on the desk as Joe realized it was a reality check for Thom. Big business. He'd have to prove himself to this big corporate monster. The unknown can be frightening, Joe knew.

Joe looked at John. He wanted to ask what would happen to Thom and a few others he cared for. He knew that would be useless. Joe then spoke.

"So, Mr. Holbrook will be gone until, Monday."

"Yes, he has many facilities to oversee."

"Well, I guess I'll call him Monday. I have

questions regarding the future of some employees here."

John nodded then said. "There's enough opportunities in the XO food company for qualified people."

"Yes, I am certain there is." Joe said halfheartedly and decided to let that question go.

He picked up the second envelope and immediately felt the difference in the thickness of the paper and the raised lettering of the company name. He opened and took out an engraved invitation that had raised lettering as the envelope. Joe looked at the letters and wondered whether it was real gold.

The card read that they invited Joe and his wife Carol to the sixty eighth-birthday party for the Co-Chairperson of CZ Corp., Nicolas Bokanawski. Joe looked at John.

"I don't want to sound too dumb but, who is Nicolas Bokanawski. I had met Eva Bokanawski."

Joe noticed a visual change in John. He grew happier.

"Yes, Eva is the boss. She is the CEO and President. Her father is the Co-Chairperson."

"I see. It really is a family business."

"Yes." Was all John said and smiled.

"What time's the party? I did have plans for the weekend." Thom said. Joe and John looked at him.

"It's just for me and Carol." He told Thom then asked John. "Are others invited?"

"I would say not. They usually invite the principles." Thom's facial expression dropped slightly, and Joe knew the unknown was starting to sink in. He hoped Thom could handle the future.

"Do bring the invitation because, security is tight at the estate." John said.

The word estate struck Joe with a surprise. Still holding the invitation admiring the weight he read the notation on the bottom that pointed to the back of the card. Turning it over he saw the estate address that had a picture of a little castle. That little picture spoke volumes to him as he caught his thoughts and looked at John.

"Okay John, let me give you the first-class tour of Bergen foods and get this assessment done."

The three stood and Paul came into the office. This surprised Joe. Paul normally would knock and be polite.

"Ah Paul. This is John Selvecki. Paul Letter. Human Resources director."

They shook hands. Joe felt something was not right with Paul. Holding a paper in his hand and he held it up to John.

"Why's this posted down on the bulletin board? It's still Bergen foods until he tells us otherwise." Paul pointed at Joe. "It's creating a problem with the workforce. They are grouped together talking and not working." Paul's face was contorted with hatred.

Joe spoke before this developed into further. "Paul, they are here just to do an assessment. I am officially selling, and I owe an apology to everybody here for not relaying this sooner. Now, I want you to post a bulletin saying that I will have a meeting soon to inform everyone. I will pay the warehouse people who shift has ended and stay for the meeting." Joe walked over and stood by Paul, so he knew this was final. He also took the paper from Paul.

"Okay. You're still the boss Joe. Okay." Paul said then left the office without saying another word. Joe then stated to John.

"Paul has a talent for hiring the right people and does wonders with getting us the best insurance for everybody. He has filled this place with some very productive people. I would advise they keep him on. He's an asset here."

John scratched his chin and seemed deep in thought about something then said. "Yes, he's like a pit bull."

They shared a laugh and looked to one another momentarily. This was an uncomfortable situation building Joe knew, he had to keep things calm until he signed off and said good-bye.

"You leading, Joe. Or you forgot already where the warehouse is." Thom said, and it helped lighten the mood.

"Yea, follow me." Joe said. He watched John's face. The man was in deep thought.

Joe felt this may not be a happy good-bye.

Chapter 18

Eva was in a dream state as she ate a light lunch in the private dining room of Senator Bob Wellington's office. The room had a sweeping eastward view of Manhattan. Eva wouldn't tell the Senator the view was grander at her office.

The conversation had been pleasant with light conversation of family and politics. She knew this invitation was not to shoot the breeze. The punch line was coming, and she would not laugh.

Eva knew that politicians took their time getting to the point, so, just coast along. She wondered why people took pride in talking a lot but, say nothing.

The assessment of Bergen foods the day before came back impressive. Eva felt it is a well-run business with a good growth rate. She knew that did not happen accidentally. Some growth came from her and Joe took advantage of it.

Eva sipped her coffee and looked out the window at the paltry view. The noise of Bob putting down his silverware on the plate annoyed Eva. The man has no manners, she thought. She hated that clanking sound.

"That was delicious." The Senator said. Eva agreed by nodding slightly. A staff member cleared off the table and left. Eva kept her cup of coffee and the Senator poured one for himself.

"Let me talk now. Eva, I know your family runs a multinational company in Europe and Russia. I know you have a few connections there." The Senator let that linger and took a sip of his coffee then dabbed his mouth with a napkin.

"I'm not trying to pry into your business. I know your father is a patriot to his country and helped the people of Russia during the Soviet Union days. I would like to take advantage of that sentiment and love you have for your country. I know there are mob groups in Russia. There's a bad group called the Reds. This group makes the Italian mobs look like schoolkids. They have a good hold in the country there and enforce their business brutally. I don't know whether you have a problem with them. What I need is help on finding out who runs that mob. I did ask a few people in government there and got a little information, but I need something more."

The Senator stopped and looked at Eva. She pretended to think of an answer.

"Well, thugs come around some businesses my family operates there trying to get money from the workers. We beefed up security and they seem to stay away. Now, I read about that big bust in the Netherlands a few weeks ago. It's said he was the largest dealer in that party drug stuff and a member of the Red mob. I hope he gets life in prison. People taking that stuff don't know what they are doing."

Eva stopped and tried not to laugh. The Senator rubbed his chin and looked serious. He then began slowly.

"I feel information we get on this Mob can be used to dismantle them. It'll be a big help for the people of Russia and probably the world. I am doing a special investigation in our Russian communities here in New York to see whether they're bothering people here. I want to know if that mob is here on American shores, if so, we will arrest them. Can't have that going on in America."

The Senator stopped, and Eva sensed that he wanted to say more. She needed to keep this going.

"I am relieved to hear that you want take action. You know the Russian government is trying to combat corruption but, they're new at this sort of thing and it will take time. How may I help?"

Bob's eyes brightened. Eva realized he must have been talking and probing too much on his trip to Russia. Maybe the reason Aunt Catherine wants him dead, Eva thought.

"You can help by getting any information on the inner workings of this mob and the top people. I did contact the Netherlands police but, they wanted to just arrest that person expecting to stem the tide of that drug. They did not question the guy much, Oleg something. They said he was the kingpin and he will do some jail time. They didn't investigate enough. Arresting the top guy, they think all will be okay now."

The Senator stopped, shook his head in disgust then continued. "My nephew tried an investment deal in Moscow with real estate. He lost ten-million dollars on a real-estate scam. The police there said it was probably the Red mob. I hate to see this happen to others. He's a good kid and let it go. He chalked it up to not knowing the right people there. So yes, you can say this crusade of mine is a bit personal."

The Senator looked out the window. Eva knew that the ten million dollars was a hurt for the Senator and his nephew. But she enjoyed taking the money. They do not realize that Russia is not America and people there do not want foreigners coming into their country and buying everything on the cheap. She was not going to tell him this bit of information. She will give key information on the Red mob. That will help her and give Bob Wellington a sense of righteousness.

"Yes, it probably was. They muscled their way into some businesses there. Like I said, we pay for a security team to keep them away from our businesses. When the time comes, and the police do something it'll be a welcome relief. I am concerned that this Red mob will trade their souls to terrorists. We don't need terror attacks happening in Russia, and I'm sorry to hear about your nephew and the scam."

Eva looked sad at the Senator. He quickly jumped in.

"No, he does not blame all Russian people for what happened because of a few bad ones. He works as an investment banker and is earning that money back and learning to forget. I feel the best way is a formation with the Russian government to combat this and other mob groups. People have a right to live in a free environment without predators intending to gain from their hard-earned money."

Yes, and be at the mercy of elected politicians who want to control people's lives for their enjoyment. Yes, raise taxes and let select corporations buy their favors so the poor will stay poor. Yes, you chosen ones play god and tear apart other companies while ruining people who do not suck-up to you elected ones. And you're not a mob yourselves? Eva thought and smiled at the Senator and knew she would without doubt give a little information to help contain and rattle the Red mob.

"Yes, that sounds good Bob but, how will you sell that to American's who don't care about what goes on in Russia. I mean, some may wonder why you want to combat a crime group that doesn't affect people here.

Like you said, they prey on the weak in Russia. I appreciate it with the people of Russia." Eva finished with a smile.

"Yes Eva, I realize that apparently, it will look a little unusual a U.S. Senator being interested in global crime. My reason will reveal itself in time. Then all including you will understand. Yes, it's personal, they took some of my family's money. It opened my eyes. It'll be a big help for American companies me starting this push now. It'll work."

"I look forward to it. It'll be a welcome relief for people in the world who want to earn an honest income and keep it."

A silence started, and Eva felt Bob wanted something more or he wanted to say more. Yes, Aunt Catherine knew something about this Senator. Eva knew this great push would not affect her family because few know of the Czarina and her business.

"I thank you for coming today Eva. Now, watch the news. I have an announcement coming.

Bob lifted his big frame from the chair and Eva also was up. She looked gingerly up at him. "What's the big announcement? You can tell me."

"I don't want to say just yet. You'll be surprised, and I won't forget friends who have been by my side all along."

"You're going to run for President." Eva said.

Bob put a sheepish look on his face then

straightened.

"Wait for the announcement."

"Okay, I will."

Eva shook hands with Bob. He then escorted her to the door. Eva turned around and looked at him for a moment. "I think you'll be a good one."

Bob nodded his head. "Just wait and see."

Eva left the building and got into a Lincoln limo. Ivan was in the front seat next to the driver. He waited inside the car. His presence was not needed in the office building. It would create a stir when people saw his physical stature. Besides, a few casual observers working for the family were in the immediate area of Eva. So, Ivan knew her every move and would be there in a New York moment if needed.

The limo moved through the streets of Manhattan as Eva looked at the foot traffic on the sidewalks. She knew that her family dealings were unknown, and she planned on keeping it that way. She understood now. Senator Bob was going to run for President and pull the lid off global crime. He did not realize that some did not want that lid to open.

The limo stopped for a traffic light and Eva looked at the newspaper stand showing the daily front stories. Her mood darkened at the thought of her or anybody in her family being in those papers like the Italian mob always was. No turncoats in her family. No pictures or stories about her will ever be read in the newspapers. She turned her head away from the newspaper stand and will wait for Aunt Catherine to make her move.

Chapter 19

Bob was sitting behind his desk when a call came in. He lifted the phone and knew it was his nephew. The kid as he mentally called him was not as smooth as his father, Bob knew. His brother set him on the political track. His brother was an exceptional stock broker and helped finance his first campaign years ago. Introducing Bob to many big business people who were behind him to this day. Bob in return helped pass laws that helped the big business make more profit. He helped them, and they helped him with every campaign to get reelected. A delicate dance that could go on forever. Bob needs them and Big Business in New York needs Bob Wellington. However, Bob wished his nephew had at least an ounce of brains his long-departed father did.

"Hi Don. What's up?"

"Hi. I hear you had a lunch with that Russian bitch."

Bob wished he knew who the leak was in his office.

"Yes, she is a big contributor to my

campaign."

"Did she give you your money back?"

"She doesn't owe me any money, Don."

Bob rolled his eyes and listened.

"Like I said, she is Russian mob. I told you about a guy I met in Moscow."

"Yes, Don, he told you she was Russian Mob and he disappeared. The man was probably just a drunk and looking to start trouble. Like I told you, I had a quiet check done and she and her family are clean."

"Yea, they probably paid the right people."

"Don, the point of this call?"

"I have more money for you. That leaves five million left to pay back."

"Okay, thank you Don."

"Your check on her came clean but, I am doing my own and will show you who she and her family are."

Bob was ready to yell but, he knew he should just let Don run his course and find out for himself. Just let it go.

"Okay, Don, do what you are going to do. Bye."

"Bye."

Don sat behind his desk at a major brokerage firm in downtown Manhattan. His father had been a major player on Wall Street some years ago. It ended with an automobile accident that was his fault. The post mortem tests revealed a high alcohol content and the lady he was with also died. The lady was a personal assistant of his dads from the office. Don's mother never recovered from that day. He was young at the time and when he did find out the truth years later, he pretended it did not matter but, it did.

He decided to leave that buried in the past and take a job at the firm at which his father had help found. For Don knew it was his ticket to riches. He went to a New England university and earned the proper degrees that opened the door to the firm. After a few years he had an office a desk and some good clients. He did make a bundle trading in his own money through the firm. He was financially earning his own way. Not as fast as Don wanted the money to build but, he could not complain until a year ago when he met a lady who knew people in Russia. She talked of a vast wide-open market where he could make much money in real estate. Don though got killed, financially.

He tried to even the score by having his Uncle Bob go to Russia and ask a lot of questions in private. It was useless, the government was not concerned with the loss of money. They nicely told him that they never should have even tried such a thing right now. The opening and stabilization of the real estate market there was still new and open to fraud.

Don decided to take matters in his own hands. He hired a private detective, and both went there. They met a man who was drunk half the time that talked of a powerful mob there that was well hidden, and nobody spoke of them. The drunk man was not to be found the next day when Don and the private detective went to meet him. The man had said some old lady ran the mob. He did not know any names but, Don knew there was some truth to the story.

Don circled the coming Saturday on his calendar. The birthday of the Co-Chairperson of CZ corp. A big party attended by a select few every year. Don's friend who's not invited will also be there.

A good friend of his since grade school and a freelance reporter. He wrote good investigative articles on subjects that concerned people and some that didn't. His stories sold well in magazines and newspapers and got plenty of interest by the public. That kept him doing more investigations for the people wanting something juicy to read.

Don's friend had done an article on CZ Corp. that went nowhere. There was no public interest in the story because of little solid evidence. He did maintain a website for curious readers and accepted information. Which was what happened two days ago. His friend got an inquiry from a man who works at a food service company in New Jersey. CZ Corp. Offered to buy the company and this man wanted to know who CZ Corp. was. He wanted the information for his boss who is the owner. Don's friend sent the man identified as Paul some information and Paul sent back the owner's name who was going to sell his business to CZ Corp. The last Don's friend heard is that his boss Joe Bergen was going to sell, and Paul would keep the line of communication open because he felt something was not right either. Don smiled when he heard this because he knew that is how dirty laundry gets exposed. It'll be a public flogging.

Now his friend was going to jump the fence at this weekend's birthday party and get some good photos. They always needed the pictures to send the story home to most people. Pictures tell a thousand words. The Bokanawski family was very secretive with virtually no pictures available. Maybe a few from a birthday party would cause something.

Don wanted that family crushed and exposed. He wanted them publicly embarrassed and charged with whatever crime they can accuse them of. He knew they had something to do with that real estate scam in Moscow and he was going to make them pay.

He thought back when he went to Moscow and deposited money in a bank and then searched for somebody reputable to buy real estate from. A week later after giving money to the realtor, he disappeared along with his store front and Don's money.

This guy Paul said his boss Joe Bergen was going to the birthday party and Don knew nobody gets invited to that party unless they are someone or going to be someone in CZ corp.

Don leaned back looking at the calendar and thought of one name, Joe Bergen.

Chapter 20

At an upscale restaurant the usual evening customers were happily chatting away. The laughter and food were complimentary as Joe and Carol enjoyed the night out. His stock broker was there sitting at the bar. Joe saw him earlier and wanted to talk but, he was on soft ice with Carol and attention to her was the most important right now.

He then remembered the stock he bought the other day, hadn't checked it. Maybe that was why his stock broker kept walking into view and back to the bar. He has trusted Stanley for seven years and didn't lose his principal money with the last downturn the year before.

Joe decided to make his move. He put down his utensils and sat looking at Carol. He knew she did not like when he went to hang at the bar but, he had to find out what Stanley wanted.

"I need to go see Stanley. He keeps watching me."

Carol looked at him with a jolt at first then softened.

"Go ahead. Tell him I said Hi."

Joe went to the bar area which was livelier. He sat on a stool next to Stanley.

"So how wealthy am I today." Joe asked Stanley who abruptly turned to him.

"You're up ten percent this week with the risky money you wanted invested. Or call that the money you wanted invested in risky stocks. The mutual funds are going well, nothing explosive. You should reach the million-dollar mark by the end of the year. The goal you wanted me to achieve."

Joe smiled and nodded. "I can start looking for that beach house."

"Maybe you should start looking for your own beach to buy." Stanley said between sips of drink then continued. "Joe I'm your broker. You put your money in my trust so you must be honest with me. How did you pick TWM?"

"Oh, did I lose a lot. I haven't had time to check."

"You're up two hundred percent from your twenty thousand. Yes, sixty thousand at the market close today. How did you? Come on now, tell me."

Joe shocked at first then thought back to Al. How did Al know?
"It was just a tip I got at a business meeting this past week. I'm selling the business."

Stanley sipped his drink and held his hand up. He turned on his stool to face Joe.

"Start slowly and tell me this again."

"I'm offered over one hundred million and am going to take it.'

"Who's the buyer?"

"XO food service. They're expanding and want my customer base. It's nothing but a warehouse full of food. It's about the customers. The parent company is an outfit called CZ Corp."

Stanley shook his head. "The names don't sound familiar. A private company but, one hundred mill? I would say that is a very generous offer. I would value your business at three quarters at best. Sorry."

"Yes, they seem very private and family owned. I met the CEO and you would kiss the ground she walks on. Gorgeous doesn't even begin to describe her."

The bartender came down the bar and Joe waved him off.

"Well now, I think we need to sit and go over your investment options. You will need more than just mutual funds to realize the full potential of your money. I can get you an interest income of ten percent, that's flexible though. To get you into better involves risk."

Joe just smiled and knew Stanley was being the sales broker.

"Stanley, you still have my business and we'll talk when I have a check in hand."

"Very good, I'll clear my calendar when you call."

They laughed and settled into a warm

area.

"So, you heard about this stock at a business meeting."

"Yea, they told me not to tell anybody. It was at CZ Corp. headquarters in New York. A guy named Al from the accounting department mentioned it. He said buy it and sell by Friday. I won't be let down."

Stanley was in deep thought for a moment then took a sip of his drink and began.

"You had a tip on a meteor. That's what we call it. No rhyme or reason why this occurs. It's huge. What I'm saying is some companies stock around earnings season rise meteorically though their quarterly report is nothing unusual. They rise almost one hundred percent. Now, investigations lead nowhere. Stocks are bought by a huge swath of people who have no connection with the companies in question. Also, they sell after a period and profit. I'm talking over a million people that buy all sorts of amounts of the stocks of the companies in question. Nobody gets burned when it happens though. That's why there's no criminal investigation. No dots to connect and nobody is losing money or getting burned when it happens. There's nothing for the SEC to go after. You my friend were touched by a lucky meteor. A shooting star."

Stanley finished and looked at Joe blankly.

"This been happening long? I mean you said no body was getting hurt by it. What do you mean it's huge?" Joe asked quietly.

"Like I said. A large group of people around the world for no rhyme or reason all jump in certain stocks and then out of them in a few days' time. It's huge. I've watched this for about five years now. The SEC mentioned it in a meeting a few years ago and said they find nothing wrong. I myself have did some checking on Internet bulletin boards and blogs. I found no place online where anyone gathers to plan or decide which ones to buy. There is no known sign of collusion."

"Am I going to be in any trouble for buying that stock? Investigated?"

"No. If in the slight chance, they ask you. You just liked the company and bought the stock." Stanley smiled an evil grin and sipped his drink.

"Wow, how did this guy at CZ Corp. know." Joe looked puzzled at Stanley.

"I would guess he liked the stock also. Don't question it, my friend. You just made a handsome profit, and nobody got hurt. Sell the stock and take the money. Nobody gets burned."

"You sound almost like you like it. Or know something, Stan."

"I'm in the brokerage business and if people get scared and lose their money then they won't come to me for investment of their money. I know of no information on why this happens. It's good for my line of business though. You understand. But, would I sell my soul to know ahead of time and profit from it, no. They would investigate me. Not good for business. There's big interest in investing since this has been occurring. A plus for us brokers. We just need to stay away from it."

Joe nodded and smiled lightly at Stanley.

"I understand. You had me scared for a moment."

They were quiet for a moment. Then Stanley broke the silence.

"Now, my best customer. When can we spend the day going over the planning of your estate? I have some good financial vehicles that you may like. Yes, Joe, I have some glossy brochures for you to take home to Carol."

Joe laughed at Stanley's sales smile. Then realized he was here a few minutes too long. Yes, Carol, he needs to get back to his table. Joe extended his hand to Stanley.

"I need to get back to Carol. Things have been rocky lately. Oh, keep it quiet, the sale. This place is a customer. Don't want them pulling out before the sale."

"I will and I am the keeper of secrets my friend."

Both shared a laugh.

"I'll be at your office soon."

"Go take care of business at the table. I don't want to have to divide assets."

"Right."

Joe left the bar area and headed back to his table and hoping Carol was not irritated. He turned the corner to the dining area and saw a man sitting at the table, in his chair. He saw Carol was chatting happily and smiling. Jealously raged inside Joe for a moment then quickly went away.

As he approached and Carol saw him, the animation left her face. The man stood smiling.

"Hello. You must be Joe. I'm Bill Shea. I'm the new manager at the bank and remember seeing Carol there today. Just thought I'd stop by and say hello."

"Good to meet you." Joe said and shook hands with Bill. He put more pressure than was needed. Bill did not visually respond.

"Well, I must be going. Joe, we do have some good investment instruments that may interest you at the bank. Stop in someday when you have time."

"I already have an investment adviser and he does a great job with my investments."

"Okay then. Joe, Carol. Bye."

Bill walked away and Joe sat looking at a knife and decided too many people knew him here. He lost his appetite and looked at Carol. She stared at him blankly.

Joe raised his hand for the waiter who was quickly there.

"I think we're finished here." Joe said and Carol nodded her head yes.

The waiter snapped his fingers for someone to clear the table.

"Would you like dessert, Mr, Mrs, Bergen."

They shook their heads no. The waiter then left and returned quickly with the bill in a leather case. Joe opened it and written over the two hundred-dollar meal was, no charge. Joe did go into his wallet and leave the standard tip. Though his customers do not charge him, he still left something for the workers.

As Joe and Carol were leaving not known to them a couple who was casually watching them from another table. As they left the dining area, the lady took out a cell phone and dialed a number then spoke rapidly in Russian.

Chapter 21

At home a while later they both were settled in the entertainment room. Joe sipping a drink and Carol reading a novel.

"So, what's will Bill the banker."

Joe felt foolish saying that, but he already said it. When another man put a smile on Carol's face it irritated him.

Carol closed her book.

"He's the new bank manager and was just being friendly. He received a promotion and transfer from another branch.

"Just trying to be pleasant."

"I would guess that's why he is the bank manager. He speaks very well and is knowledgeable. In the bank he talked with all customers, regardless their standing."

"Maybe we should change banks. I prefer a larger one. If he talks to every one of every station in life, I don't want our account holdings being general conversation." Joe said with slight anger.

"I don't think he would be going around like some old biddy telling others what we have in the bank. He didn't tell me of any other customers account holdings."

"Well, we should change to a larger bank because, we're going to be beyond the services of a local bank."

Carol looked at Joe with squinted eyes.

"Are you jealous? Are you trying to insult me?

Joe knew he started this and should have just bit the bullet.

"No, I'm just a little nervous about tomorrow. I don't know any of these people or the old man."

"Don't change the subject. Tomorrow is just another business engagement disguised as a party.

"I'm not afraid. I just thought they would buy the business and leave. Now I have to attend a party before they sign the papers." Joe stopped and looked directly at Carol then continued.

"I'm ready to retire, so we can spend time together and plan a better future."

Carol stared at Joe with anger in her eyes.

"Since when are you concerned about our lonely childless life."

Joe took a slow sip from his drink and hoped this did not explode. He needed to change the direction.

"What are you wearing tomorrow?"

Carol lightened her facial features a bit.

"I picked up something new. That's why I

went to the bank, to get some cash, and, we know the rest."

Joe felt a little foolish. She was indirectly doing for him and he was trying to accuse her of something.

"Well, you can surprise me in the morning."

Joe glanced over at Carol who was looking at him with a slight smile on her lips. She then got up and put her book on the coffee table.

"I'm off to bed."

"Goodnight."

"Goodnight."

Joe watched her sexy body leave the room. First time this week that she did not go to bed mad. Bill the banker he still did not like though.

Chapter 22

Arrangements were tedious and time-consuming but finished on time for the meeting. The room was in a chic hotel owned quietly by the Czarina which meant that hotel security wasn't concerned in this certain room. That rented for thousands a night.

They had been together an hour, and, Eva wished she had taken a pill earlier. Her nerves were getting frayed. The emissaries for the mobs were also a little frazzled due to the very short notice.

They wore slight coverings, the men, sunglasses, while Eva and the only other woman from Spain used headscarves with sun glasses so to keep their identities hidden. Though not totally, they just did not want to know each other's identity. They were people who held clean jobs and were decent if anyone looked at them. Using clean people enabled the mob groups to communicate and negotiate.

"I feel the Red mob could pose a problem if this is true about the nuclear bomb."

England had said for a second time and Eva was ready to yell at him.

"There's information showing that is the probable course they are on." Eva repeated.

"When they are on this path, we can decide. They move closer we can move closer. The Czarina has not provided us with solid evidence. We appreciate her concern, but we need more than just assumptions." England said and looked around as the others nodded slowly.

"The Czarina will keep you posted on developments." Eva said wishing this was over.

"I hope this emergency meeting wasn't just for that?" The person from France asked.

"No, a senator here in America will run for president. He will take a stand against global crime. He has targeted the Russian mobs already with little help, but as president he could pose a threat. He already knows of the Red mob but little about us or you. This person will be taken care of by the Czarina. No discussion on this." Eva finished and waited.

"The senator's name?" Spain asked.

"Senator Wellington."

"Ah, yes. I have heard of him." Spain answered.

"Yes, very popular. Is this really a good thing to do?" England asked.

"Doesn't matter livelihoods are at risk here. It'll be as stated." Eva said.

"We can publish information afterwards that reveals the senator involved with something questionable. We can make that can happen." Germany said.

Eva smiled. "Czarina will like that."

"Thank the Czarina but we have nothing to offer. We keep away from those situations and keep neutral." France said. It always bothered Eva the way the French mob drew a line in the sand.

"I will tell the Czarina."

"Thank her for the help. We just do not want blood of politicians on our hands. We are open for anything else though." France said.

"I think we all understand that and respect you for that." Eva said.

"I think we are all in agreement on the Czarina's decision to take care of that problem. I offer help if any will be needed." England said.

"I will let her know. That what Germany has planned will help put him to rest sooner. Any help is always appreciated."

"Money hidden in a bank with the Senator's name owning it could be damaging." Spain volunteered.

"Kick-backs from electronics firms would be suitable. He is one of the lead Senators for the missile defense shield." Poland said.

"Bank accounts can be set up." Switzerland said.

"The cooperation will help." Eva said and then changed the topic.

"Has everyone received their proceeds from the real estate deals?"

Everybody nodded. Then France spoke. "That was really dreadful. Many lost their homes. The money was great though."

Eva smiled and continued. "We did not start it. We just took it to a higher level and profited. Now with the economic downfall in most countries I suggest a lower price in the drug area."

"Already did that. Must help the poor." Spain said.

"Yes, we started the price discount with good results." Germany said.

"We do like Wal-Mart." Poland said and that made a few laughs. Eva was hoping France would not say anything.

"Yes, market conditions dictate a lower price now." England said.

"Good. Next delivery will be lower in price. Twenty percent lower." Eva said.

"People will still pay if we left it alone." France said.

Eva stared at him but held it in.

"Yes, we could but that would create a crime wave that no one needs. That's counterproductive to our businesses." Eva responded.

"Yes, we have a responsibility to help society." Spain said.

"A crime wave will bring the law enforcement after our people." Germany said.

"Umm, a happy user is a good citizen."

Poland said.

"Okay, we lower our prices." France said.

"Finally, TWM, made a profit for everyone?" Eva asked and everybody nodded and knew smiles behind the veils.

"Risky isn't it? We like to remain hidden and this is something the press is broadcasting every time it happens." France said.

"The profit outweighs the risk." England said.

"Yes, not illegal one million people buying into a stock. There's a cult following out there. People begging to find which will be next." Germany said.

"Yea, it's kind of sexy to be famous." Spain said.

"Well, you look sexy just the same." Switzerland said.

"Thank you." Spain said.

"Okay now, yes the money is good, but I don't like the fame." France said.

"I understand it was supposed to be a one-time deal, but success keeps it going." Eva said.

"Take the profit as long as it lasts." England said.

"Absolutely. And with that said, this meeting is over. The Czarina wishes everyone prosperity and good health." Eva said.

"We wish the Czarina the same." Spain said and winked at Eva.

The timer started and a few stood to

stretch their bodies. At five-minute intervals one would leave the suite. The five-minute hour glass was then reset for the next. To get on an elevator and leave took five minutes. Eva and Frenchmen were last in the room. She wished the clock would drain faster.

"I know I must sound like a jerk. It's just. We like to stay hidden. The Czarina has done great bringing us together, but we have our natural tendencies. I hope you understand this." France said.

"Yes, it works. We're liberals, conservatives and some are main streams. That keeps us together and one step ahead." Eva said and liked the oneness.

"So, no misunderstandings. We are with you." France said.

"And we're with you."

The sand drained off. The French man stood and bowed to Eva and said. "Good bye."

When the door closed Eva took her head scarf off and let out a breath. She then went into the bathroom and downed a few pills followed with water gulped from the sink. It would take a few minutes she knew as she went into the main room and looked out the window.

The meeting discussions would be reported to Aunt Catherine. The no vote for wiping out the Red mob, Aunt Catherine would not like, Eva knew.

A door opened and closed, and she saw

Ivan in the reflection of the glass window.
Eva turned and looked at him and said.
   "Time to relax."

Chapter 23

Music blearing, people dancing, the light show mesmerizing. One celebrity dancing was always in the news for her free-living life style. Eva knew the young woman would be out of the camera eyes in her club. The young lady would be safe here, tonight.

"Ivan." Eva said.

He was immediately in the chair next to her.

"Bergen, what's the latest."

"Him and wife did dinner at a restaurant. He talked with his broker and then had a few tense words with a new bank manager. Man was sitting with wife when he returned from talking with broker at the bar."

Eva instantly made a mental picture of that and nodded to Ivan. He then got up and took his usual position of seeing everything in the immediate area.

Eva thought for a moment about that situation. Mr. Joe jealous? Was his wife cheating on him? She didn't want to get involved. Eva liked her men free and clear, not in between. No rebounders.

Relationships for Eva are with men on the upside side of life. No day and night. No, I must bed for work in the morning. Not. They have always been extravagant occasions that play out on warm sunny islands or the insides of mansions. Rarely men from common means made the grade. That was too boring for Eva, but Joe Bergen had her interested.

Eva relaxed back in her overstuffed seat and watched the bodies dancing down below. Mia and Mya were like two teenage girls chatting and watching the men.

She thought about the Red mob. They really going to buy and sell a nuke? Was Andre not telling or getting information she wanted?

Eva drank her orange juice and pushed those thoughts aside for now. The music caught her attention again and she was enjoying it. Ivan stepped over and bent down to whisper in her ear.

"It's ready."

Eva nodded. "Okay."

Eva followed Ivan past private booths that had little private parties going on. Once pass the booths and beyond the sight of prying eyes they went through an opened doorway that immediately shut behind them. A short hallway and another door opened that lead into a lounge type area. A private room for people who had the need and money to entertain privately. The room like the club;

swept for any type of hearing or seeing devices. So, anyone entering could feel secure and speak freely.

Her family sat there. Uri, Max, Tatyana, Mikal and Olga.

"On time as usual, Uri." Eva said with a smile as she took a seat on an over-stuffed couch. She leaned back and her dress pulled up farther than would be acceptable in public. She did not care. She was with family

"Sorry, traffic, it's Friday night." Uri said sheepishly.

"Yes, and Tatyana is horny." Mikal said.

A muted laugh from Max and Uri.

They were all adopted when babies by Eva's father and mother. Eva's mother couldn't bare children after giving birth to Nicolas and Eva. Her father and mother then went on to adopt from Russia. Being the Soviet Union at the time it did not deter them from having the large family they always wanted. Eva knew them well and helped raise them.

She and the family took trips to the former Soviet Union when she was young, and Aunt Catherine always showed the most favored status to Eva. Aunt Catherine and her father operated a business of importing and exporting products from one country to another and others. Her Aunt was something special even back then Eva remembers. People called her the Czarina back then, quietly by her friends.

On every trip her Aunt Catherine showed

her how to fight and think on her feet. It was a magical time for Eva for she was impressionable at the time and did learn quite a bit. Eva went on to raise her adopted brother and sisters in the same manner. She formed a loyal group that lived by their own rules and answered to her. Except Nicolas, he was the book worm and the movie goer and did not see a need or desire to join with Eva.

Eva's fondest memory was when they did their first coordinated attack on some local Italian mobster years before. They were kids at the time and gathered in their father's basement to hold meetings. They had been following a newspaper story at the time that featured a local mobster who was famous for terrorizing the neighborhood. His name was Tony the butcher for he liked using knives on his victims. Eva's father once had a disagreement with Tony, but he had muscle of his own for protection, so, Tony never bothered him again. Besides, Eva's father had a few connections of his own within the Italian mobs and was for the most part left alone or anybody with a little common sense left him and his business alone.

So, Eva and her little mob choose Tony. They planned and executed it. One night when Tony came home, they were waiting. He parked his Cadillac in a reserved spot in front of the building where he lived. Nobody dared parking in that spot for fear of getting their car and face damaged. He was visibly drunk as he walked up the stairs of the brownstone. They were waiting for him inside as he climbed the stairs and mumbled to himself. He stood in front of his apartment door and fumbled with his keys and tried to open the door. When he finally opened the door, he stepped in and felt for the light switch. Then life changed forever. Eva grabbed his arm and yanked him to the side as Tatyana grabbed his other arm and pulled him to the other side. Both then pulled him forward and tripped him over Olga balled up on the floor. He hit the floor with a thud then Max, Mikal and Uri beat the life out of him with baseball bats. He moaned at first but that soon faded into a coma and then death. When they finished the beating, he was a bloody mess.

Max took an arm to check for a pulse and shook his head no. Tony was dead. The six then gathered around the dead body and no one spoke at first. Eva remembers thinking that he was not all that tough. She remembers learning that rumors built a person to a level that was not true. They all looked over this supposed tough guy then Eva spoke. "I won't lose sleep over this." She looked around at her brothers and sisters.

"No."

"Not at all."

Another shake of the head no.

"Never."

"Fuck him."

They then all laughed and started to look in his pockets. Where they found two rolls of bills in rubber bands. In a closet with a false floor they found a cigar box with more money and jewelry.

They deposited the money into a bank account and added to it as the years passed. They went attacking more mob people until they had the respect of most in the area. The one factor that kept them feared was that nobody knew it was just a bunch of kids. Everyone thought a new mob was around and some higher ups in other mobs tried to contact them and set up a territory deal. Nevertheless, that did not happen. They established a new order; a mob was in town that did not deal with others. They took what they wanted. Eva had front people who acted as messengers so to have a little communication, but, other than that she, her brothers and sisters ruled, and nobody knew who they were. All those years ago she learned the real export of what fear of the unknown can do to people.

"Okay, what's up." Eva said.

Olga dressed elegantly for success. Mikal dressed classy. They spread money around to higher people in governments and made inroads that helped the family. Max was the rough and tumble one who immediately formed the security team and Uri was the fast talking slippery one that stayed near Eva for he was the official drug person. Tatyana though went to the edge. Her latest dealing was real estate that had fake offices and sold the mortgages to banks that did not exist. They made money.

Chapter 24

Eva started. "We have one hundred fifty million this month." That money is always split three ways. Aunt Catherine and their father each get one third and they split the last third.

Olga turned her head and gave Eva a happy look. "I want to redesign my house in London and the new spring fashions are great."

Eva eyed Olga with a kind smile. "Sounds nice."

"Yea." Olga said with a coy look.

Mikal leaned forward. "Eva I need...."

Uri cut Mikal off. "Fuck you Mikal. You still didn't fix me up with that Spanish lady."

Mikal looked at his finger nails and then back at Uri. "If you had some class my brother and dress right, I could fill your nights with pleasure. A different lady for every day." Uri looked at Mikal and then at his clothing. Being the nervous one he didn't live life like the others. So, Eva protected him when they ganged up. The shortest of them all and sickly when young he always had a special place in Eva's heart.

"Leave Uri alone or I'll pay you in Mexican Pesos." Eva stated elegantly then looked around at everybody.

"Okay, I'll have the fake Polish loan ready for the food service company. Any time frame?" Olga said changing direction.

"Don't know just yet. I'm waiting to sign the papers for the last warehouse. In fact, the owner will be at dads' party tomorrow." Eva said. The group looked at her for a moment. Then Tatyana asked.

"Who's the owner?"

Eva looked around at them. "Joe Bergen."

"Alley boy?" Tatyana asked.

"Yea, he is." Eva said in defense and realized that. "He kept his mouth shut and I might hire him on. I had Al get in his head and he just may be a good prospect for us."

"A good prospect for who, sister." Tatyana asked sarcastically.

"We may need an outside loyal person for the future. Something I've thought about."

"Something you've thought about. Thanks for running it by us, we'd like to hear the plans also." Tatyana said a little harshly. That was her style. She always challenged a decision. It was her way of showing loyalty and Eva always looked forward to her ideas at meetings. She also loved that Tatyana always looked pissed off and acted it.

"I am right now Tat, and, I'm sure this really is not new information to you." Eva replied smiling at Tatyana.

"Ah yes. I remember. That goofy looking guy that happened in the alley when you were taking down that Italian pig." Olga said nodding.

Eva took it on the chin. She did not think Joe Bergen was goofy looking then or now.

"Yes Olga. I did do that job myself because of poor planning by others. Didn't think I had it in me? Do you care to challenge me again to do something or challenge my leadership?" Eva said in all her glory.

Olga shook her head no, keeping eye contact with Eva.

"Well now, I look forward to seeing this guy. You said he'll be at dads' party tomorrow, cool." Mikal said.

"Yea, and, I hope to start him off slowly. He'll be CEO of the XO division, it'll be easy for him and I'll get a good idea of if he'll work out. That's if he agrees to join the company." Eva said solemnly.

The others nodded in agreement for they never doubted Eva and her way of testing people. They knew if he did not work out to her standards, he would die by her knife.

"Now, I saw Aunt Catherine and she has something that she wants done." Eva paused a moment to see all seriously at attention now. Any word from Aunt Catherine carried a lot of weight. "Word is the Red mob is going to buy a nuke weapon and sell it. That's just word. I have someone inside this mob and that may not be happening." Eva paused to let this sink in. "We think they may be shopping for one, but I've yet to hear that it's happening. If they do, we'll have to eliminate them, or they'll be a witch hunt for all of us."

"Yes, I also have someone in that mob and it's just talk, right now." Max said.

Tatyana said. "They killed one of my gang in Moscow, a low-level one. That doesn't sound like a Mob that is hitting the big money. They're still keeping their street presence."

"Do we wait or go for the kill now?" Mikal asked Eva.

"I was with the other mobs earlier and they want nothing to happen until we have solid evidence." Eva said and they understood that it was a no for now and they needed to find evidence. Eliminating the Red mob without telling them would void the cooperation they have with one another. It'll send everything back to the dark ages.

"So, we watch and wait." Olga stated.

"We have no choice. Aunt Catherine isn't happy with that either." Eva replied and everybody sat in thought. She noticed that Uri was looking nervous.

"Okay, we need increased surveillance on the Red mob." Mikal said.

"Already people in place near the Red leader and a little closer wouldn't be a problem." Max submitted.

"Yes, get closer. I have Andre but I think he's useless. I'll take care of him later." Eva said to Max and then changed the topic.

"Okay, now, Olga have those people in Poland ready for the loan. I want to get that operation going soon. No use having money sit around. But I want to start with ten million and build up the amount as time goes by. With XO food service up and running we can start with specialty foods from Europe and launder some money that way. Then fake sale invoices down the road to increase the laundering." Eva paused a moment then said to every one's surprise. "I want to buy a house."

"Eva, since when do you want a house?" Mikal asked.

"I may want to plant flowers and be a domestic person." Eva said with a smile.

"I guess the five apartments just don't cut it. Uh sis." Olga asked.

"No, they don't. They're owned by CZ Corp. And it's eight apartments."

"Are you getting mushy and falling in love with someone we don't know about?" Tatyana asked.

"Not. Don't need to own a cow to drink milk." Eva replied.

"Okay, sounds good, buy a house Eva." Max said seriously.

"I figure you for a California hilltop over-looking L.A." Olga said.

"No, I was thinking more tropical, sultry." Eva said.

"Yea, nude beaches." Tatyana said.

"Cuba?" Uri said and they erupted into

laughter. When it settled down Eva looked at Tatyana. "Tat, now the real estate is done for now, what's your plans."

"Oh, I was looking around at various options. My people are getting itchy and want something to do. You have any suggestions." Tatyana replied with her all-American smile and blond hair.

"Yes, I have a suggestion. Next time don't fuck over someone close to us." Tatyana's smile faded and her eyes hit the floor. Eva continued. "That fucking idiot nephew of the Senator invested in Russian real estate and lost ten million. Did you know about this sister?" Eva was serious.

"Afterwards. A big mistake." Tatyana said somberly.

"Yes, big mistake. They kept it quiet and we reinforced the Senators desire to combat global crime. Not to mention he is going to run for President." Eva paused as everybody was watching her closely. She continued in a quieter voice. "Aunt Catherine is not going to let him."

Everybody looked shocked at first then regained their calm looks.

"She's really going to do it." Max asked and Eva nodded.

"Tatyana use Max next time to screen people. That fucking nephew is a wild hair and I would love to kill him, but the Senator has the focus. Two deaths, same family will be questioned." Eva finished.

"Okay. I will use Maxi next time, so I have

no bleeding problems." Tatyana said in a mock English accent. Everybody erupted into laughter except Max who put on a confused look to heighten the laughter.

Eva stood and pretended to have a sword, she tapped Tatyana on the head and said in a husky voice. "You are learning my child."

"Cool." Tatyana said. Eva sat back down as Max asked. "Can someone please explain?"

"I think she said you're a cunt." Mikal said.

Max looked to Mikal and then to Tatyana. "Okay." He said thrusting an index finger going toward Tatyana. She tried to fend him off, but it was no good. Max tickled her until she slid to the floor in hysterics. Her dress hiked up and everybody whistled. Max let up and went back to his seat. Tatyana fixed her dress, hair and calmed down. "Nice panties." Uri said.

"Yea, they look like the ones old women wear." Olga said.

"Fuck all of you." Tatyana said in half a laugh.

"Okay." Eva said and then continued. "Yes, Senator Wellington's death is when Aunt Catherine decides. It'll help us down the road. On his last trip to Russia he was stepping on toes, I guess. It probably dealt with the real estate scam of his nephew. He also stopped in the Netherlands and questioned authorities on Oleg. They feel they got the kingpin and all the drugs will stop. Adds up though, a global crime fighter wanting to be President. Not going to happen."

Nobody was surprised, it's the nature of their business.

Mikal then asked. "How's Oleg and how much we paying him?"

Eva brightened. "Yes, our friend in the Netherlands. He agreed to take the fall and be a drug kingpin. He has given up his life for a prison sentence that won't be all that long, but, still, he has done well for the Czarina and will retire wealthy with twenty million. He had no reservations about doing it."

Max laughed and added. "I doubt Oleg knows anything about drugs."

"No, he knew nothing and so the interrogations yielded nothing." Eva said.

"He'll get an early release in about ten years. He also expressed an interest in going to a warm island when released. I thought he was a good pick of mine." Tatyana said.

There were nods around; Eva knew Oleg would never tell a word. She then decided she was ready to leave and said. "Okay, after I pay the bills everybody will be getting the usual bonuses from CZ Corp. I know at this point; I'll be a half-billionaire in a few more years. Everyone investing wisely."

"You have such class, sis." Olga replied.

Eva gave Olga the middle finger

"All right, what's news I haven't heard. Anything I need to know." Eva asked hoping there was nothing.

Everybody shook their heads no slowly.

"Okay, then, I need to get up early for dads' party." Eva then bent over laughing. She regained herself as everyone looked at her questioningly.

"Last week he called me to say he received a check in the mail from social security. A letter attached said that he had to start receiving payments and needed to limit his work hours, so he doesn't incur a tax liability."

Everyone laughed knowing their father had access to hundreds of millions.

"I guess he'll have to take a pay cut from CZ Corp." Mikal said. That made everyone laugh even harder.

"Yea, the silly things we must do." Uri said. Everyone agreed as they wiped their eyes.

Olga then looked at Mikal and said. "TWM was great."

Everyone looked at Mikal with admiration. They waited for Mikal to speak. "Oh, you know the market is full of risks." Tatyana threw a pillow at him. A happy gesture taken as such.

"Okay, TWM was better than expected. It's the new investors that made it rise higher than expected. Did you guys get any?" Mikal asked looking around. Everybody nodded yes like little kids answering a parent.

"Good, now, I will have another next

week. Be nice, I'll tell you who." Mikal finished and everybody nodded yes again. He giggled at this display and continued. "I'll send through the usual connections."

I'll be waiting." Uri said looking around. "We'll all be waiting." Everyone said.

Mikal happened on something some years ago. Instead of spying on brokerage firms and investment banks, he found it easier to bid up a company stock. Not like the usual scam of selling or pushing a penny stock that nobody heard of and had no real earnings. People get burned that way and law enforcement gets involved. Mikal instead took a huge amount of money and gave it to a huge number of people. They're directed to invest in a certain blue-chip stock, on a certain day for a certain period, after the earnings report. Afterwards everyone sells the stock at different times so all get a good profit. Nobody gets burned. When finished, the stock settles to a normal price.

It's only at quarterly earnings time. It still did raise eyebrows, but, no one complained, and the SEC only scratched their heads. The reason it worked so well, and no investigation ever found any wrongdoing is that it involved over one million people around the world. These people were just average persons who happened to invest in a certain company for no reason to the outside world. They invested in different amounts to keep it random. Result, a handsome profit for all.

It is Mikal's golden goose. His reward is the ten percent that filtered back to him.

Eva heard the beat of music in the distance as her brothers and sisters gathered around Mikal to express their thanks.

Eva watched and seriously liked the idea of having a house of her own, a personal thing. She knew that Joe Bergen's wife liked to work around the yard when he was at work. Maybe she could use a hobby and get a little exercise. Eva got up to leave and looked back at her brothers and sisters joking like little kids.

She opened the door and Ivan was there. He immediately fell into step with Eva out of the club and motoring down the road. She needed sleep and knew a high dosage would be necessary tonight. Her hand was starting to shake but she ignored it. She knew what she was doing.

Chapter 25

It was a bright spring morning as Joe and Carol motored along a country road in Westchester County New York. The few homes they saw were huge. Driveways long and winding.

"Sure, is a beautiful day." Joe said to Carol who looked good today, he thought. Then added. "A few miles more."

"I hope this meeting doesn't get too boring." Carol said casually. He liked the tone and her attitude. She was coming around.

"Well, it's a birthday party, some family run businesses like to get to know who they are buying from. Oh, I did a stock trade that netted about forty grand." Joe looked over at Carol smiling. "Yea, I looked at the account yesterday, good move. How did you know?" She looked over with an impressed look.

"Oh, just a little research." Joe knew he just made a mistake. He should have just told her of the tip and what Stan told him. He needed to stop doing that.

"Good. I think I can find something to

buy." Carol giggled.

"It's just pocket change." He shrugged.

"Yea, okay Mr. Big. So, they're planning on hiring you on, and, we'll have a long-term friendship with some very wealthy people."

"I don't know, but, sure would be cool to have friends like them for occasional visits."

"If they do offer you to stay on, it'd be okay for a while. I mean you've always been working and to just stop with a lump sum of money might be a jolt for you. How many days can we relax on a beach until it's boring?" Carol stated.

"True, we need a purpose in life." He was relieved she was opening today. The day should go well. She always did like meeting new people.

He and Carol have always been practical in the way they live and the few friends they have. Now, they were going to see the excessively wealthy and how they live.

A few days ago, Joe met Eva and she was the only one he knew of in the company and family. He was getting a little scared because he did not know who he was going to meet. Would they be arrogant or down to earth people? He felt like he met Eva once before, but being she is a beautiful woman that is a natural first reaction.

"We're here." He said slowly and Carol's eyes went wide.

He slowed the Lexus to take in the view. In front of them was an ornate double gated entrance ballooned with the colors of a rainbow. As they pulled in the entrance, the gates opened in grand style.

Two land rovers were parked on either side of the huge driveway. Joe pulled in slowly and saw a guard building that was hidden behind the left side stone pillar. He stopped and a man in a dark suit stepped out and walked over to Joe's window. He lowered the window and saw this was a serious looking man.

"Hello. We're here for the birthday party."

The man did not acknowledge, in the slightest. He spoke in an accent that Joe did not recognize. "Your invitation please." His hand out.

He handed the man his invitation. He scanned it and returned it to Joe.

"Welcome Mr. Mrs. Bergen. Please continue down the lane following the balloons. You'll come to a parking area and be escorted to the party."

Joe looked over at Carol and noticed another man standing near the passenger side of his car. Good security, he thought.

With the car back in gear he slowly followed the balloons attached to huge trees. They looked centuries old, something one saw only on the best of estates. The branches were big, strong and overhung onto the wide lane. They shaded the roadway as they passed under them. If first impressions mean something, this was a good start, Joe thought. He looked over at Carol who just smiled brightly with the same expectation he had.

Close to a quarter of a mile later, the lane curved right and opened to a spectacular view of a huge mansion that resembled a castle. They saw the huge parking area on the lawn. The area filled with almost two hundred cars already. Another man in a dark suit was signaling Joe over. As he approached, he saw the man had dark glasses on with a curled wire going to his ear. Nobody was going to crash this party today, he knew.

He pulled next to the man and lowered the car window, again. "Welcome Mr. Mrs. Bergen. Park in that lane." The man pointed to an aisle that was half empty.

"Okay, thank you." Joe said then drove the car to the area. He looked over at Carol who had a hand covering her mouth. She was giggling. "I don't think we belong here." She said jokingly, while admiring the huge home in the distance.

"We aren't in Kansas anymore." Joe said as he pulled into a parking spot.

They exited the car lingering a moment taking in the sweeping lawn and the home. He felt uneasy. He was out of his league.

As they stood looking around a noise was heard coming from behind them. Joe and Carol turned around to see a horse and carriage coming toward them. This was unreal he thought, the carriage stopped next to them. The man driving it was dressed in some old-style European costume. He tipped his hat at both. They stood in disbelief. The man then bellowed.

"The Czar awaits your presence." He motioned for them to get in the uncovered carriage that was done in bright colors with gold highlights. They climbed aboard. Carol took Joe's hand. She was happy and excited. He wanted to thank these people because this is just what the doctor ordered.

The man whistled and worked the reigns as the horse pulled the carriage smoothly for the ride to the house. Carol leaned over whispering. "For real?"

"I don't know. I hope so. I hate to think we're going to wake up at home."

As the mansion came closer it was bigger and grander than they knew. The sound of the hooves was magical and soothing on the cobble stone lane. Joe wished he could ride all-day in the carriage.

The mansion had a main section and two wings going in opposite directions. The sound of music was coming from somewhere, a live band perhaps. Music from the 1950's without vocals. He knew the song, an Elvis tune, Wise men say....

The carriage arrived at the grand front steps. A man dressed in the same period costume was waiting. He sported a twisted end mustache and the air of someone happy to be at this place right now. The lady standing next to the him dressed the same. The carriage stopped and the waiting man opened the small door. He held his gloved hand out for Carol to step down. Joe exited the other side. He walked around to see Carol beaming in the presence of the huge man. The lady stepped over toward them and curtseyed. "Welcome Mr. and Mrs. Bergen. The Czar awaits you." She said motioning for them to follow her up the grand steps.

Carol whispered in Joe's ear. "The Czar is a Russian king."

"I guess that makes us peasants," He replied

Carol let out a laugh and held onto Joe's hand. He felt on top of the world. Looking at the huge home he wished this was his world.

They followed the lady up the steps to the top and stopped for a moment looking at the huge doorway. The doors opened and the music was louder.

They followed her inside, down a hallway passing a grand staircase. Around a corner, down another hallway to a huge ballroom filled with people talking and laughing. The far wall consisted of glass showing a view of the back side of the property. A conductor leading an orchestra under a canopy was seen and heard. On the sweeping patio some people were dancing. The scene was intoxicating.

Joe and Carol stood taking it in and not knowing where to go first. He turned to ask the escort a question, but she was gone. A man dressed in the same period costume approached holding a tray. He had a full beard with twisted mustache ends.

"Drinks?"

"Cola." Joe said looking at Carol

"I'll just have water."

The bearded man left; Carol nuzzled up to Joe whispering.

"Do you know anybody here?"

"No." He replied looking around at the people talking in groups and the dancers outside. "Well, not yet. Let's mingle."

They started walking casually through the room. Some people looked on happily nodding as they did the same.

At a table filled with cards and small wrapped boxes, Joe took the card from his suit jacket and added it on the pile with the rest. "I wonder if he'll read all these cards."

"Maybe we should have bought a gift." Carol never liked being cheap with gift giving.

"What to buy someone we don't know and probably has everything in the world?"

"Good question." Came a voice from behind them. They abruptly turned to see a red headed lady standing there. Joe immediately recognized Eva. She was much prettier than he remembered from the office. Wearing a tight-fitting blue dress that complemented her slim but shapely body.

Eva extended a hand to Carol. "I'm Eva Bokanawski. I'm glad to see you made it. Did you find the place okay?"

Carol shook her hand saying, "I'm Carol."

"Yes. Missing the gates was impossible."

Joe said.

"I apologize for the little game at the office. I didn't present myself properly. I wander the building sometimes to see people. It's a casual but productive environment." Eva said to Joe.

"No need to apologize, it was interesting. Rich Holbrook told me who you were at the meeting. I just hope you didn't take Thom as too gruff. He's great with numbers and thinks the world revolves around his opinion sometimes." He knew her from somewhere. He could not remember where, but he met her before.

"No problem. It shows you have well-picked people working for you and I reviewed your numbers, the market share, impressive. Acquiring your company will be an honor. Now, do feel your VP of finance will be a good president for the facility." Eva asked as Carol watched.

"Thom Heller. Yes. I would put my full faith in him." Joe felt a little uneasy, he thought they were going to ask him to stay on.

"Good. I like if we can talk later about an opportunity for you to work at XO food group. You built a great little facility. Now would you like to try your talents at running fifteen facilities." The uneasy feeling left as he tried not to seem eager.

"Sure." Joe glanced to Carol who was beaming.

"You don't need me to answer. It's

something you love to do." Carol said looking to Joe then Eva.

"Okay. We can definitely talk later." He responded. Eva smiled.

"All right, I'll find you later. For now, I want to steal Carol and show her the house."

"Sure." Carol smiled leaving with Eva. The bearded man returned, Joe took his cola and sipped it. He stood looking around the room, A few people acknowledged him with a serious nod. He took it to mean they were already grooming him, and some knew that.

At different areas around the room were big men in suits. One glanced at Joe; he wasn't bothered by it. They were protecting the Czar, he knew.

He strolled to the wall of windows and looked out over the sprawling property. Hedges, statues, an orchestra playing its heart out, the wonder of it all.

Chapter 26

J oe guessed living here must be heavenly. Who wouldn't like being worlds away from the real world.

"Nice view, huh." A gravelly voice said attached to a burly body with wolf's eyes. He dressed in a silk suit, and, had a calm air.

"Yes. I was just thinking, that living here every day must be heavenly." Joe said to the man who looked direct at him with wolf eyes.

"Yes, it's beyond heaven. I'm Nicolas Bokanawski." They shook hands.

"Joe Bergen."

"Ah yes. Bergen foods. Eva has told me about you and your business. It's good to see there are still honest businesspeople out there."

"Thank you. I just decided long ago that I was going to succeed no matter what."

Nicolas smiled at him. "Yes, it shows."

"Well, let me wish you a happy birthday." Joe said feeling in uncharted waters here.

"Thank you, Mr. Bergen. I stopped

counting after age fifty."

"You can all me Joe."

"And call me Nicolas."

A bearded man came asking for drinks both declined.

"I like the period costumes; my wife loved the carriage ride from the parking area. She's with Eva right now" Joe glanced around.

"Yes, they're chatting like songbirds. Eva is showing off my house. I saw them in the main hallway."

"Yes, they always talk about something." Joe said sipping his cola.

"The costumes are copies of the aristocratic period in Russia." Stopping for a moment. "I came here as young man to escape the Soviet Union regime. That was a low period in Russia and I saw America as an escape. I love this country, it has been good to me and hope I will be remembered as good for America." Nicolas coughed a laugh, then continued. "With a few dollars in my pocket and friends' home in Russia without the basics in life, I started an import and export business. Over the years I made some good contacts in Europe and after the fall of the Soviet empire, I made a killing in Russia buying businesses for pennies and the rest is history."

Joe felt impressed with the rags to riches story. Heard of many doing it, but, right next to him was a real story.

"Yes, you've done well. I think you'll be

remembered as being good for America."

"I can say that business is ruthless. I have done and seen what I am not proud of on occasion but, nobody knows but me what needed to be done." Nicolas looked at Joe for a moment.

Feeling a little uneasy Joe replied. "Silence is golden. I had done a few injustices so I could be successful."

"Right. A secret should stay a secret." Nicolas confirmed then waited a beat. "Joe, I know Eva wants to ask you to come aboard the company. One item of import, we like to be discreet in our business dealings, and, we don't want to be a public company."

"I understand. Eva had mentioned she wants to talk later. I look forward to having the opportunity." Joe said sincerely.

"You're going to receive millions of dollars and instead of running away to a tropical island you're going to take a job. Can I ask why you would consider a job in my company?" A turnaround in the conversation that Joe found challenging. Nicolas watching him did not make him nervous.

"I'm looking forward to overseeing an operation much larger than mine. I look forward to the challenge. Now, I had visited your headquarters the other day and it impressed me, the work environment. People seemed productive and happy. That doesn't happen by accident. I don't want to retire or live detached from life now. My self-and Carol will put some of that money to personal perks, a new house, vacations. The money is a big comfort. I still want to do something."

Nicolas smiled and nodded. "Good answer. Now make sure you tell Eva that. She's the tough one." Both laughed.

"Yes, she seems on top of everything." Joe added.

"Yes, Eva and the kids know how to earn money and wisely use it for the good of the company. Some of them have concerns about you, but, along as Eva has faith..............." Nicolas stopped speaking, a noise on the other side of the room got his attention. A man about the size of Nicolas approached. He had a twisted end mustache and looked serious and capable. He whispered something in Nicolas's ear, the man's face brightened. He looked over at Joe and said. "Nick Jr is here." He went in the direction of the laughter and commotion.

Joe saw everybody heading over in that direction. His mind was racing now. What did Nicolas mean, some of them have concerns, as long as Eva has faith? Who's some of them? Joe has yet to meet them and they already do not like him or have faith in him as Eva does.

Joe did not see over the people he did hear Nicolas laughing as someone said he would not miss this party for the world. He heard a birthday wish to Nicolas and some people clapped. The people thinned out and he saw Nicolas with a younger man that looked a lot like him. He had a gorgeous woman by his side. Then Eva came and gave the man a hug. Then others came and hugged and shook his hand. Joe figured the man was Nicolas's son and the rest were the kids. They all looked like a happy group, a family.

Nick Jr, Eva were the focal point of their father; A strong sense of family or something was on display. For wealthy people, they did not have the stiff upper lip attitude.

Carol appeared next to Joe. She was watching the scene also. The crowd parted and thinned as the orchestra's operatic sound floated back in like a breeze. The dancers resumed right with the music.

Most guests went back to their groups, chatting. The focal point was still there, Nicolas Sr and Jr talking. Three men close by, were listening to their conversation. Eva with two women Joe did not know were also listening to Sr and Jr. One lady, a blond, was looking at Joe and he did not like the look she gave him. He decided not to stare. He was not family, just another employee, maybe.

"So, where'd you two go." Joe asked not looking back at the family, best to let them have their private time together.

"Oh, we took a fast walk of the house and I met her two sisters. Good people, down to earth for the obvious wealth that they have."

"I met and talked with the father. The

older man in the group." She looked over at the gathering. Nicolas Sr glanced at Carol giving her a slight nod. She moved closer to Joe and spoke quietly. "I got the impression you're known, when Eva introduced me to her sisters, they acknowledged something. Like they knew you."

"This is a large family company and Mr. Bokanawski seems to like my business." Then Joe remembered that some of the kids did not have faith in him, Eva did. He didn't mention that to Carol, she would not understand. The lines in the sand were drawing already. Joe then continued. "I like the father. He is a rag to riches story and very shrewd. He came from Russia at a young age and started an import and export business and as you can see the rest is history."

"We getting get a house like this." She asked beaming up at Joe.

He laughed kissing Carol lightly on the lips. "If you want. Let's go mingle."

They walked out onto the sweeping patio looking down at the people letting go on a dance floor setup on the lawn. To the left, on the lawn, a huge tent with spires had tables set up inside. Servants were setting the tables dressed in the period costumes. Farther away were people playing tennis. A little further away some people swimming and in another direction, people were playing volleyball, and some watched a tennis game. Very exciting day.

"I guess we're going to eat outside." Joe noted.

"Yes, just a little cookout served on real China and silverware." Carol said smiling.

"See, you're going to like this, too much." He replied smiling at her.

They shared a giggle that hasn't happened in a time. It felt good connecting today and he hoped it would last when they leave this party.

A tall graying man approached from a table he was sitting at with a beautiful woman much younger than himself. Joe noticed he was slim but, at over six feet, slim was not a lightweight. He was holding a napkin around a drink. He carried himself like someone of refinement and standing in the world.

"Hello, I hear you are Mr. and Mrs. Bergen."

Joe extended a hand. "I'm Joe and this is Carol." Carol extended a hand.

"Ariel Moskowitz, CFO for CZ corp. and, a close family friend."

"I'm selling my business to XO food group and hope to be a family friend."

That produced a chuckle from Ariel. Nodding his approval of the delivery.

"I'm sure you will be. If you don't mind me saying, you make a fine couple. High school sweethearts." Ariel smiled warmly.

"No, a little while later in our lives in which case we're still making up for that loss." Joe said while Carol beamed at him.

"Yes, well put. I wish my ex-wife could have seen things that way."

Joe and Carol just nodded and smiled.

"Great party isn't it. Mr. Bokanawski always has a big bash for his birthday and we all look forward to it. He's always very generous to us peasants at the office." Ariel said with a million-dollar grin.

"Yes. Very nice party." Carol said.

"Yes, it's great." Joe said.

"I have the great luxury of seeing this estate often and dine like a king. Mr. B likes to work out of the home these days or from his yacht." Ariel said with a flourish. Joe liked this guy's style.

"Mr. Bokanawski seemed to have been very successful. I'm curious why he's going into the food service business. It can be very cyclical, I mean customers come and go very fast. Need hands on every day."

Ariel raised an eyebrow then replied. "There is a big plan for XO food groups to keep the revenue flow coming in even in unpredictable times. I of course cannot tell you that, yet. Its Eva's project and she has never failed with her projects." Ariel finished gracefully, then added. "I hear they want to tap you for the CEO of that new division. You didn't hear that from me." He finished with a wink.

Joe nodded thoughtfully. "Eva and I will talk later. Off the top though, the size of the combined warehouses will allow for large volume buying. That'll be a cost savings but being it's a new business; the up-hill sales battle will need a good staff. I see a challenge there." Joe said and Ariel didn't even bat an eye.

"Yes, I think it will be a challenge now that it's presented that way. If there's revenue, there'll be a profit." Ariel replied with a sly smile.

Carol tapped Joe on the shoulder. He looked over at her.

"We're here for a birthday party."

"Yes, Carol is right. Let's not bore her with business talk." Ariel said.

Joe nodded, his drink sweating in his hand.

Inside the huge ballroom Eva, Olga and Tatyana were watching the three on the patio. "He looks like a dork. Are you sure about him, Eva?" Olga asked.

"The wife seems like a Miss manner. My Joe would never lick my snatch until I wash it with ivory soap and pure mountain spring water." Tatyana said sarcastically. Olga snorted and Eva showed a big toothy smile.

"Ah come on. He'll work out. If he doesn't, well, Carol will be a rich widow." Eva said with a gleam in her eyes that Olga or Tatyana did not doubt.

"Just tell me he likes Russian women and he can fuck my brains out." Olga said.

"I hope you shower first, so he doesn't think we're just serfs." Tatyana said with an air of importance. Olga looked at Tatyana, smiled nicely then said. "I guess you use ivory soap and mountain spring water too." Tatyana turned her head for a moment as Eva showed her toothy smile again.

"Getting back to the original question, I will let you ladies know." Eva said looking at her fingernails. Then quickly looked at Tatyana and said. "Don't you daresay it." Olga and Tatyana looked at each other smiling.

"Do they have any children?" Tatyana asked.

"No, he must be gay." Olga said. That produced a harsh look from Eva.

"I talked with the wife, she seemed to step back when asked. Maybe there's a biological problem. There's no shame in that." Eva said and Olga nodded soberly agreeing. "No, there's no shame in that."

"He's fuckin gay." Tatyana blurted. Both looked at her soberly.

Olga spoke. "Tat, isn't there a gang bang going on somewhere."

Tatyana fixed her hair and said. "Yea, with Mr. Potruski, the man that gives it to me up my ass. Just the way I like it."

Olga glared at her. Eva looked a little surprised then asked. "Who's the new flame, Olg."

Olga looked back at Eva. "Oh, just someone I met. Nothing serious."

"What's he like?" Eva was interested.

"A fat sausage eating pig. Probably can't even see his own dick." Tatyana said.

Eva showed her toothy grin then nicely

asked Tatyana. "Tat, why don't you go arm wrestle with Ivan."

Olga laughed, spilling her drink a little. "Yes, Tat, you can compare tattoos."
Tatyana just smiled, Eva knew she likes this sort of talk. No harm done.

A huge man dressed in costume and long flowing beard blew a horn from the patio. He then announced. "The Czar awaits his guests for lunch."

Eva and her sisters headed for the patio. Through the glass walls she saw Joe and Carol talking happily and holding hands. They walked slowly across the lawn to the tents. Eva felt a little jealous. She wanted that man. She knew she could do better than Carol and could give the man anything in the world he wanted. She looked at Carol's blond hair, her shapely figure, and knew her day with him would come.

Eva stopped, looked back inside from the patio at Ivan watching her, she didn't like that. She shook her head no and waved her hand for him to go away. He just grinned. Eva knew that Ivan would make Joe's wife disappear in a heartbeat, if that would make her happy.

Chapter 27

Everybody was heading to the huge covered dining area. The tents had what looked like royal spires shooting upward with maroon outsides and chandeliers inside for lighting. The rolled-up fabric panels made so cool breezes could flow through. Extravagant looking, an average person may think though not the family, it was life as usual.

All the tables were round that seated eight to ten people. The largest table in the center was the family's seat. Nicolas Sr seated already with Nicolas Jr were talking in hushed tones. Joe and Carol stopped looking around, they did not know where to sit.

"Joe, Carol." Came a voice from behind them. They turned to see Eva. "You're sitting at the big table."

They sat as others getting seated were talking happily to one another. They were sitting at the opposite side of the table from the birthday host.

The sun was shining brightly outside the tent as the orchestra played a mellow tune, meant to relax. Joe noticed a hummer in the distance driving along the tree line. Servants in period dress costumes were already beginning to serve. They carted the food over from the house on runway platforms that made it easier.

"Hi." Came from Joe's left. "I'm Tatyana."

"Hello Tatyana." Joe extended a soft hand.

"Hello again, Carol."

"Hello Tatyana."

"Let me introduce you to everybody. Next to me is Olga, Mikal, Max, Nicolas Jr, Eva, Uri and the girlfriends for my brothers are new ones so I don't know their names yet." She pointed each out. Tatyana said this loud enough, so the girlfriends looked at her with contempt. Joe knew he was going to like this. He looked at all of them.

Uri sat next to Eva. He had greased back hair, the look of someone out of the nineteen forties, with a constant sneer on his face.

Max on Uri's left side was of size and in shape. He had dark hair with a plain face that one would forget easily.

Next to him was Olga who was tall and shapely, the hair long and dark. She had almond-shaped dark eyes that resembled an Arab women.

Next to Nicolas Jr was Mikal also of size but slimmer. He had blond fly away hair with chiseled facial features.

Next to him was Tatyana. She had long blond hair with sky blue eyes. Healthy looking. One that you would see walking on a California beach.

Nicolas Sr at the center was a sturdy rough looking man of average height with wolfs eyes.

Nicolas Jr a carbon copy of his father but younger with wolf eyes. They oversaw everything going on.

"Hello everybody. I'm Joe Bergen and this is my wife Carol." Everybody around the table said hello to them. Eva liked this, she was showing a toothy grin at Joe. He also saw Nicolas Sr looking on with approval.

Carol sitting on Joe's right started chatting with Tatyana on Joe's left. He just loved being in the middle of some women conversation. He looked over at Eva viewing this, rolled his eyes. Eva smiled nicely and thought that this was the first moment of a secret. A beginning.

"Joe, are you going to take the offer." This came from Max. Joe felt confused at first, he didn't know which offer.

"Um, which offer." Joe asked innocently.

"The job. We can use someone familiar with the food service business." Max said reassuringly.

"I haven't thought about it yet. I mean myself and Eva haven't spoken yet." He didn't like this.

"Eva will make you a juicy offer. I'm sure." Came from Mikal. Carol and Tatyana stopped talking to look at him.

"Okay. Joe and I are going to talk later." Eva broke in then continued. "You'll have to excuse my brothers. They can be pigs." Eva stressed the word pig.

Carol softened her look, Joe replied. "I have no problem with the candor of language."

"See. He'll work out well." Mikal said to a few giggles and nods of approval from around the table.

"You'll have to excuse my brother Mikal. He has no manners." Tatyana said nicely and the rest of the table looked at her with open mouths. Joe caught on that she was the dirty mouth one.

"I have no problem. He knows how to cut through the preamble." Joe said and Carol nodded.

Eva was following this as she chatted with her father. The servants started filling the plates with food and everyone started to taste it. Joe tasted his and noticed that everybody put down their utensils and looked to Nicolas Sr. Joe also noted the one named Uri only spoke to Eva and Nicolas Sr. He stayed out of the general chat.

The servants finished serving the food. Every conversation stopped and Nicolas Sr stopped talking to Eva and Uri. He looked around the tent and automatically stood up.

"We will have a moment of silence to thank our god for the fine day he has given us to celebrate my birthday." Standing, Nicolas Sr bowed his head as everyone in the tent followed. A silence even the band obeyed. Only the birds chirping and the breeze flapping the sides of the tent didn't obey. Then Nicolas Sr raised his head, and everyone followed. The orchestra started to play a mellow tune that was not intrusive.

"Nice." Carol whispered in Joe's ear. He nodded.

The conversations started again as everybody started eating. The meal consisting of assorted meats and potatoes and vegetables seemed a little heavy for a lunch time, Joe thought.

Max and Mikal were joking about some women and a beach in southern France as their woman friends were looking on with sour looks. Joe felt comfortable with the conversation because if they talked about the opera and golf he would have felt out of place.

Nicolas Jr and his lady were in their own conversations. Joe liked that beginning world of love for each other, he wondered if they were newlyweds.

Olga on the other side of Carol spoke to Joe.

"So, Joe are you enjoying the party. In case you forgot I'm Olga."

"No, yes I did forget your name. Sorry, the parties great though." He liked the deep sexy tone of her voice.

"We picnic every Saturday." Olga said.

"You can invite me and Carol. We love casual cookouts." He replied smiling.

"Do you have any children?" Olga asked. Eva's head turned to Olga.

Joe saw that reaction and Carol was also looking at him now.

"We don't, not yet." He said feeling a little off guard. Carol jumped in.

"We're thinking about adopting. In time we'll decide." Joe did not like Carols answer, so he jumped back in.

"Yes, but I have reservations on adopting, we cannot return the child if say the parents were drug users or if the child has some problem. I don't want us to have a problem that'll more anguish than joy." Joe immediately sensed a quiet fall over the table and the surrounding tables. He realized that he said something not acceptable. Nicolas Sr was looking directly at him.

Nicolas Sr cleared his throat, looked at Nicolas Jr, Eva and then the rest of the table.

"Joe, I understand your concerns but, you haven't seen the other side. I know as a businessperson you explore all sides before a decision. Adopting is different in that wife does not give the birth and the man doesn't go running to the hospital. There're disadvantaged people in the world that have no choice but to give up their child for adoption. I'm sure it tears their hearts out. Now, that child put up for adoption had no choice; no choice to be born into this world. If by unfortunate reasons that child was born with something due to genetics or substance, that's not the child's fault." Nicolas Sr took paused. "If you and your wife had a child born with something wrong from genetics from a distant relative, I don't think you would get rid of that child. Would you. Okay. I didn't want to give you a speech but, Joe, it's not a business decision like you usually make. It's having a child and raising a child for good or bad. We can talk later Joe. If you want." Nicolas Sr looked direct at Joe for a moment, then raised his glass to drink as conversations slowly resumed.

Carol was trying hard not to look like a winner. She put her hand on Joe's. "Maybe you should talk with Mr. Bokanawski."

"I think I just decided." He whispered to Carol giving her a kiss on her cheek. Joe looked up to see Eva watching him. She went back to talking to Uri.

"Joe don't worry you didn't piss my dad off. You did hit a nerve though." Olga said to both.

"I don't feel bad; I still think the world of him. I want to thank him later. Something about the way he said it made me understand."

Olga smiled, nodding. "Yes, dad can do that."

Joe leaned over to Carol. "I know what you're going to say, but it was you who helped me decide." She whispered back. "I know that. I know, sometimes." She kissed him on his cheek. With that said, Joe felt solid inside, he knew this was the real Carol. She's back.

"Do I hear whisperings." Nicolas Sr asked looking at them, then continued. "There'll be no conspiring in secret at the Czar's table." Finishing with a wave of his hand around the table.

"Mr. Czar, I was just asking my peasant husband if we were going to have Jell-O or ice cream for dessert." Carol replied elegantly.

Nicolas Sr threw his head back in laughter with everyone else at the table laughing heartily. Eva laughed but, was a little jealous at this display from Carol. She would let that go and keep her feelings hidden. When the laughter settled Nicolas Sr replied. "Carol. You can have whatever you heart wishes for dessert, and your peasant husband also." Carol put a hand to her mouth and blew Nicolas Sr a kiss. He caught it in his hand and put it in his pocket.

"Okay, Nick has brought a new movie for anyone who wants to view it in the theater room." Nicolas Sr proudly stated looking at his son. Nicolas Jr replied. "I hope it'll be a hit. Everybody is welcome and I hope to hear that you like it."

Joe looked at Carol with excited eyes as the rest of the table started asking Nicolas Jr what the movie was about. He held his hand up and said. "It's about a man who falls in love with a wealthy woman. The relationship heats until the man finds out that his woman is wealthy because, she runs an empire that they built with money from her Swiss grandfather. Money from people who died in the Holocaust that they deposited with the bank in good faith." He looked around the table and the neighboring tables. Everybody listening. Joe noticed the connection to his father. Nicolas Jr had that exhibitionism.

Then Olga asked. "What happens?"

"You have to watch the movie." Nicolas Jr replied making Nicolas Sr bellow in laughter.

"Are you a director, Nicolas" Joe asked.

"No, I own and run a production company that churns out movies, commercials and the like. I did try my hand at directing one some years ago, and, it was a flop. I do better managing the product than creating it." He said then came a few encouraging words from his brother and sisters.

"In time I'm sure you'll want to try again. A horse throws you, you climb back on it." Joe said to Nicolas Jr who nodded raising his glass to him. Eva liked that also, but started to dislike the -that's my husband look- on Carol's face.

"Yes, I hope to try again when that one perfect script comes along. Somebody is hard at work on something good right now. Until then, I still make mountains of money." Jr raised his glass again saying, "to the dream." Everybody including Nicolas Sr raised their glasses saying the same.

A serious looking man dressed in costume knelt next to Nicolas Sr whispering something in his ear. At first Nicolas Sr put on a grimace face then smiled and looked devious. He nodded yes as the man stood and left toward the house. He looked up smiling for a moment, lowered his head then looking at everybody in the tent. He started banging on his glass with a piece of silverware to get attention. When quieted down and the band even lowering their music to an eerie tune, Nicolas Sr spoke. "I have an announcement to make. We captured a thief on the property, who, was going to steal from the Czar's home, my home." His eyes lit up at what he just said as the orchestra hit a high tone as if on a cue. "They're bringing him here and we the people will hold court and decide his fate."

Everybody started to yell, "BRING HIM." The orchestra raised the eerie music to the chanting. Carol leaned over to Joe. "A staged scene?"

Olga spoke. "Yes, it's part of the party. It adds a little excitement." They nodded with excitement. Eva watched this as her father leaned over and whispered in her ear. "We finally got the freelance snitch."

Eva's eyes went wide for a second then said. "A great Birthday gift."

"Yes, my dear." Looking into her eyes smiling.

She looked to Ivan who was at the far end of the tent, their eyes met, he nodded and smiled. She knew this was better than expected, it had to be the freelance business writer, Brian Edwards the friend of Don Wellington Jr, how enjoyable, Eva thought. She then looked to Joe and Carol saying, "it's something we set up for most parties.

My dad the Czar captures a peasant trying to steal from him. We stage this so don't get frightened, nothing you will see is real."

Eva disliked the harmonious nodding they replied with.

She looked at Ivan again who had a cell phone to his ear. When finished he nodded again to Eva, which meant that they were sending a team to Brian Edwards home to begin the cover up. Destroying anything the man had complied on CZ Corporation, and the family. From what Eva knew, the information he had was superficial, but his computer still needed cleaning and documents destroyed. And, some new information planted that may prove embarrassing for the dead man.

The orchestra changed to a menacing tone as heads turned to the far end of the mansion. Two men wearing period costumes appeared, guiding a hooded person between them subdued with ankle chains. They were pulling and dragging the peasant, he seemed disoriented and the chains gave him limited mobility. The crowd started to cheer and chant again, "BRING HIM."

Joe was liking it, Carol put an arm in his and pulled it tight. She enjoyed the spectacle also, he knew. Eva watched this with distaste. Olga eyed her with a sly grin.

Another costumed man appeared from behind the house following the two guards walking with the peasant. The third guard wore an elaborate costume that showed he had rank. The increased chanting disoriented the peasant more, he tripped, his head darted to everybody inside the tent, the guards pushed him forward.

When they arrived outside the tent, the guards forced the man down to his knees. He was wobbly but kept a kneeling position. The guard in charge came inside and the chanting went silent with the orchestra. He took a knee in front of Nicolas Sr who standing at this point was looking outside the tent at the peasant, the guard then stood and began to speak. "Czar Nicolas. We have captured this peasant trying to enter your castle. He had designs of pilfering from the royal property. I present to you, the peasant."

Nicolas Sr walked outside to the peasant, the guards pulled the man up to his feet holding his arms. The peasant seemed wobbly and Eva knew that Mr. Edwards was drugged so he could not cause harm. He has no choice but to follow along.

Nicolas Sr looked him up and down then back at everyone inside the tents. They started to chant "GUILTY."

Nicolas Sr put his hands up to quiet everyone then back at the peasant. "Dare you come to my home with designs to steal from me and my family on my Birthday. Do you have say for you?"

The peasant tried to speak but this came across as comical, due to the gag in his mouth, everyone erupted into laughter. The laughter disoriented the peasant and he looked wobbly as he moved his head to Nicolas Sr and then the guests inside the tents. Somebody inside the tent stood and approached throwing a glass of wine at the peasant which started a riot of food and drink thrown at him. Nicolas Sr and the guards quickly went to one side as the mob went crazy throwing food and drink at the peasant. When this stopped the laughter continued.

Joe watching this felt momentarily helpless the arrogance of everybody, a mob out of control. Staged but, seemingly real, what was he missing. Looking at Carol, he saw the arrogance in her laughter as she threw something at the peasant. Something strange here, he felt.

Nicolas Sr was back in the center of attention when the food flogging stopped. The guards also resumed their positions with hard to disguise smiles on their faces. Nicolas Sr raised his arms in front of the peasant and spoke in a regal tone. "You have trespassed on my property. I'm the Czar, you trespassed on my property, threatening the lives of my family and my guests. What you say for you, peasant? Speak you."

The peasant's eyes darted around as he tried to speak again and the same garbled sound came out, the crowd erupted into laughter again. Nicolas Sr even laughed.

Joe was laughing but, he was also

observing everyone and caught sight of Eva watching him. He nodded to let her know that he was enjoying this. Eva nodded back. Nicolas Sr continued when the laughter eased.

"You have been found guilty by a group of your peers." Nicolas Sr looked at the guests, then continued. "All right, they are not really your peers. I didn't have time to scour the villages for a group of your peers. I doubt a few could be found."

That brought another round of laughter. Nicolas Sr basked in the attention. He seemed like a natural, Joe thought.

The guest's started chanting, "GUILTY, GUILTY." Nicolas raised his arm to quiet everyone down.

The decorated guard stepped in front of Nicolas Sr. He had an old rifle that used gunpowder and lead ball. The guard raised it in front of him as the crowd erupted in laughter and catcalls, "SHOOT HIM." Nicolas Sr nodded at the guard and he stood to one side. He looked direct at the peasant and spoke. "As Czar I find you guilty and your sentence is." Pointing to the forest line a distance away. "If you can make it to the forest before I can shoot you, you will live. If you don't, then God have mercy on you." The Czar finished and nodded to the guards.

The guests chanted, "SHOOT HIM."

The guards grabbed the peasant by the arms and spoke to him. The peasant was shaking his head no and the guards were nodding yes to him. They then pushed him forward as he stumbled and looked back. The decorated guard started to fill the rifle with gunpowder as the orchestra's powerful eerie tune got louder. Brain Edwards looked back one last time as he stumbled away. He tried to pick up speed but fell. The ankle chains prevented him from running. He got up and tried walking fast toward to the forest.

"Is it a real bullet?" Carol asked everyone at the table.

"No, we use those in the movies. They're plastic and splatter blood on impact. They do pack a little punch though." Nicolas Jr said to Carol. She smiled and remained looking at him a bit longer than properly expected. Eva saw and got a feel for Carol.

The senior guard handed the rifle to Nicolas Sr, as the other guards motioned for the guests to quiet down.

Peasant thirty yards away trying to run but couldn't. He glanced back, saw the rifle and tried to pick up the pace.

Nicolas Sr held the rifle. He raised it to eye level and aimed. Complete silence. A few birds in the distance sang.

Peasant thirty-one yards away.

Czar pulled trigger, the hammer went down, a puff of smoke and the lead ball was away.

At thirty-two and some half yards away, the peasant's back arched and he let out a sound, then fell face forward onto the ground. The guests roared with applause and laughter.

Nicolas Sr held up the rifle signaling victory. Joe and Carol caught up in the excitement, clapped and hooted with delight. The senior guard took the rifle and bowed to him. The Czar returned to the table taking his royal seat. The guests were still clapping and hooting with delight. The orchestra started with a celebratory type music.

In the distance two guards picked up the peasant who appeared limp and started dragging him to a horse drawn cart. The cart left slowly heading toward the house once loaded. Joe watched this amid all the noise and noticed Eva watching him. She gave him a toothy smile and Joe smiled back nodding.

With the tables cleared the serving of dessert started. They wheeled carts around with a choice of delicious looking desserts. Nicolas Sr huddled with Eva and Nicolas Jr sharing a private laugh. He then thanked Eva. For what nobody knew but them.

Nicolas Sr looked over the table at Joe and Carol. They had begun eating some ice cream. "I hope you both enjoyed the show. I like to do a little something to break the boredom of a birthday party."

Joe spoke up. "Yes, excellent, better than pinning the tail on the donkey."

That produced a few laughs from the family.

"Thank you, Joe. I'm happy you and your lovely wife came." He toasted them both.

"The man you shot, will he be okay?" Carol asked. Everybody in the family looked arrogantly happy then Nicolas Sr caught himself saying nicely to Carol. "Yes, he's on my security detail. He always enjoys doing it. I give him a day off for it."

Carol smiled. "Okay, that's nice."

Eva smiling wanted to bust out in hysterical laughter. She saw the glances from her brothers and sisters knowing they felt the same way. They were going to have a great time later tonight when the guests are gone. They were going to share a good laugh. In front of two hundred two people they killed Brain Edwards, and no one is the smarter.

Everyone resigned to eating their desserts and chatting lightly. Joe listened to the women talk about the latest fashions and hairstyles. Thoroughly bored with that, he watched Eva talking happily with Uri. Max and Mikal discussed an open secret because the words used hid what the real subject matter was. He hoped someday to be knowledgeable in their secrets.

Children appeared running about and a few concerned parents were trying to keep an eye on their own. Giving the usual command to calm down and don't do that to him or her. Joe wondered where they came from, the children. He didn't notice them earlier in the day when he arrived. He saw Carol take notice of the children running about and having fun in the sun. She asked

Joe. "Where'd the children come from?"

"I would imagine they came from their parents." Tatyana said. Everybody looked at her and laughed halfheartedly. A few of the children came running by the table. It was delightful, they added the spice to the party.

"There's another house on the estate we built like a dollhouse for the children to play in. They had a little party there. Besides, we didn't want to scare them with the peasants' entertainment." Eva said.

"The house staff and security have children so it's a day care actually." Nicolas Sr said looking at Eva smiling like a proud dad. "My little day care on the estate here is tiny compared with what Eva runs. Isn't that right?" He said looking proudly at her.

"Yes, I have an orphanage in Russia, just outside Moscow. We currently have fifty children. I won't tell you the budget there because, the number doesn't matter. The result is the children receiving the best in housing, food and education. They range in age from a few years old to teens and a few in universities." She punctuated. "Schooling is done on-site and better than most private schools. Because they have no parents doesn't mean they're not entitled to the best in education." She paused for a somber moment. "Adoptions average about five a year, sometimes more. I don't advertise in the papers or the Internet. Reputable agencies refer adoptive parents to us. You see, I don't run the place for them to be adopted. They're children who have been left by their parents and I give them the best things in the world and the best education. Adopting one of my children means the perspective parents must continue the course that I have set for them. You don't take one of my children and put them in public school." Eva finished leaving no doubt that she loved those children.

Joe feeling speechless felt everyone was looking at him but, they were not. He realized the full impact of his shortsighted thoughts on adopting. Carol didn't say a word to him, she did not have to, she would not. He realized how wrong he'd been and knew Carol won't rub that in his face.

"You're an angel." Carol said to Eva.

"I decided to do that some years ago as a hobby. I have plenty of money and wanted to put it to good use." Eva smiled deviously. "They who don't get adopted have a choice to work for CZ Corp. There's nothing like training your own employees from small up." Eva said with a shy laugh capturing Joe's heart for a moment.

"We... We're their Aunts and Uncles." Mikal said proudly.

"Yes, we are." Max said, and it continued around the table to Nicolas Sr. "I'm their grandfather." Which produced well-loved "ah" from everybody.

"I feel like a fool and apologize for my ignorance." Joe said.

"No need, you didn't know, we opened

you up today. Or enlightened you I believe they would say." Nicolas Sr replied.

Joe raised his glass to Eva, "an angel." Everyone followed.

He felt like he owed Eva a better explanation. He owed the whole family. He had to show them that he was not an ugly person. He had them wrong, they were not just a wealthy arrogant family that thumbed their noses at the world. They were real people.

Carol rubbed her elbow next to his. Joe looked at her with a defeated look. She was his wife long enough to know that he learned something here today. Tomorrow they would discuss the subject of adopting. He knew that they also found a reputable place to adopt from. A special moment had arrived at the table. Joe felt like he understood the family and they taught him something today.

The mood was broken by Nicolas Sr. when he stood and held a hand out to Eva.

"May I have a dance?"

"Why yes, Czar Nicolas. I would be honored." Eva got up, curtsied, then took his hand as they walked to the dance floor near the orchestra. Everybody inside the tents stopped talking and the sound of "ohs" and "ahs" were heard.

The orchestra started a waltz when they stepped on the floor. Father and daughter were smoothly dancing across the floor. Step step, slide. A light breeze enhanced the whole scene. They had everyone riveted to their chairs, watching. Nobody spoke, and nobody dared go onto the dance floor to interrupt this beautiful display.

After a few minutes Mikal, Olga, Max, Tatyana and Nicolas Jr and his lady friend took to the dance floor. Uri was left at the table with Joe, Carol and the two girlfriends. Everybody applauded when they all took to the dance floor. Carol bent over whispering to him. "They're well-trained dancers, look at them."

"Why don't you join them?" He replied as Carol looked at him then Uri.

"Would you like to do the Waltz with me?" Carol asked Uri with pleading eyes.

Uri smiled up at Carol and took on a strong appearance that Joe had not witnessed today. He figured he was the introvert of the family. He watched as Uri proudly got up and escorted Carol to the dance floor and they were off doing the Waltz. He knew Carol was a good dancer from the lessons she had taken but, she looked good out there, he thought.

The orchestra finished one Waltz and began another. They all quickly switched partners. Carol was now with Nicolas Sr and Eva with Uri. Joe took note that Eva seemed close with Uri because they sat together talking at the table. On the dance floor now, when they stood not knowing who to take as a partner, Eva went directly to Uri.

A few children on the grass were trying to mimic the grown-ups on the dance floor. Joe noticed a big guy in casual dress and sunglasses looking at him. He looked over and nodded. Ivan didn't react. Joe went back to watching the dancing. He noticed Nicolas Sr had good stamina for they were well into the second waltz and he did not seem tired.

When the waltz ended, he bowed to Carol, who in turn curtsied to him. He then waved his arm for all to come to the dance floor. Everybody did. Joe went to Carol who was a little winded. "Ready for me."

"I guess. Boy, he's a good dancer."

The orchestra started up a slow tune that everybody started dancing to. He held Carol tight and she responded holding him tight. They gently swayed to the music as a cool breeze came along. Carol whispered in his ear, "I love you." He responded, "I love you too."

Joe saw the family gathered exchanging handshakes that meant something. Nicolas Sr basked in some glory. Eva happy and showing a big smile. A few men dressed casually were there and thanked by the family members. They seemed to appreciate the attention from the family members. Joe couldn't imagine the going on, but it was good judging by the smiles.

When that song ended someone tapped Joe on the shoulder, Ariel. "May I have the next dance with the lady?" He asked.

"Certainly." Joe replied looking at Carol who gave him a big smile. He was tapped again on the shoulder and turned to see Eva standing there.

"Care to dance with a lady." Eva asked shyly.

"I would be honored."

The orchestra started into a little lively tune from the big band era of the nineteen forties. Joe scared at first looked at Eva who said. "Follow my steps."

He did and it all fell together nicely. They were predictable steps and not too fast. He was enjoying the dance and Eva's slim body felt great in his arms.

She was enjoying the moment. He was a fast learner on the dance floor. It may mean he would do the same dance for her and her family. He would have to follow her lead. Somehow deep down she knew Joe Bergen would follow her lead.

"There's an impression I'm being groomed for something. I just want to say I hope you don't get your hopes up too much on me." Joe said in a quiet voice.

"You sound like I asked for a date." Eva said smiling.

"Okay, that was good." Joe laughed a reply feeling a little pressure off.

"Well, if you don't. I'll just fire you." Keeping the same smile on her face. Then continued. "We'll talk later before you leave. I'll let you know what I want for XO food groups."

"Okay." Joe said then asked, "have we met before?"

"I don't think so. Unless you've been to

Moscow, Paris, London, Warsaw or any enjoyable sunny island that is private." Eva rattled off smiling.

"No, I guess not. Thank you for not taking it wrong."

"You mean as a pickup line. I picked you up."

"Okay, I'm not going to win here." Joe said smiling.

"No, let's just dance." Eva replied and they did until the song ended.

Carol arrived. "Can I steal this man."

"Sure, he keeps stepping on my feet." Eva said jokingly.

The orchestra started another song and Carol was in her glory. She loved to dance, and he knew he was going to have to stay dancing with her for who knows how long. He rather wanted to talk to Eva. He found her easy to get along with. He knew her from someplace and was sure of it. He let those thoughts go and danced away into the evening.

A cool breeze was blowing, and the servants were lighting torches around the dance floor that added a pleasant atmosphere. The orchestra area lit up also gave them an almost evil appearance. The mansion illuminated while on the vast property an array of lighting started a magical experience. A magic kingdom, Joe thought, all so pleasant here.

Chapter 28

The library, two stories tall with books filling shelves and a huge fireplace they never lit because it would dry the books. Huge leather couches and chairs were next to it and the big desk that their father used. The glow from a tiffany window nearby gave an evil appearance.

Sitting and chatting idly while they waited for their father for the-once-a-month meeting. It was the real board of directors with one person absent, Aunt Catherine. Eva, her spokesperson, and confidant spoke for her on business matters. Their Aunt had scaled back the meetings to just Eva and her father which meant it was just Eva who spent time with her and spoke for her at these meetings. That bothered nobody because they all knew Eva would be in charge someday. They did visit her very often, on their own, because she was their Aunt. They are happy times that each spends with Aunt Catherine.

The door opened and Nicolas Sr walked in and to his desk. He seated and looked at everyone. Eva smiled at him and he smiled back. She knew that age was getting the best of him, she wished he would live forever.

Nobody said a word until Nicolas Sr started the meeting. He never rushed and as usual he lit a cigar and started puffing while looking up and down at his library of books that he has read and hoped to read someday. He was an avid reader and shared his books with his sister Catherine. Nicolas Sr loved his sister but, they did not always agree on handling business. That their only disagreement because they loved the money they earned together and the secrets they shared. She in Russia and him in the USA. They made good money on their illicit businesses until the fall of the Soviet Union. Then with their brains, muscle and money they bought up businesses and loyal people. That point in time exceeded their net worth enormously but, the real gain in power came when his children became adults and spread out. They made the family into a global entity. Today it was far beyond anything he imagined thirty years ago. His sister Catherine though knew the details and every amount of money. Nicolas Sr, impressed with how she can do that because he needed Eva to keep him updated on the vastness of everything, they involved themselves in. When he and his sister pass on Eva will be in charge.

After a few more puffs of the cigar Nicolas Sr was ready. He placed it in his big ashtray and looking at everybody he spoke. "All right, what's going on."

Eva started with a smile. "We have a surplus of one hundred fifty million this month."

Nicolas Sr looked off in the distance for a moment then replied. "Okay. What about this Joe Bergen fella?" Looking directly at Eva, who appeared ready to defend her choice.

"He's a prospect I thought of. I feel he will be an asset for the XO food group. His reputation is clean and will be a good front person for that business. Now, I think we should find someone else for the Minneapolis warehouse. Anton Slotkolov oversees that warehouse and he is clean and not known by law enforcement but, he is sloppy. He still has that alcohol window cleaner running. If he's caught, we will have a big problem." Eva stopped because her father had something to say.

"Yes, I know little Anton and his sending that hooch to the Ukraine. He has all bases covered. They are paying the right people and send it as a chemical cleaner and window cleaner. I know the operation well. I have no problem with him. As for Joe Bergen, yes, a good choice to head that division. A good clean reputation and nobody will question him." Nicolas Sr rubbed his chin then continued. "Eva, if he's made aware of our real business in time, will he accept and not be a problem. There's plenty of others we could have picked from people we know. This is your call." He looked serious.

"Yes, I know." Eva took her dad seriously because Joe Bergen's failure would be failure for Eva and Eva did not fail.

"Okay, we'll go with Joe Bergen. Now, I know why you choose him. At the time he was much younger and didn't tell anybody probably because he became scared. It was a first instinct of his and I hope he keeps that same quality. Enough speculating on him."

A moment of awkward silence while Eva waited for her father to continue. He puffed away. Eva knew her father did not like changes like this but, he would accept Joe Bergen once he proved himself. Nicolas Sr put his cigar down and resumed. "Okay Bergen's in, now, what are we spending money on."

"I could use another loan to expand my movie productions and I've been looking into buying more theaters to show my own productions. Plus, there's interest in having outlets to help up-and-comers, indie artists. Like oil companies have filling stations. Twenty million would be great." Nicolas Jr said to his dad. Nick Jr happily laundered for the family. Everybody knew he lived for the movie business and accepted that.

His father immediately brightened up with the proposal. "Sounds good. We must spend money to make money. We can shovel money through the theaters. Good idea Nico. Approved."

Eva nodded her head knowing it was a small amount to spend and she wouldn't mind the extras today.

"Who else," Nicolas Sr asked looking around.

"Yea, I need another plane and some new electronics. We have that new device working and the people who invented it do deserve a bonus. I also do have a few ex-Russian security forces that I want to bring on board. They'll be helpful with surveillance in law enforcement. They have a few friends in Interpol and some extra income for them would help." Max asked and Eva nodded agreeing.

"Tell me more about the latest invention." Nicolas Sr asked looking excited. Max and Eva tried not to laugh as she started.

"Okay, we miniaturized the unit that scans an area for up to a mile for cameras. Small like a cell phone one or big as a movie camera, even hidden ones smaller than a cell phone one. When it detects an aperture, it immediately sends out an invisible laser beam that destroys the camera. Frying the circuitry inside with only a momentary burst needed to do that. Here's some pictures."

Max handed pictures to his father then stood by to explain them. "Here we have Eva walking around a park." The first picture showed. "Unit turned on." The next picture was blank. Nicolas Sr looked up at Max confused. "Okay, now look at the first picture again. See the ski hat

Eva is wearing. Hidden inside is the device. Eva allowed this picture taken then turned the unit on with a remote." Max pointed it out for his dad who nodded and smiled. "Three of us at different angles and distances had our cameras fried."

"This camera took a picture though." Nicolas Sr asked.

Max nodded. "That camera I took the picture with I hid and used another just like it when she turned the unit on. I showed the unit was undetectable and unknown to even exist. We hire the best and they are on top of every development in the tech world. My people also have designed computer chips that are one hundred times faster than available today, so with those products we dominate and tell no one. It cost a lot and we reap the rewards as you have just seen. Nobody else would give financing for such projects."

"We did though." Nicolas Sr said.

"Yes. This unit alone we can make a gold mine." Max said proudly but knew that it would forever be a secret.

"No, that will never happen. Secrets are our advantage. We must remain undetectable." Nicolas Sr stated.

"I can demonstrate here if you want."

Max said to his dad who brightened again.

"Yes, show me."

Max looked over at Tatyana who was on her feet. She put a ski hat on her head and went to the other side of the room and waited. Max took a cell phone out of his pocket and handed it to his dad.

"I have a normal cell phone with camera most people have. Open it and make a phone call." He opened and made a call to his own office phone on the desk in front of him. It rang a few times and then he stopped it. He looked up at Max and said. "Okay it seems like a normal phone."

"Now use the camera. Tat start walking around the room, you take pictures of her."

Nicolas Sr nodded and started snapping pictures of Tatyana as she walked around the library looking at books on the shelves. After a few moments Max signaled to Tatyana who pulled out a small remote and pressed something.

Nicolas Sr was looking at the tiny screen of the cell phone in amazement. He didn't see Tatyana in the picture or any view that he could take a picture of.

He then looked up at Max surprised.

"The circuitries fried." His father pressed a few buttons to no avail. A blank, nothing. No pictures to see. Nicolas Sr looked up at Max amazed and smiling. "Okay, I like this. Can I see the unit?"

"Tat, show the hat." Max said. She came to the desk, took off the hat. She carefully pulled out a flimsy pad that circled the inside of the ski hat. She placed it on the desk with the wireless remote. Nicolas Sr picked it up, holding the flimsy tiny bubbled material in his hands.

"That has over a thousand little sensors that scan an area one thousand times a second. They look for any type aperture that a camera or video camera uses. It locks on it, the target, and keeps sending a low-level invisible laser beam that fries the digital camera lens and circuitry. In a regular camera that uses no circuitry, it keeps shooting a beam that messes up the film, so no picture is usable. It neutralizes cameras that cities commonly use for street surveillance also."

Everybody looked at Max with amazement. They liked what they heard because a big problem for people like them is surveillance by law enforcement.

Max continued. "I used it today. We found the freelance reporter using this. I set units on the perimeter of the forest line of the property and it picked out a camera lens. And the next step of capture was easy. It's mountable on car, boat and as displayed, carried. Where there are cameras, people are using them. So, besides sweeping for electronic bugging, we sweep for any type video cameras." Max paused to overcome smiling. "It's deadly though. Detecting a rifle scope and the person looking through it, will be minus one eye or two if using binoculars. A harmless beam until directly focused at an eyeball."

That produced subdued smiles. Then Nicolas Sr spoke. "Sounds and looks like a great forward tool. The possibilities are endless for hiding; it'll take an expert to figure this out." He rubbed his hand over it, like it was a newborn baby.

"Name for it?" Olga asked.

Max and Eva looked at her shrugging their shoulders. "You can name it."

"Mosquito." Tatyana said to nods around the group. Nicolas Sr held it up in his hands and said. "Hello mosquito."

Max took mosquito and placed it in a

special briefcase with bulletproof lining and a lock that would take a forever to figure out.

"Taxicabs, we have many friends driving them. Behind the advertisement signs." Nicolas Sr said puffing his cigar up.

"Please keep that away from my movie production studios," Nicolas Jr said gaining a laugh from the group. He then continued. "Use against my competitors."

"The reality is the mosquito will prevent pictures of us. With no pictures, law enforcement will have a difficult time with surveillance. That's if they ever get wind of us." Eva said soberly.

Uri sat forward and looked at everyone. "I can use it on my travels in South America." Looking at Max.

"Not a problem Uri." Max said.

Uri continued. "I can impress a few people with that mosquito. Not that I'm going to show them the unit but, to make a point that will go a long way with showing sincerity."

Everybody was serious now because, they knew that unit will give them an edge. When approaching a new Mob sometimes it helps to show a magic trick or two. That always helps with gaining respect.

"Just tell me where you need it." Max said. Uri thought for a moment looking at Max. "Knock out cameras on airplanes? Like surveillance type planes."

"Yes. Can do. It would be like a moving ground unit. Add a power burst to bring the plane down in an extreme. That would raise eyebrows that we don't want, I'm sure." Max said.

"No. Just the mosquito will do." Uri said slightly smiling now.

Nicolas Sr put his cigar down and was ready to resume the meeting.

"Work with Uri on applying that for his travels. A few diplomats won't mind their luggage used to bring it in on short notice. When the need arises." Nicolas Sr said. Uri nodded. "Yes, that will work well."

"Mikal and Olga. You both are needy." Nicolas Sr said. Mikal and Olga looked at one another smiling.

Olga started. "I'm doing great with my divisions. No new pay outs needed, everybody is happy." Nicolas Sr smiled at Olga and she smiled back.

Mikal picked up. "No need here. Everybody has pockets full of money from us and they're loyal to a fault."

They surprised nobody in the room. They dressed elegantly and mingled with powerful people and could fix anything in Europe. Their respected businesses were running with perfection, never a mistake. They could launder one hundred million in a moment's notice and without notice. They were the European divisions of CZ Corp.

They were the bored and honest businesspeople, that is the image they presented. Doors opened for them when they needed favors. Both had a good life in Europe and stayed low-key.

"Okay, no new pay outs for your divisions." Nicolas Sr said. Eva then said. "Olga is going to arrange a loan for XO Food with our Polish friends. We're going to bring in expensive type foods and sell them here to start. And, the new laundering business will have Joe Bergen heading it. I think ten million to start would be good."

Her father reminisced. "Thirty years ago, I used to bring money over in a cardboard box. Today there's terrorists and we go through this maze. Yes, start with that." Eva nodded and then looked at Olga who nodded approval with Mikal.

"Now, who's getting that money in the end." Olga asked.

"That's going to be Bergen's salary. I think that would be wonderful." Nicolas

Sr said, and everybody nodded and laughed. Eva did not care for that joke, but she knew money was money.

When the laughter stopped Eva said. "Now, I have people that will look like investors for Nick's money. I'm going to bring his from a surplus we have in an Italian bank."

Nicolas Jr nodded to his sister and everybody then looked back at Nicolas Sr.

"Fifteen million enough increase for your division?" Nicolas Sr asked Max.

"Yes. That'll go a long way in keeping everything secure as usual." He said. "For now." He added with a smile. Everybody laughed because they knew his costs ran the highest. No price tags for good security.

Nicolas Sr then looked at Eva. "Okay then, direct deposit our bonuses with the rest."

Eva nodded yes. Nicolas Sr answered with a nod of his own. She wondered if he was getting too old for this. That thought she quickly dismissed and then said. "Okay. I have two jobs that Aunt Catherine has told me about. One is the Red mob in Russia, that's for us. They want to get a nuke to sell. The only problem is our sources tell us other otherwise. No suggestion that Ureinchencko is going in that direction."

Eva waited for a response from her father. He was puffing away looking off into space then started. "Russo Ureinchencko. We were friends once and he tried to kill me. Your Aunt Catherine and he were planning to marry, and he decided he was going to take over our little enterprise also. He thought Catherine would be a push over if he killed me. He was seeing another woman and I found out and told Catherine. I didn't want her made a fool of but, she was way ahead of me. She tried to kill him and almost did. A friend of his told her of the plot to kill me and that sent her over the edge. She went to his flat and the little sweet woman he had on the side was there. I don't know what happened but, the little woman turned up dead and the police were seeking Russo for doing it. Everybody loyal to him sided with Catherine. Now, with that consolidation of power, Russo took off for parts unknown. He must have made a few connections because the murder charge changed to unknown death of the little lady. I then decided to come to America."

Nicolas Sr looked at Eva then

continued. "You just born, and I and your mother changed our religion to the Jewish faith and came here as refugees. The rest is history. Your Aunt Catherine stayed and watched the man she almost married over the years. She's had plenty of opportunities to kill him but, I guess there's still something there in her heart for him. I can't imagine what. I will say though; they were a happy couple. The money changed him. We allowed him into our circle and he saw the money and power that we were beginning to get and that changed him. He thought he would take over and nobody would care. Even back then the people who knew us called Catherine the Czarina. They called her Catherine the Great, too."

Nicolas Sr puffed his cigar and looked directly at Eva. She always loved hearing about her Aunt Catherine. Even her mother she remembers would put Aunt Catherine on a pedestal when telling Eva about her. She did miss her mother though. Eva collected her thoughts and came back to the meeting.

"Okay, maybe she finally wants him taken out, but problem is with the mobs. I had a meeting yesterday and they want nothing done unless there is clear evidence." Eva said to her dad who nodded then said. "If that's what Aunt Catherine told you and the mobs want evidence. You must get evidence. Do nothing until you know for sure. Catherine will understand" Nicolas Sr said then leaned back looking intently at Eva. She nodded and went on to the next.

"Next issue is Bob Wellington. She said that he is going to run for president and he will not make it. On his last visit to Russia he was asking many questions about mob activity and the like. I guess he's still mad about his nephew, Don, getting ripped off." Eva paused with a sour look on her face. "Aunt Catherine will take care of this. She wants us to watch and enjoy."

Nicolas Sr leaned forward-looking happy now. "She knows what she is doing. He's a Senator and this will create headlines." He puffed then continued. "She does know what she is doing. To quote Aunt Catherine. 'To take down the largest tree in the forest, you wait as it grows old. It's eaten inside and falls on its own.' She will get the Senator by making it like a medical condition, gravely ill with something. That's one of her favorite ways, quietly take someone out. She did study medicine at one point before she got pregnant." Nicolas Sr stopped looking at Eva.

"She was pregnant? What happened?" Asked Olga.

"In the time of Russo Ureinchencko. That's the reason they were going to marry. Then a miscarriage occurred and the rest you know." He said looking at Eva.

"I see that for reason enough to kill that pig. A miscarriage and he was cheating on her. Enough reason for me." Tatyana said and all agreed.

"You would think she would want to see this pig die." Olga said.

"She has reasons for not wanting to do it but, I have no problem doing it for her." Mikal said.

Eva spoke. "We can't touch him without evidence. Our European mob friends have people there; they'll know if we did it."

"Accident." Max said.

"No, we must keep the honor with the other mobs." Eva said

"Catherine wants you to dig deeper. Is this source reliable? Dig deeper Eva. Keep me updated on this." Nicolas Sr said getting up from his chair. "An old friend is here, and I need to entertain her." He started walking for the door and everybody waited until he was gone.

"The Senator didn't surprise him much." Olga said.

"Why would he care? Just another sleazy politician." Uri said.

"Wow. She must hate him." Mikal said.

"I'm sure nobody will detect any foul play when it happens." Max said confidently.

"No, the Czarina knows what she is doing." Tatyana said out loud.

"Okay, you need to go. I have to interview Joe Bergen." Eva said fixing her hair.

They all got up to leave and Eva thought about the Senator also, echoing in her mind what Tatyana said. 'The Czarina knows what she is doing.' Eva hoped so. She looked at Ivan who had just entered the library. "Get Mr. Bergen."

He nodded and was gone from the library.

Eva took out a few pills and swallowed them. What's she supposed to do with the Red mob. She knew Andre was as reliable as she was going to get. Was it just personal? Then why did she want the vote of the other mobs? Confusing Eva thought, but hoped she would figure something out.

Chapter 29

The evening cooled off the warmth from the day; as the orchestra played a slow tune.

Joe and Carol took a break to meet some guests. Then returned to the dance floor. He felt engaged and back with Carol. This day was something he thought would never come. Joe yearned for this day. He saw Ariel coming across the dance floor.

"Sorry to disturb. Ms Eva would like to see you in the library. Only you Joe."

He looked down at Carol in his arms who gave him a proud smile.

"I can fill in here if Mrs. Carol doesn't mind." Ariel added.

"I would like that." Carol said separating from Joe.

"Good. That man standing by the door will take you to her."

Joe started walking over to a six-foot something who did not look like a person to tangle with. He felt a chill at first and then shook that off like he did earlier in the day. He heard a whistle from behind and turned to see Ariel giving the orchestra conductor a hand signal. The music took an upbeat jazzy tune and he caught a glimpse of Carol smiling and ready to dance.

He took the steps two at a time and across the patio to the big man. The look on his face did not change Joe noticed but, he still smiled and nodded to him.

"Hi, I'm Joe Bergen and you're going to take me to Ms Eva Bokanawski."

"Yes, please follow me."

Joe watched as the giant moved like a swift lion, effortlessly and exact. He had to take a little longer stride than usual to keep up with the big guy.

They immediately went to the nearest door and down a hallway then turned left down a shorter hallway stopping at a set of double doors. Ivan knocked twice, opened one door and entered standing to one side for Joe to enter. Ivan closed the door behind.

The room was huge, and Joe immediately knew it was a library looking up in awe at the endless shelves of books and the glass doom ceiling.

"Mr. Bergen."

Joe looked over at the leather couches in the distance and saw Eva sitting on one of them. She looked beautiful, he thought. The red hair shining from the light of the domed ceiling; her classical features giving the aura of a refined woman. "Come sit. We'll talk here." Eva motioned for the couch across from her.

He approached looking at the huge desk and the pictures hanging on the wall behind it. There was one picture of an older lady Joe noticed and thought she looked just like Eva. He sat across from her on the opposite couch and glanced at her beautiful crossed legs. The leather soft the view breathtaking. She kept a serene smile on her face that Joe could not read.

"Would you like a drink?" She asked.

"No, I'm fine."

Eva looked over at Ivan. "Thank you, Ivan."

Ivan nodded and left. Joe looked over after he left and back at Eva. "That's one big guy." He said.

"Yes, he cuts a mean appearance. His name is Ivan, my bodyguard and confidant. He would give his life for me if I wanted him to. So, don't get me mad."

Joe looked seriously at Eva. She giggled and covered her mouth. "I tell everyone that. I'm just joking."

"I still will try not to get you mad." Joe said seriously smiling.

"He watches out for me when I can't. I travel extensively and need someone to watch my back."

"I understand. There's weirdos with issues about everything these days." He replied nodding.

"Yes so, you'll be seeing much of Ivan. He doesn't talk to anyone but me so, don't take offense."

"No, not." Then continued. "Hum, I noticed the picture on the wall behind the desk. Is that your mother?"

Eva looked over at the picture of Aunt Catherine and felt like she was watching her.

"No, that's my Aunt, she lives in Russia."

"Oh, she looks just like you."

"Yes, we have similar features. My mother passed away about eight years ago."

"Sorry."

"No problem. We named the orphanage I run in Russia after her. She loved children and raising them. In fact, I'll let you in on a little secret. Nicolas Jr and I are natural brother and sister. My remaining brother and sisters are adopted. I'm telling you this to understand my father earlier today. He didn't mean any harm and you didn't get him mad. He's just irritated at some people's ignorance toward adoption. So, you owe no apology and no damage done."

"I feel like an idiot but, will recover. I'm not of the mind that I know everything and try to keep open to new circumstances that may occur. I hope you don't use today as any reference of whom I am."

"No, not. I just assume you had the right thoughts all along but, you were just afraid to take a risk without a sign or word from someone. I understand. You're okay."

"Thank you. I would like to ask about your orphanage and possible adoption. Not today. I would like to wait a bit to organize for what I need to do."

"Okay. I understand. Remember a child is only as good as you raise them."

"Yes." Joe nodded and Eva needed to change this to business.

"So, we are putting together a food service chain from coast-to-coast. It's advancing well. We have bought fifteen warehouses with plans to expand later into other areas. They're close to major cities, that's where the business is, in or around the major cities. Now, your business I'm impressed with. You have a good business model or just lucky. Tell me about your business growth."

She knew it'll get boring but, these are the times she endures.

Joe moved a bit and collected his thoughts.

"I started in the finance dept. of a family owned food service business that had many loyal local customers. The owner became ill and I offered to buy. Now, he ran a basic cash business that didn't grow much. I took that and extended credit so customers would buy more. Then I went after the upmarket restaurants because the size of the building at first didn't allow for restaurant chains orders. I didn't want to overextend with a bank. So, the fashionable places liked my service and attention to detail and business grew in that area. I hired many salespeople and concentrated on the family owned establishments throughout the state and it grew. It now covers New Jersey, New York and parts of Pennsylvania. I stayed away from the big chains because they just want someone to warehouse and deliver for a set fee. That fee doesn't increase with the rising fuel costs. Now, I joined in with a few other warehouses through a good buyer program, so I get the food product at a very reasonable price for a place my size. We share the cost of a trailer load of a product or larger and that lowers my costs. Other than that, I plowed money into a larger warehouse and good equipment. I do have a fair contract with the drivers and warehouse men and their union. That I like because it does afford them a decent wage and a stable workforce. I have maybe five people out of two hundred that leave every year. So, expenses are predictable and profit high."

Eva was glad he finished before she had to yawn. "Sounds like a model that works. The numbers are impressive, a ten percent annual profit in an industry that averages five percent; with a single warehouse. Can you do that with fifteen?"

"A larger scale but I probably could. It'll take time at first until I can assess every property. You said it's fifteen that you have bought up so, I assume there is no real communication to all them for the payable, receivable and payroll. Not to mention the buyers and sales staffs. A starting point is to string them together on a dedicated computer network. Keeping access to each warehouse open. Next the buyers, fifteen warehouses can get a reasonable price on product. Sales staff find weaknesses if any and get them out the door selling. Then a look at the pay and operations side, meaning the warehouse workers and drivers. I would give a tentative six-month improvement with a one-year goal of a set plan in place up and running."

Joe finished not knowing if he Eva impressed or not.

"Sounds good. Rich Holbrook is running the show and he's not the man for the job. He is better use as a deal maker. I send him out to buy new companies and set up divisions. He's quick minded and can fast study a market, no matter what it is. Real estate or food warehouses, Rich gets us a good deal. I need him out of that office now before he ruins something."

Eva giggled and Joe smiled then she continued. "So, Mr. Bergen you did a great job with your own warehouse and I badly need someone of your intellect and talent. I know you probably had visions of spending your money and if you can hold off on that dream I would, and CZ Corp. would like to hire you. The job consists of CEO and President of XO Food group and, private jet to get to the warehouses and for personal use. Feel free to take a vacation anytime you want with it. A driver, car and a security person for your safety. And, a ten million-dollar salary."

Eva finished looking directly at Joe. He

didn't know what to say at first. It sounded like a dream. He opened his mouth but stopped then started again.

"Sorry, you caught me off guard. I, yes will and am honored and would like to add that if I don't do as promised I will resign in one year." He hoped he didn't sound like an idiot.

"Joe, it's a mess right now. I just want to know first-hand from a central location how each does every month and we'll go from there."

"Okay."

"Now, the warehouses, some of them are run by the previous owners so, feel free to hire and fire as you need."

"Okay."

"When would you like to start?" Eva asked smiling while she thought of dragging him up-stairs and raping him.

"I need to wrap up my office and transfer my CFO to president. Thom Heller, he was with me when we met at your offices." Eva nodded. "I would say a month."

"I was hoping for a little closer, like this coming Monday."

Joe stared for a moment wondering if she was joking. No reaction so he nodded. "Sure. I mean yes. It's not like I'm going away I'll still oversee Bergen foods. Yes, this Monday will be fine."

"Done. We'll close on your business on Monday also."

"My first day would be fine."

"Good. Now the corporate office for XO Food is on the forty fifth floor. The floors yours to expand where needed, I can open more if necessary. Your offices come equipped and ready for use. There's staff that Rich hired and if there's a problem, staff with whom you want."

"Okay, no, I'm sure they're fine."

"They are good workers." Eva smiled coyly.

"Then they stay on."

"Good. Monday a car will pick you up at home at eight a.m."

Joe and Eva looked at each other for a moment then she stood, and Joe followed. They walked to the double doors. She opened one and Ivan was filling the door frame.

"Ivan. Joe Bergen is going to be our new CEO of XO Food."

Ivan extended his hand to Joe and they shook. Ivan's hand almost circled Joe's.

"Welcome Mr. Bergen."

"Thank you, Ivan."

"Now, I want you handpicking someone for Mr. Bergen."

Ivan nodded.

"Well, that's it, I'll see you soon." Eva said extending her hand. Joe took it liking the feel of her soft skin.

"I look forward to it."

"Ivan will take you back to the party."

Ivan stepped aside, Joe walked into the hallway. After closing the door, he immediately walked ahead of Joe who tried to keep pace again. His mind buzzing and wondering what he got himself into. A private jet to go anywhere, ten million a year. He wondered for a moment what he was doing.

Then the sound of music and laughter started getting louder and Joe knew his life was about to change. He didn't know what the future held but, it wasn't going to be boring.

Chapter 30

Both came through a set of open double doors with Joe still lost. Ivan stopped looking at him. "You'll find the party just down the hall on the left," then was gone.

Joe started walking down the hallway and he heard the orchestra still going strong. The sound of voices getting closer as he looked at the paintings hanging and realized he knew nothing of art. He could probably afford some works of art but, he knew nothing.

He entered the ball room and people started looking at him smiling. Ariel burst out from a group of people.

"I would like every bodies attention." The crowd quieted down. Even the orchestra outside stopped playing. Ariel walked next to Joe, then announced. "I would like to present our new CEO of XO Foods. Mr. Joe Bergen."

A loud burst of applause followed. Then one by one people came forward to congratulated him. He realized they were all employees of the company here. He shook hands and got kisses from women and started looking around for Carol. She played a part in this, he wanted her to share in this too. When the crowd thinned Ariel came back and whispered in his ear.

"Don't worry you'll do fine. Just do what Eva wants."

"Sure." Joe whispered back thinking, for ten million with private jet he'll do whatever Eva wants.

Ariel patted him on the back and left. More people stopped to congratulate him, and he grew weary of saying thank you. He hasn't done anything yet. Then he felt a hand go into his and quickly looking to see Carol standing next to him smiling from ear to ear.

"Well I guess you know." Joe said looking to her.

"Yes, many invitations." Carol said overwhelmed.

"I guess the majority here are coworkers so, meet some new people. It'll be fun."

"Sure, what's the good points." Carol asked wanting the quick description. Joe leaned over whispering. "Ten million, private jet and limo with bodyguard."

Carol looked stunned at first and said. "I better accept the invitations."

"You're one of them."

"Yes, this feels scary but, I'm sure I'll like it." She gave Joe a happy smile.

Nicolas Sr came bounding over with a drink in his hand and a lady friend about twenty-five years younger than himself on his arm. He had a big smile on. "I just heard the news. The board has final decision on you but, they agree with Eva. I hope the salary is enough and the jet is free to use for personal travel. I think Carol would love a weekend in Miami." Nicolas Sr finished looking at her in a paternal way.

"Or Paris." She replied.

"Ah, yes. You have good taste. Our larger jets have the range for that but, there's usually a waiting list."

"I think Miami will do for now." Carol replied not believing this.

Joe extended his hand to Nicolas Sr. As they shook Nicolas Sr gave him a serious look for a split second.

Then Joe said to him.

"Thank you I'll try to live up to and beyond."

"I'm sure you will, Joe. Just one step at a time. Eva knows what she wants and is doing. Obey her."

"Will do." He said understanding the message. Please Eva. He knew it's been years since working for somebody but, won't be a problem he knew.

Across the room Eva watched the happy couple basking in the attention. She felt jealous watching them hug plus the way they looked at each other. She did not like feeling jealous. Joe appealed to her since that day long ago he happened down an alley in New York.

"Well, I guess Joe's going to get lucky tonight with ole Carol when they get home." Tatyana said to Eva's blank stare.

"It'll be five minutes then they'll both be asleep." Olga said.

"I see you know that well Olg." Tatyana said smiling.

"At least I get some you dike." Olga returned the smile to Tatyana.

Eva looked at both saying. "Can you two shut up" Both looked at her smiling. They are going to gang up she knew.

"I bet ole Carol goes down on him until he screams hee haw." Olga said smiling at Eva. Then Tatyana weighed in. "Yea, then he rams her hard until she screams." Tatyana licked her lips moaning.

Eva broke a smile. "You two are so sick." she said innocently.

Tatyana moved closer to Eva saying. "We can arrange and do it fast. Then he's all yours. Comfort him in his grief."

Olga nodded agreeing.

"Stop. I got plenty to choose from." Eva replied to them.

"We're just looking out for sis." Olga said.

Max stepped into the group. "Am I disturbing some girls talk?"

"No. Tell me something I don't know." Eva said looking at Tatyana and Olga.

"All right, that piece of shit that crashed the party." Max started and paused sipping a drink. "We injected a few shots of something and, he's gone forever. Searched his home office and there wasn't anything of damage to us. They did find a scribbled note that said he was to meet Little Donny Wellington tomorrow at a downtown restaurant. That other little shit still won't let go. We can have him disappear, just say the word." Max finished looking at Eva.

"No. Aunt Catherine has a plan in the works for his uncle the Senator. You know that."

Max nodded reluctantly.

Eva knew that Donald Wellington the nephew of the Senator is a problem. He only touched the surface, though. The best he could do is have a friend try to take pictures. She also knew that his calls to the FBI went out the window. No concern right now.

Eva looked away from Max to Joe and Carol talking quietly together. She guessed they were planning their first trip in their own private jet. What some people think is exciting, Eva thought.

"Oh, another little nothing. The HR person from Bergen's place sent a few emails to the now-deceased photographer activist. They amounted to nothing but since we're going to own that place, we need a little cleaning. His name is Paul Letter and we don't need him thinking about us."

Eva quickly looked at him knowing he was not joking. Also, she was mad and needed an outlet to relieve some stress.

"Do it. Use one of the warehouses in Jersey City. In fact, grab the wife if there's one. Then cook the books at Bergen's company and make this Paul look bad so, they'll be no love loss from our new CEO. Hey, let me know when. I need to relieve some stress."

"Done" Max smiled at Eva knowing this would take care of a problem before it starts. He stepped away taking out his cell phone.

Eva went back to looking at Joe and Carol knowing the early death of his wife would hurt him and he would carry that a while. She didn't want damaged goods in a man. She wanted him free and clear. Eva knew she needed a different plan to capture this man.

Olga bent whispering to Eva. "He's a fox. I don't blame you. The problems we have." They looked at each other laughing. Tatyana just shrugged. "See you."

Chapter 31

After countless good byes and looking forward to working with you, Joe and Carol were finally driving down the road toward home. He did not remember most of the names of people he met; they all seemed happy and secure though. More like a club than a group of fellow workers. Joe couldn't figure out why, everybody appeared of European decent. Young and old alike all seemed like one in a real way. No talk of work, no talk of deals or sales of anything. Just people having a good time.

Joe looked over at Carol daydreaming. She looked over at Joe and smiled lightly. Overall it was a great day for her, he knew.

"Why don't you take the interstate, it's faster?" Carol said with a look in her eyes that Joe knew well. Eager to be home sooner he veered to the on ramp for the interstate joining in the race.

"Have a good time." Joe asked her.

"Yea they're cool people. Money is no object there. Do you think you can work for them? I mean the jet and money is great but, you haven't worked for anybody in years."

"I'll like it. Couldn't tell if Eva was joking or not but, she was begging me to take the job. They bought up fifteen warehouses and have no one or a network in place yet. I guess they were looking as they bought warehouses and I happened to meet their needs."

"Sounds like it. I mean why hire somebody off the street when you had a good running business showing you knew what you were doing. I'd hire you."

"I already know you would."

"When we get home, I want your services, free."

"We're getting there."

"You're a lucky man."

"I have a job ahead of me there." He paused to let out a laugh. "That's cool because, I get to set something in place and watch it work. It'll be an ego trip. Interested in a quick weekend to Miami? On my private jet."

"Sure Mr. ego. I'll fly with you anywhere."

"Two more exits."

"Hurry. I love you long time."

They both laughed hard, Joe keeping his eyes open so he could see the road.

Not much later Joe pulled the BMW into the garage. Carol was already out and heading into the house when she stopped and looked at him with a sexy pose. "Five minutes' big guy."

Joe walked through the kitchen and down a short hallway to his den. He threw the car keys on his desk and saw a light flashing for voice mail on the phone. Sitting behind his desk he hoped it was nothing dumb or an emergency he wanted to get upstairs. Holding the receiver to his ear he listened to Paul's voice. "Joe, Paul. I found something interesting you may want to read about that CZ company. See you Monday unless you want sooner." Click.

Joe felt irritated hearing that. He had a great day, and somebody wants to ruin it. Yes, he'll read it tomorrow. Since he'll be working for them, he wanted to know who was leaking information about the company. Yes, Paul. I'll read that tomorrow, Joe thought.

"Hello you?" Came Carols happy voice from upstairs. Joe hit the delete button and got from his desk. A new house, this place is too small, Joe thought as he climbed the stairs.

~~~~~

Don Wellington was in his New York City penthouse angry. Angry because he could not reach his friend. He slammed down the phone and looked at the television which did not satisfy him. A young woman named Cheryl he was dating from his job came in the room. She stood and looked at Don with a cute smile and a sexy nightshirt on.

"You coming back to bed." Cheryl said licking her lips.

Don looked over at her not wanting another round of caressing and sex. He felt satisfied with their first session. He wanted to know about his friend Brian who went to the Bokanawski party. Don looked over at the huge wall clock, 2:00 a.m. What's up?

"Hello." Cheryl said sweetly.

"What? I'm busy now. I had a good time. You can sleep here if you want." He went for a beer in the kitchen and returned looking at Cheryl. She remained looking at him with no expression.

"Go back to bed I'll be there soon." Don said nicely then took a big swig of his beer. She looked mad and walked away slamming the bedroom door. Don shook his head in disgust. He had sex with her three times a week. He figured her dating him was because of whom he is at the brokerage firm. If she wanted a promotion, he would give her one. The bedroom door opened and slammed again. Cheryl fully dressed walked past him and to the front door. She stopped and looked back at Don.

"Don't call me anymore. Don't come near me at work. You're a." She stopped shaking her head and slammed the door behind her.

Don lifted his beer and toasted and took another swig. He went into his library office and sat behind the desk. He powered up his computer and waited for the desktop to appear. Looking at the desktop clock, 2:10

a.m. Brian, where are you?

Don opened the messenger program and clicked on Brain's profile. A picture of a dog-named snoop appeared. He typed in the message box; "Hey snoop how was the party. Did they invite you in? Did you get pictures? Call me when you get home." Don pressed the enter key and waited. Knowing if Brian was home, he would be on his computer. Still, no reply came from the messenger only a blinking curser.

Don closed out the messenger and sat looking at his computer screen. He was starting to have concerns because, he did not know what was happening. Brian caught by security at the Bokanawski estate? All he had to do was say he got the wrong house. The pictures were just going to be a prank anyway, Don smiled. Him and Brian were going to set up a website under anonymous names and post the photos with a few words. Just a little fun but Brian isn't reporting in.

Don opened his mail program and looked again at the emails that Brian sent him. The first one was from some guy named Paul Letter who worked for a small food warehouse in New Jersey.

> Hi, I read your website and found the information about CZ Corporation interesting. My interest in the company is that they are buying the business I work for through a division of theirs called XO food service. I

searched the Internet and found your website. You written the company has bought businesses and closed some down putting people out of work. You state that they bought the businesses after the owner or owners had some bad luck.

Concrete information showing unsavory business deals is my interest. Some large corporations do engage in questionable practices but, no one comes forward to stop such practices. Now, you feel they did something unlawful to buy these businesses and then layoff the good workers. The company I work for is going to sell to them. I need more information to show the owner here.

Paul Letter
Human Resources
Bergen Foods.

Don finished reading that email and opened the second one that he sent the next day.

Thank you for the reply. The information is interesting. I am going to show to my boss. His name is Joe Bergen, a great guy to work for. He would feel bad if something happened after he sold his business. Now, you referred to Russian mafia, are they?

FBI aware of this? I am interested reading what else you may have. I need a little more concrete evidence that I can show my boss. Time is running short. He is going to a big party this weekend at the family's house. Please help. I don't want to work for bad people.

Paul Letter
Human Resources
Bergen Foods

Don finished reading leaning in his chair and sipping his beer. He picked up a pen and wrote Joe Bergen's name on a notepad and circled it. He closed out the email program and opened the Internet browser. He typed in Joe Bergen's name and went from there. In moments, he read a few articles about his food business. A few lame awards and yes, the home address.

Don quickly had a map showing the direct route to Bergen's home in New Jersey. He printed it out, turned off the computer. He sat looking at the printed map that showed only an arrow pointing to a spot.

Don needed a look at the house. He wanted to see this innocent owner who the Russians were wining and dining. His friend Brian had been keeping track of the latest venture of the Russians and this Joe Bergen goes to the old man's house. Other warehouse owners were kicked out and given little for a buy price.

Don remembers one warehouse that Brian told him about, in Minneapolis or someplace. The owner strong-armed into selling or so Brian said. He did keep watch on this buy up of warehouses and planned a good story when they completed. He was going to show how the Russian mob strong-armed their way into the business. Brian tried interviewing former owners, a few felt happy and many did not want to talk to Brian. So, he had to go on private documents and noticed a big price disparity in the buying. Some did get little money, or they were just plain dumb, regardless. A smoking gun not found yet. They were wining and dining this Joe Bergen guy though.

Don looked at the time then went into the living room. The room had a sweeping view of upper east Manhattan. He watched the traffic for a moment then went to the kitchen tossing the empty beer in the garbage. In the bedroom he fell onto the bed. He thought of Brian and fell off to sleep.

Chapter 32

Don slowly hung up the phone for the one hundredth time. Brian was still not answering. He's either hurt or playing the usual game of taking his time because he got some good pictures to show. Either way Don was mad because, he woke too early and the day had not gone as expected. After many calls, no Brian. Then a pleasant call to his uncle the senator, he jumped down his throat.

His uncle knew about his friend Brian and disapproved of his strategy in getting a story. Saying that's liberal journalism to the extreme and not fair reading. Leave investigations to the law enforcement. Also, Don made a mistake of saying he went to the old Russians birthday party. The old man threw much money at his uncle for campaigns. Still, he did not go to the old man's birthday party. Did he know about the Russians? And, he's going to run for president.

Don laughed. He knew that his uncle had

discussed it with his daughters who were Don's cousins. They always talk to Don and tell him everything. So, it is time to limit his exposure to questionable people if he's going to run for president.

Don glowed at the thought of his uncle being president. He could leave the boring brokerage firm and start his own hedge fund. Money will flow in his direction. The world will be his. Instead of being at a brokerage firm that his father helped build and then took his name off it when he died. Because the firm wanted to present a fresh image and having the name of a dead person on the building did not go well with the new image. For now, though, Don took the five million a year he worked for with commissions and waited. His time was coming to be his own man.

Don went over to the huge windows and looked out over Manhattan. It was a bright sunny day. A good day to go the club upstate and play a round of golf or something. Not today. Don wanted to get this smear campaign under way and watch the Russians cringe. He wanted to see the looks on their face when they see themselves posted on a website as criminals. He looked forward to that coming day. All they needed were some good photos of the birthday party. Put name tags on them and the company name and they will be history. He walked back to his desk and was getting mad, mad with Brian.

Don sat behind his desk and wondered if he should try calling Cheryl. He didn't treat her good last night. The story, when first circulated at the office, about his failed investment in Russia, Cheryl was one of few who did not take part in the slanderous rumors. She treated him nicely and did not follow the others. He felt bad about last night.

How was he going to call her and tell her that? Don decided to just let it go for now. He will bump into her soon and apologize. She would accept it because she is decent, Don knew.

He opened the web browser and read the headline news. The latest, a bombing in the Middle East. Don read the story and thought for a moment then smiled. Searching the Internet for bombs, he spent the rest of the day reading about bombs.

The day faded to dark with only the light from the computer lighting up his office. He printed many pages that explained making one. The best placement and the blast effects of many different ones.

Don rubbed his eyes and stopped reading liking what he read, but too much to remember. He did not have the means to make one but, he did have a few friends from school that went bad and might know. They can attribute a well-placed bomb to terrorism with no more questions asked. Now, who. Don leaned back and thought of Nicolas Bokanawski and Eva Bokanawski.

Which one?

Chapter 33

A warm day for April, Joe noticed walking outside to get the newspaper. Casually he looked up and down the street for his ride to work. He assumed they knew where he lived.

Walking back to the house he glanced at the headline and folded the paper back. I'll read on the way to work. The thought made him smile, read the newspaper on the way to work.

In the kitchen Carol was finishing the cleaning from breakfast. She looked over when Joe came in. He tossed the newspaper on the table and stood looking proudly at Carol.

"Your school bus here yet?" Carol asked smiling.

"No and I don't want to be late my first day." Joe replied sitting down.

Carol returned to washing the remaining dishes humming something Joe did not know. She was happy.

"Why you washing the dishes. Is the dishwasher broke?" Joe asked looking at her from behind.

"No, just wanted to wash them with my own hands." She turned slightly to smile at him.

"Okay." Joe said slowly.

They've been living a dream since the party. They took a fast ride to Atlantic City to take in some gambling and a show. They quietly walked along the beach both enjoying a moment they hoped would last forever. He knew life was going to move fast now. The subject of adopting wasn't mentioned since the party but, Joe knew it would happen and he was ready. Then he remembered Paul. He did not call him back.

Joe went to his den and sat behind the desk. He dialed Paul's home number and waited. The voice mail picked up he hung up. Then he dialed his office number and there was no answer. He did not want to call Thom at home because he probably was having a great morning, like himself. They last talked early yesterday morning and Thom felt elated with the promotion. Paul can wait until he had time later today.

Joe decided to call Thom any way. He was nervous because he did not know what to expect today. Thom's home phone picked up on the first ring.

"Thom, Joe."

"Hey, what's up."

"Ah nothing much yet. Waiting for my ride to New York."

"Sounds stressful already."

"Yea. I can't wait. I always hated driving to work."

"Okay."

"I called you because I want you to give Paul a message. Tell him I'll talk to him later today."

"Sure. Anything I need to know."

"No, he just did a little research on CZ Corp. and I think he's gotten a little carried away. No large company ever has a perfect past."

"Got it. I'll give him the message."

"Now, I know it was a moment decision but, do you want the top job there. Isn't going to be fun always. I can find someone else. If you have doubts or just want to be like you were."

"If you keep talking like this I'm going to hang up."

"Okay. Sorry."

"Joe, I'm proud to step into your shoes and I will do a great job my way. I learned from you and I will apply that in my style. I look forward to it."

"Your bringing tears to my eyes."

"Fu too."

"Okay, this happened fast and so we need to tell everybody there. I will contact you later today and let you know what time for a meeting. We need to address everybody and answer questions."

"Sounds good. When I get to the office, I'll have Paul draw up a statement to post that I'm in charge and you have sold to XO

Food service company. I'll keep it basic. You'll tell the rest when you get there."

"Sounds good and, have a great time. I did."

"Okay, thank you Joe and see you later today."

"Yep."

Joe hung up realizing he built something that will be there forever. Joe felt a satisfaction.

The front door bell chimed, and Joe had a moment of subdued panic. He heard Carol heading for the door. The door opened then closed and they exchanged greetings.

"Joe, your ride is here." Carol yelled.

"Coming." Joe replied and got up from his desk. He grabbed his briefcase and suit jacket. He took a deep breath and let it out and walked to the living room.

As he came up the hallway, he saw the look of a big guy in a finely tailored suit. He looked professional and fit, the look in his eyes told that. The man extended a big hand to Joe. "Hello. My name is Sevan. I'm your bodyguard." He said with an arrogance that Joe liked.

"I'm Joe Bergen. You can call me Joe."

Both nodded. Sevan did a quick look of Joe up and down and Carol then asked. "Any other family members."

"No, just us two. Oh, this is Carol." Carol smiled and gently shook hands with him. Sevan then looked at them for a moment then said. "Please excuse me for a second."

Sevan backed up a bit fast dialing a number. He spoke rapid in what Joe thought to be a European language. Finishing he stepped back forward.

"Sorry, I am in charge for your security. That means you and your wife and property. Do you have a house security alarm?" Joe and Carol looked at each other shaking their heads no.

Joe spoke. "No, this is a good neighborhood. I never saw a need."

Sevan nodded. "I'll get one installed today. That's if you do not mind. We or I would appreciate if you did."

"No, I see no problem with that." Joe looked at Carol who just shrugged.

"Okay, placing someone here I see by the neighborhood would stand out. Having a van out-front. You see. I like to have full twenty-four-hour coverage."

"I feel an alarm system will do for now. We'll be looking for another home soon." Joe said as Carol nodded. Sevan looked skeptical but slowly nodded.

"Please. Near future. I have a responsibility for your lives." Sevan smiled. He then pulled out two cell phones and handed one to Carol and one to Joe. "The red button in the center. In case of emergency press it and help will come. They have strong GPS. So, we will find you."

"I guess we'll cancel the ones we have." Joe said.

"Okay, now you have limousine service or

any car you want, at your service twenty-four seven. Also, that service is available for you Mrs. Bergen. Someone else will be your bodyguard." Sevan said.

"Well, if we are going to catch a show in the city or someplace important to go. That'll be good. For the usual errands we'll use our own." Carol replied.

Sevan did not like the answer, Joe saw. He assumed Sevan wanted to keep him and Carol in a bubble.

"Okay, that covers the basics. Mrs. Bergen security people will be here shortly to install the security system and will show you how to operate it."

"Okay, I'll be here. Tell them to knock hard. I'll be doing some gardening in the backyard." Sevan looked in that direction nodding. "Yes, I tell them Mrs. Bergen."

Sevan then turned to Joe. "Whenever you're ready sir." Sevan picked up Joe's briefcase and went outside.

Joe and Carol covered their mouths to contain the laugh. Joe looked out to the stretch limousine in their driveway.

"Wow. It's big."

"And now you're a big man. It did seem like a little much but, I guess they know from experience. We need to be mindful of our safety." Carol said sincerely.

"Yea, I'm entering the big leagues today. People will be envious. We need another house. Start looking today." Joe smiled and kissed her.

"What price range?" Carol asked.

"Five million. Better yet I'll ask Sevan. He's the security expert and might know what we need."

"Good idea. I'd be happy anywhere. As long as I'm with you."

"Same here." Joe straightened himself picking up his suit jacket then stopped.

"What." Carol said.

"I need a newspaper to read on my way in." He said smiling going to the kitchen. He came back with the newspaper. Kissing Carol again he stepped outside. She watched him from the door.

Impressive seeing a stretch limo in his driveway. Sevan was holding the back door open. Joe climbed into the back as Sevan closed the door and walked around to the passenger front seat. Once inside he turned to speak to Joe.

"Our driver, Anatoly, he's capable." The driver nodded." The buttons on the ceiling control everything you may want."

Joe nodded looking up then back at Sevan. "Sevan, what country are you from. I notice the accent."

"Russia, sir." Sevan said proudly.

"Okay."

"We have a schedule to keep if you're ready."

"Yes. Get me to work."

"I'm going to raise the partition for your privacy. If you don't mind."

"No, not." Joe said.

The partition raised up and Joe sat in complete silence as the limo started moving. He looked to the newspaper deciding not yet. He did find the radio controls surprised to see it was satellite. He spent a few minutes going through the stations deciding to try the radio another day. The TV was next and already set on a business channel. Life was happening.

Chapter 34

Anatoly handled the limo expertly in the New York City traffic. Joe liked this and was enjoying the ride. Then halfway down a street that had little traffic the limo turned to enter an underground garage. A gate raised as the limo slowly entered. Joe did not catch the look of the building he would be working in. He made a mental note to walk around outside later.

The limo drove past parked cars and SUVS'. It was a large parking area, Joe thought. The limo continued past a bank of elevators stopping at another gate that opened. When opened, the limo, entered another parking area that had limos and high-priced cars. Stopping near a bank of elevators a man standing in front looked like security, Joe assumed.

Sevan was out and opening Joe's door. Stretching a bit, he looked at him and said. "Nice ride."

He just nodded replying. "Ms. Vera is on her way to meet you."

"Okay."

Joe then followed him to the elevators. The security man nodded to Sevan first then extended a hand to Joe. "Welcome Mr. Bergen." Joe shook hands with the giant wondering where they grew these people. Then an elevator door opened and out stepped a beautiful petite blond. Joe's heart skipped a beat trying not to stare but, he stared. She walked over to Joe and extending a hand.

"Hello and welcome Mr. Bergen. I'm your assistant. Vera Johnson. I'll show you around and get you up to speed."

"Thank you and hello Vera. I'm ready."

Vera glanced at Sevan and the other security guy smiling. She then headed for the elevator and Joe followed. When the elevator door closed Vera asked. "Good ride in?"

"Great."

Vera nodded.

The elevator streaked upward stopping on the forty fifth floor. Joe followed Vera out. She stopped outside the elevator looking at Joe proudly. "This is your floor. Right now, you have finance, sales, and operations departments. I'm sure we're going to grow. I'll take you through and meet everybody."

Joe nodded. "Lead the way."

He followed Vera who stopped at the finance department first meeting the finance director. Then the sales department meeting the director there. The final department was operations and Joe said the same, he will meet with them and talk later.

Joe followed Vera to a big reception area and wondered how he would find his way back to the elevators or the departments he just was in. He quickly knew the best way was to invite them to his office.

They walked to an area Joe assumed was his. A secretary looked up with a pleasant smile. She seemed young to Joe, maybe in her mid-twenties. She stood and he noticed the shapely body trying not to stare.

"You must be Mr. Bergen. I'm Alexandra. I'm your secretary and look forward to working with you."

"Glad to meet you Alexandra. I'm looking forward to working with you also."

Vera then said. "Door on right is my office."

Joe looked at a doorway that was smaller than the double doors to his office. He nodded then looking at Vera who motioned to the double doors.

"That's mine I guess."

Vera nodded with a smile. Alexandra did the same. Joe opened a door on the right. Looking inside the size of the office surprised him.

"Are you going in.?" Vera asked smiling.

Joe nodded. "Yes."

Stepping in he walked over to the huge desk that had the stuff from his office at Bergen Foods. He looked back at Vera.

"My stuff." Joe laughed.

"Yes, we took the liberty of moving your stuff. The bottom right hand drawer has your whiskey." Vera said smiling as Alexandra nodded.

"I don't drink it much. It's for celebrating new accounts." He relayed to the ladies in an offhand manner.

"That's okay. We celebrate also." Vera said and Joe took comfort in that.

Standing by his desk he looked out at the two-sided view from his corner office. A view of office towers in the neighborhood were his to enjoy. Then looking around his office at the leather couch with table and chairs for small meetings next to a fireplace gave him a start. On the other wall was a wood bookshelf fully stocked.

"Let me show you your private rest room." Vera said waking over to the bookshelf and pulling back a book. Joe looked at the title, The Great Gatsby. The bookcase opened automatically to an eighty-five-degree angle. Joe followed Vera in. To the right was a full bathroom, tub and shower with Jacuzzi. He followed her to the left that had a dressing and bedroom with a king-size bed. He wondered if he would be putting in long hours.

Vera opened a closet that was full of suits, sport clothes and casual wear. On the doors hung a selection of socks, ties and under garments.

"It's kept stocked with clothes in case you have a late meeting or dinner engagement.

The sport clothes can be used for the gym on the fifth floor. We guessed your size and can exchange them if you need." Vera finished turning back to look at Joe.

"Okay. I'll try them in time and let you know." He said following Vera back out to the office. She pushed the book back in and they stood watching the bookshelf close.

Looking back at Joe. "Any questions."

"No."

"Oh, yes. You have a small conference room." He followed Vera to a door that blended in with the walnut wood of the office. She opened and they went into a small room that had a square table seating about ten.

Pointing at the end with a phone, "that's your seat. The buttons operate the windows and walls. When pressed the walls and windows emit a white noise that prevents any listening in. It's a secure room."

"Okay." Joe nodded.

"You have a big screen also for videoconferencing. It's a CZ Corp. network and encrypted."

"Great." He said looking around the room feeling secure in it. Then he knew it was time for business. "I would like to have a meeting with all department heads tomorrow. Say about nine a.m."

Vera nodding opened her day planner she'd been carrying. She was going to be a good assistant, Joe knew.

They left the conference room and went

back into Joe's office. He sat behind his desk liking the size of the desk and the positions of the two computer screens. After opening a few drawers, he saw everything was in the same place he had them at Bergen Foods. He laughed. Vera kept a somber look on her face.

"I'm laughing at the precise placement of my stuff in the desk drawers. Same place I had everything at Bergen foods."

"Yes, we wanted you to be comfortable and ready."

"I'm ready. Okay, I want you to contact Thom Heller at Bergen foods and tell him I'll want that meeting today at three p.m. I haven't told everybody there that I sold the business. I need to have a meeting to answer any questions."

Vera jotted that down while asking. "Anything else?"

"No, I need to get to work now."

"Okay, there's a button on your desk phone for when you need me. In the top center drawer are the ID's and passwords for the company computer network." Joe opened the drawer and took out an envelope.

"Security wants you to memorize them if you can. If not, you have a small strongbox in the bottom left drawer."

He opened the bottom left drawer nodding seeing a strongbox with an electronic keypad. "Okay."

"And, Ariel Moskowitz would like a meet at

ten." Joe remembered him from the party. The tall gray-haired fox that liked to dance. He did say he was the CFO.

"Tell him ten will be fine."

"Good, I'll let him know." Vera said leaving.

When she went out the door, Joe looked around the office laughing. He made it but, can he keep it.

Looking at the preset buttons on the desk phone. It started with Mr. Bokanawski then Eva, then Ariel, then his department heads. The list included one for home. Joe wondered if it was his home number. He picked up the receiver and pressed it. It rang twice and then he heard Carol's voice.

"Hello."

"Hi. I made it to school on time."

"Cool. How's it?"

"A fantasy."

"Sweet."

"My office is like an expensive suite with a private bath, bedroom and closet stocked with clothes."

A silence. "You're joking."

"No."

"What's the bed for?" She asked slowly.

"A nap when business is slow. Sleeping on-the-job." Joe laughed.

"Okay," Carol said slowly.

"I guess the real reason is for social business engagements. Some rest, shower and fresh clothes to wear. I am a CEO."

"Yes, you'll have to be Mr. social now. Oh,

the security people are here putting in the alarm. They're European or something but, good people."

"Good. I think they're probably Russian. Sevan is."

"Fine people."

"Yes and, I'll be home about six or earlier. Do dinner out."

"Sure, where."

"Nino's."

"They're expensive."

"Really?"

"Right, I'll see to a reservation."

"Okay."

"Bye."

"Bye."

Joe put the phone down looking with a start seeing Vera standing there.

"I made the meeting for three p.m. at Bergen Foods."

"Thank you, Vera."

Vera left with Joe watching every step she took.

Chapter 35

Looking at the landscape from his office window, Joe knew he made it and would be used to the view in time but, right now though, it impressed him. He jumped when he heard someone clear their throat from behind him. Joe turned to see Ariel standing there with a devious smile on his face.

Joe smiled and asked.

"Do you always do that?"

"You mean sneak up on people."

"Yea."

"Yea."

Joe bent his head down and laughed. He looked up at Ariel and tried to keep a straight face.

"You're all right Ariel."

"I haven't had a woman say no."

Joe laughed again. Ariel stepped forward and extended a hand. Joe stood up and took it.

"Welcome to our world." Ariel said with a curious look in his eyes that Joe did not understand.

"Thank you."

Ariel took a seat in front of the desk as Joe sat and leaned back.

Ariel began. "Eva wants a meeting in her conference room at ten for a formal introduction to the other division CEO's."

Joe nodded saying. "Vera said you wanted a meeting at ten."

"Oops, I meant a meeting upstairs. Not her fault."

"Okay, I'll be ready."

"No Joe, you'll never be ready for Eva. She's a self-made woman who cuts threw the formalities. She doesn't want kiss ass or niceties. Be your honest self-with her. If you don't know something, tell her that. She understands that but, do give her a time when you will have an answer. That's just the broad strokes about the boss."

"Understood." Joe said figuring she was just being pleasant at the party and will be different here.

"She'll be expecting you to learn who she is. She'll be expecting you to understand her from this first meeting." Ariel hesitated then continued. "Don't get me wrong. She's not a bitch. We work here knowing everybody is performing their job without a doubt." Ariel hesitated again. "They're paid more than they'd earn else ware, so, they go beyond here."

Joe nodding said. "A good policy that I'm sure works."

"Yes, it works." Ariel replied.

"I met my staff and they seem of European decent." Joe asked slowly.

Ariel smiled. "Yes, they're from greater Europe and Russia. In which case they're minorities. So, we exceed the federal rules. To answer your question more clearly. We're not xenophobic. We feel and get good results from people that are of the same historic background and, they work together seamlessly. We don't have any employees with a harsh word to say about us and, that makes for a good workforce."

"Now that's different. It gives me a good feeling whether I do good or not it won't be rumor on the street."

Ariel smiling. "Yes, a good feeling. It's Mr. Bokanawski' s idea. Starting with a small import/export business years ago he found he had better workers when they came from the same place. They think the same, like a family. We're a family all loyal to CZ Corp." Ariel finished beaming.

"I hope I fit in here." Joe said.

"You're Polish and Lithuanian you will fit. Your wife told me when we were dancing."

"Okay." Joe nodded.

"Yes." Ariel said looking satisfied.

"I'm curious. What does CZ stand for?"

Ariel smiled. "It's for Mr. Bokanawski. He's kindly known as the Czar. Now, his sister Catherine is the Czarina. You will meet her someday. She lives in Russia and takes care of the Russian business for the corporation."

"I see."

"Yes, the small import and export business they started has a sister in Russia that Catherine runs."

"They grew quickly with the fall of the Soviet Union." Joe added.

"Exactly. Now Eva picked you for this position and you will answer to her. She's your boss. We're equals, with the other division CEO's."

"Sure."

"Just listen to Eva."

Joe nodded sincerely asking, "what's the number of divisions here."

"Oh, six. They cover all categories of the business world. Food, Real estate, Commodities, Technology, Entertainment and Finance."

"Wow. That's quite a line up."

"Yes, and they have sub categories. The whole operation is large and profitable."

"Must be profitable?" Joe said feeling good to be here.

"Yes, connections help and business can be different outside the USA." Ariel said looking off for a moment then continuing. "Now XO food is going to take on a loan from a Polish Bank. Our European division will buy food products there and you're going to sell it here. And, yes, pay the loan back."

That caught Joe off guard but, didn't show it. "Why, I mean there is plenty of food here in America."

Ariel smiled and relaxing his face a bit. "Joe, that Eva decided. Probably to help small companies there. Quite a good selection of food in Europe that we could sell here. Sell to the best customers."

Joe was confused. "Okay, if she decided then I need to speak to her on it. Yes, there's fine foods there."

"Yes, speak with Eva on that. Now, the loan I'll be handling since you're still new. I'll let you know when this happens. You will need to sign a paper or two. As for the paying back it'll come from your money. It's already set up that CZ Corp. will debit the payments. Nothing for you to do but sell some fine food."

"Sounds good if that's procedure." Joe said wanting to know more about this.

"Yes, clean cut-and-dry. I guess Eva wants XO to sell products from around the world. Do what the competition doesn't."

"Sure. I like the sound of it." Joe started wondering if Eva was going to meddle by telling him how to do his job.

"All right then. Eva wanted me to get you up to speed on that. She'll answer the rest of the questions." Ariel said smiling.

"Yes, it sounds good but risky. The prices will have to be reasonable."

"Go over that with the boss, now I need to run and get some papers for the meeting. Eva hates when she doesn't have the numbers."

Ariel stood stretching a little then extended a hand to Joe and saying. "Welcome again and don't worry you'll do fine."

"Thank you again. See you at the meeting."

"Probably not. I have a private with Eva beforehand and usually don't stay for the general meeting."

"Okay, Vera should know the way. I'm still lost on my own floor."

"Be with you soon." Ariel said as the door closed.

Joe sat at his desk taking out the ID/Password book to get to work opening the balance sheets. He saw a few big deposits from some warehouses that seemed unusually large. His own didn't generate that much net income. A visit to these places is needed to see how they do this, Joe thought then heard a noise. He looked up to see Vera standing in front of his desk.

"You have to give me an early warning. I might be doing something private." Joe said smiling.

"Yes, sorry. They have told me you also have a meeting in the general boardroom at ten o'clock. I just found out myself."

"Yes, Ariel told me that it was a last-minute thing." Joe saw the let down in Vera's face. "Vera, you're doing great job. It was a last-minute decision."

"Yes, but, I'm still sorry. I like when they give you enough time to prepare."

This admission slightly moved Joe and he liked it.

"I'll be prepared enough. I'm sure

whoever planned the meeting knows this also. It's okay Vera."

Vera nodded walking away and he was back in the numbers.

The first facility that didn't show good profit was Minneapolis. The spread sheet had a side bar note stating, it was an ongoing problem. Joe sat back looking at that entry. He lifted his phone and called over to his VP of finance.

"Hello. Jack Miller."

"Joe Bergen here. I know we have a meeting tomorrow but, I was looking through the numbers and I see Minneapolis is sending in low amounts. Also, the note of an ongoing problem."

"Well, yea. I had mentioned it to Rich but, he was just temporary and said the next guy would take care of it. So, I did e-mail Eva on it and she pretty much replied the same."

"Yes, okay. I will take care of it. How big is that place there in Minneapolis?"

"We've owned them about a year and a few months. The original owner left and somebody new is running it. They have sales in about three hundred fifty million range with an employee base of a little over four hundred. That's the best information they sent. We're not directly hooked up to the warehouse servers, so we don't know right now."

"I see. I need to go there. I need to visit all the facilities. Now for tomorrow, if you can, start with the lowest earners and work down to the best. Break down everything in the numbers. I want a complete picture."

"Sure, I'll have based on information that we have at this point."

"Fine, crunch the numbers you have and give me a picture."

"Got it, it's spotty though. They send the reports by courier and I have not received from all them at this time, for last month. What I have will give you a break down from two months ago."

Joe didn't like hearing this. He's in charge of businesses out there with no current data of spending or profiting. Welcome to work, he thought.

"Just bring what you have. We'll go from there Jack."

"Okay then. See you tomorrow at nine."

"Bye."

Joe placed the phone down looking at the computer screen. The profit from the Minneapolis warehouse is only one hundred thousand a month. It should be at least a million or better, Joe knew.

He then thought about Eva's plan to sell high-priced European food. He needed to get his jet going and start visiting these warehouses.

Chapter 36

Eva's limo was making its way through the streets of lower Manhattan to the office. Her father was in charge but, he never went there. He took care of business from home. He only took care of the illegal business and left the laundering up to Eva and her brothers and sisters. She wished he'd take bigger interest in CZ though.

The TV tuned to a business channel and the world outside her limo was busy. Eva's phone buzzed surprising her that it was this late in the morning before anyone called. The ID showed Ariel's number.

"Hi Ariel."

"Good Morning Eva."

"Is Joe settling in?"

"Yes, he's getting in place."

"Excellent."

"He's probably cramming as we speak."

"Good, he'll probably see the first problem, Minneapolis."

"Yes, he should."

"Okay, we'll let him take the first step there. Dad told Slotkolov he was free to invest but, he's taking too much. I hear he's invested in real estate out there and I want it."

"I understand. It's the families' money

and your father didn't mean for him to take that much."

"Exactly and Joe will get the money returned for us."

"Yes."

"Now Ariel, let Joe know that he has choices when dealing with Slotkolov."

"I understand."

"I'll see you soon. Bye."

"Bye."

Eva wanted that real estate Anton Slotkolov was investing in. She knew her father approved doing it but, her father would change his decision if she told him the money was not in real estate. Eva thought smiling.

Joe Bergen is just the person to get that money. He would gain favor with her father and Eva liked that. She wanted Joe to have a good standing in the family.

She continued smiling at the thought of wiping out Anton Slotkolov Jr. She hated the man since childhood when they were friends. His father worked for Eva's father, he stole from her father in Europe and they killed him. They then sent Anton Jr to live with his uncle in Minneapolis being he was a child at the time. He did well for himself over the years. Still, Eva hated him and cringed when her father wanted Anton to run that warehouse. She felt that time has come. She decided who did well who did not. Anton was gaining too much favor with her father and she would show the apple didn't fall far from the tree.

The limo drove into the underground garage stopping at the elevators. Ivan was out opening the door for Eva. Mia and Mya were waiting by the elevators. Eva stepped out looking at the twins.

"Good morning ladies."

"Morning Eva." Both said in harmony stepping into the elevator. Ivan stayed behind keeping watch from a distance.

Watching the numbers going upward Eva was feeling good today. She was looking forward to moving and hiding money today. Her most difficult job was laundering money under the disguise of a big company. That was her success for the last fifteen years. Not bad for a girl from Russia, she thought.

When the doors opened Eva with the twins headed for her office. Greetings from people who worked on the top floor with her she returned along the way.

In her office the reports of the weekly and monthly updates on each division in Europe and America were waiting. She had final say on how each division ran. In America and Europe, she had the final say. The only area she did not was Russia. Aunt Catherine kept that a secret and shared it with no one. They put the profit money together every month but, no one knew Aunt Catharine's holdings. Nobody ever asked either not even Eva's father. Aunt Catherine put in her profit every month and left it at that.

A simple equation, after the expense

money the rest was profit. Uri did the drug running and had a team to pay. Mikal and Olga mainly laundered and made payoffs. Tatyana had a big team that dealt in insurance fraud, Internet crimes, real estate scams and most anything else she could take. Max was the security person who provided security for all of them and he had a big team. After expenses was profit.

Eva sat behind her desk and the twins went to their office. Her secretary came in presenting Eva with a report.

"A late one, sorry. It's XO Food and not complete Ariel told me to say." Uma told Eva in her heavy Russian accent.

"No problem. I hired a new person for the food business and he should be up to speed soon."

"Yes, I heard Ms Eva. I hear he's a handsome one." Uma smiled.

"Yes, he is, Uma." Eva said smiling.

Uma nodding left the office.

Eva began reading the reports wanting to know everything before the meeting. Ariel left some notes on the reports as usual. Most divisions earned good money on their own. He wrote on one. Eva smiled at that.

She was looking where she could bring in an extra few million. The food division was number one right now and they would launder ten million through it. She then thought of Joe Bergen and wondered if he would ask about the loan from Poland. He probably will, she thought. Every new CEO always asks once, Eva knew.

The rest of the report read as expected. The European divisions were holding too much cash. She needed to bring it home to CZ Corp America and pay out some bonuses. Everybody liked money. It's makes life comfortable and people loyal.

The Italians made their people earn and give to the upper bosses. In the Czarina's family, the top ones earn and give to the lower ones. How can they expect someone to work a scam and possibly getting caught, then expect them to give to the higher-ups who took no risk? How do they expect that person to be loyal to the boss who takes no risk? Eva never understood the Italian mob's method of doing business in their families. She only saw bitterness created.

Eva cringed at the thought of having a label of mob boss. It rarely occurred to her that she is. She does the impossible, so it won't happen. Bonuses.

Eva liked the family feel here at CZ Corp. Walking the halls here she knows what each person has done for the family. A dainty brunette in the payroll dept. who shot out a car tire causing a car accident that killed someone who was snooping around where they did not belong. To the scared looking man who works in the accounting dept. who accidentally bumped into a banker and injected him with a poison. Bonuses.

She finished the reports placing them in the shred tray on her desk. Now her day was whatever she wanted to do. She looked at her diamond encrusted watch touching it gently. She had thirty minutes and never remembered being happy for the monthly meeting. It was Joe Bergen she knew that had her watching the time. She liked him and was going to do what she could to help him succeed in the family. He was going to need to do something for the family though to prove his strength and loyalty. The ritual, she thought, yes, she'll be there to make sure it's a fair job for him to do.

The twins came into the office each taking a seat in front of her desk looking at Eva.

"What's up." Eva asked.

"You have a meeting in half an hour." Said Mia.

"Yes."

"Mr. Bergen's' first." Said Mya.

"Yes."

"He's a fox." Said Mia.

"He's married though." Said Mya.

"Okay, stop it." Eva said.

"Oh my." Said Mia.

"Remind me five minutes before." Eva said smiling at the twins knowing she would be watching every minute go by on her own.

They shrugged shoulders getting up to leave. They looked back at Eva smiling leaving her office.

Eva didn't take offense to their method; they were twins and always in their own world. She did not care if they thought she liked Bergen, she did not mind their playing around at all.

Eva picked up the New York Post off her desk flipping through it when a picture of Senator Wellington stopped her. It showed him giving that polished smile and wave as he was leaving a restaurant. Looking hard at the picture she knew this may be his last one, alive. When it was going to happen, she did not know. For the fund-raiser with the Mayor of New York, she will send somebody else. She didn't want to be nearby if bad may happen. He sometimes showed up to shake hands with the businesspeople. No, can't make it, she thought.

Eva closed the newspaper and getting up from her desk went to her private rest room. She wanted to look good today for the meeting.

Chapter 37

Vera standing near Joe, his eyes glued to the computer screen. A pad scribbled with numbers next to him. He had just planned on reading and getting an idea of the profits coming in but, the numbers varied widely. Curious. He didn't know what but, he'll figure it out.

He looked up at Vera smiling. "Yes, I'm ready now."

"Eva likes her meetings to start on time and she......"

Joe put his hand up.

"Show me the way." Joe getting up and putting his jacket on.

Vera came around the desk to close the computer program. She then tore off the sheets from the pad putting them into the shredder.

"Close and shred when done." Vera said looking Joe up and down like a child.

"Wait I need to use the rest room." Joe said going over to the bookshelf. He started looking for the book when Vera came over and pulled it. "Please hurry." She said.

He came out a few moments later. Vera took him by the arm guiding him toward the door. Once on the elevator she looked him up and down again. When the door opened Vera led the way. Everybody who passed by said hello. They turned a corner and went past an arched office area.

"That's Eva's office." Vera said. Joe thought the entrance reminded him of a Roman something. They stopped at an alcove. The chairs had a few women sitting in them. Joe assumed they were other assistants by the look on Vera's face. She winced seeing the chairs almost filled. He knew right away he might be late.

He followed her to the double doors. She stopped looking at Joe. "Show time." Vera said.

"I'm ready." He said giving her a comforting smile. Vera opened the door and Joe followed right behind her stopping a moment looking around the room. A large table, the largest he ever seen in a conference room full of people. Eva occupied one end of the table. Joe nodded and she nodded back then went back talking to the person on her right.

Vera guided Joe to the only open seat at the opposite end of the table from Eva. Vera then withdrew from the conference room. Joe looked around nodding at the others seated. The conversations automatically stopped with everybody looking at Eva.

"Okay everybody. I would like to present our newest member of the CZ family. Mr. Joe Bergen." Everybody clapped as Joe stood taking a short bow. Eva continued. "I like my meetings to start on time Mr. Bergen, for future reference. Mr. Bergen is the CEO of XO Food group. He brings with him plenty of experience. He is replacing Rich Holbrook who is off looking for other business for us. Now we will begin with the monthly reports."

"The Real estate market is starting to slow and does present plenty of opportunities for buying." Joe listen to the man reporting. He was of average age no older than Joe. He finished after ten minutes. "In closing I see an opportunity to get a foothold in Miami and other resort areas."

Eva replied. "Yes, I see some good deals in those areas and approve." She then nodded to the next. When that person finished Eva gave a few comments and her approval. Then the next CEO started and an hour later it came time for Joe.

Eva weighed in. "This is Mr. Bergen's first day and we will not be hearing about XO Food group today."

"Well, I would still like to say a few words." Eva raised her eyebrows nodding to Joe.

"I would like to start by saying I'm happy to be working here for a world-class company. I reviewed in the last few hours a summary of how business is at XO. I can say that sales margins are good and profit margins are good. Rebranding is still underway to the XO name. A visit to all warehouses to meet the presidents and tell them of a new secure server connection. Direct connections with each warehouse will tell me daily where were at with sales and costs. I will do central buying from here for each warehouse that will lower costs. There's an increase in the cost of food do to fuel this year I need to hedge against that by buying in bulk. I'll update on the progress in the coming months." Joe finished and felt like a fool at first. But the looks and nods from his fellow CEO's made him feel better.

"Thank you, Mr. Bergen. I must say that is impressive for the first day on-the-job." Eva said with everybody agreeing. She continued. "I have reviewed and will refer to Ariel the capital needed for these projects. For those of you who need no money we'll be expecting the deposit." Eva smiled in a kindly way. She then continued. "We're done with the meeting for this month."

Joe had a line of the CEO's shaking his hand. They said their names but, he was not going to remember them now. He did remember seeing them all at the party. As the last one left Joe did realize, they all had Russian, Polish or European names. Eva was talking with someone as he started to head for the door when she said.

"Joe don't leave yet. I owe you money." She motioned for him to sit near her as she continued talking to her assistant. He took a seat just to her right and forgot how beautiful she looked. Hair tied up with slight makeup on. The assistant left and she turned to Joe.

"Great job for the first day. You sound like you got a grip already." Eva said.

"Yes and no. Scanning the profit from the warehouses." A knock on the door made Joe stop. The same looking assistant in a different dress came in escorting a man. The man took a seat across from Joe. Eva thanked the assistant and she left.

"This is Mark Jacob. He's from the law firm of Rosenberg. He has papers and a check for you."

Mark extended a hand and they shook.

"Okay, yes. The warehouse."

"Forgot already. You're a millionaire today." Eva said brightly.

"Yes, I am."

Mark took out papers and Joe spent ten minutes signing away. Eva then took an envelope out of her briefcase and handed it to Joe. He opened and saw a bank check for one hundred fifty million dollars. Largest amount he ever saw on a check with his name. He felt good, free. He looked back at Eva.

"Don't worry it's real. I hope you're not going to quit on me."

"No, I just never saw a number so large and it's for me." Joe said.

"Well. I'm done here." Jacob said with a bored voice. He shook hands again with Joe and left the conference room.

"I can have that deposited in an escrow account if you like. With any bank you choose." Eva said.

"Yes, my local bank will gasp at the amount."

"Okay, I'll have Ariel get one of his people to you today."

"Good." Joe put the envelope in his jacket pocket trying to pay attention.

"Okay back to business. Ariel has told you about a loan from a Polish bank. I'm doing that to buy some fine European food at a cheap price. I want you to sell it through XO. I'll be getting the product at a deep discount and only want a mark up to 5 percent. I want to give our customers what the competition can't."

"All right. You're doing the buying."

"Not me. Our European division. I have some food people there and a smaller version of an XO food group there. I'm doing it this way for the first buy. In the future you'll be doing the buying. I don't want to overwhelm you right now."

"Okay, I have no problem with that. I'm curious why a loan from a Polish Bank. With ninety days payable or on consignment deal would probably be cheaper than a loan." Joe asked and feeling relieved that she wouldn't be meddling.

Eva liking the question replied. "I like when the divisions pay fast when buy anything. We buy from smaller businesses that need payment fast. In the future they will then extend credit to us if we hit a soft spot."

"And I sell something the competition doesn't have."

"Exactly. Now the setup of CZ debiting and paying the loan I do because the bank is an old friend. In time I'll leave that to you to do." Eva said trying not to laugh.

"Understand. I appreciate it. I need a little time to get familiar." Joe said feeling impressed.

"We're a private company. It's owned by my father and my aunt. They built up many business relationships in Europe that will lend us money whenever we need. And I tap those relationships to try new and everybody makes money."

"I see the advantages there."

"Yes, we are a cash rich company. So, the idea of making a huge profit on one deal we don't do. We make much profit doing many smaller deals." Eva said elegantly. Thinking she did like this man.

"Being a private company, you don't need to satisfy shareholders every three months." He said smiling. Eva took comfort in the quick response. She knew he would work out as he learned more of the family business.

"Okay, I'll let you know more by the end of the week when we'll do Poland."

"Got it," Joe replied feeling relaxed with her.

"We're done." Eva said.

"Oh, I need to travel this week to see a few of the warehouses. There's one or two I need to see. Nothing important, no red flags. I just need to see some people face-to-face."

"Sure. Vera knows how to arrange the trips. XO Food has its own jet sitting in New Jersey. It's small but, enough for travel around the country, and, you don't need my approval. Like I said, it's at your disposal for business or private use."

"Thanks."

A slight knock and in walked the twins. Joe remembered them from the first meeting last week. Seemed like a long time ago.

"These two are my assistants, Mia and Mya. I rarely can tell apart."

"Yes, hello. I remember you two from last week."

"Hello, Mr. Bergen." Both said harmoniously sounding angelic to Joe.

He got out of his seat and shook Eva's hand gently. He liked the soft feel of her hand again. He left the conference room seeing Vera the only one sitting in the alcove. She stood walking next to Joe until he realized he had no idea where he was going.

"I'll lead the way." Vera said.

When they got to his floor, he knew the way to his office. Once inside his office he took a seat behind his desk. Vera went to her office then came back and sat in front of his desk.

"The meeting went well." Joe said.

"I'm sure you did fine. Ariel called and wants to do lunch in the café at noon."

"Okay, I can do that. If you show me the way."

"One of his assistants in finance called and would like to meet in half an hour to set up an account for you."

"Oh, yes, payment for my business. They're going to give me an account with the money in it."

"Done for now," Vera said brightly.

"Yes, let me get back to work here. From noontime on I probably won't have a chance." He said standing to remove his jacket off.

Joe went back to the ID and passwords, then the spread sheet of balances. Scrolling down the entries to Minneapolis he stared for a moment. He wasn't going to let one warehouse bring him down. One man one warehouse was not going to ruin his job here. He knew he had to confront this person. Joe looked at the entry for the warehouse president and saw a name, Anton Slotkolov. Me and Anton are going to talk. Joe told himself. He looked at the phone.

Chapter 38

A dark colored SUV swiftly maneuvered its way through midday Manhattan traffic with Eva in the backseat. The freelance reporter from her father's party was dead but, this new person communicated sending emails wanting information. Max had assured her that this was the last person of interest.

The SUV crossed over the GW bridge into New Jersey when Eva's secure cell phone buzzed. "Yes."

"Max here. This person you're coming to see had a small file in his home, it was superficial but, he could have gotten more in time. There's a few articles about the buy up of warehouses. No damage but, the emails to the peasant are probing. He wasn't going to stop."

"Okay, good job. He tell anybody you know of?"

"No. His wife is present also."

"Sounds like we caught and snipped this

problem." Eva said glancing out the window at the run-down neighborhood they were driving through.

"Yup and they're waiting here for you."

"I'll be there shortly."

~~~~~

Don Wellington finished a meeting with a wealthy client. He talked through the usual rate of return and the best mutual funds he feels they would like. The client signed the papers and left the usual deposit of five million. Don's secretary collecting the documents glanced at Don who was not looking happy. After finishing she sat in front of his desk.

"Don. I don't take much stock in rumors. Cheryl is just a young woman looking for the fast track without using her brains. I don't believe what she says; many others here feel the same way."

Don looked at his secretary ready to berate her for bringing the subject up. Cheryl was not even a passing thought in his mind.

An opportunity was presenting itself here Don knew. He quickly knew that Cheryl spreading the rumor he was a mean person on a date, would cancel her out here. The Senior partners would eventually hear of it and have no recourse but to fire her. The Senior partners were happy with Don and the business he brought in. He earned good revenue for the firm and in time will be a Senior partner like his father. Don wasn't afraid of rumors but, sympathy would always be welcome to help him along here. Everybody knew of the deal gone bad in Russia with his uncle's money. He did show backbone by paying it down. The good qualities the Senior partners liked in their people.

Don scratched his head and looked a little sad for effect.

"What does Cheryl want with me? I took her out and we had a great time." Don moved in his chair deciding to get a little nasty. "After the show, she wanted something. Nose candy I think they call it. I don't do that stuff." Don put on a pleading look. She looked at him shocked.

"She wanted illegal drugs. Young people think the world's a joke or something. Couldn't get what she wanted so she's going to spread rumors. I don't think so." Don's secretary said getting up in a huff. "Cheryl thinks she is getting away with this." She finished then left the office.

When the door closed, Don covered his mouth to muffle the laugh. He knew she'd immediately be on the phone telling her friends in the building. Cheryl will never look in his direction again and eventually not work here either.

With no more business for him to attend to today, he took a printout from his briefcase. Looking at the phone number from a website that sold all kinds of weapons he lifted the phone and dialed. A gruff sounding voice answered on the second ring. "Hello, Every day Firearms."

"Hi, I'm looking for something with power." Don hoped it didn't sound dumb. "Okay. What are you planning on shooting? How much power you looking for? What's your sport? For protection or hunting?"

"Just for fun in my backyard. Target practice."

"Well, I assume you live in New York somewhere and that's unlawful except at a licensed target range."

"I see. Not a good law in place."

"No, it isn't friend."

"What if I wanted to destroy an old barn on my property. Does the law prevent me from doing that too?"

"Probably. I would suggest calling someone that takes apart buildings."

"Right, and then file papers and pay for something I could just do with a few sticks of dynamite."

A silence for a moment and Don hoped the guy didn't hang up.

"Okay sir. What exactly are you looking for? A gun or rifle or something to help clear your property."

"Clear my property."

"Okay. Give me a phone number and I'll get back to you."

Don froze for a moment. Then gave his cell phone number, yes, he'll just say it's lost or stolen.

"Okay, you got pen and paper."

"Yep."

Don gave gruff voice his cell phone number. The gruff would call back soon.

He hung up hoping he didn't make a mistake. He quickly dismissed that thought. After gruff calls back, he'll go out for lunch and leave his cell phone somewhere reporting it lost.

Chapter 39

After dialing Joe waited.

"Hello." Came a female voice.

"Hello, is this XO or Great Northern Food service?"

"Yes."

"I would like to speak to a Mr. Anton Slotkolov."

"Who's this?"

"I'm Joe Bergen. CEO of XO food group." He said with pride.

"Oh?"

"I'm Mr. Slotkolov's boss and would like to speak to him."

"Hum. Hold on."

Music played in Joe's ear as he waited. He was going to keep his cool. She might be new.

After five minutes Joe hung up and dialed again.

"Hello." Came the same voice.

"I was on hold for five minutes. I'm calling from XO Food Group and need to speak to Mr. Anton Slotkolov."

"Oh, yea. Anton just left for the day."

"Does he have a cell number?"

"Hum. I don't know."

"A home number?"

"I'm new and don't know it."

"Can I speak to the VP of finance?"

"What's that?"

"The persons office nearest Anton's I can speak to?"

"I don't know and need to ask Anton if you can do this."

"What is your name?"

"Me, I'm Cindy."

"Cindy. I'm Joe Bergen and I work for and I am the CEO of XO Food Group. XO Food Group owns Great Northern Food service. And, I need to speak to the person you go to when Anton isn't there." Joe was trying to keep calm.

"I don't know. I'm new." Cindy said in the same monotone.

"Cindy. Can you leave a note for Anton saying that I called and want him to call me back as soon as possible?"

"Okay. You are"

"Joe Bergen CEO of XO Food Group."

"Okay wait."

Joe listened as she wrote it down and he heard other calls beeping for her.

"Okay, I got it."

"Cindy, you have a great day."

"You too Mr. Bergen."

Joe slowly placed the phone down looking at the spreadsheet on the computer.

The phone buzzed. It startled Joe at first as he pressed a button. "Yes, Vera."

"Mark Urlbeck is here from CZ Finance." Vera said.

"Okay, show him in."

Vera came in with a man of slim build following.

"Hi, I'm Mark Urlbeck from CZ Finance. I'm here to give you an account."

Joe stood and extended his hand.

"Okay."

Joe sat back down. Mark zipped open a personal case taking out some papers and coming around the desk he placed them down in front of Joe.

"Okay. Documents for the transfer of a cash amount to you." Mark flipped over the documents. "Creation of the account into your name." Mark flipped over the documents to the last batch. "Name of the bank and your account number." Joe quickly read the bank name and account number.

"Where do I sign?"

Mark stacked the documents back.

"On the bottom, next to my name, sign and date." Mark said walking back around and sitting in front of Joe's desk. He looked over at the windows as Joe began the signing.

"Cool view. I'm higher up and don't get a view. Finance department has no windows."

"Yes, I can't complain." Joe said as he signed away.

After a few moments, Joe finished signing.

The day starting to wear on him. He was getting hungry and knew today was far from over.

Mark reached across the desk flipping through the papers checking that everyplace had a signature. He left the last document with the bank and account number on Joe's desk.

Mark went back and put those papers in his zip bag and took out another paper and came back around to Joe.

"Now, I'll need the check they gave you." Mark said sounding bored.

Joe pulled the envelope from his jacket giving it to Mark who stared at Joe for a moment before ripping it up.

"It's always cool ripping up a multi-mil check." Mark said with a smile.

"I wouldn't know." Joe said smiling.

"Okay. The paper I gave you has a cash account for the sale of." Mark looked down at the paper reading for a moment. "Bergen foods to XO food group." Joe nodded. "And that's it Mr. Bergen. That document there on your desk has your information. There's an account at the named bank. Also, a gift of the check I ripped up set in glass as a paper weight. It's a something special we do after we buy a business."

"Sweet." Joe said with a big grin. Mark let out a big laugh then said. "Yes, Mr. Bergen."

Joe came from around his desk and shook hands with Mark walking him to the door. Once the door closed Joe stood for a moment looking at his watch. Thirty minutes until lunch with Ariel and he was hungry now.

Back at his desk Joe took the paper with the bank information and put it in his wallet. Remembering the id and password he was back to work. Until, his phone buzzed.

"Yes."

"I have Max Bokanawski on line one for you."

"Thank you."

Joe looked at the light flashing on line one and thought fast because he didn't remember who Max Bokanawski was. Joe lifted the phone and pressed line one.

"Hello, Joe Bergen here."

"Hi Joe, Max Bokanawski. We met at the party. I run the security for every business in the CZ corp. family."

"Okay, yes, Hi Max."

"I'm sorry for the phone call but, I'm on the road right now and just wanted to touch base with you. Now, Sevan has given you and your wife the new cell phones. Please carry and use them. Like he showed you, the red button on the keypad alerts us if you're in trouble and number two on the keypad connects you to security. There's always somebody there to answer in case you need something. Any questions."

"No, you just explained what Sevan did earlier and I understand it. I do have a question though. Why do I need a bodyguard?" Joe asked feeling he should not have one.

"To open doors for you and take care of situations you won't have to."

"Okay, it's just that it's new to me." Joe said.

I feel it's good for every CEO to have one. I know Sevan and he's one of our best. He'll never be where he's not needed." Max said with an arrogant voice.

"I'll adjust to it."

"Good. Now, if you find that you and Sevan have a chemistry that doesn't work. I will send you somebody else."

"No. Sevans cool. Me or my wife have no problem with him."

"Good. Now, the security network installed in your home, please use it. For your wife if she needs somebody while you are at work for any reason, just have her dial number two on the phone and we'll send somebody. Sometimes women like to go shopping to buy expensive items and maybe she'll want somebody to watch her back. It's all free and goes with your job. Your safety and security and your wife are my job. Please us it."

"Yes, I will Max, and thank you."

"Good. Gotta go. Enjoy Mr. Bergen."

"Bye." The line went quiet.

Joe looked back at the computer screen and the numbers staring at him. He rubbed the back of his neck and resumed analyzing the numbers.

Chapter 40

The SUV stopped next to an abandoned brick building in a distressed area of Jersey City New Jersey that had no hope of revitalization anytime in the future.

Eva sat patiently in the backseat while Ivan and his crew secured the area. He emerged from the run-down building opening the back door of the SUV. Eva stepped out looking around to the other cars protecting the area so she could take care of business here.

Eva followed Ivan into the building. It smelled like old wood and dirty water. They walked through a doorway crooked from age. The walls and ceilings were peeling. In the distance, she heard a woman sobbing.

Eva and Ivan entered a large area that must have been a factory work area in better times. Men were up ahead in a loose circle. In the center a man and a woman tied to chairs with a harsh light focused on them. Max was nearby standing over a table looking at a pile of papers.

Eva stepped in front of the light looking

down on Paul and his wife Wendy. Both looked up squinting at the harsh light. His face was bloody hers not. Eva thought Wendy a looker and Paul was not half bad, a little geeky.

She went over to Max who was reading a computer printout. He looked over at her and just waved a hand over the table. Eva picked up a paper and started reading it. After a few minutes, she finished reading and knew this was not good. She didn't know these people, but they were compiling information on her family business. It made Eva furious.

Walking back to Paul and Wendy she saw the wet spots in their crouch areas. Must feel uncomfortable.

Eva pulled out a stiletto knife from her person. She bent over looking directly at Paul who looked well beyond tired.

"What the fuck you doing gathering information on my company." Eva yelled in his face.

Paul shaking took a moment to answer. "I was checking on who and what your company is, I wanted to know why you're buying who I work for." The words labored out.

"You better give me an answer I want." Eva hissed. Then sliced the knife across Paul's chest. He screamed out a high-pitched yell.

"Who's seen those papers?" Eva yelled.
A line of blood was seeping through and

going down Paul's shirt. He looked at Eva with a sneer saying. "I showed them to everybody, police, FBI, newspapers, you bitch."

Eva stepped back examining Paul for a moment.

"Okay, you need a little motivation I see."

Eva walked to Wendy smiling down at her. Wendy looked up sniffling.

"You're a real sexy woman huh. Does your man satisfy you? I don't think so."

Wendy tried to say something but.

"Yes, that's it. You never had five guys at once have you, lovely Wendy. What do you think Paul would say? Would he still love you?"

Wendy wailed more as Eva looked over at Paul. He tried saying something but, was overcome with grief. She stepped back laughing. Then in a booming voice announced. "All right guys, she's all yours. Make her feel like a woman."

Three men came forward lifting Wendy out of the chair and carrying her to a side room. She fought as best she could while crying out loud. Then the sound of clothes tearing, screams, a punch, and the sounds of sex. She was now crying in a rhythmic sound.

Eva walked back in front of Paul smiling down at him. "Think she's enjoying herself?"

"Fuck you, Fuck you. You hor, you slut." Ivan's steel punch hit Paul in the side of the face.

"Did that hurt big boy, there's more if you want?" Eva said to Paul's glazed eyes.

In the other room, Wendy's rhythmic crying ended when one man came out of the room fixing his pants. He walked over and said something to another man in Russian standing guard which made him laugh.

Eva looking at Paul watching that exchange saw his face drop. Eva added to his pain. "He said. She's a good fuck. Is she a good fuck Paul?"

Paul started working the ropes holding his hands and feet looking up at Eva glaring.

"Yes, tough guy break loose and save your Wendy. She thinks you're a faggot anyway."

Paul worked his hands and feet more. He looked up at Eva trying to say something but, showed too much pain on his face when he tried. Eva's laugh echoed throughout the area. She then motioned to Ivan.

Ivan gripped Paul as another man cut the ropes holding Paul's hands and feet. When finished Ivan quickly pulled the chair out from under him. Paul hit the floor with a thud.

Eva approached cautiously like a cat. Her body movements were careful and agile while maneuvering the knives in her hands.

Paul rubbing his arms got up off the floor slowly. He made a feeble try of a boxing stance that was wobbly.

Eva stood watching this with a smile on her face. She raised both of her arms to show a knife in either hand looking like claws. She lowered them back approaching Paul in slow cat like steps.

Paul not steady approached as Eva approached. He threw a punch out of time and range almost falling over from the force he used. Eva took the opportunity to thrust forward, spinning and slicing Paul's back. He immediately made a noise arching his back.

Eva came back toward Paul as he threw another punch ill-timed and out of range again. He went with the motion of the punch with Eva slashing his back again. Paul again screamed arching his back. He fell to the floor leaning forward. After a few moments, he stood back up.

Eva watched him gather his strength. She was like a cat watching a mouse. Paul steadied himself letting his arms dangle loose by his side. He bent over a little making the stance of a wrestler. Eva surprised he had the energy to do so.

Paul approached slowly. Eva closed both knives putting them in her back pockets. She then slowly approached Paul. He then came fast with both arms outstretched. At the right moment, Eva fell backwards, her hands cushioning the fall and kicking one leg upward that caught Paul in the groin area. He immediately stopped falling to the floor letting out a high-pitched scream holding his crotch area.

Eva jumped to her feet looking down at Paul. Wondering if she kicked him too hard.

If so, they'll be swelling up like grapefruits. She put a hand over her mouth.

Laughing started.

A man came out fixing his pants and looking at Paul on the floor curled up. The laughing increased. Ivan told the man in Russian to bring her out.

Two men dragged Wendy out from the room. She was nude with blood dripping from her face. They dropped her next to Paul on the floor. He tried reaching to touch her, she was trembling. When Paul did touch her, she pulled away.

"Well big guy, she's in love with somebody else. Wonder who?" Eva bellowed as everybody fell out laughing again. Paul's eyes rolled around as Wendy trembled more.

"All you had to do was mind your own business. Now you're a mess." Eva said letting the place fall silent for a moment. "You have not respected the Czar and Czarina. Now, the bad news is you must die."

Ivan handed Eva a handgun butt first. Taking it, she slid the slide. Stepping over to Wendy saying. "All good girls go to heaven." Eva then put a bullet in her head.

Paul looking over at Wendy had a pained look on his face. All they had to do was mind their own business, Eva thought. She handed the weapon back to Ivan stepping back a few feet.

The men lined up taking pistols out. On a silent cue, they started firing. When done,

Eva said. "Toss this shit."

Exiting with Ivan, Eva heard laughs from the men as she left the building. It made her happy.

Chapter 41

Joe looked at the phone wanting to call Carol but, he did that earlier. He remembered telling her he'd take her to dinner and regrets saying that now. He thought of the bed in his private rest room and decided not to, first day and that was not acceptable to Joe.

His phone buzzed. "Hi Joe. It's almost time to meet Ariel for lunch." Vera said.

"Yes, five minutes."

Joe went to his private rest room glancing at the bed knowing it looked inviting. He finished and went back to his office to Vera waiting.

"Ready?" Vera asked.

"Show me the way."

He followed Vera through his department. A few workers who saw him said hello and by the look on their faces they genuinely meant it.

They got onto the elevator going to a higher level. Joe, saw they went up fifteen floors. When the door opened, he caught a whiff of something tasty.

"Smells good already." Joe said.

"Yes, we have a chef that directs the menu every day. It's a good mix of healthy food with no trans fats or the like. The chef is like our mother. He makes sure we eat healthy." Vera finished giggling. Joe saw emotion for the first time from his personal assistant. It was warming to see her laugh.

Walking past glass doors to an outside eating area looked exciting to Joe. He liked the trees hanging over the tables and flowers everywhere. Joe's attention diverted to ashtrays and people smoking. He stopped and looking at that for a moment then Vera spoke.

"They allow smoking here in the building. On our floor is a smoke lounge that's approved by the family."

"I used to smoke and enjoyed it; I never saw a reason for the intrusion from groups and the government but, that's life." Joe said smiling as Vera lead the way on.

Turning a corner both sides of the hallway hung with paintings. Old masters or so Joe thought.

Vera spoke. "Copies that Mr. Bokanawski wanted put here. He felt one should eat and see the best works of arts. Eating is a celebration." She smiled at Joe.

Ahead two frosted giant doors slide open as they approached them. The delightful smell of food came out.

Walking in a sign posted to one side read:

'Beware of the chef. Do not bring your own lunch in here.' Joe smiled reading that.

"Yanni, the chef, takes it personally if you bring something from home. He'll make whatever in the world you want." Joe nodded looking around the room. Frosted glassed room for smokers with a door for the outside balcony. The nonsmoking section looked as comfortable with overstuffed chairs and solid wood tables. A fashionable restaurant, Joe thought. The curtained windows and potted plants with trees gave it a comfortable feeling. With tables well placed giving an air of coziness.

Vera upped on her tippy toes smiling. "I see Ariel."

Joe looking over also saw him. Vera escorted the way passing tables with people happily eating and talking. Joe noticed a glass or two that looked like beer. He dismissed that.

"Joe, you made it." Ariel stood with a glass that looked like a mixed drink.

"Traffic was horrendous."

"Right." Ariel motioned for him and Vera to sit.

"Can't, I'm sure you have stuff to talk about that I don't need to know. I'm going for a salad and a smoke." Vera said.

"You sure. I always love the company of a beautiful lady at lunch."

Vera giggling said. "Thank you, Ariel." Vera nodded to both leaving.

Both sat as Ariel took a sip of his drink.

Joe thought he smelled alcohol but didn't say anything.

"How you like our little café." Ariel asked proudly.

"Impressed. Great place. I can just imagine the menu."

"Anything in the world you wish. Yanni has daily dishes that if followed are healthy for you with cholesterol and the like."

"Cool. Who's the supplier?"

Ariel laughed. "You are. Years ago, when they bought the building and built this café, Mr. B had a small warehouse built in the lower level that supplies the café. Not sure if you control it. Research on a slow day."

"Sure. I'll get better prices. I see the workers are enjoying this." Joe said seeing a little frown on Ariel's face.

"Joe, use the word people here. Worker sounds so degrading."

"Right." Joe liking the idea himself picked up the menu reading a lunch menu on the front. Quickly glancing down the first page at the food items available. Full course meals. Looking on the other pages he saw desserts and any side dish one could want. On the last page, Joe saw a list of drinks that included hard alcohol to lite beers.

"Beer." Joe asked looking at Ariel.

"Yes. Mr. B wanted that on the menu. He felt responsible adults won't abuse it. There's been two in fifteen years and they're transferred."

"Transferred?" Joe asked.

"Europe somewhere. There's family businesses that aren't as pleasant as here. You see, the two weren't punished. Just placed in a business with less limits. They weren't able to carry their weakness well so there's places for such people in the family business." Ariel said straight-faced.

"Doesn't sound legal? I mean there's laws against discrimination." Ariel immediately stopped Joe by cutting in.

"Joe, they put those laws in place for people that have weakness they could not control. Why hold employers back wondering if employees will crack under stress? You see all the people eating in here. They will have a drink or two relaxing with a good meal. Now, when they go back to their jobs, they will perform excellently."

"Understand what you're getting at here." Joe said playing with his utensils.

"Look at the young people here. They go out to clubs and snort coke, do x and whatever else. They enjoy life on the edges sometimes but, they bring themselves back. When they show up for work, they're in good spirits well rested. They take the time to get ready for work. I see no problem with people doing their own thing on their time. We employ half the people here than others in our group size. That's because they work hard here, because they want to. Because we have faith in them and they are loyal to us. Doing the random drug testing and following that rule; most here would be gone. Then we'd have lazy people telling their bosses every little dirty story they could think of so someone gets fired. There would be no loyalty or family feeling."

"Made some good points Ariel. Now, I ran my own business and had the problems you described. The laws for nonsmoking and drug free workplaces only created new problems."

"Yes, they do." Ariel smiled sipping his drink.

"With that said I'll have a lite beer." Joe said looking at Ariel.

A waitress took their orders. She wrote their names and what they ordered. When she left, Ariel continued.

"You see, Joe. The people employed here know you're a boss and I'm a boss. I don't walk the halls here expecting or wanting people to feel I will fire them if they talk to me wrong or any other reason. They do their jobs well and they know who their boss is and give them the rightful respect they should have." Ariel toasted.

How do they weed out the good from the problem people?" Joe asked with a pleading look. Then stopped when the waitress came with his beer.

"Good question Joe." Ariel said smiling at Joe. "Can't tell anybody this. We don't run advertisements looking for people. We go to them and offer them a job. HR does the work looking for people. They call many businesses doing many background checks on people employed in other businesses, without their knowledge. Not illegal. We're not doing identity theft or anything for the sort. HR has a model personality type and other qualities they want. When they get a match, they go after this person with top dollars. They don't want people looking at us and saying I could do a good job for you. They go after people that would probably never consider leaving their present job. That's why we have the people we do here. You'll see in time."

"Did I fit a certain model? They offered me a job here." Joe asked sipping his beer.

"Eva hired you that I don't know."

Joe sipped his beer more. The server came with their lunch. Surprisingly fast. They stopped their conversation and began eating. Joe looked and found Vera on the balcony talking and smoking with women her own age. They sipped drinks eating light salads laughing. Gorgeous women just being themselves and having a good conversation.

~~~~~

A few miles away in midtown Manhattan Don was at his usual eatery. Waiting for a seat as usual. The restaurant had a high turnout for lunch and Don would take a secretary occasionally. He's been taking Cheryl but that's over and she's fired soon. He prided himself for the quick thinking earlier in the day.

Don was lingering in the waiting area he didn't have rank to get to a table fast. The door opened as a grayed haired man dressed for success with his entourage walked through the waiting area. He immediately disappeared to a table. Don not liking that said nothing. He knew the day would come when people will cater to him. Someday he'll be somebody.

Don's cell phone rang startling him at first. "Hello, Don here."

"Hey." Said a gravelly voice.

"What's going on?"

"You called about taking down a barn."

"Yes."

"Okay, go to the Biggity bar at ten tonight."

"Who do I meet?"

"I'll meet you. Go to the bar buy a beer and sit there. Got it."

"Yea."

The line went dead. Don stood a moment holding the phone to his ear. Then put it in his pocket looking at the others still waiting. Knowing he had to rid himself of the cell phone. He'd go back to the office telling his secretary of the theft. That'd cover him in case of anything in the future. He needed a place to throw the phone. Hudson river or subway trashcan. Here wouldn't do.

"Mr. Wellington. Your table is ready."

Don looked at the man.

"Don't want the table now. Took too long."

Looking shocked at first, he immediately

checked his list for somebody else. Don walked out into noise and traffic of the afternoon. His mind racing trying to think of a good place to toss his phone.

Chapter 42

Joe burped slightly. "Good meal. I liked it."

Ariel waved to an available server. She came over and he started whispering to her. She left then a portly man came out from somewhere. Wearing the typical chef outfit with the stovepipe hat.

"Ah, Ariel. How do you?"

"Fine, fine. I want to introduce you to our new CEO of XO Foods."

Joe stood shaking the man's hand. "Joe Bergen."

"Yanni. Just Yanni. Happy to meet you. You like lunch."

"I did. I'll lunch here every day."

"Good. Good. Now you look like healthy young man. You follow my menu every day and you have good insides. I put number one, health. Food should be enjoyable and not harm you."

"I agree. I will follow your menu."

"Good. Good met you Joe. I got work to do. Ariel."

He waddled back to the kitchen waving as

he went.

"Excellent chef." Ariel said.

"They must pay a fortune for him."

"Yes, I don't know. I guess Yanni had a successful restaurant somewhere and had problems. Mr. B hired him with no questions asked. Only cook good healthy food for everyone here."

"That he does. It doesn't feel like I ate a steak lunch. How does he do that? I feel full but not stuffed."

"Yes, I hope it stays this way." Ariel said sipping his drink.

"What do you mean?"

"Well, Mr. B hardly comes here anymore and looking to the future his job will be open. Eva will take over. Her brother and sisters have no interest in it. They run their divisions and control the board. She is close with their Aunt in Russia who has a big empire herself. Now, her Aunt doesn't like the liberal way we run the business here. So, birds of a feather."

Ariel looked off for a moment then Joe spoke. "I don't know Eva all that well. I can't imagine she'd change something that works. Somebody went through much work here and it's a great place."

Ariel shrugged his shoulders. "You haven't met the board of directors yet. They're all family members and tight. They may give you a rough going over so, keep your wits about you."

Joe sensed a hurt with Ariel. He let it go.

"I see no need to change this." Joe said sipping his beer adding. "I'll do fine."

"CFO fifteen years now and never asked to sit on the board. I guess I'll retire when I decide to leave."

That's it, Joe thought. A disgruntled employee of sorts.

"Maybe the future will hold a surprise for you."

Ariel looked at Joe seriously saying. "No, I'm not royalty. They haven't asked me into the field to show my worth."

"You're in the field every day here proving your worth. I'm sure they have a surprise for you down the road." Joe knew he was missing something here or Ariel is drunk. He didn't know which.

"I'll say though, it's been a great fifteen years. Just don't expect to move into CZ Corp. anytime soon. What they hired you for they keep you in. Overall it's a great life here." Ariel gave his million-dollar smile making Joe felt better. He figured Ariel was just letting off steam. He finished his beer as Vera walked up. "Meeting at one."

Joe looked at his watch. "Ariel, let's do lunch again, soon."

"Sure."

They got up to leave with Ariel saying. "Always want to leave a tip. I have to remind myself I'm at work."

Joe and Ariel nodded and headed different directions in the hallway.

"Interesting man, Ariel." Joe said to Vera

once on the elevator.

"Knows everything at CZ Corp. He's in charge when Eva's out. He's the only one that goes to see Mr. Bokanawski. He may be in charge someday."

"I see."

"Unlikely though. The family won't let him. They always choose who they want where."

Joe was nodding and wondering why. Maybe someday as he gets to know the family better.

Vera continued. "He's wealthy in his own right though. Has a party once a year at his mansion on Long Island. It's right on the beach and a dream." She finished with big eyes.

Joe smiled looking forward to seeing Ariel's mansion. Why the complaining then, He wondered. The elevator door opened, Joe knew the way now.

Chapter 43

Eva and Ivan were heading north on the sprain parkway in a red Ferrari with Eva at the wheel. Ivan's big body squished in the passenger seat. She, smiling as they moved along in light traffic. Eva was just over the speed limit passing cars with ease. She looked over to Ivan who was watching every move she made. A black Ferrari was not far behind for extra security.

"What's up Iv? You look nervous."

"Yes, Eva. I feel better if I drive."

"Well, you know I'm not going to let you do that. It's my car." Eva said smiling to Ivan.

Eva pushed the car faster on a clear stretch of road. Ivan made a quick call to someone then closed his phone.

"Road's clear of police up to our exit." He said.

"Thank you, Iv."

Eva pushed the car faster as everything passed by in a blur. Smiling and enjoying the feel and power of the car.

The road ahead had no police which

meant that she had five miles to open her up. That information came from people who worked for Eva with a little help from the local and state police.

Eva powered down to exit off noticing the black Ferrari right behind her. She liked that they kept up, next time she'll make it a real race. She drove at an almost normal speed now. The winding county road dictated that.

Shortly, they were at the gates of her father's estate. Eva always thought it her father's house, though he called it the family home. Not since her mother died did Eva see it that way. The spark had left the place. Her father she loved but, her mother was the more personal one in her life. Now her Aunt has taken that place.

The estate still had its lush gardens and fresh flowers throughout but, someone was missing, and Eva still felt it after seven years. Clearly, no one else has because, her brothers and sisters lived here often.

Eva sped up the car on the private drive to the house. She cut every turn close coming to a screeching halt in front of the house. Eva looked over at Ivan smiling.

"Cool or what Iv."

"Yes, cool, Eva."

Out of the car giggling up the steps she turned to see Ivan still trying to get his body mass out of the car. Opening the front Dimitri stood to one side as Eva walked in.

"Hello, Ms Eva."

"Hi Dimitri. Where's everybody?"

"At the outdoor pool, Ms Eva."

"Cool."

Eva used the hidden elevator up to the second floor. She dashed to her room tearing her clothes off. She put on a thong bikini and silk robe to cover.

She dashed down the backstairs to the first-floor veranda. Eva saw her father sitting in a cushioned wrought iron lounger under a shade tree. She headed in that direction. Along the way she saw three in the pool and two lounging by the pool. Everybody except Nicolas Jr. That bothered her, she knew her father envied him, and he was never here. Always in California or traveling to make movies. Excuses.

She quietly approached her father who was reading a newspaper.

"Hi." Eva said as Nicolas Sr jolted up a bit, then smiled at seeing her.

"Eva's here." He announced putting the paper aside. Eva bent over giving him a hug and a kiss on either cheek.

"Hey Olg." Eva said to Olga who came walking over.

"Hey." Olga said taking a seat next to Nicolas Sr.

"Tat." Eva said. "Trying to get that sexy tan." Tatyana showed Eva the middle finger. Tatyana being the tomboy of the girls dismissed any mention of being feminine quickly.

Eva saw Max, Mikal and Uri playing dodge ball in the pool. Hitting each other hard with the ball, Eva thought.

"Hey guys." They all stopped looking at her.

She took off her robe placing it on a lounger. The moment she did whistles and catcalls from her brothers came from the pool. She responded by showing the middle finger. That made them erupt into laughter.

Eva stopped looking at Max. "Got here fast."

"I have my secrets." Max said.

"You used the helicopter." Eva said.

"Yep." Max said smiling.

"Damn." Eva said looking in the distance at the helicopter on the landing pad. She looked back to Max asking. "Did you dump that trash."

"Disposed of properly." Max replied seriously then nailed Uri in the head with the ball. Which caused a new battle in the pool.

Eva sat down. Nicolas Sr was looking at her smiling. She knew he liked the one-on-one about family and business. Like she has with Aunt Catherine.

"So, what's going on dad."

He thought for a moment then spoke. "Was that necessary this morning?"

"You mean the couple."

He nodded yes.

"Best way to end a problem." Eva said looking at him.

"Reporters are the problem. That guy and his wife were just secondary. Without the first there'll be no second."

"I thought it necessary." Eva hoped he would let it go.

"Yes but, too many will raise eyebrows and it won't look random."

"Mr reporter's body parts are scattered and the couple won't be found. They erased his computer putting new information to throw off the trail he was researching. The couple stole money from our warehouse before we bought it. Joe Bergen will take that personally and not suspect nothing. They also fixed the computers there."

Nicolas Sr thought then asked. "Mr reporter was researching what?"

Eva smiled. "Italians in Brooklyn. They still control the trash business after all these years. It still hasn't stopped."

"You're beautiful." Nicolas Sr said picking the newspaper up.

"I try." She said with an innocent face. Nicolas Sr laughed then said. "Nico is on his way to Russia. Aunt Catherine wants to see him, I hope he stops by to visit." Raising his eyebrows to Eva. Meaning she needs to relay that to Nicolas Jr; visit Aunt Catherine.

"I'm sure he will." Eva said making a mental note to call him right away.

"Olga when you going home." Olga put her magazine down.

"I am home. I'll be going back to Poland in a few days."

"Okay." Eva replied.

"When's Mik going back?".

"Probably soon, I don't know. His girl

wants to go back so, they wouldn't surprise me if it was tonight."

"How's the new guy?" Nicolas Sr asked Eva.

"Bergen, he's fine, getting up to speed with the warehouses. I heard he's already questioning Anton Slotkolov's numbers." Eva watched but he didn't change his expression.

"He's using the warehouse to store some alcohol he ships to his friends in the Ukraine, tax-free." Nicolas Sr said casually.

Eva sat up on the lounger. "He's running a risk with our business."

Nicolas Sr raised his hands. "It's all safe and secure. He has barrels of glass cleaner that he converts to Vodka when chemicals are added to strip away the cleaner look. They explained it to me a while ago and I said okay until he gets another place to store the stuff."

Eva didn't like this. She did not like that he was storing those barrels there. She did not like Anton.

"Dad, he's in his late twenties not a kid anymore. Scraping for a few dollars on a scam. If the place is raided, it'll be a big problem. And he's been holding back legit profit money from the warehouse."

"Eva, I gave him my word. Profit money from the warehouse is going in real estate there. It helps him get into something different and I get a little legit profit." Nicolas Sr laughed continuing. "The kid knows of a good tract of land cheap that he can develop into estates. I gave the go-ahead and that's final."

"Dad, the barrels. It's not the nine eighties and he's running a risk that can lead back to us."

Nicolas Sr thought for a moment. "All right. When Bergen goes there and if he finds this out, give him full power to set it straight. Now, if he doesn't and a bust comes on those barrels of alcohol, that's Joe Bergen's problem. He had something going on we didn't know about." Nicolas Sr finished looking at Eva who was mad. Joe Bergen was not going to take a fall. That's not going to happen. The barrels she did not like and did not want them in that warehouse for another day. Joe Bergen wasn't going to find out either.

"We have a good honest business that is perfect for money laundering and that kid in Minneapolis is running a risk of ruining it for us." Eva said as a statement.

She didn't like someone running a risk like this.

"Okay, I understand your concern."

"I understand that and expect him to do his business elsewhere than at one of our businesses. He's just an employee for us." Eva said seriously to Nicolas Sr.

"It's my company and you're just an employee of mine." Nicolas Sr said in a serious tone. Eva had an idea. "Okay, I understand the barrels stay. Have you seen the real estate?" Eva asked calmly.

Nicolas Sr looked up to the sky saying. "No. It's the beginning stage. They have built and sold a few. In time I'll have a look."

Eva knew much to her jealously that Anton was onto something good. She couldn't and wouldn't tell him that.

"Okay, in time you'll go there."

Nicolas Sr squinted his eyes. Then said. "Eva, if you know something tell me."

"I don't. Bergen will be going there soon. We'll let him tell us."

"Okay, we'll let Bergen tell us." He said rolling his eyes then going back to the newspaper.

"Ariel showed me the numbers today and we're doing well without the laundered money. Max says there's no red flags and no interest in our company by law enforcement. We'll need to slow the laundering a pace or two. The real estate drop and mortgage mess is taking a toll and being too profitable might be bad. We must look like the legit ones, for a few months." Eva watched her father hoping for something.

"Good idea. Slow down the laundering a pace or two. We can always stock pile gold or diamonds and launder later." He said while reading something.

"Okay. I'll let Aunt Catherine know when I go back."

"Why does Catherine want this Senator dead?" Nicolas Sr glanced over at her.

"My best guess, the last trip he took to Russia. He must have stepped on some toes asking the wrong questions. We ripped off the nephew there so I guess he wants to see what he could do to bring justice to that. You know how Americans can be. They think everybody cares about them when they're hurting. He talked to young liberals there making waves with talk of protests and rights. I guess Aunt Catherine didn't like who he talked to." Eva finished leaning back on the lounger.

"The man is going to run for President. It's obvious by the news talk and she wants to kill him."

"Aunt Catherine never wants to do anything. She just does it."

Eva knew where her father was going with this and knew she could talk to her Aunt Catherine but, it would be no use. Her Aunt would only see her as weak. She wouldn't do that for even her father.

"I hope she knows what she's doing." Nicolas Sr looking at her for a moment.

"I'm sure she does, dad."

"She's going to be the death of me." He said laughing lightly. "See the latest stand in she's using."

"You mean the tattoo one. Old Russian mob." Eva said wide-eyed.

"Yea." Nicolas Sr laughed.

Eva knew her Aunt could have done better. Law enforcement is always looking for bad people. They know there's drugs and stealing going on and they look for who is the boss responsible for it. They don't look too deep when they tag a person the boss. It's thrust forward for the news media to feed on. Aunt Catherine is the brain behind the idea of using someone that fit the profile. She always has a thug appearing he's the crime boss and playing along. When they arrest him and a little prison time later keeping his mouth shut, they reward him handsomely. It's time to satisfy the law enforcement officials again with a new stand in. This time Aunt Catherine picked a man that had the worst record to date and feared by many, old school mob. He was keeping a low profile and will last for a couple years.

Eva liked the way Aunt Catherine developed that scheme. That lucky man will have a few million dollars when caught but won't happen any time soon. Aunt Catherine always liked reading about it in the news. She says watching the chase is better than the arrest.

"The Red mob must go per Aunt Catherine." Eva stated and continued. "Him and his gang are easy to get. They won't be a problem. We're more advanced than them. In fact, we can do them right now but, we need to show that they have a nuke. The mobs from the meeting won't go along otherwise. That would make distrust. We do get hundreds of millions from them selling the drugs we import to them. We could never get the product sold without the other mobs because we don't have the street level like they do."

"I know. We need them and they need us. Find what you could on the Red mob. If it's a no, then go tell Aunt Catherine." Nicolas Sr said while reading. Eva didn't look forward telling her Aunt Catherine that she found no evidence.

"Maybe set them up. Do you know where to get a nuke weapon from?" Nicolas Sr asked.

"No, too risky." Eva said thinking.

"True. Don't do that." Nicolas Sr said turning a page continuing. "Catherine will probably be let down. Just be strong with her. She'll understand if you have every informer you can get telling you it's a no."

Easy for you to say, Eva thought. She wanted to be Czarina someday

Nicolas Sr laughing said. "Ureinchencko is a slippery fucker. He'll have precautions in place and will use them. Someone once tried killing him and he was ready to take his own life with that person with a bomb. That person let go and he eventually got him later. The Red mob probably stands for the Blood mob, and they will spill it."

"What happened?"

"Cornered in his car with a bomb. He showed the bomb and it was acknowledged the other guy wanted to live. He started that some years ago, he vowed not to be taken alive or have someone kill him and get away. He always did love bombs."

Eva remembering the last pictures she saw of him. He and his entourage were getting into a car and he had a briefcase. Eva thought that was a ploy to make people think he was a businessman.

"Thank you for information." Eva said realizing it may be a concern.

Eva thought about Andre knowing he did not mention anything about this. She needs to talk to Andre again for the last time.

"Maybe that's why no law enforcement in Russia wants to touch him. They know he'll make a mess. Now, they are talking about this nuke he wants to buy openly." Eva said thinking out loud.

"That tells me he has no plans on getting one. I knew him a while ago and he would use false information to throw off his real enemies." Nicolas Sr turned another page. Eva thought for a moment.

"Does Aunt Catherine know this? She must, she almost married the guy. Why's she believing the rumors. I don't get it."

"Maybe a different ploy. Everybody who knows him will think it's just talk. Maybe he's changing and using what people think they know to his advantage. Find out and decide."

Eva knew Andre had a high ranking in the close circle of Ureinchencko. She had promised Andre that he would not be touched if he provided the information. He knows when the Czarina asks for something and it's done, he'll be provided for and safe.

Eva looked in the distance at the trees swaying in the breeze. The sound of a yell made her and Nicolas Sr look at the pool. Uri was holding Mikal from behind as Max hit him with the ball. Mikal yelled in a laughing tone as it hit him.

"All right you girls. I'm trying to read." Olga yelled.

The three stopped looking over at Olga. Max held the ball he was about to throw at Mikal and put it under his arm. Uri let Mikal go. They climbed out of the pool walking over toward Olga. She watched them approaching and yelled.

"Don't, I'll kick your asses."

That didn't deter the three as they got closer. Olga stood. "I just got my hair done. I'll kick your asses." She said. The three circled her. They started to mimic the way she was standing. Uri playing with his hair said. "I just had my hair done," in a high-pitched voice.

Olga looked to Nicolas Sr who was enjoying it. In a half laughing voice. "Dad."

Nicolas Sr shrugged looking at the three around her. "You're outnumbered my angel."

They moved in. Olga got a punch into Max's stomach which did not faze him. The three grabbed and raised her above their heads counting to three. Then threw her in the pool.

Max, Mikal and Uri laughed. Then took seats by Eva and Nicholas Sr, while Olga splashed and yelled. "Fuck."

She climbed out of the pool touching her hair yelling. "Fuck."

She came walking over to where they

were giving each a hit or smack. They laughed too hard to protect themselves.

Olga finally sat in her lounger looking at Nicolas Sr. He was smiling kindly then said. "I'll pay for your hair."

"Thanks, but I can handle it dad." Olga said sneering at the three while toweling her hair.

"I have another toy you can play with." Max said to his father.

"Tell me." Nicolas Sr asked putting the paper down.

"It'll work in time with the camera blocker." Eva interrupted Max saying, "the mosquito." Max wrinkled his face then continued. "Yes, the mosquito. The new system silences noise. A government project invented years ago that never took off. My people refined it and made it work. It locates conversation or noise in a certain area. A computer then matches the sound and vibration level canceling the noise." Max finished glancing around.

"Okay. What do we do with it?" Uri asked.

"I adapted it on poles right now. Four poles placed in a square. Noise canceling inside and mosquito on the outside. No sound no pictures in a confined space." Max drew that in the air. "Speakers facing in opposite directions. One set listens the other set drowns out sounds it hears. A confined area preventing conversation from being overheard with mosquito preventing pictures."

Nobody said a word. They just looked at Max picturing what he described. Eva was the first to speak.

"Silence bullets or bombs."

"Yes. Depending on the size of the bomb but, guns, yes. You see, they played around with this sound device about thirty years ago, but computers were crude and humans had to adjust the noise canceling. It didn't work. Now though, computers we use are faster than any human can hear and adjust."

All eyes went to Nicolas Sr who loved technology that Max invented. A smile slowly developed on his face. He then started laughing. "You're telling me I can take the device late at night to a suburban neighborhood, discharge a gun and nobody would hear it."

"Nobody would stir, not even a mouse." Max said.

"I want to see this. I want to see this." Nicolas Sr said with everybody nodding.

"No problem. I'm working on one step better. I'm trying to develop a total bubble. Square setup canceling noise and pictures but, I want the square area blocked out from nobody being able to see into it. I'm experimenting with having bright lights or a cover to blanket all four sides and the top so there's no visual." Max said looking around.

Eva spoke slowly. "The military invented a LED blanket with tiny cameras that shows the scenery behind it. Making an object seem invisible."

Max's eyes went wide in thought then spoke. "Good but, it's a physical and can't be used quickly. I want something that we can adapt to say four cars or people to make a square or triangle. Take care of business then vanish."

Eva spoke up. "Sounds good Max. Thinking about it, if you use it like you said as four people or four cars. We may need it in Russia. I need to show it to Aunt Catherine."

Uri spoke up. "There's times when moving drugs, we are exposed. I can use that."

"I had you in mind when I built it." Max said to Uri. Both touched fists.

Eva agreed. Uri is the drug exporter importer to any country in the world. He's the most profitable. A slight jealously exists but with the life of luxury they all have, nobody lets that show.

Eva looked at Mikal who was silent. He was looking at Max and Uri. She knew the joke was Mikal was one of the laundry girls.

"Mik, what's the latest take on the stock?" Eva asked as everybody quieted down. They knew already it was for their father's sake.

Mikal clearing his throat made a show of moving himself on the lounger. "Last count I would say a profit of thirty million. That will be ready for collection next week." He looked around at the smiles.

"Any who don't pay?" Eva asked.

"No, I allow for an allowance. That is, someone wants to buy a new house or car.

They then pay extra next time." Mikal said.

"No police or governments are close to figuring it out, according to our sources." Tatyana said. She helps Mikal with that at times. She devotes much time to corporate crime.

Mikal nodding said. "The thanks go to all the common people involved. I got the idea from the Italian mob except that we pump up good solid companies."

"Tell me again how it works." Nicolas Sr asked.

"I pick a stock at quarterly report time. I then send a message to one group to buy it until I send a message to stop. I then send another message to another group to start selling, now this second group has bought the stock slowly over the last three days prior. At a reasonable level, I then message group one to sell what they bought. Now, the first group makes a profit and the second group makes an even bigger profit. Ten percent follows these thumbs." He pointed thumbs at himself. "It's a run up and down and nobody is in the burn."

Nicolas Sr looked off in the distance. Eva knew her father did not like stuff like this. He wanted them to do real to earn. Her father always thought Mikal as weak, Eva knew. Her father then asked Mikal. "How many people needed?"

"I have a little over a million people that take part. It's all voluntary. They're spread throughout Europe and America which makes it difficult to keep track of for Government officials." Mikal said looking at Nicolas Sr.

"All these people do this, and you trust them." Nicolas Sr asked.

"Yes, I have locals that do the collecting. They open a trading account online and we give them money to deposit. They trade a little with their own money but, when we send the message, they invest in what we tell them to with our money. They keep fifty percent of the profit. Now, they are common good people that work regular jobs and live a middle-class life. They're not associated with the companies I choose. Nothing unusual at all. If one of them buys a stock and makes fifty grand, they have no problem paying twenty five grand to someone who gave them the tip."

Eva knew this was much for her father. She knew he came from a world and time when nobody trusted anyone. Nobody trusts today either but, for the sake of money people come together.

"Well, it sounds complicated but profitable. I'll tell you some of what I hear talked about scares me but, you understand the world today. I'm blessed with some good children." Nicolas Sr said. They all sat looking at their proud father.

Eva was already thinking about how she would discredit Anton to her father. She must do it. She will think of something, she knew.

Chapter 44

He stepped from the limo looking at the building with his name on it. Joe knew it would be changed soon, to a shiny new corporate logo with no feeling. An old friend moving on. The memories, good and bad, mainly good. This place had given him money and a life he would not have known if he did not take a risk. Today was the reward and so, risk is good he thought.

Joe saw Sevan also looking at the building.

"Saying good-bye to an old friend." Sevan asked.

"Yes." Joe said not looking at him. He then asked Sevan. "You are coming in."

"Yes sir."

Both walked to the front doors. Sevan opening the first then the second door. Joe was going to like having someone opening doors for him.

"Hi Cheryl, the boss in?"

Cheryl already standing and smiling said. "Yes impatiently."

Joe and Sevan climbed the stairs to the

executive level and down a short hallway. Nearing his old office Joe heard Thom on the phone. He stepped into the office seeing Thom turned toward the window talking on the phone. He quietly took a seat and Sevan stayed by the doorway

"Yea, I know, and she thought it was a case of apples. Now, they said it will make them change the whole menu." Thom said into the phone laughing slightly. "Yea, it'll be all right."

Thom turned around catching sight of Joe he immediately sat upright. "Ah, yes, tomorrow. I must go now. Bye."

Thom hung up the phone and out of his chair. He walked to the front of the desk and bear hugged Joe. Then settling in chairs next to each other in front of the desk Thom asked "So, how's the big life.".

"I can't complain and probably never will." Joe said fixing his tie.

Thom turned to look at Sevan for a moment.

"He's my personal security person and friend." Joe said.

Thom looked back at Sevan saying. "Hi."

"Hello." Sevan said back.

"You left everything in good shape. I almost have nothing to do."

"Well, if everybody does their job you won't have much to do." Joe said.

"True. I typed a letter to tell the customers of the merger."

"Good. I'll leave that to you to tell them.

The names going to change that's all. Oh, you'll be receiving funds for the name change also. I'll try to send more your way for expansion.

Joe said getting down to business.

"Good." Thom said wanting to hear more.

"I'm going to upgrade the computer networks, so my staff has access and knows the daily numbers. And video connections for meetings once a month."

Thom nodded. "What's the total warehouse count now."

"Fifteen and growing. I plan to do some central buying for larger commodity items, cheaper in bulk. I'll leave regional type food to the respected warehouses. Also, a line of European foods is coming." Joe said happily knowing Thom will do better than he thought.

"Great. I'm right there with you on these changes. European food line." Thom said aloud.

"Yes, at reasonable prices to knock out the competition. Now, Thom, we've worked together for years. Please don't give me this new hire. I'll do anything shit. That's not you." Joe said and both laughed for a moment.

"Sounded good though, didn't it?" Thom said smiled.

"Yea, it did. But we're friends and I know you'll go with the new way of doing business."

"Just let me know what you need done

and by when."

"First, name change by end of the month. If there's any money left over, give yourself a bonus. No need to return it, I'm already going to count the money as costs."

Thom nodded thinking about a bonus. Joe continued. "It's not my personal money anymore. That's how we big shots get bonuses."

"I'll share the money with my staff." Thom said and Joe liked that even better.

"So, what's it like. Bigger game of politics."

"No, I already have a full staff and the place it amazing. Very organized. They specially choose people to work for them. Very good system they have." Joe said looking out the window for a moment thinking of what Ariel said. Keep it in the family

"Why'd they choose you then?" Thom asked.

"I don't know." Joe said seriously.

"I was just joking." Thom said.

"I'm not." Joe said and both laughed for a moment. He then looked around asking.

Where's Paul?" Before Joe finished Thom change his facial appearance.

"Don't know where he is. He hasn't called or shown up today." Thom said with a helpless look.

Joe remembered with a lightning bolt the phone message from Paul saying he needed to see him before Monday

"Have you called his house?"

"I have Cheryl doing it until he answers."

"I forget the last time he took off work. Not like him to do this. I know he has family in New Hampshire. Maybe something happened and he dropped everything to go there." Joe said.

"Maybe. He's close to his mother. She just about raised him by herself." Thom added and Joe nodded agreeing.

"If he doesn't call tomorrow or show up let me know. I hope he wasn't expecting something with this merger." Joe looked away.

"No, that wasn't Paul. He was happy in HR."

"Yea. Let me know when he shows up." Joe said not feeling right he hasn't shown up for work.

"I'll stop by his house tomorrow if he still doesn't show up and then give you a call." Thom said seriously.

The desk phone buzzed. Thom got up pressing a button.

"Yes Cheryl."

"Everyone's in the conference room."

"Thank you."

Thom turned looking at Joe. "We're ready."

Joe stood up looking at Thom.

"Let's do it."

They left the office starting down the hallway with Sevan in tow. A few office staff were still at their desks. Thom stopped and whistled for everybody to follow. A few congratulated Joe as they walked along in a group of fifteen people. He glanced at Sevan who had his eyes planted on him.

They entered the conference room. Joe and Thom last to a slight applause. Sevan stepped in closing the door and remaining there.

Joe stopped momentarily looking at everybody, he knew most of them and liked all of them. The questioning looks on some faces he will answer soon. Where's Paul though.

Joe raising his hands quieted everyone down.

"Thank you. As you know or have heard I have sold the business. I have sold to a larger outfit call XO Food service. We now consist of fifteen warehouses from coast to coast and growing bigger. They have offered me, and I have taken the job of CEO of the company. I have a farther drive to work now." A few laughs. When that stopped Joe continued. "I have chosen Thom Heller to replace me here as President. I know you'll give him your best as you have done for me. Now, for the Union members there will be no change in your contract or work hours or conditions." A little applause from that group he noticed.

Then continuing another twenty minutes with questions for another thirty. He felt happy with the understanding he got from everybody. They were no longer a stand-alone warehouse on their own. Now part of a big team with more money available for upgrading equipment and the like.

An hour later Joe sat in the limo listening to the rumble of the exhaust. Sevan looked back from the front seat. "Back to the office, sir?"

Joe looked at Sevan then handed him an address. The limo started moving.

Chapter 45

It was a middle-class neighborhood with picture-perfect lawns. A pleasant place to raise a child and feel safe as one can be these days, Joe thought. The limo stopped in front of the house. A bi level with big oak shade tree in front. Joe didn't realize he paid Paul this well, but his wife worked also.

Sevan opened the door. Joe climbed out saying. "Stay here. I'll be fine." Pausing a second. "He's the HR person from my company and hasn't shown up. Just a personal call."

"Okay sir." Sevan said closing the door.

Joe walked up the driveway done in intersecting blocks that looked nice. The shrubs well-fed and green sculpted. Flower boxes on the porch gave a welcome feeling. Joe liked the feel of what he saw.

In the distance, the sound of children playing merged with sound of a lawn mower. Looking at the darkened front windows he pushed the doorbell and heard a series of chimes. It sounded pleasant.

Joe pushed the doorbell again. Still, no

one answer. He opened the outer storm door and tried the door handle. Still, he heard no sound of movement. He let the storm door close and looked at the darkened windows again. The mailbox full. He just wanted to see Paul. Concern was filling him.

Stepping off the porch he walked over to the garage. He cupped his hands and peered inside the small window. Paul's BMW was parked inside, and the garage looked clean and organized. That was Paul, Joe thought, always neat and perfect.

He went over to the next garage window and saw no car parked there. He didn't know if Paul's wife drove a car. It looked eerily quiet.

He backed away from the garage looking the house up and down wondering why such a big house and no children. Joe knew he had no right to ask that question and turned to walk back toward the limo.

Sevan opened the back door. He turned and took one last look at Paul's house. Joe did not have a good feeling but, he knew that it was just a feeling.

Back in the limo, he made a mental note to call here tomorrow and then his family. He wanted an answer to this.

Sevan looked back at Joe. "Home Sevan."
"Yes sir."

Joe thought for a moment if Paul staged, he's fired.

~~~~~

Miles away in New York City Don traveled slowly along a brownstone street. Not a part of Manhattan he visits often. Always meeting his friend Brian at a club or his place on fifth avenue. As he got closer, he saw police cars parked on the left side. Two black and whites and one unmarked.

Don for froze a moment at seeing the police cars. He slowly drove past the neighbors that were standing around watching. A quick glance and he saw house number thirteen fifty-three. The house number correct, that was where Brain lived. Renting a top floor apartment for home and work. He kept his files and digital pictures there not using a cloud service. Don remembered trying to get him a better place to live. He always said when a major newspaper or magazine hired him full-time, he would. He liked being around common people like himself.

Don turned a corner looking for a parking space. He found one farther away than wanting hoping nobody will steal his land rover as he locked it and started walking. He wondered if he should get close. If he says he was a friend the police might want to talk to him right there, depending on what happened. He scanned every newspaper earlier and didn't find a story of a body being found. Maybe he was dead inside his apartment.

Approaching the crowd with caution he tried to look uninterested trying not to attract attention. A few stares came his way because of the suit he was wearing. He just ignored them and hung out looking for that one person. That person that looked like she lived here her whole life and knew everything.

Don slowly moved in her direction until he was close. He heard an older looking woman saying something about late parties and women. Then Don found his opening.

"Did you say he was a drug dealer?" He asked the old woman with concern on his face. She looked at his face then his suit putting a relaxed look on her face.

"He was always having parties till late in the morning. Some big shot investigative reporter. I think he stuck his nose where it didn't belong."

Don nodded pretending to take this all in.

"Was he murdered?"

"No." She said shaking her head. "He rented an apartment from Kelly. Sure, didn't make much money for an investigative reporter."

Don wished she would get to the point.

"What are the police doing?"

"Oh, the rumor is they found parts of his body and got his ID from it. So, they come here checking the apartment he rented from Kelly. An investigative reporter renting an apartment. We played in this field when I was young. If I saved my money, I could have been rich right now." The old woman said to Don with a serious look.

His mind already digesting that his friend was dead. The police would search him out. His number was on Brains phone and email in his computer.

The conversations increased as the police carried out his friend's computer and other personal items. Don was getting sick watching this display. A police officer placed the computer on the ground and it fell over as he opened his trunk. Don remembered the pictures Brain had secretly taken at a party. Pictures of somebody that had challenged his uncle in the last election and lost due to those pictures. The challenger was not discreet with his affairs of heart. People will know who took them now and probably connect him to it. This is not good, Don thought. He needs to talk to his uncle.

The old woman was looking at Don, but he was done here. She supplied enough information. A part of his body was found. Don wondered for a moment what part. He then turned away and started slowly walking, he didn't want to know. He lost a good friend and the Russians were to blame.

Not remembering walking to his land rover and getting in. He looked at his watch counting the minutes until he met whoever at the bar tonight. They stepped over the line this time. Don banged the steering wheel then started it thinking only Russians and revenge.

Chapter 46

Later that night finally relaxing in the living room Joe thought about twelve hours earlier when his day started. It seemed like a longtime ago. He was sipping on a drink and happy. The owner of the restaurant earlier that night approached with congratulations on Joe selling his business. The owner hoped he would still get the same price and service. News got around fast, he thought.

He glanced over at Carol curled up reading a novel. Unless he was tired, he didn't remember hearing or seeing her turning a page. The office seeped back into his thoughts. He knew he had a project ahead of him with setting up the computer network and doing the buying for the warehouses. Once done it'll work well. Then the thought of this guy in Minneapolis he wondered what his problem was. Carol had not turned a page yet, he was watching from the corner of his eye. He turned to see her staring at him.

Carol closed the book tossing it onto the coffee table and smiled at Joe. He turned off the TV, finished his drink and stared at her.

"Okay, you first." Joe said.

Carol's smile went uneasy as she went to the other room and back. She had a few pamphlets in her hand handing them to Joe. He looked at them one at a time reading each title. He finished placing them down on his lap.

"I don't know." Joe said.

Carol's eyes narrowed and was about to speak but Joe spoke first.

"I don't know why you got these pamphlets. They tell everything we already know but why there isn't a child sitting on the floor or here between us dribbling food all over the place. I want to see dirty handprints on the walls. I want a child."

"You." Carol said jumping over and hugging him.

"I have a business trip coming up I need to go on. Problem warehouse. Now, it was my first day and I want to ask Eva more about adopting from her orphanage in Russia. How do you feel about that?"

"That's fine where ever they're from."

"Exactly. I feel a child born and put into adoption was for a reason. You know things aren't that good in the world, we can adopt one and bring him or her to America where they'll have a chance in this world." Joe said smiling.

"I didn't know you felt that way. I feel the

same. Plainly we can't have on our own so let us help a child tenfold with home and future in a good country."

Carol kissed Joe feeling happy. She pulled her head back and looking in his eyes. "When are you going to see Eva?"

"Tomorrow. I'll do it. I want this too. She'll let us know on the procedures for adopting from another country."

Carol rested smiling at Joe. "I'll be waiting word. I'll try to contain myself. I know this will take time. So, how'd the meeting go at the old place."

"Good. Happy being part of a bigger organization that's my take away."

"Thom's happy with the new job."

"Oh shit. He's right in his element. He'll be better than I thought."

"What did Paul have to say?"

"Don't know. He didn't show up today. Thom had his house called all-day not a word. I stopped by and nobody was home."

Carol sat up looking at Joe. "Something wrong? Did something happen to Wendy? I'll go over there tomorrow."

"If you want. I hope he's not mad because Thom got the top job."

"You mean he might be jealous?"

"I don't know."

"I'm still going over there tomorrow."

"Whatever."

Joe knew she'd go and chat with Wendy eventually getting Paul thinking differently. That is if Paul wanted to change his thoughts, Joe knew.

"Let's go to bed." Carol squeezed Joe's hand smiling. She waltzed out looking sexy in her nightgown. Joe turned off the lights heading for the stairs.

Carol called from the bedroom. "Hurry. You're going to need a good night sleep when we finish."

~~~~~

The city noise didn't stop at night, Don knew looking off at the distant twinkling lights. People bedding down for the night. He wished for a moment his life was that easy. Taking a swig of beer to get his nerve up for who he was going to meet in two hours.

His uncle jolted his nerves into high gear. Pictures on computer.

Don finished the beer going into the kitchen. He threw it in the trash then headed to his den. Sitting behind the desk he looked at the picture of him and Brian hanging on the wall. It was a hiking trip to Mt Hood Oregon that Don had paid for after college. I will do this for my friend, Don thought.

Don picked up the phone pressing a preset that picked up on the second ring.

"Hello." It was Don's Aunt.

"Hi, Aunt Katie."

"Oh, Hi Donny. How are you doing."

"Good. I was calling for uncle Bob. Is he

awake?"

"Oh yes. He's doing work down in his office. Hold on."

She put Don on hold. He knew they had a telephone network like an office. A minute later his uncle.

"Yea."

"Hi uncle Bob. How's things

"What's it Don?"

"Okay. You remember Brain my friend from college. He took those pictures of Jim Catalan from the last campaign."

"Of course."

"Well something happened to him. The police took everything from his apartment including his computer, and, I don't know if he erased those pictures. I thought I should let you know."

A silence then his uncle spoke.

"It's already taken care of. I got a call earlier from the chief of detectives and it's gone. Your friend they're still finding pieces of him all over the city. I would tell you to stay away from him but, that's done."

"Okay, I don't know who or what he was doing."

"Good. Now you tell the detectives that when they come to see you. Your email and phone numbers were all over his place. I didn't have that squashed because once it hits the papers it'll help with my push for tougher jail sentences. A little closeness always helps. Sorry, I knew he was your friend but, life goes on and there's an election coming."

"Yes, Uncle Bob I understand. He wasn't cautious. He mentioned something about those Russians and I don't know if." Don couldn't finish; his uncle weighed in.

"You never said that to me or anybody. They're good people and good Americans. When those detectives come to question you, you know nothing. Right."

"Yes, Uncle Bob, nothing."

"Exactly. Have a good night."

The line went dead. Don slammed the phone as tears came to his eyes. He wasn't going to let the Russians get away with killing his friend. No evidence to prove anything so he'll do this on his own.

Looking at the desk clock he still had another hour and forty-five minutes.

Chapter 47

On a darkened street on the lower east side of Manhattan Don walked into Biggity Bar. Inside music came from a jukebox not of a good quality. A sign read some bands played every weekend and open mike on Tuesdays.

Don took a seat at the bar waiting for the bartender. A local couple were laughing in hysterics. Some other tables had either full time drunks or drunks just wasting time over a drink. To his surprise no one seemed hostile or interested in him. Don relaxed.

A woman many years past beautiful looked over at Don and he hoped not. She waved smiling at him and he nodded.

The bartender was checking his lottery numbers and threw them into the trash can with disgust. He was a big burly fella that can probably settle any problem in the place effortlessly. He looked over at Don putting a pained look on his face. He walked over to in front of Don asking.

"What'll it be?"

Don guessed this place did not attract customers for the atmosphere.

"Molson."

The bartender put on a look of tired.

"Only American here."

"Okay, then a Bud."

The bartender went into action filling a glass from the tap. He then placed it in front of Don taking his money. He returned with his change looking at Don.

"I'm waiting for somebody."

"We're all waiting for somebody. Anything from the menu." The bartender pointed to a chalkboard.

Don looked and read fast shaking his head. He then lumbered to the far end of the bar sitting down. A man whispered to him and the bartender laughed. The bartender looked at Don then shrugged to the man.

Don sipped his beer getting into the low chat of the place. He watched the local news on the TV. After a while he looked at his watch and saw fifteen minutes past already. He took a sip of his beer as someone sat next to him. He didn't remember hearing the front door open or close but, a man was sitting in the stool next to him.

Don looked at the guy then the bartender who was watching them. The guy just nodded to the bartender who nodded back to him. He then looked at Don.

"Hey." The guy in the leather jacket said.

"Hi." Said Don.

Don sipped his beer wondering if this was

the guy who was watching him closely.

"You're looking for something." The guy said in a gruff voice.

"I need a barn destroyed." Don said looking directly at the gruff now.

"Are you a cop.?" A few people in the bar looked in their direction putting Don at attention.

"No, I'm not a cop. Safe talking here?" Don took a risk figuring this was the guy. The guy continued looking at him.

"Safe as any place. Take your cell phone out." The gruff guy said.

Don took out his new cell phone placing it on the bar.

"The battery." Don did that placing it next to the phone on the bar.

"All right," the gruff guy said moving his stool closer while glancing around at everybody.

"What do you need?"

"A powerful something that'll take down a barnlike building, has to be powerful."

The gruff man's eyes didn't change. They were ice-cold.

"You need a powerful bang that will take out a house or car."

"A barn." Don corrected.

"No, you listen to me. I don't care who or what you want to get rid of. I'm just a manufacturer of a product. How you use it is your business."

Don nodded. "Ok."

"Good. It's plastic explosive with timer so

you have time to get away. That's what I sell. Easy to use. You interested."

"Yes."

"Good. It'll take a few days." The gruff man said.

"Day after tomorrow?"

"No. The price is twenty thousand in large bills."

Don thought for a moment. Price not a problem. He wanted it sooner.

"How about thirty thousand and in two days."

"I said a few days. And since you don't want to wait the price just went up to twenty-five grands."

The gruff guy stared at Don.

"Okay. How will you contact me?"

"Get the cash tomorrow when the bank opens and keep that cell phone next to you. It'll be about a few days."

Don took that in wondering for a moment. Then asked. "How do I know you're not a cop running a sting?"

The gruff man took on an even meaner look. He inhaled deeply and exhaled saying. "How do I know you're not a cop?" The gruff man mocked. "I know this much about you. You'd be bleeding to death outside if you were. Do you think I am?"

Don shook his head feeling scared. The gruff man continued. "So, a deal."

"Yes." Don said.

"Good. Keep the phone and money close and I'll be in touch."

"Okay. The number has changed. I lost the other phone."

"Good idea. Now, what's the new number?"

Don said the number as the gruff man nodded then said. "Now, I'm going to leave. You're going to finish your beer wait fifteen minutes then leave."

"Okay."

The gruff man looked one last time at Don before getting up and going to the back area of the bar where Don saw signs for rest rooms. He sipped his beer looking at his watch. He took his cell phone and battery pocketing them.

He finally relaxed thinking of Brain. His friend had taken a risk for him and his uncle Bob. He will reward that by getting the people that killed him. Don sipped his beer fixed on the thought that his friend's death would not go unjustified.

Chapter 48

The next morning Joe was irritated with the Minneapolis warehouse. No call back from Mr. Anton Slotkolov. Not acceptable for a warehouse President. He also waited to hear from Vera. He put her on the task of finding a home number for the warehouse President.

The meeting of his staff ended on a positive note. Fourteen of fifteen warehouses were doing great. Sales department has problem with one warehouse. Finance department has a problem with one warehouse. Human resources department that was getting off the ground had problems with one warehouse. Minneapolis. Joe shook his head.

A good note Joe liked was the added cost savings he would get from having the HR department buying the medical insurance for all the warehouses. A secret to surprise Eva with. He liked the handpicked staff by CZ Corp. He would keep them all and need more.

The phone buzzed. "Your wife on line one."

"Hey." Came Carol's voice. "Am I disturbing you?"

"No. I just finished a staff meeting. What's up?"

"I went over Paul and Wendy's; the police were there. Paul and Wendy were supposed to visit his sister this past weekend didn't show up. A party for the sister's daughter they always show up. His sister said. I talked with a Detective and gave him your name because you were his employer. I'm scared for them now. Maybe it's not what you or we thought."

Joe didn't know what to say at first. "Okay. Not what we thought. What else did you hear."

"Very little. I guess they expected them at the sisters Saturday for a Sunday party and didn't show. She called the police and the rest is happening."

"Okay I need to call Thom and see if the police contacted him. Where does the sister live?" Joe asked and looked out the window at the neighboring building.

"Ah, Connecticut."

"That's a few hours' drive depending what part. Yea, they should've arrived there. I guess something is wrong. We'll just let the police take care of it."

"I feel a little bad. We thought badly of them now something may have happened to them. I hope they're okay."

"Worst case, car accident, in a hospital somewhere. I'm sure the police are checking on this." Joe looked down at his desk. The polished wood.

"Sorry to give you this bad news at work."

"Don't worry. I'm used to hearing bad news and still business goes on. Yea, in about two hours I'm to meet with the Board of Directors. I guess they want to meet me and approve my hiring." Joe said with a little smirk on his face.

"Oh. Okay. Sounds good. I'm sure they'll like you."

"Well, they're all the family we met at the party." Joe still smiling.

"Okay then. They're good people and you shouldn't have a problem."

"Yes. I haven't talked to Eva yet about the adopting. I'll try to catch her later today."

"That's okay. Business first. I just want to know more about Paul and Wendy. I feel helpless and wish I could help. I hope nothing bad happened." Carol was sounding guilty, Joe noticed.

"I'll give Thom a call and see if the police contacted him. We just formed an opinion based on assumptions. You understand."

"Yes. I'm okay."

"Good. Now let me go to the bathroom and make sure I don't have a hair out of place." Carol laughed at hearing that. Joe smiled.

"You look fine and I'm sure they don't care about your looks." Carol said joyfully.

"Yea."

"I'm going."

"Bye."

"Bye."

Joe held the phone to his ear and dialed the direct number to his old office.

"Bergen foods. Thom Heller speaking."

"Hey. It's a different name now." Joe said smiling.

"Oh, yea. What's that name?"

"Okay. Wise ass. What's up?"

"Fielding some calls. I wanted to try to get that new restaurant in town where I live. They've been there for three years and don't buy from us. I take that personally now." Thom said half joking.

"I've had situations like that for years. People own restaurants and people can be unpredictable."

"True. Why you calling. Homesick?"

"No. Carol went over to Paul's house a little bit ago. The police are there, and it appears he and Wendy didn't show up at his sisters this past weekend." Joe said solemnly. Silence a few moments. Then Thom spoke. "Shit. I hope they're okay."

"Yea. I guess the sister lives in Connecticut. Not a long distance to travel."

"No, it isn't. I guess the Police will be here soon."

"Yes. Let me know after they come."

Thom sighed, "yea."

"Thom don't let this get around the place. We don't know anything yet. He was popular."

"No. Business goes on. I'll let you know when they come."

"Okay. I'm going to meet the Board of Directors today. They're going to approve my employment. Should be a breeze. We met at the party."

"Do it. Show them what a Jersey boy can do." Thom boasted.

"We're global now dude. Think global."

"Well, I got work to do Mr. Global."

"I want big sales coming from there." Joe said laughing.

"Right. What you see what you get." Thom replied laughing.

"Call me later."

"Will do. Bye."

"Bye."

Chapter 49

Soft music eased into the conference room secured with buzzing windows and walls so no one could listen in on conversations from the outside. Also swept daily for listening devices.

"I guess I go see Aunt Catherine and tell her the news." Eva said looking out the windows.

"I got nothing to go on that says Ureinchencko is buying a nuke." Max said.

"I have nothing either. I think he's playing some game. Maybe to get attention. Who knows." Tatyana said sitting cross-legged on top the conference room table.

"They're still buying plenty of drugs to sell. My team touches base with them for small talk. They say he has enough bombs." Uri said leaning back with his legs on the table.

"The sex ring of his is running great. They skirted a bust in Belgium." Olga said sitting upright and proper in her chair.

"In Paris, I watched a man of theirs. I

guess they were checking out a jewelry dealer. Maybe to rob." Mikal said nibbling on food near the windows.

"Nothing. And your man is the closest to Ureinchencko." Max said looking at Eva.

"Yea he's worthless. What does Aunt Catherine know? She wants us to find something." Eva said looking at the others.

"Could be she's just pissed for what he did years ago? Maybe she thinks about him from time to time and wants us to find something." Tatyana said.

"We should kill him just for cheating on her." Olga said taking a drag from her cigarette.

"Can't. The mobs won't allow that." Eva said.

"Eva, go see Aunt Catherine and tell her it can't happen right now. We'll keep a watch and let her know when something surfaces." Mikal said. Eva looked at him nodding. "I leave for Russia today." Eva said heading over to the buffet. She approached Uri taking a plate and grabbing what he did. They all took casual seating and ate. When finished Eva buzzed the twins. Mya entered the room.

"Tell Vera were ready."

Mya left the conference room and Eva deciding the time was right. "There's a problem with Slotkolov. He has dad's approval to take profit money from the warehouse and build homes. He's taking too much I feel. He also has that shitty glass cleaner stuff going on." Eva said.

Olga stuck her tongue. "Yucky. That stuff is crap."

"Yea, I heard that a few get sick from it." Mikal said.

"The man has no class." Tatyana said and everybody looked at her.

"Well, I'm going to give Bergen approval to fire him if he must." Eva said.

"What'd dad say?" Uri asked.

"If he's caught, you know what that means." Eva said not smiling.

Everybody nodded.

"The houses. Are they selling or is he building any?" Max asked.

Eva knew this was her moment. "I had someone check them out. Garbage. Property's on wetland. It'll flood with the first bad rain. He has people building them with the cheapest wood."

"Well, that comes close to stealing. And, we don't like that." Max said smiling at Eva.

Everybody nodded and Eva knew they would take her word on that. None of them ever bothered checking on what, she said. Except Max. Eva knew he knew something and would help her.

"Then fire the little shit. We'll do dad a favor." Tatyana said.

"Yea, he has a soft spot for little Anton. Take care of it sis." Olga said.

Eva won this one she knew.

"I can send someone to give him the news." Max said. Eva waited a beat then said. "No, I'll have Bergen do it as a company thing. If little Anton wants to take it a step further, I'll have people there to enforce the termination." Eva said with a small smile.

"Why'd dad kill his father and now have a soft spot for the son?" Mikal asked.

Everybody shrugged.

"Okay. We need to give approval of our new CEO of XO Food group." Eva said feeling good she got them to believe her.

"Who?" Olga asked.

"Oh, that dork." Tatyana said.

"He has a great looking wife." Mikal said.

"She must have hairy armpits then." Uri said to Mikal.

"Fuck you." Mikal said to Uri. Uri just nodded as Eva watched this closely.

"All right. Joe Bergen is our new CEO of XO food group and we'll approve him." Eva said loudly. Everybody nodded. Nobody liked when she raised her voice. They knew who's in charge it was reality.

The steno lady entered taking her seat. She looked up when seated smiling at everybody. Her family was from Lithuania and worked for one of CZ Corps companies, good people. Eva liked them, she went to their home occasionally for dinner. It reminded Eva of when young and her father and mother had ethnic gatherings. Those days are long gone but, the memory remains. Eva nodded to her.

"Max." Eva said.

Max sat up and everybody followed suit. He then began. "This meeting is to vote for Joe Bergen as CEO of XO Food Group. All those voting yes raise your hands." Max looked around counting. Uri abstained.

"Okay, all those voting no, raise your hands." Max stared at Uri. He did not raise his hand. Uri smiled at everyone. They all knew he liked to be the odd one. Eva knew he always liked to do this but today it meant something more to her.

"Okay, I have a proxy vote from Nicolas Jr and will open it." Max opened the envelope reading. "Nicolas Jr has voted yes for Mr. Bergen as CEO." Max finished looking at Eva. She turned in her chair pressing a button. The wall behind her opened and a big screen showed. Her father was sitting there staring at the camera. He gave a big grin waving hello.

"Okay, we have Mr. Nicolas Bokanawski Sr present. Sir how do you vote for Mr. Bergen." Max asked.

"I vote yes for Mr. Bergen as CEO of XO Food group." Nicolas Sr said.

"Okay let the record show there were six yes votes and one abstained for Mr. Bergen as CEO of XO Food group." Max said.

"All right who didn't vote." Nicolas Sr said. Everybody looked at Uri. He raised his hand smiling.

"And why no vote." Nicolas Sr asked.

"I don't know this person. I don't know that he'll do a good job." Everybody looked at him thinking. This is a money laundering business.

"I respect your decision, Uri. I know never to run for office." Nicolas Sr said bringing laughter to the room. Eva laughed knowing if they were at father's house, he would have pressured him to vote yes.

Chapter 50

Vera walked in saying. "Joe, the Board is ready for you." Joe forgotten but not totally.

"Any phone numbers for Anton Slotkolov?"

"I called his uncle's house. He's the only main number." Vera said looking blankly.

"And?"

"A man answered and said he has no number for Anton Slotkolov."

Joe looked off in the distance saying. "Day after tomorrow I am going to that warehouse. Make it happen."

Vera nodded.

"Okay this is it."

"Yes."

He got up putting on his suit jacket. He looked at Vera who looked stressed.

"How do I look?"

"Great." Vera said smiling. "Now hurry and follow me."

The top floor seemed quietly active. Top of the world Joe mused to himself. He followed Vera remembering some of the way from yesterday. They got to the conference room door and Vera stopped looking him up and down saying sternly. "Good luck."

"Thank you, Vera."

She turned and knocked on the door. Mya opened it exchanging smiles with Vera. Mya motioned for Joe to enter.

He stepped into the same conference room, but the faces were different from yesterday. Mya escorted him to a seat at the head of the table. Joe sat and relaxed as best he could. Everyone was staring at him unsmiling. Eva smiled at the other end.

"Welcome Joe. We are the board of directors of CZ Corp. We have all met you at my father's house over the weekend."

Eva stopped a moment as Joe looked around the table smiling at everybody.

"We want to ask some questions before moving forward here." Eva finished.

"Sure. I'm open to any questions. However, if I may, I'd like to say a few words." Joe stopped and everyone nodded yes. "I forward to working for a great company. Having run my own for ten years with great success I plan on doing that here. Granted it's on a larger scale but that's a challenge I look forward to. I will leave after one year if I do not achieve my goals that I have set. I set a goal to increase the profit margin ten percent than it is today. I will not do that by playing with the numbers, I will do that with good old-fashioned hard work and sales." Joe instantly saw he impressed no one. He figured they heard this before and hoped he could do ten percent.

Tatyana spoke up. "Mr. Bergen. The ten percent seems like a big achievement. I'd be happy with five. Let's be real, the food service business is competitive, and we don't need salespeople just wasting time making you look bad. That happens when goals are set too high. I'd go with five percent, and I'm Tatyana in case you forgot."

Joe nodded replying. "Tatyana, I agree with you on the sales part but, I can get ten percent."

"Mr. Bergen I'm Mikal."

"Yes. Hello Mikal."

"I have a question or two depending on how you answer. Excuse my rude family but, there are eats and drinks if you like." Mikal waved an arm behind him at a table. Joe looked feeling ready to talk for now.

"Not now, I'm fine."

Mikal looked up for a moment and collected his thoughts, Joe thought. He also noticed the fine tailored silk suit. Priced in the thousands.

"Joe. Have you ever in your years at Bergen foods smoothed over the numbers? Bad year but needed a good profit and done so with a creative accounting." Mikal smiled gently. Joe knew right off this was a good question.

"Yes and no. Let me say right off the numbers you see are accurate. You bought a solid business. To answer the question.

About seven years ago I was expanding or had plans to and needed financing from the bank. Six months before I did make a few false invoices to show donations and damages so I could get a tax break and show more profit." Joe looked at Mikal who was still smiling.

"And you got the bank loan?"

"Yes. I was nervous but the loan did help to expand the warehouse and I never did that again." Joe was feeling a little nervous.

"If you didn't take that route to get the loan what would've happened." Mikal asked.

"I'd have a much smaller warehouse and wouldn't be sitting here today." Joe answered.

"True. You used personal ingenuity and it paid off. You took a sure risk and prospered. We're a private company with numerous divisions and need to move money from one division to another. Because we like to keep the tax bite low. How would you feel if we gave you fifty million to add to your books at XO and incorporate those funds to look like earned income?" Mikal finished smiling. Eva thought that was a good question.

"Like you said this is a private business and I understand the need to move money around for tax purposes. No problem with that. Increase income from the warehouses for a start. Fake invoices can be done in case of an audit. I'm here to work for CZ Corp. and help the profit level. I do love America but, sometimes corporate taxes can be a bit much." Joe hoped he didn't go overboard. He noticed Eva smile and nod. The guy next to her with the dark slicked back hair had a sneer on his face. The name was Uri, he remembered. Funny how one remembers the evil ones, Joe thought.

"I liked your answer Joe. I believe you would like a little intrigue in the workplace. Yes, I love America too and do find the tax bite a little much. I'm glad to hear that you have the right frame of mind."

Joe nodded as Mikal looked at the others. A lady Joe met but forgot her name put out her cigarette and leaned forward. Her breasts were touching the table top showing cleavage.

"Hi Joe, I'm Olga. I know you remember my name." Everybody snickered and laughed at little. Joe noticed Eva roll her eyes.

She spoke with a deep sexy voice that held Joe's attention. Dark pulled back hair and deep tan.

"I'm happy we found someone capable to run the XO. I remember meeting your wife and thinking she is a lucky lady." Joe nodded as Olga took her time.

"Have you ever done things with other women and remained loyal to her?" Olga had beautiful dark eyes like a wolf, Joe thought.

"I have been on business trips where a one-night stand took place and the next morning I still loved her and always will."

"Thank you for the candor. Now in that same relationship with your wife I expect you to show the same loyalty to CZ Corp. Think of them as the only two women in your life. If you cross one you get a divorce. If you cross the other, I will be your worst enemy." Olga had one of her few serious looks on her face. Eva was trying not to laugh.

"I understand, Olga."

"I'm sure you will do fine. We built this company and plan on being in business forever. I demand loyalty and respect for me and all who work here. That's why we are a successful business and only hire the best." Olga finished smiling at Joe. He didn't know how to take her though, he looked forward to talking with her more. She's a beautiful woman he'll never sleep with but, would be just as happy talking with.

"I understand and accept the rules of CZ Corp." Joe didn't know what else to say. Olga nodded giving him a sexy wink.

"Mr. Bergen I'm Uri."

"Hi Uri." Joe didn't like in this one.

"If you had an opportunity to kill your worst enemy and nobody but God and you knew about it. Would you, do it? I mean a bad enemy who wanted to do harm to you and your wife. He wants to take away your livelihood and good name."

Uri was leaning forward sneering. Joe really did not like this one of the family.

"Figuratively speaking I would. Being it's the scenario you just described." It hit Joe that Uri was asking if he would commit murder. Joe didn't like this guy. Uri smiled an evil look then said.

"How would you feel. Could you live the rest of your life normal after doing such an act?"

"I would think so. If only I knew. I mean I have never killed anyone but have seen some things. I went to school at Columbia here in the city and saw city life in the raw." Joe said wondering what Uri wanted to hear.

"What did you see?" Uri asked Joe who thought he sounded like evil.

Joe moved in his chair a bit. He glanced around and they were all looking at him.

"I saw drug deals and women selling their bodies. I watched a fight two against one and didn't help because I didn't feel it was my business." Joe stopped.

"I see. That's normal stuff but, did you ever see something bad and you never told anyone."

Joe did not like this one bit, but figured they wanted to know him well. He would go along as he thought about a day over fifteen years ago.....

The relief of getting out of the apartment felt good. A sunny warm day between the buildings where the sun slipped through. The street noise and activity of people going about their business helped him forget his studies. A detachment or distraction, he was not sure. It helped relax his mind.

A little quieter was what Joe wanted as he

crossed the busy avenue. He didn't know the street, but he knew the river to the west of where he was. Being in New York City for three years attending Columbia University for business he still didn't know the streets and avenues. Streets ran east to west and avenues ran north to south. He knew that much. Knowledge from his father to help him get around the city. Somehow that did not help him remember the names of streets or avenues he mused to himself. The noise of the busy avenue faded behind him.

With the sun blocked out by the buildings the air felt cooler along the street he walked. Like walking through a tunnel that leads to sunshine at the end. About halfway up the street a noise caught his attention. It sounded like a cat scream. He stopped at the entrance of an alleyway. It's where the noise came from, but he wasn't sure. Not caring to venture down the dark alley for a wounded animal he waited. He heard the noise again.

With his eyes adjusting to the darkened alley, he carefully started walking up. Then he heard the noise again. This time it sounded more like a puppy scream. He stopped and peered ahead at what may be a Cadillac parked up ahead.

He saw movement near the car as he approached. A man dressed in a suit hunched over forward. A young girl appeared from in front of the man. Staring wide-eyed at the man who had a grip on her arm. She plunged something into his lower torso with her other arm. She squealed and he grunted as she struggled to free herself from the man's grip. He raised his hand from the torso and tried a swinging punch at her, but she ducked he missed.

At this point Joe unfroze and started fast for the man. The girl looked over at Joe as he came running and she appeared surprised. He got closer and the look of the girl surprised him. Her clothes. Not typical clothing of the people living in this area. Her hair was red and braided with the braided end wrapped around the top of her head.

Joe's first reaction when reaching them, was a hard grab at the man's arm that was holding her. The handgrip let go of the girl.

The man kept his other arm holding his lower torso as he tried to take a swing punch at Joe. It missed and the energy used took the man to the ground.

With the man on the ground Joe looked back to see the girl standing behind him with a knife in her hand. Her eyes were wide and glaring. He slowly turned to face her.

"Why you do that." The girl said. Joe was quickly reassessing the last few moments. Which he didn't have time for.

The girl started moving towards him with the knife in the forward position. Like a cat swiping its claw in the air. She lounged forward with the knife.

Joe jumped back trying to think. He needed a moment to figure out what he walked into. She stopped relaxing a bit. Her eyes were darting from Joe to the man on the ground moaning.

"I was trying to help." Joe managed to say. Her eyes fired up again. Almond shaped and dark blue fire. Her age looked that of a young teen. Her clothing of a wealthy young teen. She didn't reply verbally but a look of acknowledgment settled on her face. The intense eyes looked over Joe's face as if searching for something.

Then she broke eye contact and darted over to the moaning man. Kicking him in the side that gave a thudding sound. He screamed out in pain. Then in a quick thrust she plunged the knife into his left side. Which caused him to emit another half of a scream before his body went still, no movement.

Joe stepped back, the horror sinking in. He didn't see this or wanted to see this. He didn't understand.

She held the knife in her right hand and rummaged through the man's suit jacket and pants pockets. Finding what she was looking for she put it in her tight pants pocket.

She was back on her feet looking at Joe. The look of a question on her face and a knife in her hand.

Joe started to realize he happened into a situation that he should not have, and this girl didn't need help or witnesses.

She stood straight up and cautiously walked toward him. Like a cat stalking prey. Her eyes fixed firmly on him as she took *careful steps toward him.*

Joe wishing, he didn't wake up today wondered what to do. Hit this young girl. He imagined the news reports. 'A man killed and a young girl almost molested.'

Approaching closer with knife in the forward position. Her eyes taking in everything. Joe was in her sights, watching every movement. He wondered if she could read his mind.

Stopping a few feet from him a puzzled look appeared on her face. Stepping from side to side eyeing him up and down then directly into his eyes. A calm serious look many year ahead of her age.

Joe wondered what happened to her to make her look like a natural born killer. She just isn't right, he thought. He tried thinking of anything that could calm her.

"Look, if he was trying to hurt you the police will understand. I can be your witness. I will help you."

Her body relaxed a little. She took the knife in her other hand and Joe thought he saw the beginnings of a slight smile as she continued staring at him.

"Um, I was just trying to help you. I have no money. Just trying to get through college. I have no credit cards; do you want to see."

Joe made a motion to take his wallet out. To his surprise she nodded yes. So, he pulled his wallet out from his back pocket. He started opening it but in a flash, it was taken from his hand. Taking a few steps back to examine its contents Joe noticed her hands. Thin with long polished nails, a clear gloss. This is weird he thought. She isn't a girl from poor upbringing judging from her clothes and looks. Yet she just killed a man.

She stuffed the wallet into her jacket pocket.

"I will find you if you are one of them, pray you are not." The girl said.

She motioned to the body lying on the ground behind her.

"I'm sure you will find I'm not one of them."

He also motioned to the body behind her.

With the momentary lapse, Joe tried to figure what accent she spoke with. Her voice was direct.

She started taking careful steps backwards as Joe glanced at the dead man then into the shadows where she had gone.

"Well, thank you." Joe said in the direction where she left.

"And I thank you." Joe heard from a distance. He froze for a moment considering the shadows.

He looked at the body a few feet away dressed in a nice suit. He didn't know much about suits, but it looked expensive even with the bloodstains. Maybe try to get the man's wallet and call the police but she took that. He might have family waiting for him somewhere.

He heard a car drive past on the street. He swung around but didn't see it pass by.

Looking at the alley entrance to the body on the ground, he knew he needed to leave, fast.

He knew nothing of what happened here. Sorry fella, I can do nothing that would help here.

Joe looked at his own clothing for any blood stains. He looked decent. He fixed his hair and started for the street.

The light got brighter as he approached. He would leave this behind and never tell a soul. Not his problem. Going to the police would make it his problem and that isn't going to happen. Some things a better left alone.

Chapter 51

Joe said, "I did see something once in a dark alley a girl and a man. I didn't get a good look at either. I guess it was a pimp and his women but, the guy was on the ground bleeding, so I guess she did it." Joe looked around and they were listening to every word. He hoped he didn't just lose a job.

Eva was ready to bust in laughter at the thought of Joe thinking she was a prostitute. She thought back to that day. They staked out an Italian mob guy because he had always had much money on him. They said he liked young girls and the police wanted to bust him. So, they felt it would be a welcome relief if he's dead.

Max and Tatyana had followed him to the private club. Eva remembers not feeling well that day. Drinking too much the night before didn't help being ready. Uri was the one that wanted to do the killing, but Eva remembered that she told him no. A girls needed to attract him. Olga, not, too polite back then and didn't get her hands dirty. Tatyana did not want to do the attracting part either because she and Max were the lookouts. Mikal and Uri were the ones that were going to go to the guys house and rob him blind while Eva was taking care of him.

She was going to attract him to the alley getting him out of the car. Max and Tatyana were to shoot him with silenced guns then leave them behind to make it look like a rival mob hit. The Fat Italian bookkeeper for the local mob always had cash on him. So, the first part went well. Eva attracted the guy into the alley and talked him out of the car. She remembers the guys eyes lightening up when she told him they would do it on top of the car.

The problem occurred when the guy parked the car. Wrong spot and he wouldn't move it because mud puddles would get it dirty. That left Max and Tatyana without a clear shot. Eva resorted to plan B. She knew they could not get him because they were to shoot him when he got out of the car. He got out of the car and approached her like a wolf licking his chops. She waited for the shot then took out her knife. She was not feeling well, and her timing was off. The fat guy was quicker than she knew because he grabbed her and the arm with the knife. She remembers trying not to scream but something came out of her mouth in the struggle. Then fatso looked back toward the street momentarily. That was when Eva took advantage and plunged the knife in the fat guy a few times.

Eva then remembers seeing this guy walking up the alley and assumed it was a friend of the fat guy. Ready to plunge the knife into him but held back realizing he was not a friend of the fat guy. He helped her. A moment when she thought she was going to die by the fat guy, he helped her.

When they all gathered later to count their winnings, her brother and sisters did not know what happened at first. Max and Tatyana had left the roof for the street because they couldn't get a shot. In that time frame when nobody was watching Joe Bergen saved Eva. To this day she knew that they would never leave her alone in a problem again.

Then Eva thought, Yes. I want to thank you for that, but I cannot, right now.

Then Uri spoke again.

"And you never reported or told anyone."

Joe instantly remembered his wallet. She had taken it.

"No. I didn't see a need of getting involved. First off. The guy did not look like a good person. The girl I guess wanted away from him. That's what I thought. If I reported to the Police and they found, her and she ended in jail I would need to be a witness." Joe stopped for a moment. "She wanted away from him. By me not reporting maybe, she did get away from him and that life. Maybe now she's a mother with a family or dead from drugs. I felt I did right. Besides, I didn't witness much."

Joe looked around the table and felt a little strange, he did not know why.

Eva looked at him and liked what he said. Yes, that girl did do good in the world, thank you, she thought.

Joe did not remember the face of the girl he just realized. Being so long ago it didn't matter anymore, he thought.

"Well, thank you Mr. Bergen. I never had anyone answer that question quite like that. I myself feel you did good by that girl." Uri finished looking at Eva.

"You never told anyone." Olga asked with her dark sexy eyes.

"No, I just hope I did good by her." Joe said.

"Your secret is good with us, Joe. I'm Max."

"Hi Max."

"Now, I'm not going to try and analyze or fuck with your head, like my brother and sisters like to." Max hesitated, and Joe was impressed by the size of this fellow. A forgettable friendly face but, the size of him would stop a train. He had combed back hair and a manner like he belonged here in this conference room on the top floor. A definite corporate Titan, Joe thought.

"I'm just telling you that I'm in charge of security. I am security for CZ Corp. and all her sister companies. I know everything everywhere. Nothing gets by me. If someone steals, I'll know, if someone copies files I'll know. I'm the last person in this company you want after you. And, I'm a nice guy." Max gave a big toothy smile to Joe not doubting what Max just told him.

"Okay. I understand." Joe said.

"That's my opening line to scare the shit out of people. Now, I will be in charge and arrange with Sevan every detail, so no one bothers you in your daily life with obstacles. We are a large corporation and never know when some sick person wants to kidnap or hurt one of our employees. I stay on top so you can have an enjoyable productive life here. I have spoken with Carol and she loves the alarm system, please use it. I have seen your file and I am impressed with what you have done with Bergen foods. I'm not one of the great thinkers in business like my brother and sisters. I just protect everything that's ours in my own style." Max finished and Joe did not doubt a word that he protected the kingdom.

"Thank you, Max., Yes, we used the alarm system last night. It works great."

Max nodded beaming with pride. The table was silent. Eva began.

"I guess it's my turn. I don't have any questions for you, Joe. What you have said here tells me what we can expect of you. I'm sure everybody feels the same way. Let's see if co-chairperson has any questions." Eva pressed a button and the wall behind her slide open. Mr. Bokanawski was smiling on the plasma screen.

"Hi everybody. Hi Mr. Bergen. I see they asked some good questions of you and I appreciate the honesty in your answers. CZ Corp's a private business and we keep that privacy when not at the workplace. We make a lot of money and pay for the best people to work for us. We're all family here and like to keep it like a club. There are many perks the company gives and I hope you and Carol take part of them. With that said, Welcome to CZ Corp., Mr. Bergen."

Joe nodded saying. "Thank you, Mr. Bokanawski."

"If that's all, I have a plane waiting."

"Yes, thank you dad." Eva said as the screen went blank and wall closed behind her. She then looked at Joe.

"Okay, we have already taken a vote before you came in. There's seven for you and one abstained." Joe nodded. Eva continued.

"The abstained one is Uri but, don't feel bad. He always does that. One day we hope to get a vote out of him." Everybody looked at Uri.

Joe said. "May be in time Uri will want to vote for me."

"I doubt that." Uri said. Both locked eyes but Joe gave in. He was in no position to play games with a family member.

Eva took over. "As CEO of CZ Corp. I close this meeting." The steno lady started packing her stuff. Everybody started getting up.

"Joe, come get a snack." Mikal said. Joe went over and looking at everything grabbed a plate. He took a seat back at the table. Mikal sat next to him.

"To bad Eva got you. I could have used you in Europe. I have a few businesses there and need a good person." Mikal said.

"Maybe in time. They are part of CZ." Joe asked.

"Yes, everything is when you tire of food service let me know. I have food place and technology and others."

"Sure. First let me get my feet wet here." Joe said.

"Sure. You're not going anywhere." Mikal said then lowering. "Don't let Uri's attitude bother you. He's always that way. You won't see him much any way."

Joe asked. "What does he do, I mean what does he run for the company?"

"South American operations." Mikal said.

"Okay. Produce I guess." Joe said.

"Yea, it's the only thing we could find for Brother Uri to do. He's always impatient." Mikal laughed a bit. Joe felt reassured he can talk to one of the family. He felt that was a good start.

Then Mikal said. "I'm in town for a few days. Maybe you and Carol want to dine out have nice evening together. My girlfriends with me from France. She's trying to learn English and a night out with English speakers would help."

"Sure. It'll be fun. I need to check with Carol and I'll get back to you." Joe said wondering how to act at dinner with a family member.

"Cool. I'm here until Saturday. Eva's secretary, she'll know how to contact me."

"Okay then." Joe said looking forward to dining with a family member. He felt like he was about to rise here. He continued eating and felt someone rub next to him. Looking over Olga with her dark sexy eyes was looking at him.

"Hi." Joe said.

"What're you two whispering about?" Olga asked. Joe mesmerized by her beauty.

"Nothing Olga." Mikal said forcefully, and Joe got the message. Wealthy families have strains within too.

"We're discussing what baseball team looks good in the coming season. I think Boston will do it again." Joe said taking a bite of food.

"Boring." Olga said.

"I think Boston will do good this year. Time to win another." Mikal said. Joe guessed right and felt a bond beginning.

Olga said. "Your new girlfriend coming back on the plane with us?" Looking past Joe at Mikal.

"She made me forget we were flying at thirty thousand feet." Mikal smiled back at Olga.

Joe decided it was time to leave. "I need to get to work. Olga, Mikal it's nice seeing you both again."

"Nice to see you again Joe." Mikal said and shook hands.

"Nice to see you again Joe, tell Carol I said hi. Oh, I'm going to be sending her a catalog for the fall fashions. Tell her to buy her heart out."

"I will." Joe shook hands gently with Olga.

Joe took the plate over to the table and walked to shake hands with the rest. He wanted to ask Eva about the orphanage but, this was the wrong time. He stepped over to Eva and Uri. Both stopped talking and looked at him.

"I want to thank you both. I'm going back to work."

"And I thank you, Joe." Eva said as they shook hands. Joe liked the softness of her hands and the bright blue eyes that enhanced her pale skin. Her red hair tied up and professional looking. He extended a hand to Uri and he just looked at Joe saying. "Have a nice day." Joe backed away to where Max and Tatyana were sitting and talking.

"I want to thank you both. I'm going back to work." Joe said.

Max stood towering over Joe a good foot. He extended a bear paw of a hand. Joe noticed that Max moved swiftly for a man his size.

"Welcome aboard Joe." Max said.

Joe extended a hand to Tatyana who grabbing firmly said. "Welcome, Joe, and we do have a gym fully stocked on the third floor. Do you play racket ball?"

"Never tried." He replied as Max weighed in. "She's looking for somebody she can beat."

"I usually practice at seven if you're in early, I'll look forward to it." Tatyana said. Joe had an instant liking for her. Dressed elegantly with no makeup like her sisters. A healthy glow showing exercise and a healthy persona. The sparkling blue eyes and long blond hair. A model for clean healthy living, Joe thought.

"Bye all." He said heading for the door. He exited hearing a few murmurs of work hard and see you soon.

Joe stepped out letting the door shut. He let out a breath looking at Vera who was instantly there smiling.

Chapter 52

The conference room bubbled with laughter.

"He's probably nervous as hell. Mikal did you invite him out." Max asked.

"Yea, I'll give him a call if he doesn't call me." Mikal said. His chiseled face showing a smile.

"And he thought that girl was a prostitute." Tatyana said. Eva did not feel bad with that, she knew it was coming. They all fell out laughing.

"He was just guessing." Eva said with little volume.

"All right. In case nobody was listening, he did say in a few words that he's with us." Olga said.

Uri said, "what's so special about that?"

"You look and see if you could find someone who'll follow along with us. Most turn into whistle-blowers. I suggest we take care of him like we do the others that work for us." Olga said, and everybody quieted down.

Uri said forcibly, "he's a citizen and not able to digest our business or life."

"Alright. He's an employee and a citizen and we take care of him like all the others. The future will tell if he could move forward in our world." Eva said.

"He did okay for the moment, Mikal." Olga said looking at him.

"I need to get him and the wife out and gage them." Mikal said.

"Well hurry. He's leaving for Minneapolis in a day." Eva said.

"Make sure we get the Vodka barrel operation." Tatyana said.

"Kid stuff." Mikal said.

"Hey, I can use that and his friend Mona. If she can disguise Vodka, maybe she can do other stuff." Tatyana said looking around.

"I like you sister. I can use another way to hide the transport of drugs." Uri said.

Eva forgot Mona. "Yea, we can use her." Eva said remembering that she and Anton were good friends.

Mikal said, "anyway, getting back to Bergen. Let's walk with him for now."

"Okay. Let's give it time. We brought him in to take over XO and he should do that. We need him to understand more about us and don't need him to increase sales and the like. We just want him to follow along." Tatyana said.

Max said, "yes. Mikal take him, and wife out get an idea. I'll have Sevan find the right moment and see if he goes for it. Then Eva it's up to you."

"Sounds good." Eva said thinking about Mona. Anton's chemist and cheap lay. She then had a thought, make it look like an accident.

~~~~~

A few miles away in his office Don Wellington was fielding a call from a wealthy customer. Most of his days are on the phone, he then sends orders to stock and bond traders to buy or sell for a customer. Then he reaps money in fees. With that call finished he closed that customer for this month and calculated his commission mentally.

Don's secretary buzzed. "Don. There's a police Detective here to see you."

"Show him in."

Don decided to keep the papers on his desk from the latest client call. The numbers in the account page on top should impress the low civil worker Don thought.

A quick knock door opened. A man in dark suit looking tired walked in.

"Come in." Don said as he played with a calculator for good effect.

The man walked over to the Dons' desk looking out the window behind Don then him. He then took out a billfold and showed his badge.

"Mr. Wellington. I'm detective Mensing."

Don stood from behind his desk shaking hands with the guy. Then motioned for him to sit. Don noticed the Detectives eyes looking at the papers on his desk and going into a thinking pattern for a moment.

"What can I do you for you Detective Mensing? Retirement funds maybe?" Don said with his best business smile.

Mensing said, "no. I'm here to ask you a few questions." His stoic face looked old enough to be retired. Taking out a notepad, he began. "Do you know a Brain Edwards?"

Don doing his best at caution, "yes. We attended college together and been casual friends since. What's happened?"

"He's dead. An apparent murder."

"Murder." Don repeated.

Detective Johnson remained stoic, "a gruesome one at that. We're still finding pieces of his body. We got an ID from the hands we found."

Don said with his best showing of remorse, "who would do that? He was just a freelance reporter."

"We don't know that yet. When was the last time you talked to him?"

"Sometime last week, I believe Wednesday. He'd been preparing a shoot for Sunday." Don leaned forward continuing. "Ed did investigative reporting and liked to show me before it went into print. I tried getting him to go mainstream at the Post or the Times."

Don relaxed then, for good effect.

Detective Mensing wrote something down asking. "Do you know what his latest interest was or who?

"I think a Russian mobster. He didn't tell me directly. He liked to keep it secret so, nobody would get the jump on him. That was his paranoid side, I guess. He explored the Italians and I knew he liked mob stories as a moneymaker." Don tried looking sad.

Detective Mensing wrote asking. "Do you know where he was going?"

"No. He liked showing me before he was ready to send to the paper. I never knew before."

"He was the reporter that exposed the man challenging your uncle in the latest election."

"Yes, shocking when I saw that one before he sent it in."

Detective Mensing stared at Don momentarily then asked. "Well, he did go to some dangerous areas to get his stories. The murder so far looks mob type and you had no idea where he was going. How do you know he was going after a Russian mobster? Did he tell you something?"

"Ah, he was joking about Russians. He called me a comrade the last time we talked. He learned the makeup of what he was going after. Like an actor getting ready for a script."

Detective Mensing wrote saying, "and he never said who or where."

"No. Have you contacted his family? I believe his mother lives in Connecticut."

"Yes, and she and him weren't close. She

did mention something about drug use. Did Brain do any drugs that you know of?"

"No, not for years. We did our thing in college but, not to my knowledge did he do anything lately." Don lied.

"Do you know any of his girlfriends?" Detective Mensing asked now looking bored.

"No, he had many casual ones. I don't remember him being with the same one twice."

Detective Mensing wrote then stopped reading his notes. Then began. "A possible Russian mob or member he was investigating. Not good, they are very dangerous people. We did not find anything in his apartment or computer. I assume he got the pictures and then he did the story. So, we have no way of knowing where he went Sunday. We ran his name at DMV and his car hasn't been found." Detective Mensing finished.

Don asked. "How will you find who murdered him? I mean it sounds hopeless from what you read off."

Inside Don was beyond mad, beyond angry. He knew who did it and knew he would get them.

Detective Mensing closed his notebook putting it in his jacket. Then saying. "Mr. Edwards did a story about seven or eight years ago. The story was about Police corruption. A uniformed officer was his story. The man was five years on the force. He had family members on the force and retired ones. He had two young children and a wife who loved him. Mr. Edwards followed and photographed him until a story developed. He ruined that officer's life. His wife divorced him, and he never saw his children again. They never saw him again. They sentenced him to ten years in prison for taking bribes. They found the guy that gave him the bribes. He was dead. The jury convicted just by the pictures alone." Detective Mensing stopped for a moment before continuing. "He committed suicide in prison or, so it was said. Prison can be a bad place for ex-police officers. The officer was also married, to my daughter."

Detective Mensing looked hard at Don standing up saying. "I don't think your friend's murderer will be found. Thank you for your time Mr. Wellington." Detective Mensing left the office.

Don looked at the door lost in anger. Don knew who murdered his friend and will take care of them.

Chapter 53

Joe and Vera back from lunch stepped off the elevator when Joe spotted Eva and the twins talking with a few of his employees. His mind went to full alert.

Walking toward Eva and the twins. Joe overheard her joking with a man. He felt lost, he didn't remember who that guy was, and this was his floor.

"Joe." Eva said.

"Eva." Joe said continuing. "We just had an early lunch."

"Good, hunger slows one." Eva gracefully smiled continuing. "I'm here to let you know you're to go to the mayors' party tonight."

Joe asked surprised, "mayor of New York."

"Yes, Joel Klein. He's a great guy. I select one division CEO and it's your turn. Can you make it?" Eva asked, her blue eyes sparkling.

"Sure. Me and Carol had nothing planned. I'm sure she'll be happy to go."

"It's a fund-raiser for dance classes the city sponsors for after school hours. It's fun.

Eat, drink and dance. You'll be representing CZ Corp. They'll be from banking and insurance and brokerage firms."

"Sounds great. Carol will be thrilled to meet the mayor."

"Good. I left an invitation on your desk. Now, if you don't have time use your company card to get a suit. It's black tie only." Eva looked at Vera saying. "Vera. Dress Joe up."

"Will do." Vera said.

Eva said, "call Carol and tell her a gown is needed. Tell her I'm sorry for the last minute."

"I'm sure she'll find something."

Eva looked to Vera who was already mentally noting it, "have one of my personal shoppers go to his house. It's a company expense."

Joe said, "okay. Let me call and tell her."

"Tell the Mayor may be next time I'll be there." Eva said giggling. Joe figuring a private joke.

Eva said, "thank you Joe."

"No problem Eva." Joe said remembering about adoption knowing not the right time again. He did have another problem though.

"Eva, if you have a moment. There's a Mr. Anton Slotkolov at the Minneapolis warehouse and I cannot get in touch with him. Vera searched finding no other numbers for him. I'm just feeling this out, but I think we may need a replacement there."

Eva thought for a moment. "Anton

Slotkolov is an old family friend. His father died while working for my father. So, we hired Anton Jr to take over as President in Minneapolis when we bought that place." Eva paused, and Joe wasn't liking this. "He has an arrangement with my father to take some profit money and invest in real estate to build homes. Dad's decision. Now, that leaves you under pressure."

Joe knew why the small profit being wired. "Well. You answered one question. His profit coming in has been lower than the rest."

Eva said, "however, he's not showing respect to you. You're his boss. So, replace him if you see fit. You can sell the real estate to our division here." Joe didn't feel good with that answer.

"Your father okayed this, and I don't want to get in a family problem. Maybe if he could talk to him."

Eva said softly with a smile. "Joe, I'm giving you permission to fire him if you want. In fact, I agree with you, it should be done. I'll square it with my dad. I'm the boss."

"Understand. Thank you for clearing that up."

"No problem. Do the right thing and don't worry." Eva finished giving Joe a sexy smile. "Gotta go, have to leave for Russia today, be back in a few days."

Joe impressed with the casual way she said it. "Sounds nice."

"Yes and no. I have business to attend to. I'll see you when I get back and I hope you have good news for me." Eva said waving and walking away with the twins.

Joe stared for a moment thinking about those last words. 'I hope you have good news for me'. He knew what that meant feeling relieved.

Looking at Vera they went to his office. He inside his and she disappeared into hers. Joe saw the envelope on his desk and opening it saw an invitation. Placing it down he sat behind his desk. Within minutes Vera was coming through the door with notepad.

"I have a group coming to fit you for a Tux. They'll be here in an hour and I have Eva's personal shopper going to your home for Carol's fitting." Vera said looking blankly at Joe.

Joe said still amazed how fast she did that, "okay, let me call Carol." Vera left. Joe picked the receiver watching Vera leave.

~~~~~

Eva was back in her office huddled with Ivan. She had him paged and he sat waiting for her to speak.

"Tell Sevan to keep a watch tonight at the mayor's party. See if Don shows, the Senators nephew. If he does, try to see what he does or says to Bergen. He likes showing up for these parties."

Ivan nodded Eva continued. "I don't want him touched, Don." Eva said rolling her eyes. Then continued. "Make sure all goes well. I don't want him near Bergen."

Ivan nodded again. Eva watched his nods and knew he'd take care of it. She knew she could make him disappear right now but, her Aunt Catherine has something planned for his uncle.

"I also want you to come up with an accident for Anton Jr in Minneapolis. A 100 percent accident. He must have a funeral, no disappearances."

Ivan nodding said. "I'll confer with my best people."

"Bergen's' going there in a day. I want it done fast even if Bergen is there."

Ivan said, "Friday accidents happen. People drink and lose all reason."

"He's building houses and if one happens to collapse." Eva said, and Ivan raised his eyebrows saying, "or burns in a fire."

"No, he must have a viewing and leave a good carcass."

Ivan thought for a moment then said with an arrogant smile. "Bridge collapse, he plunges in water and dies."

Eva smiled, "that's evil Ivan. What about innocent people."

"That'll make it believable."

Eva laughed saying, "do it."

Ivan nodded.

"Is my plane ready?"

"Yes."

"Get Steve that guy I had last week. He's always looking for fun. I need someone to keep me happy for the trip." Eva said with a big smile. Ivan rolling his eyes pulled out his mobile phone.

Chapter 54

The orchestra played classy standards with sounds of laughter and kinking glasses coming from the tables. Placed between an insurance executive and a banker was Joe and Carol. He liked the tux; the fit was perfect.

He found easy conversation with the insurance guy and the banker. They knew each other and gave Joe their cards. Joe found business cards of his own in his pocket and knew Vera put them there. He gave his own and wondered if they would ever call. Few of them heard of the startup food group but, a few winks told him it would be successful.

The mayor was at the next table talking with guests. Joel Klein was in his last term as mayor of New York City and probably trying to do favors for big business in town before he stepped down. Maybe hoping to be hired by a big business represented here tonight.

Joe looked over at Carol who was chatting away with the insurance CEO's wife. He heard new house, vacation in the Bahamas and private jet. She was fitting in better than Joe thought she would. They were currently talking about children and the insurance wife complained about their daughters first years in college and the money she spends. Carol's smile told Joe she was wishing she could have those problems to deal with.

Joe felt a hand on his shoulder, he turned seeing the mayor standing there. Joe stood up. "Hello, Mr. Mayor."

"Call me Joel."

"Okay, Joel. I'm Joe Bergen of XO Food group. A division of CZ Corp."

The mayor smiled, "Eva has stood me up again. Tell her time is running out."

"I will sir."

The mayor asked, "how is Mr. Bokanawski."

"Good. I just saw him this morning." Joe said thinking of the Board meeting earlier in the day. He took an envelope out to give to the mayor. "This for you sir."

Joel handed it to his assistant. "Thank you. I also want you to extend a thanks to Eva and her father for the vacation last summer."

"I will sir and I would like to introduce you to my wife, Carol." Carol stood.

"Hello Mr. Mayor."

"Joel."

"Yes sir."

The mayor said smiling, "I hope you dance Carol. It's required for ladies to dance with me tonight."

"I had lessons in my teens."

"I'll be looking forward to a dance with you then."

Carol said smiling, "I'm honored, sir."

The mayor gave Carol a lite kiss on the cheek and moved on to the insurance man. Joe and Carol sat. She bent over whispering to Joe, "thank you for tonight."

"Thank you for coming at the last minute. How's the gown?"

"Heaven." Carol said leaning closer and smiling. "You want to show me off."

"Sure. I met the mayor and my job's done."

Carol got up and Joe followed her to the dance floor. Couples of all ages were dancing as they saw fit to just enjoy. The music a slower classy tune got Joe right into the groove with Carol, they were dancing cheek to cheek. Joe saw an elderly couple and it appeared they were standing still. Carol also saw, "that'll be us someday."

"Yes."

Joe felt a tap on his shoulder.

"I always dance with the new ladies first." The Mayor said.

"Be my guest," Joe said. The mayor whistled a hand motion. The tempo of the music increased. He took Carol in his arms like a gentleman and they were off dancing.

Joe watched thinking, not bad. The mayor he assumed to be fifties or early sixties with the energy of a young man. Joe backed farther away standing next to the mayor's assistant.

"Quite a dancer, the mayor." Joe said.

"Yes, he and his ex-wife won a few dance competitions in their younger days."

"Cool." Joe said impressed.

"He likes dancing with the younger ladies to relive those days, I imagine."

"Carol loves dancing. She's trained in ballet and ballroom as a young girl."

The assistant said, "pray she doesn't tell the mayor that. He'll invite her to every dance competition in town."

"Well, if she does. He'll have a new friend."

The assistant said, "as mayor he has a new friend every day. The man does not slow down."

"Problems." Joe said. The assistant took on a serious look, saying. "The mayor has known the Bokanawski family forever and if you work for them then your wife is okay to attend dance competitions with the mayor. It'll save time for us who watch out for him." A pause. "People every day are trying to get close to the mayor for good and bad reasons. It's overwhelming at times."

"I understand." Joe said and for the first time understood the circle of people that look out for the mayor. He also knew the mayor's political party he never liked. Right now, though it's meaningless. It's about people.

The band finished, a few couples clapped

in the mayors' direction. They came walking from the dance floor, talking fast and laughing.

The mayor said, "now she can dance."

"I was just following your lead trying to compliment your steps." Carol said. The mayor gave her a serious look saying. "What are your styles?"

Carol said elegantly. "I'm trained in ballet, modern and ballroom dance. That was years ago."

"Dancing is a free art form that expresses emotions. It's a passion of mine. Now, once a month I visit school dance classes when my schedule allows. I love watching the young ones. I have an entourage that goes with me. They are people like you that encourage and support. We would be happy if you could join us; the young ones would learn so much."

Carol looking surprised said. "I'd be happy to." Joe jumped in. "Mr. mayor, I can help provide transport compliments of XO Food Group."

"That would be nice but, I already have transport in place provided. God knows. Every company wants their name on the list. Thank you though Mr. Bergen." The mayor then said to his assistant. "Get her number and address."

"Joe, Carol. Thanks for coming. Carol, I look forward to having you with us."

After shaking hands Joel left to meet other guests. Joe felt the glow of something special go with him. He enjoyed the center of the world for a little time.

Joe and Carol welcomed a few congratulations from the Insurance and Banker couple. The wives bent forward chatting with Carol as the husbands sipped their drinks. Joe came back to earth needing to use the rest room.

He was finishing washing his hands when a young executive type came into the rest room. The man walked to the sink next to Joe just looking in the mirror.

Joe noticed the man standing there and did not bother looking. Young executives have big egos he knew. Taking a few towels and drying his hands he glanced at the young man.

The young man spoke first. "Your wife is a good dancer."

"She does it as a hobby. Better than drinking I always thought." Joe said.

"Very positive." The man extended a hand to Joe saying. "I'm John Train from Mutual Life."

"Joe Bergen. XO Food group." They shook hands as Joe wondered what's with all the insurance people.

"XO Food. Never heard of it. A new startup." Don asked.

"A division of CZ Corp." Joe said trying not to show off.

"Ah, yes. The mysteries' CZ Corp. I've tried selling insurance there and always get the closed door."

"Don't know. I'm new there."

"I'm going to keep trying. I met the lovely Eva Bokanawski once. Quite a babe, uh." Don said smiling.

Joe immediately felt uneasy; A young executive with too much to drink.

"I suggest you keep trying. Ms Bokanawski likes a good deal." Joe said putting his hand towels in the trash can.

"I'll do that." Don said.

"Nice meeting you Mr. Train." Joe said leaving the rest room.

Don watched Joe leave thinking, we're going to be good friends Mr. Joe Bergen.

He checked his look in the mirror and left the rest room. Walking back out into the dining area he noticed an average height but solid-looking guy watching him. Don stopped for a moment to look at the guy. He kept staring at Don not changing the arrogant expression on his face. Don gave in and headed back to his table. One of the Russians, he thought.

Joe back at the table didn't give the man in the rest room another thought. Carol was chatting with the ladies about her years of dance. The husbands huddled, and Joe got up to go join them.

~~~~~

Somewhere over the Atlantic Eva laid in bed. Her nude body half covered, and her friend Steve sleeping. She had a movie on the big screen. A knock on the door and Ivan entered. She did not bother covering herself.

"Bergen and Don; rest room together; party. Sevan does not know if they talked." Ivan kept eye contact not looking at her body.

"Shit. What's the guy's problem? Nothing we can do right now. Ask Sevan to keep Bergen away from Don."

Ivan left the room.

Chapter 55

The next morning in his office Joe fielded a few calls. The Insurance CEO tried selling his insurance products and Joe asked him to send over documents and he'd look. He still got weekend invitation to his mansion in Connecticut.

Joe was reviewing the last month's numbers again for anything he missed when Vera came in quietly standing by his desk.

"Yes Vera."

"I'm to remind you about dinner with Mikal." Joe looked up realizing he forgot.

"Yes. Make it for tonight at whatever time is good for Mikal and let him choose the restaurant."

"Good." Vera said smiling.

"Also, I need you to upload these business cards." Joe removed a bunch from his jacket. "List the categories. I may use them in the future."

Vera nodded holding the cards, "anything else."

"No."

Vera left as Joe watched smiling slightly. His phone buzzed. "Joe, Mr. Heller on one."

"Thank you."

Joe lifted the receiver. "What's up?"

"Joe. Um, Paul's sister is here and has filed a missing person last night."

"I see. No sign of him or Wendy."

"No, she entered their house with police and there's no sign of foul play or the like." Thom said Joe noting a sadness in his voice.

"Cars missing?"

"Yes, Wendy's'. The police were here yesterday afternoon and collected some information."

"I see, did they have or say anything."

"No, right now, maybe they took off somewhere. Police are taking it casually. They said they'd like to speak to you. It was too late yesterday and I'm telling you now."

"Okay, I'll stop by on my way home today." Joe said feeling a ping in his stomach.

"You want to see a Detective Burns." Joe wrote that down.

"Right."

"They're running the plates from Wendy's SUV and putting out a bulletin. They don't suspect anything foul yet. His sister came here yesterday after the police leaving me a little sad. She's all twisted up nervous. I pray Paul and Wendy didn't do this on purpose or I'll kick his ass." Joe noted the sadness disappear from Thom's voice.

"I agree. You don't put people through

this. On a good note though, I met Mayor Klein last night at a fund-raiser."

"Klein, cool. He did the city good. Fitting in already with city life."

"That's just the half of it. I'm having dinner with one family member tonight. I can't say it's been dull."

"Remember us little people here in New Jersey."

"You know I will." Joe said with a smile.

"Tell me more about Klein." Thom asked.

"He has a passion for dancing. The fund-raiser was for after school dance classes in the public schools."

"That's good stuff. That's why Klein did good for the city. I feel he should go for President." Thom said proudly.

"I'll pass that onto him if we meet again."

"I got to go. An appointment with the family that runs that chain of European restaurants here and upstate New York."

"Wait a minute. How did you get them? I've tried for five years."

"I got a call yesterday and I'm ready with a smile and brochures."

"I hear you've been holding out on me. I'm going to cut your budget in half."

"I'll need to get more business then, bye."

"Later."

Joe hung the phone leaning back in his chair. He felt mad and confused. The week Joe is gone they get a good account he was trying to get for years. He then thought for a moment that Thom knew the owners and quickly dismissed that thought. That would be Paul, he knew. He wished that guy would show up and end this drama.

Joe punched the button for Vera immediately hearing her voice. "Yes."

"Vera, come here I have something I need you to do."

"I'm on the way." Came her soft voice. Moments later Vera came with her notepad.

"I want you to call the police department in Hills Point and ask for a detective Burns. An employee from Bergen foods is missing and he wants to talk to me. See if he can be there at three p.m. today. If not tell him I'm leaving for a business trip and will contact him when I get back."

"Okay and your reservations made for eight tonight at the French Life. Mikal will meet you there. I suggest you be on time or earlier." Vera said as Joe nodded thinking no problem. Vera turned and left.

Joe dialed his house. Carol answered on the first ring. "Hello."

"Good news again. Dinner tonight in the city."

"Okay, why."

"Mikal Bokanawski. We talked yesterday; he wanted to do dinner. He's here for a few days. His girlfriend speaks spotty English and wants to learn more of it. I guess because I'm new and he wants to get to know me better also." Joe said hoping Carol wouldn't decline. He knew she would not but, a good frame of mind always helps.

"Sure, no problem. I need something new to wear." Carol slowly said.

"My thoughts exactly." Joe smiled into the phone.

"Okay. Yes, I think I remember Mikal. Blond hair not good a dancer. Where's his girlfriend from?"

"France, I think. Well, his sister Olga didn't care for her. Point is he's a family member and we are not to judge his girlfriends."

"Ah, yes, I see." Carol laughed.

"He's a boss."

"Joe, no problem. I guess we can relax with him. That's cool."

"Exactly."

"What time."

"Eight at the French Life and Sevan will take us."

"Good."

"Also, Thom called. Paul's sister is at his house and she filed missing report. I need to stop to talk to the police on my way home." Joe said noting a sour noise from Carol.

"I hope this is real. I don't know. I'm going. I need to go shopping."

"Okay. Bye."

"Bye."

Joe relaxed taking note of Carol brushing off the news on Paul. He didn't blame her. It's a drag. Next, he'd tell Thom to start interviewing for a new HR person.

Looking at the clock on his desk and ten a.m... He was ready for a break when the phone buzzed.

"Yes."

"Joe, you have five minutes. MS Catherine Bokanawski is here." Vera said.

Joe's mind went blank for a moment.

"Bring me up to speed fast. Who's she? I know but I don't."

"Catherine is boss overall. She rarely comes here from Russia."

"Okay she's going to have a meeting?"

"No, she's coming to see you in five minutes."

"Okay."

Joe went to his private bath to check his look. Back into his office he felt nervous. Aunt Catherine he remembered in the library at the father's house, the painting. She looked like Eva. Joe remembered the picture now. He walked out of his office and stood by Alexandra's desk. She was busy typing something when Vera showed up.

"Five minutes." Joe said.

"Yes, one of her people alerted me."

"Okay."

Joe stepped from his office area looking out at the other offices. Vera followed as they slowly turned a corner. The elevator doors opened and out stepped five people. Two women and three men. Joe picked out who Catherine was. Her hair was red and next to her was an assistant who had black hair and younger.

He went forward to meet her with Vera following. They got closer as Catherine went to a cubicle area and started talking with employees. They all seemed happy to see her and Joe held back to let this happen. She was attractive looking a lot like Eva but, older. The slender figure the red hair and that smile.

After a few minutes Joe approached. Catherine looked directly at him and he felt intimidated. The eyes were like Eva's, Joe thought as he extended his hand.

"Hello I'm Joe Bergen."

Catherine stared pleasantly smiling. "I'm Catherine," holding Joe's hand for a moment.

"My assistant..."

"Vera." Catherine said before Joe could finish. "How you doing girl."

"Oh, you know. Getting along and getting." Vera said with a blush.

"Joe treating you well." Catherine asked.

"Yes, a great boss."

"Good." Catherine said looking at Joe who felt weak.

"Mr. Joe Bergen. How do you like my little company?"

"It's my first week but I love it."

Catherine smiled saying. "Good. I want all my people to be happy."

Joe looked at her gorgeous assistant and the three men. He figured two were bodyguards and one he could not figure out.

"Come to my office." Joe said.

"Yes, first I have others to see."

Strolling slowly Catherine stopped at

every office and every cube. It surprised Joe that they all knew her. Everyone talked to her like old friends, she knew wives and children's names.

A while later Catherine and entourage entered Joe's office.

"A bit small but I'll get you a bigger one in time." Catherine said.

"It's fine, Miss Bokanawski."

Smiling nicely. "Call me Catherine. Miss Bokanawski makes me sound old."

"Sure. Why don't we sit, would you like anything to drink or eat?" Joe said.

"No thank you. I came to see you and get to know you."

Catherine sat on the couch and Joe sat a little distance away. He liked her. She's a classy lady.

Catherine looked at her people. "I want to speak to Joe alone."

Three left and one remained. Catherine looking at the one-man Joe could not figure out said. "Dimitri. Please."

Dimitri nodded and eyed Joe as he left the office.

Catherine looked to Joe. "You did a good job with your own company. I saw the numbers and my niece Eva speaks highly of you."

"Did my best to make a profit." Joe said and noting Eva.

"Yes, you did, and I expect the same good management here. Eva you will listen to. She's the boss here. Do what she asks, and you'll have no problems. However, I'm going one step further here. My brother is assistant Chair and I'm the Chair overall. You're under my wing. That means if you do not do as described by Eva, I will fire you. That also means if you have a problem you can call me directly."

"Understood." Joe said wondering where this was going.

"My brother Nicolas takes little interest in the business these days. He's made bad decisions sometimes, so you call me if he makes what you feel is a bad call. No harm will come to you. He spends his days in leisure. He doesn't care." Catherine said like a queen.

Minneapolis, Joe thought

"I don't want to step on toes, but I'll call if I know a different decision can achieve something better." Joe said hoping it made sense.

"Good, that's done. Eva someday will control this empire, so, I suggest you never leave her side or disagree with her. Maybe try to make her see how a better decision will work. Stay close to her and you will rise with her."

"Okay."

Catherine laughed saying. "She's on her way to Russia to meet me and I'm here. I didn't tell her I was coming here. She's going to be a little mad, but I did it for a reason. She'll handle it well and do what needs to be done there."

"She seems like a well-balanced person." Joe said.

Catherine smiled. "Yes, she'll be fine. Now, you're going to Minneapolis to see little Anton."

"I tried calling and can't get through to him. His profit numbers are low but, I found out he had approval to invest in real estate. I just need to go there to see what's going on." Joe said hoping for the best.

"Like I said, my brother and his decisions sometimes. Go there and see."

"Yes, and Eva had told me to fire him if I feel the need to."

Catherine smiled. "Do what she wants. She's the future."

"Yes." Joe felt good going there now.

"Enough business. I hear you want to adopt. I have some lovely angels in my orphanage."

"Me and Carol because of medical reasons can't."

"I can make it happen in a week. Let's say, two months from now. I'll contact you."

"Sounds good."

"You need children. They are a joy. I have a wonderful family in my nieces and nephews. They're the spice of life." Catherine said smiling to Joe.

"I look forward to it."

"Good. Dinner's at my place tonight. You and Carol. Sevan will know where to bring you. It starts at six. I'll have strange guests and interesting people to talk to there."

"I'll be happy to go. I did have a dinner engagement with Mikal."

Catherine laughed a bit. "Don't worry about Micky, he'll be there."

Catherine stood up and Joe followed. "I need to carry on my journey here. I love meeting the new ones and seeing the old friends. See you tonight Joe."

"Look forward to it."

Joe opened the door for Catherine. They stepped out as she turned putting a hand to his face. She said quietly to Joe. "You could be Czar someday."

Catherine then walked away with her entourage. Joe watching her go felt good. Vera stepped next to him and Joe said. "She's nice."

"She's the Czarina." Vera said with quiet respect.

Chapter 56

The flying palace landed a few hours before at the main commercial airport in Moscow. Eva had Ivan got Steve a return trip to America on a commercial flight. She would have had one of her planes fly him but, he did not satisfy her on the flight. The Kremlin in full view as Eva looked out at it in the distance from her high-rise home. The day was late, so she was going to do some shopping tomorrow. She liked the new outfits in the stores for spring. Eva liked to buy her personal cloths on her own at the store.

The shopping would help put her back in a good frame of mind after seeing Aunt Catherine. She had to report to her tonight that no evidence was found on the Red mob. Eva knew when she told her news that was negative it upset her. Aunt Catherine had good instincts and expected her to follow through.

Eva shook her head no slightly and thought. There was no evidence. The mobs wouldn't approve it. They needed their approval, or it risked hundreds of millions in drug money.

Ivan entered the room and stood near. She looked over at him. "What's new?"

Ivan waited a beat. "The Czarina's not here."

Eva looked at him with wide eyes. "What!"

"She left two days ago and is in New York."

Eva turned walking up to Ivan. "What!"

"She left message saying that she knows of no evidence."

"Where is she in New York?"

"The office. She's having Joe Bergen and wife for dinner."

Eva glared at Ivan punching him in the stomach. He did not move or make a sound. She hit him repeatedly until he backed up and defended himself. Eva had a knife in her hand. Ivan shook his head no. She thrust the knife forward and Ivan dodged it. He grabbed her arm on the second try and held it. She hit him repeatedly with her free hand, but it was no use. Eva screamed "Fuck!"

Ivan held her arm until she dropped the knife and she fell to the floor crying. "Why does she do this? She played a joke on me. I don't like when she does this. I try to do what she wants." Eva sobbed.

After a few minutes Ivan helped her from the floor. He picked up her knife, closed the blade and handed it to her. Eva wiped her face and looked up at Ivan. "I'm sorry."

"No problem." Ivan replied.

"You're getting better." Eva said with tears in her eyes and a smile on her face.

"I learn." Ivan said smiling that made Eva laugh. She let out a breath and regained herself.

"Would you like to see Andre?" Ivan asked.

Eva looked at him with an evil smile. "Yea, somebody must pay for this."

Ivan nodded.

"I need to freshen up first." Eva said and left the room. Ivan smiled and took out his phone.

Chapter 57

Joe was sitting in the small waiting area of the local police station. He'd never been inside this old looking building before for all the years he lived and worked in the town. As he sat there, he saw officers moving about and the static of the call radios. Very active for a small-town, Joe thought.

Uniformed officers went in and out of Detective Burns office. Joe was starting to get impatient.

The door opened and a gruff looking old guy looking years beyond retirement filled the doorway. He waved Joe in.

Inside Joe took a seat on a hard-wooden chair. The big guy sat behind his desk looking directly at Joe the way police do. The serious casual look that masks the information seeking brain.

"I'm Detective Burns. You can call me Henry."

Joe nodded. "I'm Joe Bergen and you can call me Joe."

Detective Burns nodded then started.

"Paul Letter's sister Cathy filed a missing person's report on her brother and his wife. She reported his employment is at Bergen Foods which you have recently sold. I have spoken with Thom Heller who is in charge there now and he recommends I talk to you. Now, what can you tell me about him and his job role there."

Detective Burns flipped over a paper and read for a moment. Joe began.

"I recently sold the company to an outfit called XO Food Group. The parent company asked me to take over that division. I'm now CEO of that division."

Detective Burns started taking notes. Joe continued.

"And with my new job I needed to promote a new president at Bergen foods. I choose my VP of finance who is a capable guy. Thom Heller."

Detective Burns finished writing.

"Paul Letters reaction to this?"

"I don't know, it was moving fast. I appointed Thom running it by the board of directors through an email to get a fast approval. I didn't say anything to Paul and left that to Thom. I didn't think Paul would have wanted that position. As VP of Human Resources that's not a position or did he have the qualifications for President of a warehouse. Sales, operations, buying and budgeting for everything can be complicated. Paul never showed that he had an oversight of the business. He also never showed interest in such at the company. So, I didn't feel the decision would bother him."

"He never showed interest in those sides of the business." Detective Burns asked.

"No. He was excellent with hiring and keeping employees. The warehouse is union and he did a great job keeping that smooth with the men there. He strongly influenced the union contracts with getting a fair deal for both sides. Never knew him to be flustered, an easygoing personality."

"He never showed an interest in the business side. I mean the sales and profit numbers."

"We had budget meetings and Paul was there when we went over numbers but, he didn't show a big interest. He did have the medical benefit's coverage for everybody to deal with. And I must say he did keep his budget inline, never over."

"What did he get when his budget was inline."

"A bonus."

Detective Burns jotted some notes and then looked back at Joe. "Okay he's well trusted. Did he have access to books, computers that have money and able to write checks?"

Joe started to wonder where this was going and answered. "Yes. He filled when Thom needed help or was between employees in Finance. He did know the passwords for the computers in that department. We're a small company and trusted each other in the executive area."

"He had access to money of the company." Detective Burns said, and Joe's interest got the best of him.

"Yes, we trusted him. He did payables sometimes and never had a problem."

"Did Paul or his wife have a drinking, drug or gambling problem that you know of?"

"No." Joe said and thinking for a moment answering again. "No."

Detective Burns closed his notebook and rubbed his eyes. He then looked at Joe for a moment then opened a desk drawer and put a folder on his desk. Written in bold letters on the folder was money. He opened the folder and handed Joe the first paper from it.

Joe took it and saw the letterhead from his company. He started reading and discovered it was a plan to steal money. It was Paul's handwriting, Joe knew his handwriting from the millions of notes they left each other in the office.

How to steal small amounts of money from the company and covering each transaction. It went as far to fire employees for some fictitious reason if they discover it.

Paul took small sums from receivable accounts giving it to himself as a bonus. Accounts skimmed entered as discount adjustment to customers.

Joe immediately wondered if Thom was part of this. He looked up to see Detective Burns watching him closely. Joe spoke without thinking.

"Did he do this?"

Detective Burns shrugged and handed the whole folder to Joe. He quickly started flipping through the papers. Organized and started two years ago. Joe remembers a few months ago when Paul suggested he change insurance carriers. He made money there. He flipped and read fast and felt the life come out of him. Joe looked back at Detective Burns who said. "We'll need it back. If you do file suit that will change the missing persons to an arrest warrant." Detective Burns said blandly.

Joe couldn't speak at first. He didn't know what to say but spoke anyway.

"I need to review this more and see what happened. I need to cross-reference with the office files." Joe closed the folder feeling numb. "How'd you get this?"

"Cathy Letter let us in the house and free to search. She let us take those. As former owner and still boss of that facility, it's for you to decide if a crime was committed. We cannot file charges unless you find he has done what's stated there. So, the status is still missing persons."

"I need to check and see that his has occurred." Joe said knowing deep down that it may be true, and he didn't want to think about what he would feel.

"Well, here's my card and call me if you want to pursue that or hear from Paul and Wendy."

Joe took Detective Burns card and

pocketed it. He held the folder tight in his arm. He left the police building and saw Sevan get out as he approached the limo. Joe climbed in. Sevan got in turning to look at him.

"Get me to Bergen Foods, fast." Joe held the folder in his arm refusing to let go of it.

Chapter 58

Joe was out of the limo heading to the front doors of his old business. A few people mingling nearby in the smoke area said hi and Joe stopped calmly to say hello to them. No point throwing problems on others if they're not involved. The smokers are innocent he mused.

Inside the lobby Joe stopped to say hello again to a few and calmly went up the stairs to the executive suite. Down the hallway to the old corner office Joe stopped in the doorway. Seeming like long ago but, only a few days.

Thom saw Joe and waved him in to take a seat. Joe looked direct at Thom and maybe a little too seriously for Thom's facial expression changed and he began trying to end the phone conversation. The phone call ended.

"To what do I owe this honor." Thom said graciously.

"I need some answers." Joe said a little

too sternly. Then said. "Close the door."

Thom was up closing the door. Then taking a seat next to Joe eyeing the folder in his lap.

Joe talked fast relaying the same Detective Burns had told him. Then handed the folder to Thom.

Thom read the first page and looked up at Joe with the most serious look he ever saw the man have. He read more pages reddening with each page.

Joe knew this man longer than Paul and did not think him involved but, he wanted to see what he would say or do. He needed a concrete reaction from Thom, this was a moment that would define his future. Joe watched as Thom read intently. On the numbers page Joe could see his mind was in overtime. Stopping and looking up at Joe and reading something on his face, Thom closed and placed the folder on the desk.

"Hey, wait a minute here. Follow me." Thom lead the way to his old office. A few people chatting from the adjoining office. Being late afternoon Joe knew it was the slow time for the finance department.

"Hi everybody we need this office for a few minutes." Thom said nicely as ever. An old-time employee that was the mother hen of the office looked at Thom and Joe saying. "Aren't you fellows married?"

Thom looked at Joe who replied. "Marge. Thom will give you a bonus if you don't tell anybody." That caused laughter from the small group. They all filed out Thom closed the door.

Immediately Thom down to business. Sitting behind a computer terminal he opened the folder and taking out a spreadsheet that showed numbers Thom said calmly.

"Let's, go back six months ago." He fingers typed away as a spreadsheet appeared. Thom scanned down a row of numbers. His finger stopped at a number as he looked back at the spreadsheet on the desk mumbling. "What the fuck."

Joe observing this never realized how fast this guy was. He also never heard such language from the guy. He saw the printer in the corner working as Thom was going through another screen for the payables. He mumbled the same word again as the printer continued to work.

Thom collected the printouts spreading them out on the desk. He took a pen and circled numbers from one spreadsheet to another. Joe knew what he was looking at. The numbers matched up. They were of one thought when Thom blurted, "what the fuck is the guy's problem."

"I don't know." Joe said slowly.
Both stood looking down at the printed spreadsheets. Thom slowly looked at Joe saying. "If you think I had knowledge of this I'll step down and leave the company."

Joe slowly shook his head no. Thom continued. "He had access to these systems and it's possible he did it. And, I guess that may explain the disappearance."

Joe slowly shook his head yes.

"I recommend that we get an outside audit done for an exact number."

Joe slowly shook his head yes and said. "It's your company now."

Thom nodded saying. "Judging the dates, he went in after I closed out each month. Smart. He knew there was no reason to go back and look at past months. We keep good records and he knew I wouldn't look back at previous months. Amounts small enough not to raise eyebrows. Looking at the last six months, he took about thirty thousand."

Joe continued staring at the computer printouts thinking about the nice house Paul had. He cleared his throat, "Thom, you're in charge of this warehouse. Fix the numbers quietly and I'll cover it at my end. I know you had no knowledge of this. If you did, you wouldn't still be driving that old BMW. Also, no outside audit. It'll create rumors and questions. Best to keep it buried until Paul shows up."

Joe continued. "In fact, don't fix anything, leave the numbers as they are in case, he does show up." Joe stopped stepping closer to Thom whispering.

"I would kill that fucker if he walked through that door right now."

"Not if I got him first." Thom whispered back with hatred.

"Destroy that printout and wait and see

what the future brings." Joe said walking to the far side of the office staring at a picture. Remembering when bought years ago. Showing a man on boat during a violent storm. Joe looked at it and knew he must remain calm.

Thom walked over to Joe saying. "I guess piss tests don't reveal everything these days."

"No. I should have suspected his meticulous personality. He was working double time and I took that to be intelligence." Joe stopped looking at Thom. "Do me a favor. He was collecting stuff on CZ Corp. Stay late and destroy everything you can find in his desk and computer. And, advertise for a new HR person. He's officially gone. Anyone asks he abandoned his job."

"Will do."

Joe liked Thom and realized it then. He knew he made a good decision with him.

"Also change locks and passwords." Joe said.

"I was already going to do that when you leave." Thom replied.

Joe looked at his watch. "Dinner tonight with the Chairperson of the business. We must never let this story be told"

"Nope. You go have a great time at dinner and don't worry about it." Thom said slowly.

Joe walked over to the door looking back at Thom who was already shredding the printouts. Joe nodded to him and left the office.

Passing a few employees in the hallway he put on a smile saying hello. Even though his stomach dropped out and he felt shallow, he preserved his pleasant manner.

Down stairs he smiled with the staff shaking hands saying some nice words. For some odd reason he thought about the warehouse in Minneapolis remembering what Eva had told him. 'I want to hear some good news'. Joe knew right now he's not going to go through this again. He wasn't going to cover up or tolerate this again.

Chapter 59

The old building was in disrepair, in a complex of similar looking buildings. The planned living experiment that was part of the old Soviet government. Eva looked around the twentieth-floor room they were in. It did have great view of the city.

Nearby buildings were still lived in by mostly elderly residents that probably did not have the means to move. They were a product of a government system that taught them to depend on the government. Now they waited silently for something.

A distant lone figure was walking and stumbling along. It clearly was a drunk person from a neighboring building. The sight of that person gave Eva a chill. She hoped never to be alone and in disrepair like these buildings that they forgot. The government here hoped the buildings would just disappear like the people that live in them.

Another sound of fist hitting face and groaning came from behind Eva. She turned to see Andre' half crying and bloody. Ivan watched the beating of the man with his people doing it. The two men were good, they alternated so at any onetime Andre was getting a beating.

Eva walked over near Andre, he was a bloody mess. Trying to breathe through his nose that was maybe broken. This was a technique Ivan's men liked. Gag beat until they die of lacking breath. Rather crude, Eva thought.

Eva watched this in disgust, she was in disgust because she gave the man money and a place to live and he took it for granted. He didn't get information that Eva wanted. She knew now there wasn't information to get. It made her mad that it came from the Czarina.

The two men stopped the beating as Eva moved closer to Andre.

"So, Andre, you don't know anything more about the Red mob. You tell me their selling bombs and have military connections to get them. That was good and all you gave me. I wanted to know about a nuke they were trying to buy, and I found from other people that it ain't so. You did not tell me this. I was paying you and you deceived me."

Andre's eyes went wide shaking his head no. Eva expected it, the man was gifted to talk away any situation. The gag helped her from listening to him for the moment.

One man hit him in the side of the head, he went blank for a moment then refocused on Eva.

"The Czarina is unhappy with you. She expected you to grow as a family member and you went backwards. She is very unhappy."

Andre shook his head slowly looking down at the floor. He looked back up pleading shaking his head slowly. Eva motioned for someone to take the gag out. She at least wanted the man to have a last say before he faces his sentence. They pulled the gag. Andre worked his mouth saying.

"Ms. Eva, I did not hurt the Czarina. I try to get her more information but they quiet down and nobody speaks. They are going to buy a nuke bomb from the military. The Red mob keep quiet and I can get nothing more. I tried."

"Yes Andre, they are keeping quiet and you have no way of getting information. I hired you to get information because you are a high-ranking member with them. But they keep quiet now."

"No, no. I'm going to meet Ureinchencko tomorrow and discuss business with him. He trusts me, and I know he will tell me." Andre said with blood coming out of his mouth. Sad, Eva thought. He won't live to get that information.

"Then I wait, and you tell me what I already know and have a party, with my money."

Andre shook his head no saying. "I use your money to pay for my daughter in the university. I use my money to party."

Eva knew this man could talk shit and she almost wanted to believe him.

"All right Andre. I don't have the time to listen to you lie to me."

"I no lie. I get the information."

"Shut up." Eva yelled as one man hit him in the side of the face. Andre shut up.

Eva looked behind Andre at the window. Nighttime sky was clear, and the stars were shining bright. She walked overlooking out the window liking the clear night.

"Come here." Eva said to Andre. They untied him. He got up wobbly and approached cautiously.

"See the planet up there." Eva pointed upward. Andre nodded.

"They say the first religion was the science of the planets. And how they could predict the future. Do you believe that?"

Andre nodded.

"Good, because I believe that you have bad plants lining up for you and you can do nothing about it. That is your future that the planets predict."

Andre stared at Eva.

"The Mayans could predict people's future from the time they were born till the time they die. Not a pleasing prospect to know that you won't be successful. Do you think so?"

Andre nodded no then yes.

"I see your planets predict that you have come to the end."

Andre deflated.

"No harm will come to your daughter if you do what must be done. She will have her university studies paid for and an enjoyable place to live and given every opportunity to succeed."

Andre kept staring at Eva.

"That comes from the Czarina and you know the Czarina keeps her word."

Andre nodded slowly.

Eva stood looking at him wondering if he would do it on his own. Probably not.

"If you need help let me know."

Andre continued looking at Eva sadly. He started crying falling to his knees saying, "please take care of my girl."

"I will Andre, but you must take that step."

Eva looked to Ivan who motioned to the men. Four came over each grabbing an arm or leg and held him up. They were twice the size of Andre and had no problem holding him suspended by his arms and legs.

"Ten." Ivan said.

The men started swinging Andre back and forth starting the count.

"Good-bye Andre." Eva said.

Andre blurted out. "Please take care of her." That was all he said because the count reached ten and out the window he flew. Screaming as his body twisted and turned. He hit the ground with a thud.

Eva watched as a man down on the ground walked over and put a bullet into

Andre's head. Extra measures to make sure he is dead.

Eva looked over at the four men saying. "I say a 9.4. you see the twist he did."

One man said. "8.0."

Second man said. "7.4."

Third man said. "8.5."

The fourth man shrugged making Eva laugh and they all joined in. She then thanked them, and they showed the utmost respect. They each bowed to her and started to leave the room.

Ivan stepped in with Eva as they walked down a hallway that had peeling paint and smelled of urine. She thought about tearing this down and building a medical center. She could name it Andre medical centers.

On the steps down Eva remembered the last words. "Please take care of her." She kept repeating that in her mind and decided that his daughter would work for the new medical center named for him.

Chapter 60

The limo pulled to the front of the huge glass tower in Manhattan. Sevan was out first opening the door for Joe and Carol. He had explained to her on the way over from New Jersey about Paul. She took it as a reason to hate him and his wife forever, also, as caution she told Joe never to tell anybody at CZ Corp. Joe already knew that hours before.

Inside Sevan took care of talking to the desk person. In moments they were whisked up an elevator. It stopped opening to a private entrance. Seated big men in nice suits Joe assumed bodyguards for whoever was inside.

Sevan rang the bell and the door was answered by a butler. Joe and Carol entered, and Sevan stayed outside. The view of the city amazed them. The music classy as they approached the main room to a live band.

They smiled walking into the main room seeing guests sitting and standing filled with laughs and conversations. A server approached holding a tray with glasses of champagne. They each took one and started walking slowly around.

Near the doorway for the balcony Joe saw two women kissing. He whispered to Carol who looked smiling. "It's a free world."

"Yes, but they can get men if they wanted to." Joe said as Carol poked him in the side.

From behind them came a voice. "You both made it."

They turned to see Catherine standing there in all her glory. Dressed in a tight-fitting black dress that showed her figure. Her hair let down and flowing. Joe noticed the jewelry knowing it was all real diamonds.

"Yes, a little traffic but we made it." Joe said.

Catherine laughed.

"Oh, Carol my wife."

"Carol a pleasure to meet you. I'm Catherine."

"Pleasure to meet you Catherine." They gently cheek kissed.

"I love this apartment." Carol said.

"Thank you. I own the building. If you like I can get you one."

"Well, for now we want a larger home. Maybe in the future." Joe said.

"Okay, I'll wait." Catherine said smiling.

Then a noise from behind made them turn. Joe noticed the man Dimitri off to one side of Catherine. He was eyeing everything going on.

"Aunt Catherine." Joe saw it was Tatyana. She curtsied and hugged her Aunt. He noticed a young lady next to her, brunette and attractive.

"How are you doing my dear?" Catherine asked like a mother.

"Fine. Taking care of business. You remember my friend Mindy."

"Yes, Mindy hello."

"Hello Miss Catherine."

"I guess Eva will be a little mad." Tatyana said with a private smile. Catherine gave the same look back saying. "I'm sure she'll be okay."

"Hi Joe, Carol." Tatyana said.

"Hi Tatyana." Joe said.

"Hey, I love your dress." Carol said.

"Thank you. It's just something I picked up." Tatyana looked to her friend Mindy giggling.

"Aunt Catherine we're going to mingle."

"You girls have fun, see you later." Catherine watched them walk away close to each other. Joe thought that a little unusual.

"They've been dating for a few years now." Catherine said.

Joe stunned at first said. "It's a free world."

Catherine eyed him a moment saying. "Yes, it is Joe."

"If they're happy together." Carol said.

"Exactly. I was surprised at first but by accepting it they're happy and I'm happy for them. It's one of those things we wanted to

hide. However, find love where you can."
Catherine said in regal prose.

"True. I never saw a problem with people
who want to live that life style." Joe said.

Catherine smiled nicely saying. "Joe, it's a
shock to you I know don't worry. I
understand. Please say nothing more."
Catherine looked at Carol continuing. "Men
are so abrupt."

Carol giggling added. "And have emotions
like cavemen."

Catherine and Carol laughed while Joe
sipping his champagne nodded looking
around. "You two are great." Catherine said
as an elder looking man stepped next to her
appearing distinguished. Catherine put her
arm through his saying. "This is Mr. Leonid
Meinkkoloff. My constant companion."

"Sir nice to meet you, Joe Bergen and my
wife Carol." Leo shook hands with both.

"I see a certain famous actor has arrived."
Leo said. Catherine looked around saying. He
came." Leo nodded.

"Thomson James. I love his acting in the
love story. The gift."

"I don't think I saw that one." Joe said.

"I did it was great, and I cried." Carol
said.

"I cried too." Catherine said.

"Come Carol lets go see him." Catherine
and the three took off with Dimitri following.

Joe sipped his champagne looking around.
He saw Tatyana in the distance holding
hands with Mindy. He never would have

figured that, he thought.

Then a hand grabbed him on the shoulder. Joe turned to see Mikal standing there with a big grin on his chiseled face. "What's up bro?"

"Enjoying the party." Joe said.

"I like you to meet Suzette. Joe Bergen, he is one of the family." Joe gently shook hands with her as she looked up at Mikal with a smile.

"She speaks broken English and loves everything American. She puts this country on a pedestal."

"In time she won't." Joe said. Mikal relayed that in French to her and she shook her head no.

Mikal looked saying. "I see Tat with Mindy. Thought they had a falling-out. I guess they licked and made up."

Joe snorted a laugh. "Don't worry bro your safe with me." Mikal said.

"I'm surprised to learn that but, if it makes them happy." Joe trying not to be biased. Mikal just shrugged. "Yea, it's what she likes so that's it."

"So, where's the wife." Mikal asked.

"Catherine took her to meet Thomas James."

"Oh, he's here. My brother Nicolas helped his career by running his movies a lot in his theaters and selling DVD's. He's washed up as an actor." Mikal said in an arrogant tone.

"True, people want good action or thrillers."

"Let's, see, we have many culture people here tonight. Aunt Catherine knows everybody in all fields. Tonight, it's the arts and movies. Oh, see that dainty blond, she's the lead dancer for a show on Broadway. If you were alone, you could score." Mikal smiled.

"I'm married and happy. Thanks anyway." Mikal nodded.

"Bummer, I hear you're going to Minneapolis to see Anton Slotkolov." Mikal said sipping his champagne.

"Yea, he's not returned my calls and I hear he's been investing in real estate with profit money. Eva said I could fire him if I want." Joe said casually.

"Fire him. He's an old family friend. Well, not a friend. His father wasn't trust worthy and he's like his dad. Apple didn't fall far from the tree."

"I see." Joe sipped his champagne.

"He gave Eva a difficult time when kids, and besides you can get someone else to run that warehouse. Do what Eva says." Mikal said looking directly at Joe who felt reassured.

"When I get a look, I'll decide."

"Do it Bro." Mikal said. Joe saw his face brighten as Catherine and Carol and Leo came back.

"Aunt Catherine." Mikal said kissing her lightly on the cheek.

"How are your Mik." Catherine asked happily. Joe saw the love in her eyes for the nephew.

"Oh, you know. Kicking ass and taking names."

Catherine put a hand to his face squeezing it a bit.

"Oh, Suzette." Mikal gestured to his date.

Catherine spoke French to Suzette. The lady smiled shyly. Then Mikal joined the two and all three laughed.

"Well, I'm going to see some people. Joe, Carol mingle." Catherine said leaving with Leo and Dimitri.

"Joe said you didn't want to come to this party." Mikal said to Carol. She looked at Joe then Mikal. "I didn't say that."

Mikal giggled said. "I'm a troublemaker. Joe didn't say that."

"Thanks for warning me." Carol said.

Somebody bumped into Mikal and he turned fast and saw Max standing there with a smile on his face. "Mystery Max. Bro what's up." A slight hug. Max then extended a hand to Carol and Joe saying hello. "Having a good time." Max asked both.

"Yes, it's great." Joe said.

"Great." Carol said.

Max looked off for a moment saying. "Oh, Tat and Mindy are here. I thought they broke up."

"I guess they licked and made up." Mikal said in full laugh. Max looked at him and smiled. Carol raised her head to Mikal and said. "That's not nice, Mikal. She's your sister."

"You'll have to excuse my brother, Carol. He's warped." Max said.

Joe was grinning, and Carol hit him lightly. "That's not funny."

"I wasn't laughing at that." Joe said.

"Forget it Joe. You're guilty." Max said.

"Okay let's be civil here." Mikal said.

"Yea, I'm going to find Aunt Catherine and sneak up on her. She hates when I do that." Max said and left.

"Me and Suzette are going to mingle. Joe, Carol have a good time. Enjoy." When Mikal left Carol, looked at Joe saying. "Don't join that. Their brother and sisters and we don't belong in with the family jokes."

"I know, It was surprising what he said."

Carol nodded. "Let's walk around."

They walked and tasted the serving trays. Joe saw Ariel with a lady much younger than himself. He made eye contact with him. Ariel gave him a million-dollar smile and a toast. Joe did the same.

On another side of the room a big burst of laughter and Joe saw Mr. Bokanawski the center of attention with his sister Catherine. Joe watched this and enjoyed it.

A while later dinner was in a huge dining room. A custom big wood table with solid wood high back cushioned chairs. And a fireplace lit to add atmosphere.

They seated Joe and Carol next to Tatyana and Mindy who were next to Catherine. Leonid, Max, Mikal, and Suzette were on the other side. Down-the-line the other guests buffered Mr. Bokanawski with Ariel on his right.

Servers came and took orders. This surprised Joe and he said to Carol. "Just like a restaurant."

Catherine heard and said. "I don't like to force one meal on everybody."

"A nice touch." Joe replied.

"Yes, many here tonight are actors and dancers and don't eat meat." Catherine said kindly.

"That's good" Carol said.

"Too bad Eva couldn't make it." Mikal said. Joe noticed a hard stare from Tatyana to Mikal.

"She's busy Mik." Catherine said with a sly smile.

"Last I heard she took care of that dead end." Max said. Catherine looked to Max and Joe guessed it was new to her because she slowly smiled saying. "Thank you, Max."

"My service to you." Max toasted Catherine.

"See. Some of us do work. We don't all waste time." Tatyana said to Mikal. He flipped his hand in the air and shrugged. Mikal then said. "Aunt Catherine tell Joe and Carol about your castle." They heard a few yeses from around the table.

"I own a castle in Russia the Royals used as a summer place. I loved it and restored it." Catherine said in regal prose.

"Tell them about the tunnels." Someone farther down said.

"Oh, they were escape routes used in case of a siege. I restored them to have access to the river and the forest."

"Sounds cool." Carol said.

Then Max said. "A Czarina owns it again."

Everyone raised their glasses saying, "the Czarina."

"Carol. You and Joe will see it in a few months. I invite people from the office for a week of fun. I have rooms with every toy imaginable. One wakes in a royal bed then out onto a veranda overseeing hundreds of acres of sculptured lawns to eat breakfast. Dinner overlooking the river with the setting sun shimmering in it." Catherine said in a dreamy way that left the room quiet. Then someone asked. "Cost for a night."

"For you, the highest rate ever."

Everybody laughed and toasted Catherine again.

When dinner ended everybody combined into groups talking and enjoying the good life. Joe and Carol were seated on an overstuffed coach. Catherine came taking a seat across from them, Dimitri close by.

"You both enjoyed yourselves. I hope." Catherine asked.

"A great time." Joe said.

"This was a great night, thank you." Carol said.

"Oh, don't thank me. You both deserve it." Catherine said then looked at Joe. "You're going to Minneapolis tomorrow. Fix the mistake made there."

"Yes." Joe said.

"Keep it quiet and do what Eva wants. It'll be okay." Catherine said in a serious tone.

"I will." Joe said looking forward to exerting some power.

"Good. Carol, I liked meeting you and we will get together again, soon."

"I look forward to it." Carol said.

Joe hoped for more dinners like this. He felt the family trusted him and knew his life was getting better.

Chapter 61

Don didn't drive his personal car because he didn't want to buy another one. He had to buy a new cellphone and liked it. He wasn't going to pay much money for this mission to happen though.

Yes, he thought. A terrorist attack, they happen all the time. Then maybe a newspaper article about the company Joe Bergen works for with connections to the Middle East. Yes, Don thought. Yes.

The rental car did not handle the backcountry road well. A clunker he arranged through his office, so he didn't have to pay for it. Nobody would question a rental. Part of his job expense is renting cars to visit customers. Another pothole and the car shook and squeaked a bit.

Up ahead Don saw a for-sale signposted on a piece of property that looked old. The grass almost covering the sign. That was good, Don thought. Going faster he might have missed it. He slowed the car turning onto the dirt drive. The headlights swept the property and he saw a vast area that looked well-kept some time ago. He slowly drove up the dirt drive hearing the tires crackling on rocks. He was getting scared and hoped this was the right place.

Don saw the overgrown trees that obscured a run-down house up ahead. He slowed the car to a stop hearing the last of crunching tires. They told him to stop just before the house and he hoped this was the right house. The house had a wraparound porch that remembered many happy family gatherings. Those days were gone. Now it looked evil, Don thought.

The sound of the car idling was loud. Intruding on the quiet night. Hearing a whistle, the wave of a flashlight. He sped up slowly coming to the side of the house where he thought he saw the light come from. Stopping no more than a second, he heard another whistle and a flash of light again a little farther up. He sped up slowly again as the car went into a few dips and the sound of grass scraping underneath. An old barn came into view of the headlights with a man standing in front. He drove closer and the man yelled out. "Shut the fucking lights off." He immediately did that and stopped and shut the car off also.

He yelled again. "Out of the car come here."

Don climbed out into the pitch-black night. The star's overhead not giving enough light to see anything. The man turned on the flashlight and shone it in Don's eyes.

"Come toward my voice." Don did as told, hoping this was the right place. He hoped he did not happen onto a meth lab run by some weirdos.

"Stop." The voice said turning the light off. Someone from behind grabbed Don's right arm bringing it up behind him to keep him in place. It started hurting.

The voice in front said. "Just keep cool. I need to check you."

A pair of hands frisked him up and down then disappeared. Don's eyes adjusted to lowlight seeing the guy in front of him. Different from the bar in New York.

The man asked. "Where's the money?"

"Under passenger seat." Don said.

The big guy walked over to the car. Don tried to look but the man holding his arm would not allow him to turn. He heard the car door open and then slam shut. The big guy came walking back saying to the man behind Don. "Bring him."

He pushed Donald from behind he stumbled but did not fall. His arm was let go and the blood flow began again. Rubbing it he followed the first guy into the barn. It was dark inside until they turned on a flashlight and placed it on a table made of plywood and cinder blocks. On the table sat a duffle bag.

Don continued rubbing his arm as the big guy opened the small briefcase from Don's car. Arranged inside were small stacks of cash wrapped in bands neatly stacked. The big guy picked up each flipping through the bills.

Don turned to see where the other guy was, and an object poked into his side. "Face forward." He said.

When the big guy at the table finished looking through the money, he placed it in a canvas bag of his own. He closed the brief case and pushed it to the side looking at Don.

"You got the money now where's my bomb."

The big guy looking at Don had a twinkle in his eyes. He then opened another duffle bag and took out a square wooden box and gently opened the lid. Inside showed a digital read out with red zeros on it.

"Okay, it's very easy. You use this numeric keypad to enter how much time you need to an explosion. This red button is a bypass to reset the time to zeros in case you make a mistake. The green is to set in motion the time you set on the screen. Time is calculated in tens. So, if you want it to go in one minute, you would set the time to sixty." The big guy paused and looked at Don who was impressed with his teaching skills. He could have been an inner-city grade schoolteacher. The big guy then asked. "Any questions."

"Where's the bomb stuff? I mean what's inside used for the explosion."

The big guy looked at Don for a moment

then undid the wing screws that held the readout screen to the box. He then lifted the top out and Don saw wires going to a small circuit board and a putty like substance. The big guy said. "That white substance in the bottom is plastic explosive. I'm sure you have seen it on the Discovery channel. It'll take down a large barn this size." The big guy waved a hand. Don quickly glanced around the area and back at the plastic inside the box. He slowly nodded and smiled.

"Okay. Thank you."

The big guy put it back together expertly. Don was impressed, despite his appearance. He knew he could be making millions with the right company; life can be strange and unkind to some. He wasn't letting life be unkind to him; the bomb is the key.

Big guy finished reassembling and wiping everything off with a dirty rag. Then using the rag-covered hand to close the lid he looked at Don. "The batteries are good for six months. By the end of six months you should think of disposing it if you haven't used it. The plastic will start degrading and become unstable, and it might blow up your nice penthouse home."

The last part of that sentence scared Don. How did he know where he lived? Who were these people, did they follow him? Don had a sinking feeling. He was going to say something, but the big guy said. "And I appreciate your business."

Don moved to take his purchase but the

guy behind him put the object into his back.

The big guy in front took out a small digital clock, pressed a button and the numbers started running fast. He picked up the canvas sack with the money saying. "The alarm clock will sound in fifteen minutes. You do not leave this barn until the alarm goes off. You got it?"

Don nodded watching the numbers fly by. The big guy and his friend following walked past Don. They stopped by the door. "And Donald Wellington, I hope your uncle runs for President. He seems decent."

Both left the barn laughing. Don's head was thumping with a large flow of blood. How did they find out who he is? Don wondered in lightning speed. Now what, he thought.

If it came down to it, they wouldn't make credible witnesses he knew. He took a little comfort in that.

As the numbers were flying by Don looked at the flashlight left behind remembering the big guy wiped it down. He could get this place watched to find out who they were so, he could take care of them later.

In the distance he heard the rumble of a few motorcycles start then fade away. A silence prevailed scaring Don. He looked at the clock saying out loud. "Fuck this."

He took the bomb gently placing it in his briefcase and closing it. He gently picked up the briefcase to let the bomb slide to the bottom. He started to walk with it. Nothing happened. It did not explode.

He left the flashlight in case somebody was watching, he did not want them to see a light outside. Opening the door, he cringed as he walked fast to his car. Stumbling on clumps of grass and holes he made it. He looked around, half expecting a gunshot or something to happen.

Quickly getting in the car and starting it. He spun the wheels turning it around. He put the lights on and spun the wheels again going forward. He slowed because the bumps were making the briefcase bounce on the front seat. Once on the road he took off fast. Slowing his speed after a mile, so not bringing attention to him. He relaxed for a long drive back to the city.

Don knew he had to do something about those two. They knew too much but, first the Russians, he thought with a smile. Joe Bergen being their new darling would be the one, Don thought cruising down the road.

Chapter 62

Joe was home drinking on a good high. The evening went well with Catherine and the family. Carol had gone to her private little world of calling a few friends and telling them about the fabulous dinner with a very wealthy owner of the business.

He didn't want to admit that Paul had gotten over on him. If he showed up, Joe was not in a mind frame of welcoming him. In fact, he wished Paul would just stay away. Enjoy the little money that they stole.

The embarrassment that a court case involved was not a choice that Joe wanted. He thought of what Catherine said earlier about Anton in Minneapolis. 'Do what Eva wants.'

Joe had the History channel on but, it did not satisfy him.

Anxiety over the embarrassment it would cause if Paul showed weighed on Joe's mind. Now he knew he was getting too buzzed from the drink and dismissed that thought.

If he came knocking right now, he would

hurt him. He remembers a few fighting moves from his younger days. Older and slower, still, he would try anyway.

Joe thought of Eva wondering what she was doing right now. He wouldn't turn her down if a moment came and they were alone. He dismissed that knowing he was drunk.

He finished the drink knowing he didn't need another. Morning would come fast, and he needed to be on his toes and fresh. If someone at CZ asks about Paul, he would need to answer and have them believe him. Joe worried the family would think he weak for not figuring out sooner what Paul did. He covered it at his old warehouse and won't let it get into the numbers at the XO food. The guy in finance might report it to Ariel and Joe did not want that happening. He had his plan in place. A minor cover up to keep his good image.

Joe sighed as Carol came into the room.

"Everything okay." Carol asked. Joe realized he was holding the glass too tight in his hands.

"If he showed right now, I don't know what my reaction would be."

"I do with plenty of bleach to clean it up."

Joe stared at Carol wondering if she was serious. "Bleach?"

"Yea, after killing someone. It cleans the bloodstains from detection." Carol said innocently smiling.

Joe kept staring digesting what she said

then burst into laughter, Carol joined him. When the laughter subsided, Carol said. "You know that's a first instinct. A show portrayed a family run business and when someone took their money, they killed them. I'm not saying that it's acceptable but, you ran a business and had someone steal money from you. To take him to court is such bullshit. Only if we could just take care of it quietly so he doesn't hurt and embarrass others."

Her reaction surprised Joe. Then again, he felt reassured that his wife was close to his feelings on this. He caught his thoughts knowing he was buzzed and getting carried away.

Joe cleared his throat. He immediately remembered about the guy in Minneapolis. This is just what he needed, someone to vent his power and anger on.

"There's a similar problem going on in a warehouse in Minneapolis. He's not stealing as far as they know but, he's not sending all the profit back to New York. It's complicated in that he's an old family friend but, they want it to stop. He's been investing some profit money in real estate. I'm to go there officially have him stop and take possession of the real estate for corporate."

Carol nodded saying. "Sounds just like something you need to do."

"Yea, I need to vent on someone and this guy Anton is the one. I don't need another Paul."

Carol smiled and said. "Go show him who

the boss is."

Joe nodded, "yea."

"We don't have much time."

Joe looked puzzled and was going to ask but Carol showed him. She stood taking off her nightshirt. She was completely nude. Joe understood. Carol left the room looking behind herself at Joe saying. "Hurry."

Joe turned the tv and lights off making his wobbly way to the bedroom.

~~~~~

While eating breakfast in the sunroom of her Moscow home Eva took her cell phone dialing a number. Max answered on the first ring.

"Max, what's up."

"Nada, what's up you."

"I hear Aunt Catherine's in New York."

"Yes, and we had a party." Max said, and Eva's heart fell a little. She took a few pills earlier and would be okay.

"I hear Joe Bergen was there."

"Yep, he and the wife looked like they had a good time."

"I took care of that problem."

"I heard and it's making a statement being how you left the remains."

Eva thought of Andre on the ground all twisted up with bullet head.

"Yea," she said slowly. "Nobody will know though."

"Eva, I hear Ivan is assembling a team to

go to Minneapolis. I'm security knowing everything."

"That alcohol operation; one bust and were dust for a time with XO foods. He's running a risk at our expense. What was dad thinking?"

"I'll take care of it." Max said in a serious tone.

"An accident or dad will know."

"I know that. I'm with you. It's for the best. If we kick him out of the warehouse, he'll cry to dad causing more problems.'

"Thank you, Max."

"It'll be my pleasure."

"How you going to do it."

"Mysterious Max never tells. Just keep near a phone."

"Thank you."

"Just taking care of our business." Max said hanging up.

Ivan was standing near the door. Eva looked over saying. "Call the team off. Max will take care of Anton."

Ivan nodded saying. "The Czarina will be here soon and wants you to wait."

Eva looked at him as he stood there ready for any reaction.

Chapter 63

Don watched his rearview mirror and the briefcase in the seat next to him. Every bump in the road made him cringe. He hoped the big guy didn't set him up. Maybe he could have taken care of the Russian problem for him. He and his buddy do have a good structure in place. Another bump in the road Don looked over at the briefcase next to him. He decided to focus on the road a little better and move forward with what he planned. Maybe the big guy will read in the paper of an explosion and Don will gain some respect.

Inside his apartment a little while later Don had the bomb placed on his desktop looking at it like a parent seeing a newborn child. He smiled knowing he had the power to change people's lives. He will encourage events to happen. As an investment banker he may make money from the turmoil.

Don looked the bomb back and forth smiling. He can't get Eva, but he can get the guy Bergen. He will make a point to a few people. Looking at the pinprick of a house on Bing maps. It will blow like a toothpick house.

The bomb sat there on the desk as Don thought back to a few hours ago and the big grizzly guy. Not likely the man would tell the police he sold Don the bomb. He may even gain respect with the big guy. He seemed like a good American type, help save America.

Irritation though the big grizzly knew who he was. He felt violated and wondered how he did it. Followed from the bar. Not fair but chilling to Don to think the big guy would think of hurting him if he did.

Don downed the rest of his drink feeling it was fair enough. He got what he wanted, and the big guy got insurance. Don did know a few FBI but that isn't a good idea. He'll leave it at that, he got what he wanted.

Wrapping the bomb in a blanket he looked around his apartment for a hiding place. A giant vase in his bedroom he bought from an antique store caught his eyes. It stood about five feet tall and had fake flowers placed in it. Don took the flowers out placing the bomb gently inside. Then replacing the flowers on top, he bowed to the power inside.

He looked down at the traffic fifty floors below. Little fireflies buzzing around the streets. The world is a jungle and the strong survive, Don thought. Looking west to New Jersey he pictured a big fiery explosion.

Chapter 64

The next morning Joe was in his office a little heavy headed from last night. It did feel great with Carol, she did support him and give him that bond of trust he needed. And from what he remembered in bed last night she left him with a good feeling.

He made a few calls to people he met at the Mayors party. And, received a few invitations to house and dinner parties, he had decline though because of the trip he was taking today. These people were heads of corporations and like teenagers. No thought of tomorrow just parties every day.

Joe had more pressing concerns and didn't want the distraction. Should he tell Eva he had an employee that stole money from his company? He knew she would not find out he had covered it up as expense that went unreported. They wouldn't notice the amount, meager, compared to the sales revenue and profit. Thom, he owed a bonus, at least he could trust someone.

Joe's phone buzzed giving him a start.

"Your wife Mr. Bergen."

"Thank you."

Joe picked smile"

"Hi."

"Hey," came Carol's sultry voice. "I just wanted to say good-bye and have a safe trip, again."

"Thank you again."

"Don't tell anybody," she whispered.

"No, haven't seen anybody. I've been fielding calls from the Mayors party. They're like teenagers. The one from our table just bought a new Ferrari and wanted me to come over tonight, hang with him and his buddies. All corporate big guys."

Carol laughed a bit saying, "it's a new world we're in. Big boys have big toys."

"I guess."

"Why don't you buy one?"

"A Ferrari."

"Yea. That'd be cool, that turns me on."

"First the new house in a neighborhood that likes classy cars."

"True and I hope Paul never shows up. We don't need him ruining everything for you."

Joe smiled hearing that. "I just need time to pass. It'll never happen again."

"I'm sure it won't."

"The longer he's missing the better." Joe said sneering.

"I hope he's running scared owing money to bad people." Carol said with the same hatred. Joe liked the mind-set they were both in.

He turned his chair to the desk looking up to see Vera standing there.

"You still there." Carol asked.

"Yes, time to travel."

"Have a safe trip."

"I'll be back soon."

"Bye."

"Bye."

The elevator went to the top floor and Joe wondered why. He figured a ride to ground level to limo would be in order. When the elevator reached the top floor, it opened. They walked from the enclosure looking at the helicopter on a raised platform. Blades starting to turn, firing up. It was monster loud to Joe. They waited until the luggage got loaded. The rotors were whooping at a fast speed.

Joe didn't notice Vera watching him. "Like the helicopter." She said over the roar.

"No." Joe said.

"Relax, you'll like it." Vera said smiling at Joe.

"I wasn't aware this was on the roof."

"You need to ask more questions." Vera said.

A helmeted man motioned for everyone to come. They all started to climb the metal steps, Joe in the lead.

On platform level wind from the rotors was wild. A big entry door made for easy walk in away from that. Joe sat at a table across from Sevan. Vera sat next to Joe. He looked over at her she smiled nervously.

Inside the helicopter was equal to a living room. The chairs overstuffed and comfortable with a real wood table. After the pilot closed the door it was remarkably quiet.

The helicopter lifted off the platform as Joe grabbed onto the table. Vera looked at him smiling then back to looking out the window. The helicopter went upward for a distance then started forward.

Joe looked down at the streets of Manhattan. The cars like ants going here and there. The helicopter banked right surprising Joe, he grabbed the table again.

When he looked out again, he noticed they were heading for New Jersey. The Hudson river and GW bridge in the distance getting closer. Cruising at a level pace was better, cool. Vera's smile was looking at him.

The decent started abruptly. Joe did not grab the table this time, he tried to tough it out. An airport came into view getting closer. Joe recognized the Newark International. A familiar place.

The Helicopter slowed to stop then started lowering itself to the ground. The rotors slowed once grounded. The pilot emerged from the cockpit opening the big door. Sevan, Joe and Vera followed to the tarmac where a limo was waiting.

Joe noticed they were in a less active area of the airport. After a thirty second ride in a limo they stopped at a gleaming plane. Getting out Joe stopped looking at the jet in front of him. The color white with no descriptive markings other than a highlight of maroon.

"No company name on it."

"It's for security reasons." Vera said.

He felt a surge of emotion seeing his own jet. His pride and joy now. He looked over at the hanger at the other jet planes big and small. All looked very professional.

"They're at your disposal," Vera said. Joe turned seeing her enjoy his surprise with the planes.

"I'm impressed." Joe replied.

Turning he saw Sevan watching the driver load luggage to the plane. The sound of big jet engines started.

Joe, Vera walked to then boarded the jet. Four overstuffed chairs that make a bed when needed also a kitchenette and rest room in the back. Joe inspected all this knowing he would use it.

He took a seat across from Vera. With door closed Sevan took a seat near the front.

The plane started moving to Joe's excitement. He felt like he made it. A confidence overcame him, and he knew he would do his best for this company. Vera was looking over some papers and Joe looked out the window.

In no time the plane was rumbling down the runway then airborne. It took off smooth not having the feel of big plane wobbles and shakes. It was tight; his Ferrari. He felt excited wanting to call the CEO from the insurance company and show off his toy.

Chapter 65

The air chilly as Joe waited with Vera outside the airplane on the tarmac. He turned and looking back at the plane occasionally to admire it. The ride was fast and smooth. Now though, events were not going fast smoothly. Sevan was off getting a rental car which he insisted they needed. Joe was irritated no one from the warehouse was here to greet him.

Sevan approached driving a Cadillac Escalade. The cost, Joe thought.

Vera finished her cell phone and Joe's attention to the conversation was Vera saying. "Someone had better be there."

Joe took note deciding not to ask.

Sevan stopped the vehicle immediately out opening the back door.

"Must've cost a bit?" Joe said as Sevan drove away.

"Security picks up the bill." Vera said giving Joe a look to relax. Which he did for the ride. He was happy to see the scenery of Minneapolis. Like most cities in America this time of day. People heading home from work. They faced slow traffic on the highway.

A short while later the Cadillac pulled in the parking lot of a business called Great Northern Food service. Joe looked at the sign wondering if Sevan had the right place. He realized it was the former name of the facility.

Sevan parked the vehicle front row closest to the building that said reserved. He was out opening the door for Joe and Vera.

Joe glanced around the building and property. Loose litter on the lawn; the name proudly displayed was not XO Food Group. That put a sneer on his face. Vera had notepad out writing.

They continued toward the front doors, Joe in the lead. Entering the outer area, he smelled something his nostrils disliked. In the lobby area a couch and chairs to one side were looking old. A desk near the stairs leading to the executive area looked old too. He glanced upward then down at the lady sitting behind the desk.

She looked young speaking on the phone in language that teenagers do. Glancing up at the three of them she said, "I need to call you back."

She placed the receiver down rudely looked up at the three. "Yes, can I help you."

Joe didn't see a need to overpower her. Lacking people skills, she shouldn't even have that entry-level job.

He respectfully said. "Yes, I'm here to see

Anton Slotkolov. I believe he is expecting me."

"And you're?"

"I'm Joe Bergen. CEO of XO Food."

The young lady did lose the arrogant teenager look and seemed flustered for a moment. Then said more nicely. "Mr. Slotkolov has left for the day. But let me get Mark Milner. He's the Human Resources manager."

Joe didn't say another word or see a need to show anger to this young lady. She immediately pressed a button said something hushed and hung up.

"He'll be here momentarily." She said then played with some papers on her desk.

Hanging by the desk he looked at Sevan and Vera who kept blank stares looking around the lobby. Joe noticed a display cabinet with an award from years ago. The glass cabinet had more fingerprints than the FBI database.

At the top of the stairs came a thin man wearing glasses. He had the look of a library caretaker. He reached the bottom of the stairs looking unsure of himself, Joe thought.

"Hi, I'm Mark Milner. We've been expecting you."

He shook hands with Joe and Vera. He went to shake with Sevan, but Sevan declined. The man seemed nervous.

"Mark, where's Mr. Slotkolov today."

"He'll be here tomorrow. A family matter I believe." Mark said nodding.

"Does he have a number where we can reach him?" Joe asked more sternly than wanting.

"Um, yes. I have a number where we can reach him." Mark said fixing his glasses.

Joe remained calm asking. "The finance manager here?"

"No, he left for the day."

Mark was getting more nervous again, Joe thought.

"I see, an operations manager?"

"Well, no. He left about a month ago and we have not filled that position yet."

Then Joe asked. "I guess you've been busy then, trying to fill that position."

Mark smiled nervously. "Yes, I've been very busy trying to find new people to fill in."

Joe glanced over at Vera's blank stare it almost made him laugh. Sevan stared with his mouth open.

"Okay Mark, I guess you're in charge here today."

"Yes sir." Mark said proudly.

Joe didn't want to scare this guy. Beaten down by life already and probably kept on because he did what Slotkolov wanted with no questions asked.

"Mark, how about you show me around. I want to see the warehouse."

Mark's eyes brightened, and Joe found something he was comfortable with.

"Yes, follow me."

Joe started following Mark and heard Vera ask the girl at the desk where the Finance dept. was. Sevan stepped in right behind Joe.

A few minutes later they were in the warehouse meeting the supervision. Day shift was wrapping up their shift putting product away in the various departments. The noise of beeping horns and lite music playing was normal to Joe. The employees handling the equipment seemed unusually subdued, scared, he thought. He said a hello to a few as they passed, and they seemed nervous. Something was wrong Joe felt.

When an outside suit enters a warehouse, the men usually hang back watching and laugh at a private joke. That wasn't happening. They were working and not taking an interest in Joe.

Joe led the way through the dry goods department. Looking up at the items in storage just like a public warehouse club. Only difference people from the outside won't be walking these aisles.

A forklift beeped and drove by. Joe watched the man stop his equipment raise the product to a certain level and place it there. He pulled and lowered the forks driving away to get another pallet of food. This was done hundreds of times a day. The product put away, so the night shift crew will have properly placed products to ship out to customers. Mark was looking around like he rarely sees this work going on, Joe noted.

A triple stack of barrels caught Joe's eyes. The barrels were blue plastic, fifty gallon and four to a pallet. They stacked the pallets three and four high along the wall. Twenty stacks in all.

Walking closer to the barrels he read stenciled on the side glass cleaner. Glass cleaner Joe mumbled to himself. He looked over at Mark asking. "Trying to corner the market on glass cleaner."

Mark looked at the barrels and back to Joe with a nervous look saying. "I don't know. I don't take an interest in the warehouse stock and don't know why there's so much."

The supervisors also just shrugged.

Joe glanced back at Sevan who had a grin on his face. Joe nodded smiling not knowing who would buy glass cleaner by the barrel.

"Okay, everything looks doki doki here." Joe said seeing Mark's face smile. He took that to mean he was uncomfortable with the workers.

Casually walking up the aisle looking at product and stopping for the forklifts rushing by Joe observed one doing a professional job of putting the product away. The driver of the equipment was wearing a baseball cap with a metal badge covering the company name. The badge was from the local labor union. Joe stepped forward.

"Hi, Joe Bergen CEO of XO Food."

The man maneuvered his equipment to the side stepping off extending his hand.

"Thom Dresden former day shift shop steward. Glad to meet you Mr. Bergen." Joe liked the man right off. A worker and leader of his counter parts. He showed pride in his work; a straight up person.

"I'm here from New York to see the place. I formally owned Bergen foods in New Jersey. I had a good crew there and honored the union contract there." Thom kept eye contact and Joe liked that. Thom nodded then said after looking over at Mark. "Our union was bounced out and we don't know why." Thom paused. "We do good work here. I heard a big outfit bought us and you're the first person to come here. Um, I might say were better under the previous owner but, we'll give it time. There's several minor issues I don't want to bother you with." Thom finished looking back at Mark.

Joe understood deciding not to make the nervous Mark any more problems. He took a business card out of his pocket and handed it to Thom, who looked at it and placed it in his pocket.

"I'm not going to override management here. I don't know them yet. So, feel free to call or email me if you feel all avenues have exhausted at your end here. I'm a fair person and recognize the work you do."

"Yes sir." Thom looked over at Mark saying. "I believe in giving things time to straighten out. I'm not like some younger workers here. I'll take up your offer if need be." Thom finished stepping back onto his machine driving away. Joe watched him leave. He stopped down the aisle talking to another on a machine who said rather loudly

"All right."

Joe knew they were workers like in any warehouse. The bottom of the food chain when it comes to decent pay, benefits and respect. Labor unions only do so much. They need good management on their side.

Starting to walk again, another forklift came past, the man operating it gave Joe a sincere nod. Joe knew rumors good or bad travel at light speed in a warehouse.

He looked over at Mark's grim face asking. "How's relations between labor and management?"

Mark's face soured. "Good, no complaints. The labor union pulled out, things have been quiet."

Unusual to have a labor union pull out. The warehouse I owned usually had complaints and grievances filed. My HR man had good negotiating skills which helped. As always unforeseen problems and legitimate concerns need attention." Joe thought of Paul and knew he had one reliable quality.

Mark looked lost saying, "Mr. Slotkolov takes care of any problems in the warehouse."

I bet he does, Joe thought, then realized they stopped walking. Joe asked Mark. "Take me back to the offices. I need to find my assistant."

Joe followed Mark ready to strangle this little geek. He realized they hired him to be a yes man and do whatever Slotkolov wanted. Joe was anxious to meet this Mr. Anton

Slotkolov.

Chapter 66

Mark's nervousness showed again in the lobby. Joe didn't care because he felt the man isn't suited for the job of HR manager. Mark asked the cute blond where Vera had gone. She didn't know.

"I would say she's upstairs." Mark said heading in that direction Joe following. Sevan stayed behind in the lobby.

Just up the stairs and over into the first office Vera sat going through some files. Mark looked at the desk with the files and said. "I don't think you should be going through these files. You need permission from Mr. Slotkolov."

Joe was going to step in when a battle ship-sized lady came into the office. She had just come in from outside, the shopping bag in her hand told Joe that.

Mark looked with shock lowering his head. The lady looked to Joe. "Hello. I'm Dinka. I'm Mr. Slotkolov secretary. You must be Mr. Bergen."

Both shook hands and Joe motioned to

Vera saying. "My assistant Vera." She looked up smiling at Dinka who smiled back unfriendly. Dinka put her attention back to Joe.

"And how is Ms Eva and her father."

"They're doing great. I just spoke with her this morning." Joe said. Dinka put a cautious look on her face.

"Okay, Dinka. How do I contact Mr. Slotkolov? I need to see him. Mark said he had an urgent family matter to take care of. If that matters resolved I need him here." Joe finished with a smile.

Dinka's glance to Mark could chill water to ice. She then said. "I'll go to office and phone him."

Joe looked at Mark who's looking at Vera, who was looking up at Mark. Joe stepped over. "Okay, thank you for everything, Mark."

Joe put a hand on his shoulder leading him to the door.

"You're welcome Mr. Bergen. I'm at the end of the hall on the right if you need help." Joe thought that a good place to keep him.

"Thank you again Mark."

Joe closed the office door taking a seat in front of the desk. Looking at Vera with few stacks in front of her was the overworked person. Joe smiled gently, rubbed his face letting out a breath. He looked directly at Vera's stoic face.

"I'm not impressed and ready to take over this place." Vera continued looking at Joe.

"Maybe the man does have a family emergency. Mark, I feel should work in a library and where is the sales manager. We went by an office downstairs and Mark tells me the sales staff are on the road. The people behind the desks just field complaints. The sales manager rarely comes in a finance manager is out. They need an operations manager." Joe stopped.

He kept looking at Vera writing in her notebook, but she said nothing. Joe asked. "What're these files?"

Vera said. "Recent payables and receivables. I see a problem already." Looking down at the open file she continued. "There's two companies here. Great Northern buys the product then sells it to XO Food. Yes, with a price mark up." Joe put his hand up for Vera to stop. He knew already what that meant. Mr Slotkolov was profiting from that money.

Joe said. "Okay, Vera. Quickly compile and come up with a number in the difference between the bought price by Great Northern and the sold price to XO. Say, for the last three months."

"Sure, I'll need a few hours."

Joe smiled. "No problem."

A knock on the door and Joe yelled. "Come in."

Dinka stepped in, closed the door, walked over to Joe. "I've contacted Mr. Slotkolov and he can meet you at restaurant in the city at six p.m.."

"What restaurant." Joe asked ready to yell for not getting him to come here. Dinka handed Joe a post it note, he didn't have the slightest where this place was. He handed it back to Dinka.

"There's a man in the lobby. His name is Sevan, please give him that name and directions to it."

"Yes, Mr. Bergen."

Dinka closed the office door. Joe looked back at Vera in a file taking notes and said.

"Why can't the man just come here? Is he trying to impress me?

Vera looked at Joe shrugging her shoulders. Joe continued. "I can't wait to hear the story."

Vera looked up again nodding yes.

Chapter 67

Joe in the front seat watched Sevan drive expertly through the city traffic of Minneapolis wondering if he'd been here before. Vera was back at the warehouse compiling numbers. He hoped she'd be fine there. That's when the thought hit Joe and he turned to look at Sevan.

"Sevan, I need an answer to something." He looked over Joe continued. "What do you make of the barrels of glass cleaner in the warehouse?"

Sevan didn't blink, he continued driving and finally saying. "Maybe glass cleaner inside."

"I never heard of buying glass cleaner by the barrel." Joe said keeping a look on Sevan.

Sevan answered. "Maybe to fill little bottles with. There's many big buildings here that need clean windows."

"Right. A need for clean windows." Joe said finally looking out at the office towers. He took his cell phone and dialed.

"Hello."

"Vera, Joe. I need you to check on something. Push everything aside and find a bill from a glass cleaner company."

"Can you explain?" Vera asked.

"Yes, there are about twenty barrels of glass cleaner in the warehouse and I need to know where they came from."

"Okay. I don't know how long it'll take."

"Call me when you find it."

"Okay."

"Bye."

Sevan pulled the Escalade into a parking lot between two buildings. A downtown area that looked trendy to Joe. Evening people walking on the sidewalk probably shopping and going to eat.

Sevan looked over at Joe. "It's halfway down the block."

They got out Joe immediately feeling the chill in the night air. Dressed only in his suit jacket he figured he could walk half a city block. Sevan didn't seem bothered by the temperature as they started walking on the sidewalk. They passed a few storefronts that seemed expensive Joe thought. Jewelry, clothing, electronics and on. He looked down at his clothing to make sure he looked fine.

They entered and stood in line behind a few couples who chatted lively as Joe looked beyond them into the restaurant. People were dining at large and small wooden tables talking happily. Cozy with an atmosphere that Joe found appealing. From his current vantage point he gave high marks. The line went down quickly. Another fine point, nobody likes to wait.

Sevan stepped forward speaking to the person at the desk. The man immediately nodded motioning for someone. A young man approached, the desk person whispered something to him. The young man smiled and motioned for Joe and Sevan to follow.

They went through a dining area and then past an elegant bar. Much hardwoods with dining booths or tables. It all looked refined with lit fireplaces and soft music playing. It gave off a special effect that attracted customers. Fashionable dresses on the ladies and stylish suits on the men.

They entered a dining area that had a few patrons at the tables. At the far side near a fireplace a table with two men. As they approached one man got up from the table. He looked at Joe and Sevan, more so at Sevan. Same weight, Sevan in height. The man had an arrogant look on his face and stood between Joe and Sevan and the table. The young man who escorted them nodded and left.

The big guy stepped aside locking eyes with Sevan who seemed not the least concerned.

The man at the table started smiling and stood. Joe was taken aback by the man's young appearance. He looked finely groomed and appeared dressed in a silk suit. Probably worked out judging by the way he fit the suit. He extended a hand to Joe.

"You must be Mr. Bergen."

"Yes, and you are Mr. Slotkolov." Joe asked immediately jealous. Why, he didn't know or have time to think.

"Please sit." Mr. Slotkolov said. Joe seated himself looking at Sevan with his new friend. Both took seats at a nearby table. It didn't look like they were going to be friends, Joe thought. He knew for some strange reason that Sevan would be just fine.

"Mr. Bergen let me start with my embarrassment at the state of the warehouse. People keep quitting. I have not any good prospects to hire. Difficult business with the labor costs and customers wanting free."

Joe didn't know where to begin. He didn't like this guy for some jealous reason he could not figure out.

"You can call me Joe."

"You can call me Anton."

"Okay Anton. You have no operations manager to coordinate the warehouse and transport. That's an important area. I would like to see us develop more sales here in Minneapolis. You took over last year and the sign in front hasn't changed yet." Joe paused. "And, I'm sorry for talking business immediately. I'm inhuman sometimes. The family emergency. What happened."

Anton's look brightened with the last thing Joe said. He had a good complexion with dark eyes. This man was a childhood flame of Eva's and Joe felt jealous he was not her childhood friend. He was here to protect her business he reminded himself.

"Yes, the family emergencies resolved. They rushed my uncle Vladimir to the hospital. He thought a heart attack but turned out a case of heartburn." Anton continued in a lighter tone. "I will be at the office tomorrow and we can talk business. I look forward to your help and advice."

Joe nodded and lightened his tone also.

"Okay, we'll save the office for the office."

"How's Mr. Bokanawski? I have not seen him for a time. He and my Uncle are close, they go back before me."

"He's fine and in good health. Eva is also doing well. I had dinner with Catherine yesterday and she speaks good of you."

Joe saw Anton's expression change at the mention of Catherine. Not sure of the meaning, but Joe was going to like it because he didn't like this man.

"I'm glad to hear. I'm glad Catherine speaks of me at all. I always wished to be friends with her. That's good." Anton said not looking comfortable. He continued. "I hear you have an assistant at the office going over files. We could have done that tomorrow. I know on the surface it doesn't look good from a business stand point but, there is profit and big profit that will come. Please understand that, Joe."

"I understand that Mr. Bokanawski had an agreement with you for investing some into real estate here. I would like to see the property. As for Vera, she's just getting some numbers and so I can see the real financial health of the company. Like you said, we can talk that at the office tomorrow."

Anton was quiet for a moment then in an animated way said. "I could show you the property, but it is dark right now." Anton said then leaned forward toward Joe. "I know builders, and this is going to be hot property for the wealthy. They are going to want to live in that area I have bought. You see. Nobody wants to take a risk, not the banks or the builders. Someone must step forward and build a few homes for others to see the idea. Build it and they will come."

Anton sat back smiling. He could not tell until he sees the property and the price paid. Joe knew he had limited knowledge of the fundamentals of real estate but, he would not throw water on it. He didn't look forward telling Anton that he was taking all that property and firing him. Maybe he could work out a finder's fee for him if it's worth it.

"I look forward to seeing the area. I live in an old neighborhood, and don't know much about the luxury market or the tastes of people who buy into that market." Joe said realizing he was going to deal a hard blow to this guy and needed to lessen the pain for him. He hated his looks as a lady's man, but he needed to be reasonable here. He knew he had the power over this guy and needed to show discipline.

"I look forward to showing you. You will like."

"Yes, I look forward to it. However, we first must go over some office stuff tomorrow. They hired me to pull together this food service chain to run as one unit. Now, I know Mr. Bokanawski hired you and I don't doubt his reason for doing so. I'm sure you're qualified. But, being the boss of XO I need all warehouses running to my direction."

Anton looked hard then softened. "Yes, I will bring it in line with what your direction is. I will listen and follow along. Yes, everything must run quietly. I'm loyal to Mr. Bokanawski and I'm sure he hired you on your expertise and don't doubt his decision."

Joe looked at Anton ready to tear into him and regretted having pleasant thoughts about him. Tomorrow will be different, Joe thought. He sat back looking around. "An attractive place."

"Yes, they have good meals here." Anton said raising a hand for a waiter surveying the room. He immediately came over waiting patiently as Joe poured over the menu.

Anton said. "I recommend the NY steak dinner."

Joe looked at the waiter. "The NY steak it'll be."

The waiter looked at Anton. "I'll have the usual and see to those two men."

Joe looked over at Sevan who was already telling the waiter how he wanted his steak cooked.

Anton asked. "How was your flight?"

"Good. Smooth and not stressful. I like my new plane." Joe tried to let go but said. "I see you are still running under the Great Northern name. Can you explain why?"

"I felt the customers would leave with a new name. I was going to work it in slowly." Anton said looking uncomfortable.

"One year is enough time to start rolling out the new name and image of great service. An opening to tell customers."

"Yes. I can start on the name change soon." Anton said and ended. "Tomorrow."

"Yes. I just want you to understand how this warehouse is going to run and under what colors." Joe felt he was getting a little too strong here. His phone ringing surprised him. He quickly opened it and answered. Vera. He got up and walked near the fireplace feeling Anton's eyes following him.

"Hey, I found the bill for the barrels of window cleaner. The company's in Kentucky. The name is Chem Clean. I checked it on the Internet and they have no website. I tried to get a phone number and can't find any. I did find transactions for the real estate. Profit from Great Northern and XO matches up with the buys. And, Anton is also collecting two paychecks for some unfilled positions." Vera finished, and Joe glanced at Anton who was looking at him.

Joe said. "Good work. Keep the files aside and bring them when I pick you up in a few hours."

"Okay. A few hours." Vera asked.

"Probably fewer."

"Okay."

"Bye."

"Bye."

Joe sat back at the table and had a drink and small salad waiting. Anton, a lady seated next to him. She was attractive. Her dark eyes and short dark hair gave her a clean appearance. He looked at the drink and signaled for the waiter. When he arrived, he told him a cola would do. Joe didn't want to drink. He was not feeling comfortable and was working and needed to show a strong image here.

"No drink." Anton asked as the waiter left.

"No. I drink on when home and not working."

"Miss Vera found out what you were looking for I hope."

"Yes. We can go over the rest tomorrow." Joe hoped she was okay there. It was no secret to the office workers what she was doing and of course they let Anton know. Good to see they were loyal to him, Joe thought. He looked at the lady and asked.

"Are you Mrs. Slotkolov?"

"No, I'm Mona. I work for Anton."

"Okay." Joe said, and Anton took over. "Mona helps me at the warehouse. Like a consultant."

"A consultant?" Joe asked.

"Yes, I pay her from my salary."

Joe decided to leave that alone. He figured she was a paid girlfriend.

Joe's cola came, and the meals soon after. Both started eating and the meal impressed Joe. The steak excellent. Halfway into the meal Joe asked Anton. "Your uncle how is he. I mean with age comes certain health's need watching over in the human body. How is he for his age?"

Anton wiped his mouth and started to go into details about his uncle's health from twenty years ago. The detail did not go well while eating, it was gross. Mona looked bored nibbling on a salad.

They talked for close to an hour finishing their meals. Then an enjoyable cup of coffee when a big man came bounding into the room. He went right up to Anton who stood and both bear hugged. They talked in Russian and glanced at Joe.

Joe stood to shake the man's hand but got grabbed in a bear hug.

Anton said brightly. "This is my cousin, Vladimir Jr. He owns this restaurant and one of our best customers."

Joe said. "I hope you get good service from XO Food."

"Yes, Anton gives me good service. He my favorite cousin."

Joe smiled over at Anton who was beaming. Vladimir then said in a lower voice. "Tell Mr. Bokanawski I say hello and am with him, and hello Mona."

Mona nodded and smiled, and Joe did not

understand the latter part but did not question it.

"Yes, I will."

"Good, Good. I must go. Meal good? You like."

"Yes, good. I enjoy." Joe said meaning it.

"Anything you want to eat here is free." Vladimir said.

"I appreciate that. Thank you." Joe said as Vladimir put a serious look on his face for a few seconds. He touched something inside Vladimir.

"And I thank you." Vladimir said then looked at Anton speaking in Russian. They smiled, and Vladimir left the room.

Joe and Anton sat back down.

Joe said. "Your cousin has an enjoyable place here. I can see he does a good business." He looked around watching Anton from of the corner of his eyes.

"Yes. Cousin Vladimir is successful. He owns three restaurants here in Minneapolis." Anton finished looking off for a moment. Smiling he returned saying. "This restaurant he bought cheap from a lawyer and doctor who couldn't keep up with it. A good deal."

Anton the unsuccessful one trying to keep up, Joe thought.

"Anton, how's the football team here. I usually bet on NY, but they haven't done anything in years."

"Ah, they good. I made a few bets and made money there." Anton said as the dessert appeared on the table. Joe didn't know if he could eat more.

~~~~~

In Moscow Eva's phone rang and she hated when it did that when at her club. She answered.

"Eva, Vera here."

"Ah, yes. How's Minneapolis?"

"Good. It's what you expected. I find no theft though I haven't seen the real estate yet."

"Okay."

"Anything else to look for."

"No, that's my only interest and Joe will take care of the rest."

"Yes."

"Good. Now, I did contact the real estate division and they tell me they found a place you may like. An old building in the city with an exposed brick wall two-bedroom top level."

Eva listened as Vera screeched saying. "Yes, Yes. Where?"

"Contact Phil in real estate."

"Um, I may be short on down payment."

"Down payment. There's no down payment needed. You're family."

"Eva, I want to thank you very much."

"Your part of a family that you watch out for and we watch out for you." Eva said feeling good saying that. Not every day she sees the good in people. Today and the moment was real.

"Yes. You name it and I'll do it."

"What's with that guy you dated is he still following you."

"Ah, no. Now that you mentioned it, I've forgotten him and haven't seen him."

"Well, you see, everything works out for the best."

"Yes, they do. Must go. Joe needs a report when he gets here."

"Bye."

"Bye."

Eva put her phone down and Ivan was looking at her. She waved her hand for him to turn away. She liked Vera. A good worker who just wants to feel protected for the good work she does.

Eva wondered how Joe was going to take care the situation there or how was Max going to take care of that situation there. She was looking forward to how Max was going to make it happen she decided.

Chapter 68

Joe full of food wanting to sleep glanced over to Sevan and his staring contest with the other guy. Joe turned back watching Anton talking on his cell phone in Russian. A good way to hold a private conversation. He looked irritated, probably not good news. Mona left earlier saying something about getting together later.

Thinking back on the dinner Joe realized Anton doesn't respond to him as a boss would expect. Joe could tolerate that because of his family connections. However, he's fired, so respect he'll get from the new warehouse president.

Anton ended his call and looked with a slight smile saying. "Sorry, my friends always call with the smallest concerns."

"No problem. Take all the time you need." Joe said hoping he wouldn't.

"Thank you. To continue. Yes, my dad goes back to the Ukraine to visit family and never returns. At first, we think he decided to stay and leave me and my brothers alone.

Then as time went by, we never heard from him." Anton stops to sip his wine and then continues. "I never felt so alone. I lost somebody I looked up to. My mother bless her. She raised us to be good citizens. My uncle he became our dad. Today I thought he was going to leave us and that scared me. I felt that loneliness again." Anton finished sipping his wine.

"I understand. You take the time you need. I'll find my way around the office and probably hire some people to fill empty positions. I have extra time I could spend here." Joe finished wondering why he said that.

He noticed Anton respond physically by moving in his seat and fingering the wine glass.

"Joe I can do hiring of minor staff that we need. You have big things in New York to worry about. I'll be there tomorrow."

"I can help if needed. I'm here to get the profit money going back to New York. Eva Bokanawski has told me that. I know you have an arrangement with Mr. Bokanawski but that has ended." Joe stopped there watching Anton look off for a few moments.

Slowly nodding he asked. "How's Eva? I haven't seen her for a few years. Did you know we were friends growing up together? She was my girlfriend. I mean preteen stuff. How's she?"

Joe felt a jealous pang not knowing why. He liked Eva, but this feeling wasn't in tune with that. He ignored saying. "Eva's fine. Saw her yesterday." Joe wanted to talk real estate.

Anton said. "I liked her when young but that was when I was young. When we get older, we see life a little better. I have a fiancé that I plan to marry soon. She's good women to me."

Joe wondered if it was Mona saying. "I remember my wedding day. It's the happiest day I remember. Her name's Carol; we have a good life together."

Joe hoped he would leave Eva alone. He knew Anton was circling and he was going to protect her regardless.

"My fiancé will make good wife. She not like Eva. She's a home person. Eva travels the world like sailor a boyfriend in every city." Anton said with a laugh.

That dug into Joe. He was ready to pounce but held back asking. "Was that your fiancé earlier, Mona?"

"No. She's a friend and consultant."

"Eva's the boss. My boss and yours. You were childhood friends, leave it at that. What she does today is her business. I don't think you want me telling her what you said. No more talk about Eva." Joe said looking at Anton who smiled and nodded.

"Sorry. I don't know her these days. Now, the real estate. I'll have no more money to invest in that project." Anton asked.

"The limit has come. Any property sold or built on?"

"I have three parcels sold and ready to build more. I can pay the rest of the way if no surprises come along. I can pay back Mr. Bokanawski for the property overtime. As I sell more, payments will increase."

Joe thought carefully. This wasn't the place to tell him CZ Corp. owns that property and not his to negotiate with.

Joe said. "I need to make a phone call in the morning and see. I'm told you're to stop investing money from the warehouse."

"Okay. You call and let me know what the terms are. I have five more lined up to buy homes. I have other property I want to buy that will sell. I know the housing market's down, but these are homes for wealthy. A whole different market. I know many people that want to buy them. I can do better than the big guys."

Anton stopped and sipped his wine. Then continued.

"I know what wealthy people want in homes. They want privacy and an excellent view in the country. In the city they want a magnificent view in the heart of the city and security. I know this. I own part of a building a few blocks away that's upscale residential. Three of those bought the first homes there. I know the market here. I started with a few old houses and repaired them and sold them. That market is up and down for the middle class. The wealthy housing market is steady. I know this property will go over great and I can build on that."

Anton looked sad for a moment then back to his arrogant self. Impressive speech Joe thought, but then a lawsuit that could go either way. For now, though he told Anton.

"I'll make a call tomorrow but can promise nothing."

"I take you there before you call. I need you to see, I show you the signed deals already."

Joe thought that a waste of time. He then knew it would be a good place to fire him.

"Okay, I'll look before I call."

"Thank you, Joe."

Joe felt he could try Ariel, but the orders to take the property and he must do. He has the good grace of Catherine also. If no signed documents show they allowed him to take the money. Theft could work into the equation. Joe took comfort in that and stood.

"Anton, I need to go. I must go pick up Vera from the warehouse. She hasn't eaten, and we need sleep."

Joe noticed a sour look on Anton's face when he mentioned the warehouse. He shook hands with Anton.

"I'll be there bright and early." Anton said.

"I will soon after."

Anton smiled and nodded.

Joe nodded to Sevan and they walked back through the restaurant toward the exit.

Joe felt the grip of cold outside. He put his hands in his pockets and tried to keep warm. He should have checked the weather before he came. They walked past the stores now closed or closing. Passing a few people Joe saw a couple lost in their own world. Sevan looked behind them often.

"Why does Anton have a bodyguard?"

Sevan looked at Joe not saying a word. He kept casually looking around. After a few moments Sevan said. "I can kick his ass if you want."

Joe looked at Sevan asking. "Anton or the bodyguard."

Sevan gave him a confident look saying. "Both, at the same time."

Joe just looked at him and said nothing. He didn't doubt it. They turned into the parking lot. Sevan did a quick sweep of the Escalade and then unlocked. They seated and left.

Joe started to think about the dinner. Anton did not show respect to a boss and did not have nice words about Eva. Firing him will take care of that. He'd tell him tomorrow at the property.

The barrels, Joe thought looking at Sevan.

"What did you make of all those barrels of glass cleaner. I know I asked already but." Sevan didn't take an eye off the road and said.

"A severe shortage wherever they're going."

"Going." Joe said and took out his cell phone. "Vera. We're on the way. One more, grab shipping files for the barrels of window cleaner. Don't make copies just bring the files."

"Sure." Vera said.

"See you in a few."

The road noise made Joe weary. He didn't realize the impact the day was having on him. He leaned back closing his eyes. He kept thinking about window cleaner and where was it scarce or bought at a big mark up. The soothing road noise made him nod off.

Chapter 69

They checked in a luxury hotel that impressed Joe. He was accustomed to chain places. He didn't ask Sevan about the price because if security was picking up the tab, he'd enjoy it. He sat on the bed looking out at the twinkling lights of Minneapolis.

The little nap he took felt good but then guilty when he saw Vera lugging files looking tired. She wanted to go over the files tonight also.

Joe rubbed his face thinking of Carol and dialed. After a few rings she answered.

"Hi. Sorry to call late."

"Oh, hey, how's the trip going." Joe knew by the sound of her voice he had woke her.

"Irritating. This guy's a piece of work. The good news though I already know what to do and hope to be home by the weekend."

"I'll be lonely. I wish you were in bed with me right now." Carol said yawning.

"So, do I. I'm just not looking forward to tomorrow. I need to tell this guy the money he's been investing from the company is the companies and you're fired." Joe said rolling his eyes to no one.

"What's he been investing it in?"

"Some real estate here. Said he knows the market for the wealthy here and wants to pay the company back for what he bought. Eva told me to take it and give it to our real estate division."

"Have you seen the property?"

"Tomorrow he wants me to go there. Says he sold three parcels with houses built on them. I don't know. He's not going to take it well but once fired I can hire. Then go home."

"Hmm, then look tomorrow. Maybe he should be in real estate than running a warehouse. How does he do as the warehouse president?"

"Not good. He has no intelligent people in place and is collecting the pay for a few positions. He's taking all he can and never there probably. The point is I must fire him. So, his real estate career will end also." Joe tired of talking about it and needed to change the conversation.

"You know what you're doing. I guess."

"Not looking forward taking candy from a kid. He did talk well about the real estate. If he'd taken an interest in the warehouse I'd have talked to Eva. He didn't, and Eva wants him gone."

"Some people take jobs they don't like until they find what they like."

"Let me let you go back to sleep."

"Love you."

"Love you too."

Joe shut the phone thinking about Anton. He hasn't changed the name, he hasn't hired office staff to keep up with business or know the business. Grounds to fire someone. What could he be doing in the real estate area? Probably not much better, Joe thought as he rubbed his face and wondered when Vera would be ready.

He stretched out on the bed and closed his eyes. He would give Vera a few more minutes and then call over to her room.

Joe imagined an empty field with holes dug in the ground or maybe three to show the three buyers. He laughed and thought of being home in bed with Carol. His thoughts faded, and he fell to sleep again, happy.

The knocking was loud and insistent as Joe opened his eyes looking around. The clock read one hour later than when he fell to another nap. There was knocking again and his cell phone ringing.

He stumbled off the bed to the door. Vera was standing there with a cell phone in her hand. She pressed her phone off and the ringing stopped from inside room. She looked a little mad.

"I dozed off." Joe said rubbing his head. Vera walked in to the table and put down the files she been carrying. She took a seat at the table and Joe took a seat at the table also. He looked at the files and at Vera who said. "Are you ready?"

"Yes."

"He's taken almost fifteen million for the

real estate. Anton listed it as a corporation. The Green Hills reality company. Paperwork's here on the money transfer. I didn't find any files for the Green Hills company. He must keep them locked-in his desk. I didn't have permission to go into his desk." Vera stopped there as Joe was digesting the information. He then thought about an empty field with some lumber laying around and three holes in the ground. It's open-and-shut tomorrow.

"What's the current money?"

Vera took out her notebook flipping a few pages saying. "Two million available. Eight hundred fifty thousand payables and receivables are two and a half million."

"That's good to hear." Joe said still feeling groggy.

"He's kept that amount since the purchase of the warehouse. He's been taking profit and investing it in real estate." Vera said looking at Joe who wished he had a cup of coffee. That would keep him awake though. He looked at Vera saying. "Good to hear. He's been doing a good job then. The real estate I drop the bomb on him tomorrow and fire him. I need to get someone to take his place though. Oh, the pay, has he been taking the pay for some unfilled positions."

Vera flipped another page. "He's been collecting two paychecks. Four thousand a week after taxes."

Joe whistled. "He's going to get a pay cut. That's for sure, and you have nothing on the real estate."

"Nothing. Like I said, it's locked-in his office desk probably."

Joe looked out the window starting to feel happy. The warehouse numbers were in order. The profit will be going to New York. They'll take the real estate and pay XO Foods. Then Phil in real estate must decide what to do with a field and three holes.

Joe asked. "What's those."

"Files going back six months. They're the buy and sell orders for the barrels of glass cleaner, no prices on them though."

Joe forgot about that.

"What do they tell you or me."

"He's been running a subunit out of the warehouse called The Mini import and export company. It must have its own books because there's no transactions on the XO, Great Northern books."

"Where're the barrels going." Joe asked curiously.

"They're shipped from Kentucky to here then sent to New Jersey for export."

"Export. That's it. No name of country."

"No."

Joe thought for a second.

"He's shipping glass cleaner to somewhere and must be making a profit. Strangest I ever heard. Glass cleaner scarce."

Vera shrugged. Then Joe said.

"A valued customer to him. Try to find who the customer is, and we'll steal them from him. Other than that, it's just a case of getting rid of him. Going as planned." Joe nodded, and Vera nodded.

"Sorry, you didn't have to bring those files."

"You did tell me to bring them."

"Yes, I did and I'm tired."

Joe's mind was stuck, and he asked.

"How much glass cleaner is he shipping."

Vera flipped her notebook a page saying. "Three hundred a month."

"Where's that stuff going and why. I mean glass cleaner is an easy product to make. We need to know who the buyer is. Is it that profitable?"

"Won't know until we see the numbers."

Joe said. "Can't see the numbers. It's his private side business." The real estate though is ours and we need to see the books before I fire him."

Then Joe said openly. "Glass cleaner."

Vera giggled with her shoulders. Joe stretched yawning saying.

"Vera, thank you much. You need to go to bed. Have you eaten?"

"I'm fine and need some sleep too."

"Go to bed. Tomorrow will be easy. In fact, list a job opening for a president of a warehouse and the rest of the day should go like clockwork. We'll in New York for the weekend."

Vera jotted that down then gathered the files starting to leave. Joe got up opening the door for her. Vera turned. "Goodnight."

Joe nodded. "Go rest."

Back in bed he lay thinking what a big help Vera had been. Then he thought about glass cleaner. The barrels danced in his head putting him to sleep.

Chapter 70

The next morning feeling refreshed Joe was ready for the task here. He was keeping his mind off Anton. The passion he displayed for the real estate stayed with Joe. The man should have approached Eva and Catherine, he thought.

Dressed and ready he hadn't heard from Vera or Sevan. When he heard a knock on the door. He opened to Sevan standing there arrogantly happy.

"Morning Sevan."

"Morning sir. Miss Vera waits in the restaurant."

"I hope she didn't order for us."

Joe saw what a smile on Sevan's face might be. There's hope, he thought grabbing his jacket.

Down in the restaurant they found Vera as Sevan backed away to the counter. Joe stopped him.

"Sit with us Sevan."

"Yes."

Joe regretted that decision because Sevan's bulk needed one side of the booth.

Vera and Joe squeezed on the other side. A waitress appeared pouring coffee handing out menus.

Joe sipped coffee looking at Vera and then Sevan.

"What's up."

"Sevan feels a problem will arise today when Anton's fired. He wants to bring in a team to help. I disagree."

Joe looked at Sevan and then back at Vera saying. "You both discussed this. Without me."

"We need to think ahead on some matters that you don't need to be bothered with." Vera said, and Sevan nodded.

"Sevan you think a team might be needed. Can you explain?" Joe asked being clueless what a team was.

"A few from our security detail can be here in a few hours and standby in case Mr. Slotkolov does not take the news well today. Mr. Slotkolov may have friends here who can maybe play rough. I'm just looking out for your safety."

Joe asked. "What can Anton do."

"We're going to see this property. I found the location. It's well in the woods and I would feel better having people close by. That's the best I can say. For your own safety and Miss Vera."

Joe sipped his coffee looking at Vera and then Sevan.

"Sure, bring a team and keep them hidden. I don't want Anton thinking I'm going to hurt him. I plan to do this diplomatically. I'm his boss and family friend or not he's fired from the company. As for his personal respect of me, I don't care. That doesn't make money in our business."

Sevan excused himself to make a call. Joe asked Vera. "You don't feel a little extra security is in need."

"I'm sure he'll blow his stack and calm down. Sevan always wants to fight. Security people. I mean last year I saw him beat the hell out of a guy outside a restaurant just because he called me a slut. I mean the guy was harmless. That's the language now a days."

"I would've done the same. I guess it's just a male thing."

Vera rolled her eyes and sipped her coffee. Joe enjoyed this little moment together. He saw the real Vera not just the efficient sexy young lady.

Then Joe asked. "You worked with Sevan before."

Vera's eyes lit up saying. "We've been together for two years. I worked in the real estate for Phil. He's the CEO and they always start the new ones with him. I like Sevan, but he's this overprotecting animal that comes out if somebody looks wrong at me or my boss."

Joe liked this saying. "He's just doing his job."

"I guess."

Sevan sat back down saying. "They'll be

people in place in one hour."

Joe smiled at Vera saying. "We can never be too sure."

Sevan shrugged, as Vera rolled her eyes at him. Joe liked personal bonding's with his employees.

"I got a call from Ariel. He's in the office if you need anything. The family members are not available." Vera said.

"Okay. Ariel's the boss." Joe said wondering what Eva was doing at his moment. He remembers the smell of her perfume and soft white hands. Then the waitress of great size returned, and Joe finished daydreaming.

Later while traveling to the warehouse Sevan made use of the GPS unit in the Cadillac. Every turn alerting him ahead of time. A good device to have in a rental, Joe thought. He wished he invented it, so he wouldn't be bothered with the mundane job that he had.

He had lazy people before, now he has them around the country in charge of warehouses. He did like the money though. Carol and he were going to live nicely. Maybe in a few years he'll retire to spend time on something more challenging. Like children.

Joe liked the idea of having a child, in fact he wanted a girl. He knew girls always liked their dads and he would spoil the hell out of her. Joe heard Vera's cell phone ring.

"Yes, Hi, Ariel. Yes, He's right here."

Joe reached taking the phone. "Hi, what's up."

"The usual rat races. How's the weather there?"

"Seventy-five and sunny but will turn gloomy for Mr. Slotkolov."

"Yes. Be firm."

"The guy has the place running like shit. He's collecting the pay for unfilled positions. He's also running some small export business from the warehouse. Now, the real estate I imagine is an empty field with three holes in the ground. However, yes, Ariel I'll go easy." Joe glanced over to see Sevan smiling.

"I'm sure you will Joe. I have a news bit though. Mr. B called saying he had a call from Anton's uncle. He said you were rude to him at dinner last night. I believe its bullshit. I know the kid there. Mr. B didn't say anything more and just brushed it off."

Joe absorbed it fast and understood even faster saying. "A little jab. It didn't bother Mr. B. That's good but, I have a verbal ruling from Catherine that bypasses Mr. B."

Ariel was silent for a moment then said. "I understand. Then do what Catherine wants. You're under her rules."

Joe said. "I'm not comfortable with that ruling. I don't want in the middle of family but, she's the boss. Eva gave the order for Anton and Catherine is backing it."

"She is. Do what she has told you. I know

nothing. She will tell Mr. B." Ariel said solemnly.

"I thought of something. Anton has the real estate in his name. Not something our real estate division can just walk in and take. I feel this could get messy, a lawsuit. You think hire a lawyer here and be ready. "Joe asked.

Ariel quiet for a moment then said. "No. The family will personally take care of that. You're to fire him and they'll take care of the real estate. Anton knows where the money came from and who's the rightful owner."

"Your right. I'll take the first stand at getting him to sign over the property. If he refuses, it's out of my hands."

"Exactly."

Joe thought of telling Ariel about the extra security but decided not to.

"I'm going to give him the news at the property. It's probably just three holes in an empty field."

Ariel laughed and then said. "Two holes. Three's much work for that kid."

"You're right."

"Right then. Do what Eva wants done and come home."

"I was thinking a trip to Florida to give my team here a rest for a few days." Joe said looking at the two. Sevan stoic and Vera smiling yes.

"Your decision. I hear Vera looks good in a bikini."

"Ariel, we're getting to our destination."

Joe said.

"Go it."

Joe closed the phone. He held onto it then Vera leaned forward. "My phone."

Joe handed it to her. He wondered if she heard what Ariel said.

He dismissed that needing to keep focus and then told Sevan. "Tell me know when the team arrives. Keep them at a distance. I'll leave it up to you after I tell Anton the bad news."

"Yes sir."

He started to realize that this young man here may try something. Maybe he'll have friends at the property to intimidate me, Joe thought. He took comfort in knowing Sevan was aware and knows what to do.

Joe then wondered why the family would not fire him. They hired him.

Chapter 71

D on felt a little dirty doing this, but one must lower themselves to win. A court of law could never bring justice. He slowly drove the rental car up the street of where Joe Bergen lived. Midmorning and sunny. He pulled the car slowly into the driveway parking under the shade of a big tree.

He stepped out grabbing his briefcase. Don listened to the distant sounds of birds and lawn mower walking up to the front door. There was no answer at first. He was going to ring the bell again when the door opened. A shapely blond stood looking at him. She had on sweat pants and a tight-fitting shirt with no bra. He had the right house. He remembered her sitting with Joe Bergen at the mayor's party.

"Hello. I'm John Thane from North Eastern Insurance. My boss told me to come to speak to Mr. Joe Bergen. They sat together at the Mayor's party."

He noticed the look change on her face

from unknown to calm happy.

She said. "My husband isn't here right now. He handles the insurance for us."

"I see. Can I leave some brochures and insurance quotes?" Don asked with kind face showing. The blond softened her look more saying. "Okay, I see no harm in getting a quote. I don't want you in trouble with your boss." Carol opened the door wider to let Don in.

He quickly looked over the inside. Dining room on the right to the left a living room. Straight ahead a staircase and a hallway leading probably to the kitchen and maybe a den.

"You work for who again." Carol asked

"North Eastern Insurance. Your husband sat with my boss Mr. Huntington at the Mayor's party and he's sent me to sell yourselves something."

Carol nodded looking ready to laugh. "I remember sitting with someone in the insurance business."

Don relaxed inside not showing it. "I haven't done street sales in a while, years. I run my own division." Don pulled out a fake card he had made. "My card."

Carol took and read it. "A division head comes to sell insurance."

"My boss wanted the best for you and Joe." Don said seriously.

Carol giggled saying. "I'm Carol. We'll sit in here."

Don followed her into the living room. He

saw big flat TV with leather couch and chairs. He took the couch having a view of the front window and the street. He knew right below the front window is ground zero.

Carol asked. "Can I get you coffee?"

"Yes. That'd be nice. We're not supposed to accept food or drink. I started that rule."

Carol laughed saying. "You made the rule and you can break it. Don't worry I won't tell."

"Thank you." Don said giving her a big smile. He then placed his briefcase on the coffee table opening it. Carol left to make coffee. He took another look around. The room had magazines, books and one well-worn recliner. It's the spot.

Carol seemed okay and he didn't like seeing her killed but that happens in war, collateral damage. Innocent people are hurt.

She returned with phone in hand sitting in a chair away from Don saying. "I want to give Joe a quick call. He's going to laugh. I believe it's your boss who wanted to show him his new Ferrari."

"He has a picture proudly displayed on his desk of it. And I drive a Chevy."

Carol laughed. Don knew he was doing great. He hasn't lost his sales skills.

"Someday you'll be CEO and buy one." Carol dialed as Don quickly ran through the names of who was who at North Eastern Insurance. He also had fake voice mail and email set up. He was ready if he had to speak to Joe Bergen.

~~~~~

Joe entered the front entrance with Vera and Sevan following. The receptionist dressed better today looking professional. She said good morning satisfactorily and let Joe know that Mr. Slotkolov was waiting. He started to climb the stairs with Vera when his cell phone rang. He looked at the readout and saw his home number. Carol knew the best times to call he mused to himself. He stopped at the top of the stairs waving Vera to go on.

"Hello."

"Hey. Sorry to disturb but you're going to love this. The insurance guy you met at the mayor's party with the Ferrari has sent one of his people over to sell us insurance. He hasn't sent just anybody. He sent the Division President for insurance policies."

Joe didn't believe this. He let out a little laugh saying. "We have insurance. We have more with CZ Corp."

"Mr. Thane is sitting here if you want to speak with him." Carol said happily.

Joe looked down the hallway and saw Anton pop his head out his office. Both locked eyes for a moment then Joe said to Carol.

"No." Joe then continued. "Listen to the quotes. Might be good. But we don't need."

"I will."

"Need to have Mr. Huntington over for

dinner." Joe said with a laugh.

"Yes"

"Okay."

"Okay. Bye."

Joe closed his phone and liked hearing Carol was having a great day. Mr. Huntington sent over an underling to get some business. He was going to be an interesting friend, Joe thought.

~~~~~

Don listened pretending to play with numbers on a calculator while listening to Carol laugh and giggle. He did look over and smile on cue when she announced his title to Joe. The phone call ended. Carol looked at Don with a warm smile. He knew when not interested but going to listen and be nice. Cold calling, he learned years ago. He liked it. He lowered the suspicion level. They'll be dead before speaking to Mr. Huntington the CEO of North Eastern Insurance.

"Let me get the coffee." Carol said leaving the room again. Don looked out the front window remembering the shrubs just below it. He knew that'd make good cover. She returned with coffee. Don took his cup placing it down on the table.

"When's Joe going to be here."

"I hope by the weekend. He's in Minneapolis right now and I hope by the weekend. He has a private plane, so he can fly back next week if he's not finished there."

"I see." Don said. Minneapolis; a private plane; he was ready to throw the cup of coffee across the room. He continued. "I can come this weekend so not upset his schedule."

Carol sort of nodded yes saying. "You call Joe first. I don't want to handle him. He doesn't like that."

"I will." Don noted this weekend. Saturday. Then the world can say prayers at church Sunday for the loss of life.

He got down into the salesperson routine rattling off life, home and car insurance that was available. Then delved deeper into the savings as preferred customers and the conversion to stock in the company once they paid the policies in full. Don then went into explaining about annuity funds and other moneymaking savings plans. He went on for close to an hour impressing himself. Carol was impressed he knew because she looked serious and read over the numbers thinking.

After the hour he had Carol interested and could sell her anything. All Don cared about was she and her husband were going to be dead customers.

He left the house a while later with Carol in his hand. He left papers and figures that would impress anyone. Too bad no insurance would ever give such a good deal even to friends. Don almost laughed as he backed out of the drive way.

~~~~~

Not known to Don, Joe and Carol the security installed in the house by CZ Corp had hidden cameras. Joe and Carol thought it was just to oversee windows and doors and set off an alarm if broken into. They didn't know of the hidden cameras around the perimeter of the house. The security people from CZ Corp. wanted the picture of anyone who broke in the house. So, to give justice the CZ Corp. way.

The signals sent wirelessly to Manhattan. In a hidden office at CZ Corp. a man sat looking at a video screen. He saw someone go inside the house and leave about an hour later. He got a video feed of the man and the car and license plate. He quickly ran the plate number and came back as a rental. The man decided that it looked okay. He joked that maybe the wife was having a fling. Nothing appeared wrong, so he filed the video in a storage server and would bring it up later if this is a recurring situation.

Chapter 72

Joe knocked lightly entering. Anton on the phone waved him in to sit. He had a moment to think. Wanting to laugh at what Mr. Huntington did. Sending someone to his home to sell insurance. He knew he had a friend there that did in a big way. Joe thought how to return the favor. He was happy to hear Carol laughing and enjoying it.

He felt elated and ready to have a good day. He looked at Anton finishing his conversation or so Joe thought being it was Russian.

Joe looked around the office. The furnishings were plain and sparse. Nothing of class or anything that shows the personality of Anton Slotkolov, he thought knowing this guy had no personality.

Vera came in and Joe watched Anton eyes glue to her. Seating next to Joe she whispered. "I put the files back and noticed some payroll ones were missing."

"Okay." Joe said not surprised Anton was trying to cover up a few paychecks.

"The finance manager's here. Seems intelligent." Joe stared a moment saying. "Take me to him."

Anton was watching the verbal exchange. He left the office with Vera and into another office. He saw a normal looking guy behind a desk.

Joe stepped over. "Hello. I'm Joe Bergen. CEO of XO food service."

"I'm Dave Thompson. VP of finance. Glad to meet you Mr. Bergen."

Joe asked. "Employed with the company long?"

"Close to ten years. I decided to stay after the buyout. Sorry for yesterday." Dave paused moving closer. "They didn't tell me until this morning."

"No problem." Joe said moving closer too. "Understand there's a few problems here."

Dave rolled his eyes. "The buyout. I have two in college and I can't just."

Joe held his hand up. "You know the buyer of the glass cleaner?"

"No. His friend Mona takes care of that private business."

Joe nodded remembering Mona then said. "There's going to be fast changes today. I'll need someone for the top job."

Dave looked surprised saying quietly. "I know this place like my children."

"Stay here today and I'll have news for you."

"Joe. Sorry about the phone call." Anton said from the doorway.

"You've met my finance guy. Dave. He keeps the numbers good." Anton said looking at both.

"Yes, good man." Joe said.

"Good, now let's go to my office."

Joe shook hands with Dave saying. "Glad to meet you Dave."

"Same here Mr. Bergen."

Joe started once seated in Anton's office.

"Let's talk business. We'll start here. The sign, trucks and all letterheads are to be changed to the XO Food group yesterday."

Joe stopped momentarily when Anton got up to close the door. "That must begin immediately." Joe stopped, and Anton began.

"Okay the switch over in names will start today. I'll order the head of maintenance to get that going. I've been interviewing for positions and have prospects I'm ready to hire. Mark's doing the needed background checks." Anton finished.

Ironic Joe thought, he'd love a background check on Anton. "I'll be going over the sales numbers later today. Keeps sales at current level. Revenue and profit numbers look good, so we'll keep that for now. Don't refuse new customers that come in though. I'm setting up a buying office in New York that'll bring down costs. Until that's in place there's no need for drumming new business on a large-scale. That will come later." Joe paused and saw that Anton's eyes were glazing over. He decided to continue so he could fine tune this speech for Dave later in the day. "I have graphics designers in New York for the company brand products. We hired a big outfit that designed the new name design and it's fresh and friendly looking. A new image a new day, that type image. If you have any ideas, you can send them to the branding desk. I want brand names for the commonly brought products, something that will show good quality and a few cents cheaper. I want to see customer loyalty with a brand name. Once in place we can go full tilt on sales." Joe stopped.

Anton cleared his throat saying. "That sounds good. I'm looking forward to those changes."

"All sale's VP's from around the country I'm going to bring to New York for a week of sales training. I have my staff working on a new program that I hope increases sales by making their job easier. A friendly approach with the emphasis of keeping customers. A tug-of-war. The sales staff will pull customers in using all their strength. I'm excited with the new program. But, first the new name and branding of popular products will need to be in place." Joe stopped.

"I'm with you on this new look and change. It'll be great." Anton said.

Joe wondered when Sevan will tell him the teams here. He knew he had no problem talking the time away and forged on.

"The issue of running two books has to

end. There's just one company, XO Food. We end Great Northern. I realize that there's tax advantages running two books but end that."

"I will faze that out when the official company name has changed." Anton said looking uninterested.

"Good. I need that done in a months' time. The second month will be the sales meeting in New York." Joe needed the team here he wanted to move forward with the real estate.

"Now if that's done." Anton said. "I've been in talks with Mr. Bokanawski and he has come up with a payment plan for the real estate, but I haven't seen it yet."

Joe wondered if it was true. He spoke with Ariel he didn't mention anything about Anton buying the property. In the dark for a moment he decided he must go forward with what Eva had told him to do.

"I spoke with a representative for Mr. Bokanawski on the way here and he didn't mention any payment plan for the property. CZ Corp. owns the property." Joe finished the last part with power knocking Anton back a little. He looked around his office. Joe knew he's scrambling for a way out or into something. He got up unlocked a file cabinet and pulled out a file.

"I'll show you the value of the property I bought. Here's the papers." Anton said.

Joe sat up straighter finally getting what he wanted. Anton took out a paper handing it to him.

"Property values from one month ago. It's gone up in value. I have three completed houses with occupants. The remaining property I have commitments for eighty percent and that's based on word of mouth from the people who bought already. I'm taking the opportunity to develop a wealthy enclave instead of a few houses in the country. Enclave has a special meaning some like. I kept it quiet because I didn't want developers moving in and bidding up the price of property there." Joe stared at Anton thinking. The property belongs to CZ Corp.

He scanned the numbers showing the buy of property and cost of building the three homes. The value of the property after three houses were built. As houses are built, the adjoining properties go up in value. Difference between buy and current value was over thirty million. On the back side of the paper he saw a number circled. Profit, over twenty million. Organization better than thought.

Joe realized talking to Eva might get Anton a bonus for his efforts. Lessen the pain.

Joe handed the paper to Vera.

Joe said. "Numbers look good. Can you tell me more?"

Anton brightened and began. "I have designs for seven different styles of houses. My customer chooses the style and I build it. My brother has a crew doing good work, they're from the old country and take pride in what they do. I've made a profit and keep that in a bank. I take out for supplies and the worker's pay. I take no pay from that company." Anton paused, and Joe knew why the four paychecks. It impressed Joe, the effort and hardship he went through to make the property work.

Anton continued. "I'm to a point of buying up the remaining property. I have a deposit to purchase the adjoining property. The problem is I don't have enough funds to build new homes and buy property. Payments are slow when building and when I build the remaining 80 percent of the property someone else will buy the adjoining property. I just need a bridge loan. The bank wants too much interest because of no track record." Anton stopped there. A good presentation. CZ Corp. will make good money from this project, Joe thought.

"Anton, all sounds good." Joe saw a darkness come to Anton's face. "I don't have the power to extend money for outside projects that have nothing to do with XO Food. I suggest that you speak to Mr. Bokanawski again. Maybe he can help you there."

The dark look remained, and Joe knew this guy wasn't going to let go of this real estate.

Joe said. "Maybe you can contact Miss Eva Bokanawski. She's the CEO of CZ Corp. and maybe can help. My job's the well-being of

XO Food."

"You're going to take the property." Anton said with a hard stare.

"The deal has ended. That comes from Catherine and Eva. That's all I know."

Joe saw Anton's face lighten. He felt a little better. Then looking at the doorway Joe saw Sevan standing there. Joe left the office.

"They're in place." Sevan said.

Joe smiled saying. "We'll go to the property now."

Sevan smiled taking out his phone. Joe went back into the office. He looked at the file on the desk saying. "Show me the property."

"Why? Your interest is in XO Food."

That caught Joe a little short. "Because I want to see what you spoke so great about." Joe said knowing it was time to terminate.

They all got up to go and Anton handed the file to Joe saying. "Please review the file on the way there."

Joe took the file. "Sure." Wondering if the numbers were real. He'll have Vera review it on the way.

Chapter 73

Riding back to the office gave Don time to think and decide if he was sure going to plant the bomb. He could use a delivery service but today packages are thoroughly checked and that's a problem. That left one choice for him. No way around it he thought.

Watching live trading at his desk and the value of his private trading account only his eyes saw the missing five million. It was the last amount he had to pay back, then he could continue earning for his own greed. Repaying the money to his Uncle kept him happy with his family.

The numbers on the monitor should've been over forty million but, he ventured into a sure deal in Russia.

It began after his Uncle introduced him to the red-haired Eva at a party. At the party he was given the name of a business in Moscow selling real estate. He fell in love with Eva and real estate from the start. Wanting a relationship, he was rebuffed, and the real estate was a scam. That added to his anger now.

He didn't want to hurt her. She's a nice lady that everybody liked. His Uncle wouldn't hesitate to search for the person responsible if anything happened to her.

However, killing an executive in her company would send a message to her and make her think. By hurting the people close to her, she would suffer also.

The numbers on the computer screen dipped into the red. Red arrows down. Don invested in a cross section of stocks with real growth potential, but the economy was slowing the markets. At this pace the last portion of money was going to take longer to earn back for his uncle.

His uncle didn't want promises or words he wanted the money returned to the blind trust.

He started shredding the papers used at Joe Bergen's knowing he still had that sales touch. A boost to bring up his self-esteem. He knew his self-esteem will soar higher with news of a house exploding in a suburban neighborhood.

He will have the world in his hands soon enough. He's ready to take the parts he wanted, like Eva. By killing enough of her key people, he could hold her as a hostage and demand money. Destroy everything she holds dear and break her down to a low point. Don liked that knowing an expanded assault will have better affects. Joe Bergen will be the first wave.

Looking at the computer screen and the red arrows affecting most stocks he thought of throwing the computer at the wall.

Chapter 74

They started from the warehouse, Anton's BMW in the lead followed by the Escalade. Joe gave the file to Vera wanting her to read and give quick highlights.

Joe said to Sevan. "Tell the team to stay out of sight but close."

Sevan made a call talking in Russian.

"Joe." Vera said from the backseat.

"What did you find?"

"Three homes sold and enough money to pay back what's borrowed. Must be elegant homes. They sold for over five million each."

Joe looked at Vera's file spread on the seat. "Fifteen million. I don't believe it."

"That's what the file states. Can pay back what he borrowed from the company."

"He's using that profit from sales to build new ones." Joe didn't know what else to say. Vera said. "Appears he put a down payment on property next to what he already owns. I see he's been declined financing from two banks. I guess he's in a bind. Needs money to build more homes."

"And he doesn't want supply and no buyers." Joe finished.

Vera said. "You are correct."

"Made-to-order file?" Joe said.

Vera didn't respond reading more of the files. Then said. "He has down payments for construction of four homes."

"I bet he does." Joe said.

Sevan put his phone away saying. "Ready."

"Thank you, Sevan."

Joe wished he thought clearer on this. Police presence maybe. He could file charges for fraud. Get rid of Anton legally.

The BMW exited off the main highway onto a county road. The day sunny and bright. The trees emerald green with rays of sunlight bouncing off. Joe liked the scenery thinking how enjoyable a country home would be.

An old barn kept up. Farmhouse in the distance. Tranquility coming through the windows. Cows grazing along the winding lane. Trees overhanging the road giving a patchwork of light and shade as they passed underneath them.

On a downhill slop the BMW pulled off to a paved side road. They immediately saw a sign that read Country Estates, and a phone number. The sign well-made and painted with flowers planted just below. The road went slightly uphill and then gently down and the view was beautiful. An emerald valley with three homes and wooded areas.

Passing the first home Joe looked with awe. Large set back on the property. Well worth a large sum and he did see a limo parked in the circular drive. They followed the BMW passing by two other homes that were equally impressive. They stopped near a house under construction.

The BMW slowed and putting a window down. Joe watched Anton wave to somebody and that someone looking to be a supervisor waved back. The BMW took off with the Escalade following. They came to a dead end with an uphill grade at the end. The BMW stopped. Anton and his bodyguard got out. Joe, Vera and Sevan parked and got out. They gathered just away from the vehicles on a grass spot under some shade trees.

"What'd you think?" Anton asked Joe.

"Impressive. An attractive area." Joe said looking at the distance homes they passed. They sat raised surrounded by trees. Slate roofs visible.

Anton asked. "Would you buy a home here?"

"I would. Thirty-minute ride. That's a plus." Joe said caught off guard. He didn't expect to see this. Beautiful. The real estate people in New York will love it.

Joe noticed a Lexus approaching. They stopped turned around leaving. Inside Joe saw an old couple. Customers, he guessed.

"Come I want to show you something." Anton started walking up the hill where the road ended. Joe looked back seeing Sevan and Anton's bodyguard keep their places eyeing each other. Vera talking on her phone.

They slowly walked up. Reaching the top Joe saw a valley and a lake in the center. It was breathtaking Joe thought. Anton said. "My planned phase two. With that lake I can command a larger price. A private area the residents can regulate. After that section I hope to go outward in either direction. Notice the uphill slopes, picture mansions up there. Lake section the most expensive homes." Anton finished looking at Joe with pride.

"Attractive." Joe said not expecting this. "The file shows you have twenty million. That's enough to pay back the money taken from the company."

Anton said. "Yes, but I need money to build the homes. Need to pay for supplies and workers. These are wealthy people that buy them and before they pay, they look and want special touches. Not like cheaper homes bought to fit the money. These people come every day wanting different appointments. That cost money to please them with those changes. But, yes, you see the profit that I made so far."

Joe asked. "How many homes total?"

"Thirty. That's the maximum I can do here in the lake area with the outward expansion. I haven't bought but there's other areas in the state that I'm interested in. There's an area I could quickly buy and put up some lower priced homes for the working class. Earn some bread-and-butter money." Anton said with knowledge of a salesperson in know.

Joe needed a change of plan here. He needed to think saying. "Need to see all the files and bank accounts with payroll and supply outflows."

"No problem. Filed at the warehouse. That file I gave you was my promotional one. You'll see the numbers add up. You see the potential here. It's much easier to sell these homes then sell food to a customer." Anton finished with a laugh.

Joe decided to start since Anton was on a high. "Speaking of the warehouse. I have bad news." Pausing to look at the beautiful scenery. Anton finished. "I'm fired."

Nodding Joe said. "Not really my decision. But, seeing the place, I do agree."

Anton looking in the distance said. "I won't fight that. It's the family. The Bokanawski's. The dad likes me, but the rest don't so I guess the majority wins."

Joe thought he took it well. He looked down over at Sevan shaking his head no. Sevan nodded.

"What're those barrels of glass cleaner in the warehouse and the export company that buys them? What's the story there?"

The question took Anton aback as he looked at the lake. He took a few moments to answer. Joe eager to hear the answer.

"I sell them to help finance my real

estate. I asked Mr. Bokanawski to help with this project, and in this business extra money helps." Anton said.

Joe didn't get the answer he was looking for and asked. "What's in the barrels? You're saying there's a shortage of glass cleaner somewhere in the world."

Licking his lips Anton looked at Joe saying. "No shortage on glass cleaner in the world. I water it down selling it cheaper than the competition."

Joe looked at the lake laughing. "You're telling me your selling watered down glass cleaner. Don't know if that's illegal but will say that's not nice."

Anton nodded yes sheepishly. "Need money to make money. I ship to Ukraine. Have people bottle and sell in a discount store. Everybody makes a profit. No harm done. Person buys bottle for a dollar gets a product that's worth a dollar. Need that income to fund my dream here." Anton waved his arm around the area stopping at the lake. Joe watched every look on his face. Anton continued. "Sorry if you think bad of me but no harm is being done."

Joe let that go saying in a low voice. "Property is the problem. Profit from the warehouse financed it. Company wants it."

Anton said. "I understand. They have no soul. They're sharks. I have enough money to pay. I see the dream here they don't. They take it over it won't work. I'm needed here to finish."

Joe waited, and Anton continued. "I'm just a little guy trying to do something honest. You'd think they would know and like that." Anton finished picking up a rock and tossing it with no great power or direction.

Joe looked around saying. "Maybe I can help. No promises. Let me make a phone call."

Anton said. "Catherine can only make that ruling."

Joe thought about Catherine and what she said. If he feels, they made a bad call he is to contact her.

"I've stood here listening to you talk knowledgeable in the real estate that you bought. I'm standing here seeing what you have done." Joe paused looking at the defeated look on Anton's face. "I can help you with your new career. That file you had given me if correct is good and maybe I can arrange something. No promises."

Anton's face showed thinking. Joe waited. Anton said. "Shortfall of ten million if I move forward with the rest of the property and building homes but, I can work around that. I can pay the company's loan and work with that. You see I build them, but they must first have inspection and until that happens, I don't get payed. People are waiting, but not forever. May sound scary to you but I love the challenge." Anton finished looking questioningly at Joe.

"Tell me there's no surprises. I want to know everything now." Joe said wanting to help.

"No hidden surprises. I'll show you everything. It's developed here one home at a time. That's how I'm doing it. When someone wants a certain one in a certain time we cannot build fast enough. I may need a bridge loan for people like that. The second home was like that. It throws off my plans temporarily when I put a larger crew on one home. I plan to build certain types of mansions but, I must build to suit the buyer. Once it's full of homes the easy job is getting the rest of the wealthy to come and buy the standard ones."

Joe said. "I'll need a few hours to turn the tide. You're doing a great job here." Joe paused looking at the vast area. "May take on a partner since you have investment money from that partner. You will have complete control. They'll be silent. How does that sound? I don't imagine they'll give you money without a partnership. I suggest that to help me convince the family."

Joe didn't look forward talking with Eva, but this could be profitable for all.

"I want a signed document. The silent partner stating the rules. I want them to stay silent and let me do this here. I promise to keep them updated and paid if wanted."

Joe extended his hand, and both shook firmly.

"Need a few hours to talk this over with certain people. Barrels in the warehouse, move them. That's a private business of

yours and I suggest you sell the real stuff."
Joe ended with a laugh.

"I'll have that moved immediately."

"Also, clear out your desk. You'll be paid until the end of the month and paid for any vacation time you didn't take."

Anton nodding said. "I appreciate that. I suggest you put Dave Thompson in charge. He knows the business well."

"Probably will. Do you have a number where I can reach you?"

Anton handed a card to Joe. Reading it said Anton was president of a reality company. He liked that thinking he didn't have one for the food company.

"Where can we meet later."

"Cousin's restaurant."

"Okay, I need Dave Thompson promoted and the warehouse in order. At the same time, I'll be calling and convincing the right people to let you continue here with this property. Leave me the file. I need numbers to tell them."

Anton said. "I hope you can do it."

"About eight tonight at the restaurant."
Joe said.

"Eight will be fine. I'd like an hour at the office to say good bye. I'll leave files in the desk that you'll need." Anton said respectfully.

"Take the time you need there. I want to look around this property." Joe said feeling for the guy.

"My brother's building that house. He runs

the construction outfit. His name is Sergi."

Joe looked in the distance at the house saying to Anton. "Call me when you're done at the office."

"Will do."

Both shook hands again. Joe watched Anton walking down the hill pulling out his phone. Motioning his bodyguard, they were gone in moments.

Joe walked down the hill slowly. He figured a call to Ariel first to get the ball rolling.

Sounds of hammering in the distance. The smell of grass and the sunshine on his back felt good. A big profit here, Joe thought.

Chapter 75

In her Moscow apartment Eva slowly hung up the cell phone looking out the window. In the distance the colorful onion shaped domes with the high spires looked enchanting

Looking over at Ivan she was sure he already knew of Joe Bergen's plan in Minneapolis. She wasn't mad at all. Anton was fired. That she wanted done.

Eva asked Ivan. "What do you think of it."

Without blinking he said. "Okay for outsider."

"An outsider. He did all right. He saw something we who hate Anton didn't but, it's too late though." Eva smiled.

"Nobody will suspect." Ivan said.

"I was going to give Anton a partnership and an accident happened."

Ivan kept staring at Eva that wasn't intrusive. She liked when he gave her visual attention.

She had everything covered. Her father won't suspect it was her. She looked back at

Ivan who was still looking at her.

"Let's go see Aunt Catherine."

Ivan was up and on his cell phone.

Eva stepped over to the huge windows overlooking the city of Moscow. A cloudy, dreary night was ending. She knew out there was a pretty sun rise. The clouds covering the old city prevented her from seeing it. She wanted to see love. She hated nights like this.

In her gilded bathroom she swallowed a pill with water. It'll give her a bit and she needed it for a bit. Things were piling up lately. Help only a pill can give.

Minutes later she was in her armored BMW moving through early morning Moscow traffic. Traffic as bad as any major city in the world. Today it bothered her more so. Everything bothered her since landing few days ago. She wasn't enjoying her time in her favorite country. It was dreary, and Eva didn't like dreary.

A while later the car was rolling fast along the country lane leading to the Czarina's castle. A bright spot in her dark mood today. Her Aunt always raised her mood in a way only a close relative can.

The sparse lighting on the road gave an eeriness to the dawn. Huge trees overhung ready to grab her car and lift it up. Luckily waved through the gates and sped toward the castle.

The car stopped at the grand entrance. Ivan opened the door for Eva. Looking at the walk of steps upward cursing her Aunt for needing everybody to use the front entrance. Eva was hating everything today.

The bearded giant opened the door giving Eva a smile. She gave half a smile back taking off her coat and giving it to him.

Eva strolled the great hallway to her Aunt's favorite room. Slowly opening the huge door, she stepped in. Her Aunt sitting in an overstuffed chair already had glasses off looking at Eva.

At first Eva dismissed the thought but for some reason Aunt Catherine looked a little mad.

Eva walked over saying. "Hello." Taking a seat in the overstuffed next to her.

"Hi Eva." Her Aunt said closing the book and putting it on the table between them. Eva looked at the title on the spine. War and Peace. That struck a note in her, but she didn't know why.

"Reading the great ones." Eva said.

"I have a few pages left." Her Aunt said looking strangely at her. Eva wondered what was going on. The dreary day strangeness was continuing here.

"I imagine more than a few pages." Eva said waving at all the books in the library.

"What's going on with Anton?"

Eva cringed, and her stomach tightened. "Nothing. He's building homes and playing with that glass cleaner Vodka stuff."

Aunt Catherine smiled slowly saying. "I'm not your father. Don't fuck with me." In a high tone that made her cough.

Eva froze inside and started. "I feel Anton's taking a risk with the export business. If he's busted, we run the risk of getting found out. That we don't need. I brought that up with dad and he said Joe Bergen would get the blame. I tried to talk to dad, but he can be stubborn. I and the others feel firing Anton is good. The export business would go with him."

Her Aunt said with piercing eyes. "Continue."

"I had Max looking into an accident to silence Anton because he will call dad and start trouble. I love my father, but I feel he hasn't changed with the times, he still likes the old days. We must be careful these days. Anton's too belligerent one bust with his glass cleaner scam could bring down our billion-dollar empire. Also bringing Anton into the family business will be bad. I feel Joe Bergen as a prospect is better. He's a clean image and not sloppy. He came up with a good deal for Anton. It won't happen though. Anton is a risk."

Her Aunt kept looking at her saying. "You thought well on that. I agree, Anton has no place in our family. I hope it's an accident beyond a doubt. His father was honorable and so is his uncle. The young Anton is lazy. He makes a modest profit from that Vodka, glass cleaner stuff but the consequences are higher if he's caught. So, let's let it happen."

Eva liked what she said waiting for her to

continue. "Russian government is examining banks, so they can be globally acceptable. So, don't stop any business coming to the bank. It'll raise a red flag."

"I read that in the news. They're trying to be like America with sound banking. And CZ Corp. will continue as usual."

Her Aunt laughed saying. "Of course. America sets the model we must follow."

Eva felt relieved asking. "How was your trip to New York?"

"Good. I wanted to meet your Joe Bergen. A handsome man. I see why you hired him. The wife is a plain Jane but that's good. We know he's not gay." Aunt Catherine said, and Eva felt a jab but let it go. She had no choice and said with little volume. "Maybe someday bring him in the family."

"In time. Time reveals qualities about people."

"If he didn't show up fifteen years ago, I wouldn't be here now. That's a quality I see already." Eva said proudly. Her Aunt smiled.

"He did help me and you. I do owe him for that." Aunt Catherine said.

Eva felt there was something more to her reply but let it go saying. "That's why in the future I may bring him closer. Phil in Real Estate I don't have good confidence in. I think Joe will do better and understand what we do."

"Philly can be soft at the wrong times. I feel the money we pay him is doing it. But, by no means fire him. He's doing great with

Real Estate." Aunt Catherine said arrogantly.

"Yes, he'll stay where he is." Eva said as a butler entered pushing a cart with tea and sweets. Aunt Catherine smiled. "My favorite."

Eva got for her Aunt. They ate and drank quietly and when they finished the cart was taken away. Alone in the library. Aunt Catherine said in a soft voice. "Andre's gone. Thank you."

"Yes."

"I'm sure you're curious why I had you do that." Aunt Catherine asked, and Eva shrugged. She continued. "I wanted to upset Russe." Aunt Catherine looked off smiling. Then continued. "Andre was a close person of his. I remember Andre from years ago when he was a lad. The tough kid who would do anything for Russe Ureinchencko. Now put to sleep and known that Andre was taking money from a rival mob. That's sure to be upsetting. I imagine Russe right now is second-guessing all his top people. It'll be confusing for a time for Russe." Aunt Catherine kept smiling and looked away.

"Why don't we just wipe him out? We have the manpower." Eva asked. Her Aunt cut her eyes to her for a moment then softened. "That's one person you would not want to kill, Eva."

"Can I ask why?"

Aunt Catherine smiled saying. "He's an old friend and I want him to live. I like playing with him now and then."

"Dad did mention you and Russe almost got married."

"I was young, and he made an impression on me. He's a handsome man. But he wasn't happy with just one woman. I found out and killed her. I sliced her tits off and put a baseball bat in her pussy. A horrible find by the police, they thought it was a serial killer. At the time I was going to kill Russe if I found him." Aunt Catherine finished laughing heartily.

Eva smiled sheepishly asking. "You still love him."

Aunt Catherine went soft in the face and knew she did. Her Aunt then said, "you would too."

"He's kinda old for me." Eva laughed.

"Yes, yes."

"Dad mentioned that you were pregnant."

Aunt Catherine looked at Eva saying. "Your father is dreaming."

"Probably needs watching over with who he puts in charge. I mean we don't want known criminals running things. And some of Dad's old friends are known by law enforcement."

"I know. I can't just put him out to pasture. He helped build this empire and he will have a say until his death." Aunt Catherine said firmly.

"I understand. I won't say that again."

"No, you have a good point. Tell me if you think something is not right. I also told your Joe Bergen to see me if he feels a bad decision is made. I will explain that to your father. I was hoping he would retire by now. He hasn't so we keep on with him."

Eva felt a spark of happiness what she told Joe Bergen. She liked the guy and wanted him to be part of the family someday and he was having a good start without knowing it. That excited Eva.

"That's fine with me. I can't picture dad not retired."

"He's like an Alzheimer patient. We must keep a watch on him." Both laughed.

"Now, when's Uri bringing in the next shipment." Aunt Catherine asked.

"Next Friday for Russia. It'll be four tons. A good supply and money for us."

"Great idea he had."

Eva liked talking business. "Yes. It's almost undetectable. We lost only five shipments since we started it."

"Versus the other way when we tried every trick in the book to smuggle and loss ten out of fifteen." Aunt Catherine said laughing lightly.

"In ten years, we have a hold on the smuggling business. Close call once. A ship boarded and searched. They sent men down in scuba gear see if anything was thrown overboard."

"I guess they never saw the underside of the ship."

"Well, we have the sub hulls painted to match the ships we use. So, unless they go up close and look, they won't know." Eva said with confidence.

"If they did, they'd be looking at one hundred million in cocaine and weed and didn't know it." Aunt Catherine said laughing.

"Everybody's paid well at the other end, so we'll have no problem." Eva said.

"Pay people so they can feel human and live a good life and buy what they see. They'll always be loyal."

"While we flood the world with drugs, and nobody has a clue how we do it." Eva said proudly.

"Not the whole world. We only have America and Europe." Aunt Catherine said sternly.

"Yes, I know. The African countries are too unstable. They want guns and the ones that buy drugs are fleeting. We had different buyers every time we sold there on a trial. That's too unstable. We'll get busted. They ask too many questions. They asked the team if they could bring in weapons. I don't want to be a gunrunner."

Aunt Catherine nodded saying. "Africa's out. Asia?"

Eva rolled her eyes. "Don't know anybody there. We need to cultivate some Asians. I mean they have their gangs, but they're all tattooed, and the law watches them. It'll lead to us if we're involved. I have someone traveling the Asian areas and in time we'll have connections with the right ones."

"I hope in my lifetime." Aunt Catherine

said with a smile then continued. "Interpol's getting interested again. We're too good. I bought another tattooed one to take the fall."

"Fifty million for a few years in prison shouldn't be a problem for him."

"He won't mind at all. But, yes, we need more buyers though. We have tons of drugs and need to expand." Aunt Catherine said in a somber tone. Eva hated this.

"In a measured way. We sell in Europe and America and have laundering operations to handle the money. Asia, we have no businesses yet, we need that first to expand there. Getting the drugs there is no problem it's the money that we need to clean. It'll look strange to have a Russian buy many Japanese businesses. You see we are strangers there. Not like Europe and America where we fit in."

"I understand." Aunt Catherine said.

"It's not impossible. I just need time. The Asian countries like to know people and the respect thing they have in their society."

"We need a partner then. That I don't like."

"I think China will be the first new area. The gangs are less respectable, unlike Japanese gangs. The booming economy in China makes finding businesses there easier. We won't be as noticeable, everybody's going there." Eva said knowing she didn't even have anybody in the area. She was winging it knowing she'd have to go forward with what Aunt Catherine wanted. They had billions now and they should just stay put with what they have. She didn't like going into areas where the language and people are different.

"Keep me updated. We need to expand." Aunt Catherine said.

"The Chinese are different, so it'll take time."

"The Middle East. Don't they like drugs."

Eva prayed for the day she was in charge.

"Very risky. They're extreme people. Yes, there's drug use but if our teams caught, they'll torture them. I mean we can, but the risk is scary if our people are caught. Here and America we can pay officials. There, it's about religion and I feel we should stay out."

"True, we deserve better for our people. We don't send anyone to do what we wouldn't do ourselves."

Eva laughed, and Aunt Catherine looked saying. "I'm glad you find that so funny."

"I was laughing because I did go with a team to unload a shipment."

"And, tell me what's funny."

Eva kept a straight face and said. "The ship stopped near a port in France. I put on scuba gear and made my way over with the team. I got over the cold water. At the ship we started the release of the sub hull. It drops suddenly. I tried to help keep it up and paddle my feet. Well, it was heavy, and I tried to keep my side up. I almost let go then felt a hand on my ass. Another team member pushed me up and I held it up with the help of his hand." Eva bust out laughing. Aunt Catherine said. "I bet you were thrilled with an orgasm in the ocean."

Eva finished laughing then continued. "We swam back like that. We got the hull attached to the retrieving boat and left. We swam to the dock and went into the safe house." Eva laughed again saying. "The man took his suit off and dressed in record speed and left. We changed in separate rooms and when we reassembled that guy had already left. I asked why. They said because he felt bad about touching my ass, but he didn't want me to fail. They said he did good but bad and left. I didn't understand this, so I had them tell me where he lives. I went there the next day and it was a cute farm with two little kids running around and a pretty wife. I asked where he was. And the wife took me inside and left. He was scared. I asked him why. He said he didn't want me to fail and held me up by my ass. He said while we were swimming back, he decided that he should quit. I asked why. He said because he touched another lady's ass and disrespected his wife." Eva paused, and Aunt Catherine smiled. She continued. "I told him it was fine and hoped he would return. He said no. I then decided to talk to his wife. She told me he never looks at another woman and she calls him her dream. I explained to her lightly that he helped me and touched me and feels guilty. She said that always happens. So, she went into the house and talked to him. They both came out and he said he will return. I guess she knows of the work he does because she told me that it happened before with Olga and Tatyana."

"He loves his wife." Aunt Catherine said solemnly.

"When they married, he told her, and she told him if they can't be true to each other they will never survive. That's why they bought a farm and live a secluded life. He then told me that goes for the Czarina also." Eva said with respect.

"Very loyal."

"Yes, I bought them another farm a bigger one. They send me produce every season. I had Uri put him in charge of the team."

Aunt Catherine thought for a moment then said. "Yes, it seems unusual people working for us have high standards. What they do does not bother them. I told you about the hit man we used. He would go to church every Sunday and never botched a job. To this day he's happily retired and goes to church. People will do anything for the right price these days. Pay them well and they will be loyal. You won't find that in colleges now a days."

Eva smiled saying. "This man has such a pristine life and he helps bring drugs in the country. How does he justify it?"

"Justify what. It's for entertainment. The first Astor to America made money in the fur business and then shipping the furs and other products. He imported opium which wasn't illegal at the time. Then real estate. Ever wonder why his children and the later generations never made the money like he did. Twenty million dollars in the 1800's when he died was an unprecedented amount of money to have. Furs and real estate didn't make all that. He may have been the first drug baron in America." Aunt Catherine said with authority.

"Understand. It's a living. Nothing to feel guilty about." Eva said thinking out loud.

"We're no different from tobacco or alcohol or other products that sell. Even foods clog the insides. We just import to the border and collect our money. We don't sell on the streets and see the good or bad that comes from the product. Like any other company." Aunt Catherine finished with a serious look.

"Understand. I'm amazed we have people working for us that are so good. It makes me feel good."

"That's why we have no theft of our product. We have many good people working for us." Aunt Catherine smiled nicely.

"I see that. They just want a living and don't care what they do to earn it."

"They don't care. Why care? Graduate college and get a job. Constant stress then retire and find out that retirement is poor. Or the company's sold and you lose your job. Find another and live by the laws in place and feel cheated." Aunt Catherine took a breather then continued. "Like all those awful movies that tell how you should live your life. Cheating wives, cheating husbands. Medical services run by people that don't care. Accidental deaths by doctors and they don't care. We vote people into offices to do the right thing and immediately we find out that a dictator holds us. The dictator is the news media. Get enough people to believe the media and watch governments cringe and do what they want. What's to look forward to in that life? What we do and the money we use to influence has never been easier. People are afraid of tomorrow."

Eva looked at her with respect and said. "It's true. We give people a way out as long as they're decent."

"We make sure they are. Some of the best citizens in Europe and America work for us. What's that telling you?"

"People are tired and fed up."

"Correct and we help the ones who can handle it. Take the man in the water with you. What's he got to feel guilty about? Swim to a ship; unhook a sub hull; transport to another. No different from a man building a missile in a factory. Where it goes doesn't concern him. They just want to live a good life and be happy."

Eva stretched her body. "I wasn't trying to give you the idea that I have a bad feeling."

"I know. You're like me explore

everything. A good."

"I like to think so."

"Yes." Aunt Catherine smiled, and Eva felt strange for a moment. The pills were wearing off and sleep was needed, fast.

"I guess I'll head back to America."

"No. Stay here for the next few days."

Eva's stomach tightened hearing that. She wanted to see Joe Bergen to toy with him and plan his future.

"Can I ask why?"

"Wellington is going to announce he's running for President, should happen very soon. I feel it best if you stay put."

"I'll stay in Russia. In fact, I'm going to take a trip to our diamond mine. I need some new jewelry made."

"Between you and Olga how am I to sell any. You girls have a contest to see who'll have the most jewelry."

"No, we just like diamonds" Eva said with a big smile.

"I bet." Aunt Catherine said showing a cheek, so Eva can kiss her. "Good-bye Czarina."

Eva left the library heading out of the house. Daylight was shining, and she hated it. She liked the night.

The car sped down the road as Eva felt relaxed. No emergency was needing her attention. She could relax and go to a sunny island when Aunt Catherine releases her. The Asian connection she'd have to start deciding who to send there. She'll decide while sunbathing on a sunny beach.

Chapter 76

Crowds were gathering in the hotel lobby roped off area. The unlucky ones who couldn't get into the ball room. The patrons of the hotel didn't mind, some liked the attention walking past the crowd. The hotel manager expectant and in control radioed to his security people not to let any more in.

People were gathering for the expected speech from Senator Wellington. He was to speak in the grand ball room. Check-ins for the all-night party would take place after the announcement.

Not a secret that Senator Wellington's interested in running for President. He formed a committee and stated to the news media he was considering a run for that position.

Don stepped off the elevator amazed at the size of the crowd. He saw the manager and approached him.

"I'm amazed at the crowd. I hope it's not a problem. We didn't expect this many people."

The manager looked at Don with surprise.

"No problem, Mr. Wellington. We put more chairs in the room and hopefully nobody's left behind. There're fire safety rules but I hope the Senator will be happy."

"I'm sure he will."

"I have a large screen so people in the lobby will see the speech."

"That's great. The speech is important."

The manager nodded walking away to talk on his radio. More people waiting outside the police were already there. Don was excited. It's going to be a serious event and he's part of it.

Off to one side a news crew was scanning the scene and taping some stock scenes. Don saw the camera with a well-known news logo on it. The female reporter stopped the manager and pointed toward Don. He froze momentarily then continued looking over at the crowd.

The news crew arrived in moments. The lady reporter stepped up to Don.

"Hi, you're a family member of Senator Wellington."

"Yes, I'm Don Wellington Jr. The Senators nephew."

"Okay, Don, would you mind answering a few questions."

"Sure."

"We're going to tape this, do you mind."

"No. Hope I combed my hair." Don said playfully putting his hand to his head.

The reporter laughed saying. "You look fine and relax."

"Okay." Don said watching the woman turn to her camera operator and say something. In moments it was lights, camera, action. Her opening remarks said where she was and who she was going to talk to. She then turned to Don asking. "Don, can you tell us, is this going to be Senator Wellington, your uncle's announcement that he's running for President."

"I believe so." Don said feeling good in front of the camera.

"Don, how do you feel about your uncle the Senator from New York taking a step like this."

"I feel he'd make a good President. He's aware of the issues facing people these days and I know he could help the country as he has with New York. Economy in decline; people losing jobs; military involved around the world where it doesn't belong. I believe my uncle; Senator Wellington is the right man for the challenges we face. He can turn this country around making us proud of being American's again. A beginning."

The reporter didn't say anything. Don looked over at her and she was talking to somebody in her group. She looked over at Don smiling. "I just got word your uncles on the way to the ball room. I want to thank you and you'll be on the news once we edit."

"I thank you also." Don said.

Immediately the lights went out as they moved to the ballroom. Don felt strange with the warmth of the attention gone.

He remained standing noticing few in the crowd were looking over at him. A few moments of fame felt good and this was the beginning. In a year and a half, he'd pick the questions asked and who asked them. He felt on top of the world. He started walking toward the ball room.

Don's cell phone rang, and he was ready to ignore it but, he saw a highlighted number that was his uncle's or someone close to him.

"Yes."

"Your uncle wants to see you right now. Come backstage."

"I'm on my way." Don said as the phone clicked off before he finished.

He walked down a hallway that went behind the ball room stage. Security people stopped him, patted him down and gave him a badge to wear. One of the security people escorted him to a room. A quick knock and Don was under the scrutiny of another security person inside.

Tv's on and people talking. Don just stood looking around when another security type came up to him saying. "Follow me."

Don followed the guy into a dressing room where his uncle was getting a little fixing up for his face by a makeup woman. She smiled at Don and went back to his uncle's face. Just like the movies, Don thought.

His uncle looked at him from the mirror for a moment and then said. "Don. I have people that do my public relations. If asked to answer a question from a reporter, just say no."

He came across gruff as he always does in private. The face lady just went about her business and ignored everything.

"I will. I was just trying to help. I only said a few sentences to make you look good." Don knew his uncle had people everywhere. That's the reason he was questioning here right now.

His uncle's look didn't change. Then said, "be ready in ten minutes. Your Aunt will stand next to me on stage and the rest will be off to the side. When I finish you, all come and form a circle behind me and enjoy."

His uncle in the same gruff manner said. Enjoy, no problem, Don thought.

"Okay."

"Now stay here, backstage until it's time."

"Okay." Don said again and left the room. He walked back into the main room listening to the conversation from the political experts his uncle employed. He found a seat by his younger cousin, Cynthia.

"I hope I look good."

"Yes, Cyn you look great. Half of America will see you and your going to be popular by morning."

"Heard you did an interview. You know my dad doesn't allow us. We must be the happy silent children."

"News travels fast."

"Yea, mom told me."

"Was nothing. I just said a few good lines."

"Hope they air on tv."

"Doubt it. The speech will take the front line."

Then Don thought again and knew his uncle would try to have it erased. With the people he knew, anything was possible.

Don just hoped he makes it to be president because he had some ideas of his own. He wanted to be the person who could erase and take care of people problems.

Almost an hour later they all paraded onto the stage. Don stayed behind his cousins because he was not immediate family. He looked over at the press and media people. They were all there including the lady reporter from earlier. She made eye contact with Don smiling.

Senator Wellington had the crowd in an uproar when the speech ended. Senator Wellington was now a contender for president. Don and his cousins stood around his Aunt and Uncle. He smiled and made it look like they were the all-American family.

Don thought about Bergen's wife for a moment and dismissed it if she did see him on tv. They'll be dead soon, Don thought, smiling for the cameras.

Chapter 77

A delicious dinner as the night before minus the Anton indigestion. His narrow-minded preset notion about the man here in Minneapolis the cause. Joe looked around at Vera, Sevan as they ate.

Anton upheld his end of the deal having the barrels moved. No connection with the warehouse now. Joe smiled when he thought of Anton selling watered down glass cleaner.

He thought back earlier in the day spent with Dave Thompson. Proud to be president of the warehouse and Joe knew he'd have a good running place here. They went over meeting the salespeople to the warehouse and getting confirmation from Dave he would make the changes needed. Joe felt good about Dave Thompson.

Looking at his watch Joe saw it was eight p.m. and where's Anton. He wanted to congratulate him for pulling out of the warehouse with no problem.

Joe realized Ariel had not called back either. The first call made Ariel groan, not a good sign. Joe tired of waiting. He wondered mildly why Anton was late and Ariel had not called. Time to step up he decided.

Joe looked at Vera asking. "We have a direct line to Eva?"

Vera answered. "For emergencies. I cannot guarantee she'll be happy."

"Dial the number."

Vera took out her cell phone and dialed. Obviously long-distance with all the numbers she dialed. She listened and said something in Russian then handed the phone to Joe. Vera smiled.

"Hello Eva."

"No. I get her." Said a gruff voice.

A moment later. "Hello Bergen. Did my warehouses burn down?"

"Ah, no. I'm sorry to disturb you at this late hour."

"It's daylight in Moscow."

"Oh, okay. I called to see if Ariel had called you about Minneapolis and what I proposed."

A moment of silence. Joe wondered if she hung up. "Yes. Ariel called. My answer is yes."

Joe had a surge of emotion. He was going to speak but Eva continued. "I don't know Anton's abilities because I have a mental block for the guy. I guess you see something I don't and will go with you on this one. Sometimes we hate people and don't see the good they can do."

"I've seen the books the real estate and

the guy is running that with expertise. Yes, I feel confident he'll repay, and we can even get a stake in other areas he wants to develop. I see an easy way to make some money for the company." Joe finished wanting to say more.

"Joe, it's your deal. Your neck. I'll have our lawyer go there with papers to sign. If he doesn't pay it back, it'll come out of your pay."

"Sure. I'll pay it back and ring his neck at the same time."

Eva laughed, and Joe felt better. She then continued. "I trust your take that Anton will pay the money-back. I was just joking about your pay. I have enough money."

Joe replied. "I'll make you even more."

Eva laughed saying. "I need love not money."

"I think I should go now and thank you Eva."

"You'll be hearing from me. Bye."

"Bye." Joe closed the phone giving it to Vera. He picked up his fork deciding he was hungry for the dessert. He looked up and saw both looking at him.

"Eva's approved the deal and the lawyers will come.

"That's great." Vera said.

Sevan just shrugged.

"Where's Anton? I brokered him a great beginning. I hope he decides to show up."

Joe talked to his cousin and he had no idea where Anton was. He left a message that if he does not show up or call by noon tomorrow the deal was off. Joe left the restaurant feeling confused. If Anton didn't want this deal, why not just say so.

Later at the hotel, Joe was taking off his jacket and he heard a knock on the door. He went over and wondered what, as he opened the door.

Standing there a lady dressed in fashionable style. At first Joe didn't recognize Mona.

"Hi." Joe said suddenly not feeling tired.

"Hello. You are Joe. I'm Mona. I am a friend of Anton."

"Yes, I remember you." Joe said.

"I have some bad news." It did not register at first then Joe caught himself and said. "Come in, I'm sorry."

Mona walked in with grace of a cultured woman. Taking a seat at the table nook near the window she crossed her legs. "Do you mind if I smoke?"

"No. Go ahead."

Joe sat on the other side watching her light a cigarette. She then looked at him saying. "Anton is dead."

Joe's mind went blank then asked. "How do you know?"

"His fiancé killed him. I supposed to meet him at six and he didn't show. I went around to his house and police were there."

Joe was tired, but this awoke him. "Do you know for sure that he's dead?"

"I have a friend in the police, he told me.

Drunk fiancé found pictures of him with me." Mona said puffing her cigarette.

"What time."

"Between five and six."

Joe heard another knock on the door. He opened to Sevan filling the frame.

"Come in."

Sevan stepped in looking at Mona. She smiled at him.

"Mona tells me that Anton is dead."

"Yes, I just heard. They tried to revive him at the hospital but no-good. The cousin called me."

Joe sat back down looking from Sevan to Mona. Neither showed much emotion.

"Where does that leave me?" Joe said out loud.

"You his employer. Nothing more." Mona said.

Sevan got the next knock. Vera came in and sat on the bed. "I guess you know." Joe asked her.

"Yea, Sevan alerted me." Vera said then continued. "Where's that leave the real estate deal?"

"The family takes it to court?" Joe said.

"His brother Sergi can carry on with the property. He's more honest than Anton and easier to deal with." Mona said.

Joe looked at her then Sevan saying. "I need to meet Sergi."

"I arrange that for tomorrow but, he may not want to talk business." Vera said.

"Yes, they are close. Maybe I can talk to

Sergi to speed deal along." Mona said.

Joe wondered if he had a fiancé wanting to kill him. Then said. "Yes. I need a number for you Mona. I can pay you for your work."

"No money. I'm happy to do it. I'm at fault here and owe you help. I know Sergi and will send any message you want."

"Need him to continue what Anton was going to do on the property. If he feels, he can do it he'll need to sign some papers. If he feels, he can't the family would like to buy him out, quietly." Joe said knowing he was overextending here, but he had to resolve this.

"Understand and will tell him. I do know him and Anton for a long time and I feel he's capable of carrying on." Mona said.

Joe didn't doubt she knew both saying. "I need to meet him at the earliest if he wants to move forward. I imagine Anton was the sole name on the property, so we might need a lawyer. Tell him that."

"The owners are Sergi and Anton. I did their books. Sergi's the owner now. Right of survivorship they signed. Mona said, and Joe liked that.

"Good. Tell Sergi the deal will carry on with him if he wants. He'll deal with the real estate division from CZ Corp." Joe said.

"I'm sure he'll want to carry on with the property. He has same dream." Mona paused then continued. "I was collecting a check from the warehouse. Anton's way of being nice. I have a PHD in chemistry and didn't need the money. I hold a few patents for some chemicals and receive a good income. I'll be the go-between, so you can leave. Sergi will be hurting. He will be at work but hurting inside. He is Russian like me and we carry on even when hurting. So, if you want, I help you."

Joe wondered how an educated lady involved herself with Anton. He then asked. "Did you invest in the real estate?"

"A little. Nothing that will set me back. In time Sergi will pay me or he knows I'll cut his balls off."

Joe taken back a bit regained saying. "CZ Corp. gets first repayment."

"I know business Mr. Bergen. I'll wait for mine. I'm not hurting."

Joe wanted to ask how she got involved with Anton but not in front of Sevan and Vera. He then said. "I see no reason to stay here."

"Send the lawyers and I get this going with Sergi. I also want my money in the future. Like I said, I know the books. There's enough money to build the first property and buy the lakefront and build there. Building expense will come from the profit of the first property. CZ Corp. does not need to send money. I can guide it for Sergi. In fact, payment of one million can start this month. That give CZ Corp. their money in two years. If they do not trust, I can get Sergi to need two signatures for any checks from the company. His signature and someone from

CZ Corp. We can arrange for honesty."

Joe impressed with her business sense said. "Okay. Sounds good. The lawyers will come and see you. Can you get an official title with the company and keep watch for us?"

"I keep watch so I get mine. Anton was slippery. He liked money and invested well but never stopped. Sergi's more straightforward and will do as he says, and, yes, I stay on and watch for you. In the future you do me a favor." Mona said smiling.

"Yes, I will be glad to do you a favor. I don't know if CZ Corp. needs a PHD in chemistry but, I'll ask." Joe said feeling awkward.

"I don't need job Mr. Bergen. I just want friends and want to meet Eva. I maybe can help her business. She will understand." Mona said and Joe did not understand.

"Okay." Joe said looking at Vera and Sevan. "I see no reason to stay. The warehouse's squared away, and we were just waiting on Anton."

Mona went to the desk and wrote her number and address giving it to Joe. He read the name, Mona Molinkolf.

"Okay thank you, Mona."

"I watch for you." Mona said.

"And someday I'll introduce you to Eva."

Joe did not know why but he trusted her. Mona left as the three sat looking at one another. Joe spoke first. "Should I trust her?"

"Yes. She's an honest lady." Sevan said. Joe surprised asked. "Can I ask how you know?"

Sevan smiled. "I'm security and they watched Anton from the day he started at the warehouse. Mona is who she said she is. She has five million in the bank and receives about five hundred thousand every six months for her patents. She won't take off with the company money."

Impressed Joe asked. "Why an educated lady tied in with Anton?"

Sevan smiled again. "He met her when he moved here as a kid. Our information tells us that she's just a friend of Anton's. They grew up together."

"That's weird. A beautiful lady and he gets killed by one who probably had mental problems." Joe said out loud.

"Being she's educated I guess that's why they never married." Vera said.

Joe looked at her and laughed then said. "Not nice. The man was murdered, we shouldn't be talking like this." Joe laughed again.

"You said you want to leave." Sevan asked.

"Yea let's go home. If the police need me, I'll come back. I don't see why they would." Joe said.

Sevan had his phone out and talking. After a few moments he said. "Plane's ready in an hour."

"Good. Let me pack."

"Yes, I need too also." Vera said and left. Sevan stayed, and Joe looked at him asking. "You don't need to pack."

"No, I wear one suit once."

Joe smiled liking that wondering why he wore his many times. Something he needed to think about. Joe caught his thoughts and realized he was tired and started packing.

Chapter 78

The thumping music came through the wall of the manager's office. The nightclub located in a more fashionable section of Moscow attracted a wealthier person. One of few exclusive clubs found there and the Czarina owned it unofficially.

Eva was behind the desk while Tatyana, Uri and Olga were lounging on the leather couches. Mikal was missing due to something that nobody knew of. Max was on a mission that she just heard the results from. It scared Eva knowing that someone could talk a person into killing someone. She wanted to see Max and hear the details.

Uri read news on a PDA device while the other two watched the closed-circuit tv's showing the dance floor. They were laughing at the drunk guy trying his best to dance.

"How's Aunt Catherine." Uri asked.

Eva broke from her concentration saying. "She's good. Wants to sell in Asia. China to be specific."

Eva noticed Tatyana and Olga straighten

up a bit. Uri did not stop reading his PDA.

"Uri, I'm going to shove that up your ass." Eva said getting his attention. "Did you hear what I said?"

"Yea, I heard. Tell me what ports and I'll make some hulls." Uri said with a sly grin.

"Yea, all that easy. I need businesses in place to launder. We can't import drugs and not launder the money." Eva said a little irritated.

"Easy sister. I know that. What're you mad about? I don't know of any businesses there we can buy." Uri said.

"Maybe a few of mine can expand to China." Olga said.

"No, that's osseous. I just don't like setting up shop there. We'll be the outsiders. I don't have a good feeling." Eva said.

"Let them pick up in Europe." Tatyana said.

"No. If they're busted, the questions will be endless. I only see us dealing with people of our own heritage. If we look different, we will stand out and that brings speculation." Eva said.

"Why sell to China?" Uri asked.

"Aunt Catherine wants to expand." Eva said thoughtfully.

"Why don't we put it aside for now. Something'll come along." Tatyana said and everybody looked at her.

"Right. Good idea." Eva said, and they relaxed. "I hear you're back with Mindy."

"Yea, we decided it was nothing of

principle to break up for."

Olga and Uri looked on with serious faces. Eva then said. "We hoped you'd get back together."

"I was. Mindy is a pretty lady and I like seeing her around." Uri said.

"And that's all you'll do is see her." Tatyana said with a sneer to mimic Uri. Everybody laughed. Olga broke in. "Okay, what happened with Anton. I was sort of not told."

"I decided with the good graces of Aunt Catherine to put him to sleep. Anton was too belligerent with his scams. We risked getting busted. Dumbass had Vodka in barrels in the Minneapolis warehouse. May he rest in peace." Eva said with authority.

"What about the real estate or something dad let him do. What's with that?" Olga asked.

"Not bad, money to made there. You see Anton was running a risk of getting busted. Now dad and his warped loyalties were going to let Bergen take the fall if Anton got busted. I don't see the logic there. For one we don't remotely need a bust or law enforcement sniffing around at all. Second, Bergen has possibilities that Anton doesn't." Eva said, and Tatyana nodded.

"Dad's going to take this hard." Olga said.

"He'll survive." Tatyana said.

"Mona we can use." Uri said.

"If she approaches with respect, we'll talk." Eva said.

"I can use her. The lady has a PHD in chemistry and designed that glass cleaner Vodka. That was fucking brilliant. I can use her." Uri said.

"She'll need to work only for us. I've had her checked out and law enforcement does not have a clue about her. Her name's nowhere on their radar. So, we'll see what the future brings." Eva said.

"That's a good first step." Tatyana said.

"Yes, she's going to liaison the real estate for now. And, in time we'll see. Yes, she would be a great asset, Uri. I'm thinking of you but, protocol first." Eva said, and Uri nodded.

"What actually happened to Anton." Olga asked.

"From what I heard his fiancé knifed him. The details I don't know yet." Eva said.

Uri laughed saying. "Remember that South American guy who was Mayor of a town and wanted too much money." Everybody nodded or shrugged. "I asked Max to help. This Mayor was a churchgoing family guy but took bribes from my drug runners. So, it turns out the Mayor liked little girls." Everybody moaned and shook their heads. "Max had pictures taken of him with his favorite little girl. Then got a trusted local who knew the Mayors wife and approached her. They talked for hours looking at the pictures and when the local left, the wife thought her husband was the devil." Uri paused, and they were all looking at him wide-eyed. "When he went home that night, his wife shot him in the head and the groin. She set the house on fire. She's serving life in prison. The new Mayor is happy."

"Anton did little girls." Olga asked. Everybody laughed, and Eva said. "I doubt that. But a devoted fiancé shown pictures of him with another woman could send her over the edge to want to kill him."

Olga said. "Great idea. An accident."

"Yes, dad won't doubt that either." Eva said knowing her favorite employee Joe Bergen wasn't going to be setup.

Chapter 79

The plane began its decent to Newark International Airport and the view of lower Manhattan thrilled Joe. Buildings lit up; it looked surreal. Minneapolis left a bad taste in his mind, but he carried out his goal. A new person was running the warehouse and Anton wasn't a problem anymore. Mona, he trusted though convincing Ariel and Eva of the same remained a question.

The plane touched down and Joe looked at his watch seeing three a.m. he didn't want to go home. He'd be talking to Carol and not getting any sleep. A few hours' sleep and a few tasks later and he'd be home with her.

In few minutes they were in a limousine heading for Manhattan. Vera sat next to Joe not saying much. Sevan in the passenger seat was talking away on his cell phone. Emerging from the Holland tunnel the car maneuvered its way through the streets of New York City. Joe amazed at the car traffic still around at this time of the morning. The city never sleeps, he thought.

A short time later he was heading up the elevator with Sevan. Vera gone home for a few hours to refresh and be back later. Lights dimmed and quiet as they walked through the general area. At the door to his office Joe turned to Sevan.

"I want a wakeup call at seven."

"Sure." Sevan said as Joe entered his office.

Once inside he stood looking at the view of the office towers nearby. Many the floors lit up probably with people working, Joe thought.

He went to the bookcase and opened the door and closed it. He went to the small bedroom and it looked inviting. Within moments he was in bed and slowly slipping away.

It seemed like a few moments later the phone next to the bed was ringing. At first Joe didn't know where he was. He remembered in a flash as he picked up the phone and heard a voice. "Good Morning sir. This is your wakeup call."

"Thanks." Joe said hanging up the phone.

He went from bed to shower picking a suit from the closet. A Brooks Brothers with a silk shirt and tie. A fine suit, he liked the fit. He then remembered what Sevan said. 'Wear suit once.' He'll do that too.

Out in his office Vera was sitting. She looked happy and refreshed with her day planner.

"Morning." Joe said taking a seat behind his desk.

"Morning." Vera said then continued. "Ariel wants to see you when possible."

"Okay, first breakfast." Joe said.

"Eat here or in the cafe?"

"Here."

"I recommend the montage. It's little of everything."

"I'll take it with coffee."

Vera was gone, and Joe called his house. Carol answered on the first ring.

"Hello."

"Hey how's it going."

"Oh, hey good. I'm getting ready to go to the bank." Carol paused then. "I'm thinking new car for myself." She added sweetly.

"I see no problem with that."

"I was thinking BMW." Carol said slowly.

"Sounds good. I'll be home this afternoon. I flew in early this morning and slept at the office."

"Oh, why didn't you come home." Carol said and Joe knew she was pouting.

"Because I wouldn't have gotten any sleep. I'm going to take an early day."

"Cool, how'd the trip go?"

"Ah, the guy's fiancé killed him. I already fired him and had VP of finance taking over. I also arranged a deal where he could keep on developing the real estate. His brother's going to continue. It's a great development. Mansions, trees and solitude. The company's going to receive a nice profit from the venture." Joe said feeling hungry.

"Christ that's horrible. His fiancé." Carol said with harshness.

"Yea, I heard she saw pictures of him with another woman and I guess she went overboard." Joe thought of Mona and decided to leave her out of this.

"I would've just left him."

"Cool, I know I won't be dead." Joe said laughing.

"Just try that and you will be dead. I said him, not you."

"Let's not go there. You know me, and I know you."

"Yes, and now I'm going to look at new cars." Carol said happily.

"Buy what you want. I'll be home later."

"Love you."

"Love you too."

Chapter 80

Breakfast and a few calls later Joe's on the top floor walking toward Ariel's office. Staff seemed friendly as he passed by. A few said hellos and he didn't know who they were.

Joe entered the alcove to Ariel's office as his secretary looked up and said. "Hi Joe, go right in."

Joe opened and walked in. Ariel talking on the phone motioned for Joe to sit. Ariel ended the conversation on the phone.

"Welcome back from the wild west." Ariel said with his million-dollar smile.

"Thank you."

"What the hell happened to Anton." Ariel asked with caution.

"Hell, if I know. The fiancé killed him for cheating on her. I had the deal set. I talked with Eva after waiting for your call. I waited for him at his cousin's restaurant. He didn't show I went back to the hotel and his friend Mona came there and told me the news."

Ariel sat back in his chair. "Mona, yes we

know of her. Very educated and the connection to Anton is a mystery." Ariel perked backup saying. "I also was waiting on the boss call." Ariel said with half a smile.

"Well. I called the boss. Anyway, Anton and Mona were friends since childhood."

"I know that but, people you grew with turn out different and you part ways after a while."

"I know. She's going to get his brother Sergi to sign papers and go with the agreement that I arranged for Anton. She does the books and says they can start paying back money right away."

Ariel smiled. "That's what I want to hear. Sounds like a good lady. What do the houses look like?"

"The place to live if you lived there. Anton had a good eye."

"Now his brother does." Ariel said with a gleam.

"I'm happy being away from Minneapolis, for now. I mean the killing and all. Not a good feeling. I flew back last night." Joe said quietly.

"Understand. Mona's in charge and guaranteeing payment."

Joe took out her number and address and put it on Ariel's desk. Ariel looked a moment.

"She'll stay on until payed back. She also invested a little so it's a personal concern."

"Very good. I'll get the lawyers on a plane tonight. I know the brother may not want to talk business yet, so they'll wait until he's ready." Ariel said with flair.

"Just did what I thought necessary. Funny, I thought Anton would kill himself when I fired him and possibly lose the real estate. A weird situation." Joe said shaking his head and then added. "Oh, Mona would like to meet Eva. Maybe a job or something once the pay back is complete. She has a PHD in chemistry and holds a few patents. Sevan has told me she collects half a million every six months on those patents."

Ariel laughed saying. "Yes, security is excellent here. It's run by Max and he likes to know everything."

"I feel secure knowing that."

"We'll do. Now for Mona meeting Eva. It'll happen in time when she's finished there. They must pay the loan back first. She is responsible for that happening. It's a Russian rule." Ariel paused for a moment then said. "I think if you do the introduction when the time comes it'll be respectful."

"Sure. I can hire her on to work in finance and then do the introduction."

"Hiring her on won't be necessary. It's a Russian rule, again. Introduce then step back. Keep in touch with Mona so you're not strangers when the time comes."

Joe listened then laughed saying. "I'll keep in touch, but I don't want Carol seeing pictures of me with her. She will kill me."

Ariel laughed saying. "I know. That wouldn't be good. I didn't mean that close of friends."

Both laughed as Ariel's phone buzzed. "Yes."

"Mr. Bokanawski is on his way to see you."

"How soon."

"I see him coming now."

"Thank you."

Ariel stood putting his jacket on. Joe also stood fixing his suit. Seconds later a knock and the door opened. Mr. Bokanawski walked in with the air of an owner, Joe thought. "Bergen." Mr. Bokanawski said extending his hand.

"Mr. Bokanawski." Joe said.

"Call me Nick."

"Sure."

Mr. Bokanawski looked at Ariel saying in exasperation. "What the fuck happened. I just got word about Anton."

"Joe was just telling me about it. The fiancé stabbed him. I guess she saw pictures of Anton with another woman."

Mr. Bokanawski took a seat motioning for Joe and Ariel to sit.

"I know the young lady. She comes from a decent family. Why'd she do it? What the hell was Anton's problem. She is a nice girl."

"I don't know. Young people and morals these days." Joe said, and Mr. Bokanawski looked at him asking. "What's with the real estate now?"

"Sergi, Anton's brother is going to carry on. I have a commitment. The warehouse loan will start being paid being this month. It should take two years." Joe said.

"I have no problem with repayment, I know Sergi will pay it back. You talked to him."

"No, I talked to Mona who is or was Anton's friend. She does the books and guarantees it can be paid. I didn't speak to Sergi. I felt it would be not correct being I did fire Anton earlier in the day." Joe said and felt good with that.

"You fired him." Mr. Bokanawski asked in a serious tone.

Joe froze and then started calmly. "I was given permission from Eva and Miss Catherine. Anton didn't change the name over. Salespeople had quit, and he hadn't hired any. He was taking their paychecks and other problems with the warehouse he wasn't taking care of. I arranged for him to keep the real estate and carry on with that business and he agreed having no problem with it. I was to meet him last night at his cousin's restaurant and the rest we know."

Mr. Bokanawski nodded and thought for a few moments then said. "I respect what you had done. Eva and my sister pulled rank and you had to follow, you did well. Now, you arranged for Anton to keep the real estate."

"Yes, I spoke with Eva and she approved that."

"Okay, I see no problem there. I won't doubt he wasn't a good warehouse president, so steps had to be taken." Mr. Bokanawski paused then said. "Joe, you're going to find the women run this business. Much like a marriage. You could leave before it deepens."

"No, I'm here for the long haul." Joe said.

Mr. Bokanawski looked at Ariel and both laughed. Then Mr. Bokanawski said. "It's your call Joe. I warned you. All joking aside, you did what you had to. Anton made a mistake to a good woman, sad as it is."

"Scary shit." Ariel said. Mr. Bokanawski looked and smiled at him like an old friend.

"I was thinking of sending something from XO Food. I don't know if that would be right." Joe said.

"No, send nothing. I'm going there. I must go there. Anton's dad worked for me and lost his life now the son. I need to go there and show my respects and help out."

Mr. Bokanawski stood saying. "Joe keep up the good work. Ariel I'm gone for a while." Mr. Bokanawski walked away shaking his head in disbelief. When he left Joe and Ariel sat back down.

"He's taking it hard. Mr. B loves people. A heart of gold but don't cross him." Ariel said. Joe nodded. "I don't doubt that." He then remembered what Catherine said; he was to answer to her. He knew now that she and Eva are the bosses.

Chapter 81

Later in the evening. Joe climbed out of bed when Carol came back in. "What're you doing?" She asked.

"Going for a drink. That's if you're finished with me."

"Yea, for now. I was just in the garage looking at my baby." Carol said smiling. "

You should've said you wanted a drink. I'll go get." Carol left the room and Joe picked up the tv remote. He scanned through the channels stopping at the news.

Joe heard a noise from down stairs. Carol was in the garage looking at her new BMW. Then the noise of ice cubes at the refrigerator and her footsteps coming upstairs. Into the bedroom she came with a tall drink.

"That was quick." Joe said when she entered the room.

"Yea, I took a quick look at my baby. It's fast and sleek and I love it." Carol said as she handed Joe his drink and curled up next to him. He took a sip, chocked and looked at

Carol. "A little strong."

"Oops, I was thinking about my baby when I poured it."

Joe loved the moment.

"And now I need a new ride."

"Are you sure. We need a house." Carol said.

"Yes, that'll come. I want a Porsche." Joe sipped his drink.

"Cool. We'll both have our dream cars." Carol said smiling.

The commercial changed as they both looked at the tv. It started with taped recording of a celebration in a hotel ballroom. The announcer started amid all the loud cheering and clapping. "Senator Wellington announced his candidacy for President. And you can see the crowd of loyal supporters here." The camera surveyed the room to the stage where Senator Wellington and family were standing. They took in all the excitement waving.

Carol jumped up, she moved closer to the tv and looking closely at the scene. "That looks just like the insurance guy who came here from your buddies' company."

"Which one."

"Guy on the end." She said pointing.

"You're sure."

"Yea, that's him."

Joe squinted at the tv then remembered seeing him somewhere before. He remembered. "Yea, I think I met him at the Mayor's party, he looks familiar."

"Cool, we know someone who's related to someone who's running for president." Carol said and left the room running.

Joe watched her go and he sipped his drink. The family on tv continued waving to the crowd. Joe thought they looked happy. Carol returned with some papers jumping into the bed next to Joe.

"His name is John Thane. A relative?" Carol gave the papers to Joe. He looked them over and at the figures and thought they were good estimates.

"They're some good numbers. I should switch insurance companies."

"No, the name." Carol said and then changed the tv to another news channel. It showed a closer view and Carol nodded. "Yea, that's him."

"Maybe John Thane's a relative of Senator Wellington."

"That's cool, and we know him."

"Well, we don't really know him."

"Oh stop. We know him." Carol said changing channels again and watching the same scene again.

Joe was looking at the numbers thinking he should switch insurance companies. He looked at the tv and remembered seeing him at the Mayors party.

"I might call him when I go back to the office."

"Yea, do that." Carol said smiling.

"It'll be a good friend to know for the long-term."

Carol looked at Joe saying. "We might go places with a friend like him."

"I guess. I just want these rates." Joe said looking at the documents.

"With a friend like him you'll have more business and the family will like you."

"They like me now."

Carol put a sour look on saying. "They want business and more billions. They don't really like you. It's about money."

"No, it's about us adopting." Joe said as Carol sobered looking at him.

"Yes, you're right. I thought you forgot."

"Catherine said she wants us to go to Russia in about two months. She also knows people to speed up the adoption. There and here."

"She did." Carol said slowly smiling.

"And we'll live nicely from the sale of my business. In time, I'll slowly pull away. I realized in Minneapolis that I'm doing the same on a larger scale. The power's addictive though." Joe said smiling.

"Okay, in time. But, make it a long time. They or Catherine is doing us a great favor." Carol said smiling.

"Yes, it's pleasant working there, so, a few years to make money for them."

Carol moved closer saying. "Let's go slow with that. The child I want but let's not be rude."

They resumed looking at the tv and another recording of the happy Senator and family waving to the crowd. Joe watched the man on the end, John Thane. He was causal looking like a decent person, Joe thought.

He finished his drink and put the light out. His hand went under the covers and touched Carol. She giggled and took her nightgown off.

~~~~~

In his latest rental car, Don slowly drove past the Bergen home looking at the shrubs below the living room window. He liked that spot. No lights on in the room. House looked dark.

Don turned right drove down and took another right turn. Slowly driving up that street he hoped to see the back of Bergen's home. Maybe a light in the backrooms. Wrong, Don thought, moving the car up the street to see the back of the house. The properties arrangement and trees made it impossible.

Looking back at the road just in time to brake for a man walking his dog. The man and his dog stared at Don as they continued crossing.

Don put the radio on and continued up the road. The radio announcer did top of the hour's news. The announcer talking fast had Don smiling when reiterating Senator Wellington's candidacy.

The future's in Don's hands. He's going to be somebody, a player. He'll be a power broker. He'll have his own investment business and pick the wealthiest for his customers. First though he must send a message to a certain person.

He swung the car back onto Bergen's street crawling up the road. Going past the house again all was dark. Maybe Joe Bergen was still away on a business trip. Gofer for the Russians. A loser, Don thought.

He looked over at the paper bag on the passenger seat and thought that his little friend would have to wait for another day. Maybe a phone call tomorrow to his Carol and some chitchat would find out when Joe Bergen will be back. Don took a left-hand turn at the intersection and decided to take his little friend home.

Chapter 82

Come morning Joe felt tired and called to let Vera know he won't be in. It's Friday and he decided to make a weekend of it. Carol and himself were lounging in the yard enjoying the day, relaxing.

The grill was cooking burgers and hot dogs. Joe laughed, he could go to any restaurant in the city and eat. He looked down at the barbecue stained newspaper and the picture of Senator Wellington.

Carol came out of the house with his phone. "Eva."

Joe put the utensil down answering. "Eva, hello."

"Hi Joe. How's life."

"Good, I was just taking the day off for a long weekend. Barbecuing right now."

"Sounds cool. I heard about Anton. It's just awful." Eva said trying not to laugh.

"Yes. I'm shocked myself."

"I hear his brother is carrying on with the real estate."

"Yes, I talked to Phil in real estate and he's sending people out with papers to sign. Sort of an after the fact loan agreement for the money owed." Joe paused then said. "Mona does their bookkeeping and says it'll be paid back."

Eva noted Mona saying. "It's sad. That's Anton's dream and it's right that his brother carries on with it." Eva covered a laugh as a cough.

"Yes, I feel good about it."

"I do too."

"Um, this Mona has expressed interest in meeting you. For a job or what I don't know."

Eva smiled knowing that's the first step. "In time. I'm aware of who she is and her education. Let her finish first with helping Sergi. It's a sensitive time right now." Eva needed to change the subject.

"Okay. In time."

"Have you heard of Senator Wellington running for President?" Eva said lacking in creativity.

Joe looked down at the barbecued stained paper saying. "Yea, not really a surprise. Word is he thought of it before but waited for the current President to finish his eight years."

"I hope he makes it. He done good for New York State." Eva said ready to end this conversation and get back to her latest boy toy waiting in bed.

"A funny thing, me and Carol were

watching the announcement speech and she recognized one of the family members. She said he came here when I was in Minneapolis to sell insurance. I think I remember him from the Mayors party." Joe said turning over a burger.

Eva stood holding the phone to her ear saying abruptly. "Are you sure?"

"Yea, I slightly remember him from the party. I believe he said he was an insurance person, and Carol said he came to the house. Mr. Huntington sent him."

Eva nodding yes wanted to hear more. She asked. "Carol's sure."

"Yes. Imagine that we may know the future president. Good for business maybe?"

"It'll be just great." Eva said and froze then said. "Joe, I'll see you soon."

"Sure. Stop and try a burger if you're in the neighborhood."

"It'll take a twelve-hour flight but thank you anyway. Bye."

"Bye."

Joe hung up wondering what it's like being anyplace in the world. He wondered how Eva deals with fatigue.

~~~~~

Eva hung up then dialed Max. When that call ended, she told Ivan to get the plane ready. She was going back to America and Don Wellington was going to die despite her Aunt's wishes.

She went back to her bedroom still in the nude. Looking at the bed and the guy sleeping. Ivan entered, and she said. "Get rid of him."

Ivan grabbed the guy waking him up. He picked him up and threw him into the hallway. Grabbing his clothes, he threw them out on top of the guy. The door closed and the sounds of hitting and cries were heard.

Eva half listened not caring. Joe Bergen's life was in danger and she wasn't going to let anything happen to him. She stood naked and the door opened, Ivan stepped in. "He's gone."

Eva looked at him and he kept eye contact. Not once did he look at her nude body. "I'll be ready in a few."

Ivan nodded and left the room.

~~~~~

In a basement office at CZ Corp. a tech just got off the phone with Max. He printed out a picture from a file and quickly went through the library of footage of Joe Bergen's home. He felt relieved that they just started watching that house and it took five minutes to find the person. He fast-forwarded and froze a still picture of Don Wellington Jr.

The man picked the phone up and dialed. "Yes, it's him. Two days ago." The man hung up the phone and stared at the picture of Don Wellington and waved bye to him.

~~~~~

Back in New Jersey Joe and Carol were finishing their picnic. Sevan came around the back surprising them. "Hi Sevan."

"Hello Mrs. Carol."

"Sevan."

"Mr. Joe."

"I'm not to go to work until Monday." Joe said starting to get curious.

"News reported a house robbery not far from here. I feel better if someone's here."

Joe and Carol looked at each other then Joe said. "There's a few burgers left if you want one."

"No thank you. I'll be in van out front if you need me."

"Okay then. If you need food or the bathroom come in." Carol said.

"Thank you." Sevan said and left.

"Well, the neighborhood is going to shit." Joe said.

"I guess we should look for another house. Sevan dropped off brochures. Every house a mansion with a guard shack." Carol said with a laugh.

"Well, I'm a CEO of a major company and it's needed. Robbers go after the rich."

"I guess we should take one. Someone named Phil called saying the company owns the homes." Carol said smiling.

"Think of the money we'll save."

"Yea." Carol said, and they took the food

into the house.

Chapter 83

The office brightly lit and intimidating with the huge wooden desk and the fireplace to the right. Don has been here a few times but never to his Washington office, he was sure it was just as scary. The credenza had pictures of his uncle shaking hands and smiling with a long list of famous and powerful people. Then on cue a side door opened, his uncle stepped in.

"Hey, you're here. Good." His uncle said plopping down in his desk chair. Don thought the picture was perfect now. The powerful man in the powerful office.

"Yes, I'm using my lunch time and they gave me all afternoon if I wanted. You have made my job easier. Could I get something to eat?" Don said and his uncle did not even show an emotion.

"When I'm finished there's restaurants down the street." This didn't surprise Don because his uncle is always gruff with him when in private.

Don's father was a high-profile

stockbroker and part owner of a big Wall Street firm which Don works minus the name on the building. His mother had taken the buyout from the firm's partners years before and the name came off the building. So, Don grown used to the underdog status.

His father died of a car accident which wasn't bad, but the passenger was a young lady from his brokerage firm. That created a scandal that put Don's mother into a depression for the rest of her life. They shuttled Don from one expensive boarding school to another. Others raised him who thought they knew him but really hated him. Being the only child, they tagged him to be like his father and his uncle was the number one person who believed that.

Don thought his father was cool. He didn't have a chance to know him well, but Don always believed in his father, he created a business and worked hard at it. In contrast, his uncle begged people to like him, so they would vote him into office to represent them. The divide comes when Don thinks how his father and friends bankrolled his uncle to get his first public office and now his uncle shows no respect or a little thanks.

Don figures his uncle thinks he will create an embarrassment like his father did many years ago. The Russian land deal that failed was a contained embarrassment that few knew about and that put a bigger divide between them.

"Now, I want you to stay on the sidelines

during this campaign. Don't take this wrong. I appreciate backing from the firm. That reminds me when I first ran for office years ago. Your father helped me and now you are. But, please just tell any press you have no comment. You know how they can be, they may dig up the past and mention your father to try to get to you. So, just no comment no matter what they say about me. I would appreciate this."

"Sure, I already had a few calls for interviews and declined." Don said with a smile and liked the little edge he had here. His uncle grunted and looked away for a moment. Don then continued. "I'll keep quiet and smile and tell no secrets. I do want to see you be president. You worked hard, and I feel you would be a good president."

Don saw his uncle's eyes brighten for a moment.

"Your dad told me the same many years ago."

"I'm sure he's looking down on us with his girlfriend and saying the same again." Don said as his uncle moved in his chair and putting a sour look on his face said. "I was never a big money person like your father and you. But, where's that sense of humor come from. Do they teach that at the firm? Make millions and anything's a joke." His uncle finished shaking his head.

"No, it helps deal with the stress. The stress of winning." Don said.

"Like investing where you don't belong."

His uncle said with a grin.

Don moved forward and glared then settled back. "Those fucking Russians are going to regret that."

"Calm down. Let's call it even. Forget the other four point five million whatever. They are good friends of mine and they took care of that person. They have told me that it was a big embarrassment to them, and that lady is scrubbing floors in an old Soviet building with no hope of her life getting better."

"Yea, they'll regret it."

"And what the hell you going to do. Have a hack writer do a bad story that nobody will read."

Don held back. He thought of the little brown bag in the vase and came to his senses. He then said slowly. "No. Brian is dead and there are no more hack writers. I mean they'll regret it if they had knowledge of it. If they get ripped off, I look forward to hearing about it."

His Uncle sat back in his chair and let out a breath. "You got to let some things go. People are going to screw one another and yes in time they'll get screwed. Glad to see your getting over it and forget the rest of the money. I'm going to have my tax returns, and everything examined closely now. So, to save anything from turning up, you've paid me."

"Well, thank you. I'm six months away from the rest. I guess I'll have money to invest now." Don said with a slight smile.

"Yea and keep it in America. I'm campaigning and the world's watching."

"And your Russian friends will keep it quiet." Don asked in a sour tone.

"Yes. Like I said they apologized and its history that will never become known. In fact, I got more support from them and money." His uncle leaned forward on his desk speaking quietly. "If I'm president, we'll all make out, the rest of our lives. Leave the little shit behind and look forward."

Don took that feeling good. The best his uncle ever told him. That's what Don wanted, guarantees he'll get something.

"Understand. I'll let it go."

"You'll have the family name back on the firms building. That's what I want to see for you. You're like your father, brilliant with money. You deserve the honor."

His uncle leaned back in the chair looking kindly at Don.

"Thank you. I dreamt that since being offered work there. And I want his picture hanging back up."

"It'll happen. We now need to watch everything we do. Don't give the press anything to write about. Now, I'm going to start a tour of the country and probably won't see you for a while. I just want you to know that this is for our family. I'm not just running for president, I'm taking our family to a new stature and we will all benefit."

"Understand. I can help with your financing dept. No point having donation money just sitting there. I can get you ten to twenty percent a month return that may buy more air time."

"I'll have my people contact you. I look forward to the help. Squeeze the pennies, get me air time." His uncle beamed with pride.

"That's easy. I'll put it in the overnight money markets, short-term paper, that'll have ads leading to your arrival in any state." Don said with a business air.

"Thank you, Don. Your father did the same for me and I won my first election. He's gone but I have his brain here in you."

"Hey, we all benefit with a winner. The money goes with the winner."

"And don't worry about the Russians, they know I can benefit them greatly by being president. Relax the immigration a little, lower the import taxes. Don't worry about them."

His uncle came around the desk and shook hands. He walked Don, to the door.

"Don't worry about money. I'll make sure it follows and keeps up with you."

"Thank you, Don."

They stepped into the outer office. His uncle telling his secretary to give Don the phone numbers of the finance dept. of the campaign.

Don looked at the names and knew some of them. Accountants who don't take risks. Maybe he'll have a cabinet position. The thoughts ran through his mind as the elevator descended. One thought he couldn't shake were the Russians.

He thought about that party at the mansion. The red head Eva was the center of attention. One of her girlfriends came to him and they used a bedroom. Sincere conversation of life in Russia and the opportunities there. The phone number and the fast trip there and then handshakes with fast-talking men in suits.

Don knew he couldn't let that go. They took something from him, and he'll take something from them. Their new CEO of the food business.

Chapter 84

The day had ended with many interviews and great general interest in Senator Wellington from everybody. Now to take time with his latest female friend.

Rebecca came into his life a few years ago. She a volunteer that helped with his last campaign to keep his senate seat. An easy win but he played it as scary to win the attention of Rebecca. He liked her from the moment he met her. The soft appearance and easygoing personality. He also liked that her husband was killed in a car accident and she was left a wealthy woman. He always liked good looks and money. She was the right woman for him to recharge on the campaign trail. He called her and asked her to join his campaign for president and she agreed. He had her watched and checked out and knew the lonely widow would do anything for him.

Senator Wellington got up from the bed yawning. "I need to get going. I have a morning interview. The press won't stop."

"When president you can stop the press." Rebecca said in her French accent.

"No, I will tell them when they can bother me." The Senator said with authority and continued. "I'll get Congress to pass tougher laws for people who drink and drive. That I can tell them to do."

"Yes." Rebecca said looking away for a moment trying not to laugh. Her husband didn't die in a car accident from a drunk driver. The mob in France killed him as a favor to the Czarina. She had to turn her husband in when he started to lose it. He oversaw a large company there and the government money laundering investigation was getting to him. The Czarina didn't know that until Rebecca told her. She loved her husband, but she loved the life the Czarina could provide even more.

"I will do that for a friend like you. I'll see that we have the toughest laws of any country in the world." The Senator said with a proud smile.

"I just don't want to see that happen to anyone else. It's horrible."

"We can't stop people from doing what they like. The right laws in place people will think carefully before walking out of a bar and driving."

"I understand." Rebecca said wondering what was going to happen. They told her this was the last time she's going to see this man as he is. Rebecca thought he was a good lover for an old man and a friend. His friendship doesn't compare to the friendship she has with the Czarina though.

The Senator went into the rest room and Rebecca wondered why the Czarina didn't like him. She met her once and found her enchanting. The knowledge and control are magical. She was enjoyable, and Rebecca felt she was an old friend. A guardian angel, watching and protecting.

She's happy being with this old man. She's happy also because she wanted to see what was going to happen. After whatever happens she'll go back to France for a time to see some old friends and family. Her younger sister's going to have a baby and she wants to be there.

The Senator came out of the rest room and Rebecca thought he was pale looking. She won't be suspect since he is a Senator and word of a lover in a hotel room wouldn't be good. Besides she's well trusted by him and his people. Rebecca did not like the nephew though.

"Gotta go." The Senator shook his head scratching his chest. "Damn indigestion, happens every time."

"Take some medicine. I don't like when you leave me in pain." Rebecca said aware that something was happening.

"Pain's not from you. I leave you happy as I came." The Senator said then laughed at the joke he made. Rebecca wrinkled her nose smiling.

"Bye Bec." The Senator said opening the

bedroom door. His security guy was waiting.

"Bye my friend."

The Senator turned giving a fake smile. Rebecca noticed his bodyguard asking if he was okay. The Senator and his pride said he was fine. She knew it was starting and did not know what but, she knew the time has come.

Rebecca thought to a little over a month ago when shopping for shoes and approached by a nice old lady. She said she was just a messenger for the Czarina. The message being her secret friend wasn't going to be around much longer. The Czarina appreciates her loyalty. Rebecca treasured those words because she knew them to be true and not just a statement. She knew sometime in the future that a great gift will come her way.

Rebecca and the old lady talked for an hour. She told her what her and the Senator do and where they go. The old lady told her to do the same and do nothing different. Something's going to happen, and Rebecca shouldn't worry.

Rebecca rose putting a robe on. She went into the outer room as the Senator and his bodyguard left. He gave her one last glance and the bodyguard smiled also. She thought the bodyguard was nice, he always treated her good, but he was too young for her.

Now the last thing they that told her was to stay put at the hotel for a few days like she always did. Security people for the

Senator will return and ask her to leave and go somewhere. Yes, Rebecca said to herself, she'll go to France.

She decided on a shower to wipe away the old man's sweat for the last time. Hoping that whatever happens will be fast because she longed to go back to her villa. She liked sitting on the veranda sipping the wine that comes from the grapes on her property. Sunshine and wining away the time.

Chapter 85

Don's phone rings.

"Hello."

"I'm calling from Senator Wellingtons office. Senator Wellington has fallen ill and is at the hospital." The bland voice said.

"Can you tell what hospital?"

"The Bethel."

"Thank you." Don said hanging up before she could reply. A cold bitch calls me instead of his Aunt.

Don looked at the grocery bag and placed it on the counter next to the refrigerator. It was late, and his uncle went to the hospital. Probably nothing but he needed to go. The old guy never got sick, Don thought. He should go and show himself.

The great Senator's ill. He prided himself on working seven days a week for the people. Hospital. What does that do with his bid for President. He goes down so does my dream, Don thought.

He looked at the grocery bag deciding to

leave it there. It's safe and Bergen will live for another day.

Don put his jacket on and left the apartment. Riding the elevator down he knew the news cameras will be there. Show concern and play it down.

~~~~~

A taxi drive by the hospital was as he figured. A multitude of tv cameras and reporters. He dropped off on the corner and began walking to the front. "Aren't you a relative of the Senator?" Came a voice. "Do you know the Senators condition?" Another asked.

Don stopped at the door saying. "We would like a little privacy right now. I do not know the Senator's, my uncle's condition. Once I know the family will issue a statement."

He then walked inside showing his ID and security took him right up. The elevator ride took forever, and they got off on the intensive car floor. Don didn't like this. One of the Senator's security people took him over to the waiting area. The man looked sad, Don thought.

In the sitting area he saw the same sad look on his family's faces. A few tears in some eyes. They looked at him no different than if he was a bum on the street. He saw his mother and wondered why she was here. Seriously. Don sat next to her.

"Hi mom."

"Donny." She said wiping a tear away.

'What happened?"

His mother looked away already tired of telling the story. "All we know is he was going home from his office and he started to breathe heavy and collapsed in the backseat. His security team brought him here. Doctor says stroke but not sure how bad." She began to cry again, and Don looked off in the distance.

A stroke means paralyzation and speech problems. Regular doctor visit and still it happened? Don could not believe he might be brain-dead. He expected him to come bounding out of one of the rooms smiling and barking orders.

Don got up and walked over to sit by his cousin Amy. "What happened, Am?"

"He was rushed here. That bitch from the office called like I was a campaign donor. I just got here, I heard it happened a few hours ago."

"Yea, me too."

A doctor came walking in the sitting area. He went over to Don's aunt. She was sad and as the doctor spoke, she went from sadness to outright crying. It must be bad Don thought. He never knew his aunt to show emotion expect when eating.

The whispers started with the sounds of oh my god. Don's other cousin came over and sat next to Amy. She glanced at Don and said nothing. She spoke to Amy. "It appears he had a massive stroke. They can detect no brain activity. Not good."

Don listened to that and he felt his heart sink. His world was over. His uncle would not be president. He would not have his own investment firm. He'd continue working at the same place and hear his coworkers whisper he's half the man his father was. They would say his uncle never had a chance.

Don sat there trying to find a bright spot in all this, but he couldn't. His Uncle's healthy. Don knew this. He remembers hearing his uncle say that his Doctor said he had the health of a thirty-year old, last year.

Looking off in the distance; anger starting. The Russians. They're low enough to do something like this, Don knew.

The room started filling with sobs. Don couldn't cry and wouldn't cry. He pictured that grocery bag exploding in front of Joe Bergen's house for starters. Then that red-haired bitch was next. He would take the rest of his life if he had to, but he'd get her.

Chapter 86

Across from Don's apartment in another expensive residential building a security team sanctioned by Max Bokanawski waited. The apartment bought long ago to keep a watch on Don Wellington Jr. High-powered digital cameras and listening abilities pointed at the apartment. That is, in the visible rooms, in the bedroom or den they lacked visual surveillance.

Team leader saw Don leave five minutes before. The news breaking that his uncle was in the hospital. They knew it was an opportunity to get inside his apartment since word came that he might try something. Getting past the desk security wouldn't be a problem. Friendly's in the building will let them in. Team leader waited and received the phone call Don was at the hospital. The team went into operation mode.

The team's search experts left walking across the street to Don's building. A man and women dressed like a night on the town. He in an expensive suit and she in elegant dressings. They entered and approached the desk. The security person right away suspected nothing and looked as if he understood who they were. "Good evening." The desk security person said.

"Hello. Can you ring Mr. Robertson. He's expecting us. We're Mr. and Mrs. Jennings."

The desk security nodded punching a few buttons on the phone. He spoke softly.

Mrs. Jennings said. "The news about Senator Wellington sounds horrible."

"Yes, I hope he can still run, who else can we vote for." Replied Mr. Jennings.

Desk security listening rolled his eyes. "Mr. Robertson is expecting you. Please use one of those elevators."

"Thank you."

They lifted to the twentieth floor and exited off. They knew no cameras were in the elevator or the hallways. The apartment owners voted that down. They returned and descended to the fifteenth floor.

They walked to the fourth door numbered fifteen zero five. The man put a key in the lock opening the door. One last look, up and down the hallway before entering the apartment. They put on lights going to the living room. The lady made a signal with fingers at the window. To alert team leader watching from across the street of their penetration. The man put a headset on that connected to a wireless network they used.

He spoke. "Going into the den."

The lady followed. Looking around

cautiously. The man moved some papers on the desk then picked the desk lock. He searched all drawers finding nothing. He spoke into the headset. "Leaving den, nothing."

"Entering bedroom." They searched around finding nothing.

"Leaving bedroom, nothing."

"Entering guestroom."

That lasted about half an hour and found nothing. One room left. "Entering kitchen."

The man and women searched the cabinets, stove and refrigerator. The kitchen took longer because of foodstuffs needing to be checked. A miniature handheld metal detector helped quicken that search. Both saw the plastic bag on the counter and didn't believe it suspect. They just moved it and kept looking for that hidden something. They finished the kitchen looking at each other with slight confusion.

Being experts at their job they didn't believe that nothing menacing was here. They always found the hidden object. Like pointers on a summers' day after the shot. They once did a job in Chicago at a high-ranking police detective's house looking for the payoff list. He was collecting money and certain people thought it best he retires. They spent nearly an hour and found hidden behind an old photo of his mother the list. It showed the people he was getting payoffs from. That finding retired the detective and promoted one the family preferred.

Finished searching they visually surveyed around slowly. They never spoke when inside a place doing a job. It heightened their senses.

She stared at the bag on the counter. The man just waved a hand to dismiss it. He had looked in it when he first entered the kitchen and saw a receipt on top a half gallon of milk. The lady slowly took the receipt out and read it. A big smile came to her face. The man looked at her then the bag with the milk container. Taking out his detector and waving it over the container light bars lit the top of the scale.

She slowly removed the half gallon out of the bag placing it on the counter. She looked at the man who just smiled and motioned for her to open it. She opened the glued folds. Spread the opening wide and looked down with a smile. She gently pulled out a wooden box and opened the lid. The smile went off her face. The man stepped forward and his smile also went away. Inside they saw the bomb. Not what they expected. They were sure a pistol with no serial number, not a bomb. Regardless the smiles returned. They knew they found the evidence.

The lady went to work. She put the box down gently and lifted her dress to thigh high. The man whistled. She gave him the finger and unstrapped a slim box and placed it on the counter. She opened and choose the tool for the job.

Chapter 87

Eva restless couldn't concentrate on anything. The movies and books didn't entertain. She slid to a window seat looking out at the blackness of the night. The jet engines noise bothered her. If anything happened to Joe Bergen, she would never forgive herself.

Ivan stepped over smiling. She looked up at him.

"Bomb found and neutralized. Max has given orders to let him follow through and grab him on the way to Bergen's."

Eva slowly smiled digesting the news. Her anguish went away, and her stomach stopped hurting. She relaxed and looked back up at Ivan. "Tell Max I want him. I want that fucker."

Ivan went back to the front on the satellite phone. Eva watched and knew she should alert Aunt Catherine. After it's done, though. She didn't want her Aunt stopping her on this.

Chapter 88

News of Senator Wellington spread around the world. No major headline since presidential election's almost a year and half away. Most people just shrugged it off knowing he probably didn't have a chance in hell.

The Czarina watched in her library on a huge LCD screen. She watched the program showing pictures of the Senator with a brief biography. He was looking old, she thought. It's been a few years since she saw him.

He a bright smiling Washington D.C. person that came after the Berlin wall fell. Like most they all came to see what's behind that iron curtain. Beauty and the beast, the Czarina thought. Real life was behind the griminess.

The Czarina laughed at the thought of how her and her brother thought they were doing well at the time. They feared the fall of the iron curtain at the time. A blessing in disguise. It allowed them to buy plenty of businesses to keep their money invested;

first step. The second came when they saw the illegal drug business open in the newly freed countries.

They already had a system of funneling illegal products to the black market that was secure. But, when they put illegal drugs into the line, the profits grew. They grew larger than one could ever dream. Life's still getting better every day.

Then seasoned Senator Wellington comes to Russia in the early nineteen nineties. The Czarina remembers how he held a meeting and invited all business owners to meet big money people from New York. Big money people told business owners the need to keep up with the world. Allowing partners. Sell stakes in your businesses and they'll grow. Your products will sell in the United States.

A few followed the big money people and were pushed out of their businesses. The Czarina and her brother set up shop in America and Europe. They had the big three, Russia, Europe and America. They were setup to launder the drug money. They did not want partners. They didn't need partners. They liked being low-key in the business world.

Then the threats from the big money American people started. The FBI raid on the New York offices but nothing illegal found. They searched the real estate division. Nothing wrong found so they moved onto every division. They tried to get help in

Europe from Interpol to examine there but, they declined. They also tried to get the Russian government to search the Russian offices. They refused them. The FBI kept up the pressure until a new president's election and the investigations stopped. Terrorists were the new targets.

The big money people gave up due to their jobs being in question. Senator Wellington then stepped out of the shadows to make friends with her brother. The Senator decided that donated money from CZ Corp. would be a big help. Being the big money people, he was using, started to have difficult times. The sands shifted, and her brother now the new friend of the Senator. The Czarina encouraged her brother to keep good ties with Senator Wellington though they knew the Senator was the problem to begin with.

As the years went by the Czarina and her brother keep good relations with the Senator. She gave him a world-class visit whenever he came to Russia. She didn't like him in the least.

There's a day when she took him to one of the Czar's palaces and he commented that it was a failed past. The Russian people should tear down those palaces and sell the property. He also said the current government was heading down the wrong course and would end like the Czarist regimes. He hinted again that she should open her businesses to American investors, but the investigations were long over, and he wasn't a threat. The Czarina saw the weakness coming to the tiger.

That was the last time she saw him in person and that was a few years ago. In that time the Russian government grew stronger and kept out the foreign powers with their ideas of owning a big piece of Russia. Too bad the nephew didn't know that, the Czarina smiled. He helped the Czar's palace restoration with ten million of the family's money. Starting with the one Senator Wellington stood in years before. The Czarina smiled broadly.

The TV showed the Senator's pictures again. The Czarina looked at them seeing a weak tiger. He didn't raise a family that could have protected him. The Czarina did. She had plenty of strong wolfs keeping her safe.

Chapter 89

Don returned to his apartment and turned the news on. There's shock and grief and he's pissed. The thirty-second clip of him earlier at the hospital showed his few moments of fame. It disgusted him the way the news reporters played like they liked his uncle. He picked up a figurine from the coffee table and threw it. The figurine shattered against the wall. Looking at the shattered pieces he knew that was his life.

The team leader sat forward in his chair and then made a call on his cell phone. His eyes on the camera monitor.

Don went into the kitchen and looked at the grocery bag. He picked and put it into a cabinet slowly closing the door. He took a beer from the refrigerator and looked at the clock. Almost three a.m.

He walked to the den looking down at the map laying there. The circle on Joe Bergen's house. He sipped beer and from the living room he listened to the announcer say:

"Senator Wellington is gravely ill."

Listening to that he kept looking down at the map with hatred in his eyes. He was impatient and getting angrier. Dark outside and inside.

The hospital didn't tell him anything new except the same, no brain activity. He knew there's a high-priced doctor that's able to bring people back from that condition. The American government does not allow such stuff, Don thought with a sneer on his face looking out the window down to street traffic below.

The time's dragging as he walked into the kitchen taking the grocery bag out from the cabinet. He took the milk container out but didn't want to open it, he knew what it looked like. She's beautiful. A device that will change his world. He bagged it carefully. Opened the refrigerator and looked at the beer. Not another, he thought and closed the door.

In the den he decided to get going. The map of Bergen's house into the shredder and then deleted all stored documents in his computer. The clock showed three thirty a.m. and it was as good a time as any he thought. He'll drive there in a rental car he got earlier in the day and place the bomb in the shrubs. Set timer for ten minutes and be a few blocks away. After explosion a slow drive back. All will be good, Don thought.

Then the anonymous email to CZ Corp. To let them know that somebody is after them, he thought and smiled.

In the bedroom Don put on an old pair of jeans and sweatshirt. The old sneakers he would toss out tomorrow. There was no rush because nobody knew he was doing this, and nobody would come looking for him.

Time's three thirty-seven; it'll take an hour to get there. Then the return trip home at daylight.

Don took the bag and tied the plastic handles. He smiled walking through the living room to leave.

Across the street team leader was telling everybody it was game time. He watched Don leave the building and walked down the street to a car. The team leader had the car make and license plate recorded earlier. He was not going to put a gun to his head for a failed mission.

Don pulled into traffic and the team leader watched as four of his people were right behind him in cars. They reached the end of the block and the team leader got ready to leave. He had his own people waiting for him in an SUV that's going to follow from a distance.

Earlier in the day somebody placed a G.P.S. emitter so they would not lose his trail. There were five different ways he could get to Bergen's house and each way had people waiting in trail cars.

Besides the G.P.S. emitter another man slipped under his car at another time planting a unit that'll cut the fuel line to the engine. They'll trigger it when Don's on a lonely strip of road. A car stopping at the right moment to lend a hand and capture.

The team leader thought of the tail cars. Each had harmless looking male and female. All carrying needles. A quick jab and sleep.

The team leader didn't know why the change in plan. Bullet to the heads easier. A phone call earlier in the day said he must be alive; then park his car near the Hudson river with whiskey splashed over the inside. The team leader didn't mind the change in the plan. He still had a boat waiting to dump the body in the ocean.

The team leader boarded his SUV and it took off. In the backseat a lady watching the G.P.S. They weren't far behind. The team leader loved doing these missions. He remembers meeting the Czar and his life has been good since. A dream he didn't want to lose.

The team leader asked. "How long."

"Judging the traffic, forty-five minutes."

"Backup's ready."

"Yes, rocket launcher ready if he slips through."

Team leader grunted. They want him alive, but mission would still be completed though. He wouldn't have failed, the team leader thought nodding. It'll be blamed on terrorists. He knew, Don wouldn't make it to the house.

"Okay, car one, three and four and two are following him over the George

Washington bridge."

"Good. Now which of five directions is he going to take." The team leader said. Already dreaming beach property in California with the five million he'll be getting.

Chapter 90

Joe relaxing on the couch thought a new house would be delightful. A mansion in the hills of New Jersey. He turned the channel on the tv.

Carol came flying into the room. "Wanna fly to Florida for the weekend."

"Sure. I'll call and get the jet ready for the morning." Joe said with pride.

"You think they'll mind."

"No, that's a standing right I have. Let's live."

"Cool."

"I looked, and Sevan has a camper out there." Joe said smiling.

"They're protecting us. I think a new house will help him."

"Yea, we need to help Sevan."

Joe stood looking at Carol. "Let me call and have the plane ready. Eight a.m.?"

"Perfect, I'll get on the Internet to find a hotel in Miami."

Carol stood, and both hugged and kissed.

Chapter 91

Midnight a day later an SUV stopped at an old warehouse in Newark, NJ. Eva eagerly looked out the window happy finally to be here. They parked next to SUV's and a car.

Ivan spoke into his cell phone then closed it. Two men emerged from the building Ivan was out of the SUV. He opened the back door and Eva stepped out. The two men came forward extending their hands. Eva shook both.

"This way." One man said, and Eva followed. The other man walked behind, and Ivan followed. They entered the building and both men lit up led lights.

Eva followed through an old office area. Smelly and well beyond useful as a business. A few steps further into the huge warehouse. Footsteps echoed as they walked. Ahead was a bright light pointed on a man tied to a chair. As they got closer Eva could see him, Don.

The man stopped at a makeshift table. He

picked up a box. Eva looked at it.

"Plastic explosive bomb. Powerful enough to destroy a house killing anybody inside." Eva held the bomb in her hand amazed. First time she ever held one. Handing the bomb back she walked to the man in the chair.

"Hi Don Wellington, you remember me." Eva said smiling looking forward to a reply. "Fuck you."

"Okay, fuck you too." Still smiling

"Fuckin red-haired bitch."

Eva thought for a moment then said. "The latest on your uncle is he'll never regain. He'll be brain-dead forever. And eventually dies."

"Fuck you." Don said slurring his speech.

"Bet your tired and hungry. It's been twenty-four hours and you must wanna go."

Don stared at Eva.

"Could let you go. Don't feel right keeping you here. I mean we did your uncle and that's joy enough."

Don's sneer disappeared.

"Yea, he was easy. You met Rebecca. She's a friend of mine. She told us everyplace and everything your uncle liked to eat. She even told us how he ejaculated in five minutes. With that we just salted his food with a chemical that makes blood clots grow and oh my, he had a stroke. I guess we put too much in."

Don's mouth hung open.

"Yes Don, we're what's called Russian mafia. Yes, we took your money and waited to get your uncle. Why? Because we wanted to. He tried to hurt us, and we mafia people don't like that."

Don looked down on the floor.

"That blond lady you dated. Took her to the In Out club about two months ago. That club I own. The coke you snorted, I imported it. You both went to your apartment and fucked for ten minutes. You then went to the kitchen and got two beers."

Don looked up at her.

"Yea Don. I know and control and love it. CZ Corp. A huge money laundering business. I know you thought we were mob and you were right. I'm the largest importer of drugs to Europe and America."

Don put a sneer on his face.

Eva leaned closer. "Your friend Brain. Caught em trying to sneak onto my dad's property. It was a birthday party and we hooded him and shot him in front of two hundred people. Nobody believed it was real. We then had his body scattered everywhere."

Don kept sneering at Eva.

"You thought getting Joe Bergen would be easy. I guess you learned a lesson. Now, if I let you go will you tell anybody."

Don's sneer faded a bit. Eva walked over to one man whispering something then walked back.

"Don. I want to let you go. I feel bad about your uncle. Would you tell anybody if I let you go?"

Don blank stared shaking his head no.

The man returned whispering to Eva. She nodded and giggled. Immediately four men grabbed Don and cut the ropes. They stripped him down and held him on the concrete floor. Eva stepped into the darkened area. She came forward moments later dressed in Doctor greens with mask. With clippers in her hands used for small gardening.

"Don. I need you to tell me that you won't tell anybody."

They were holding him down on the floor as Eva knelt next to him. She pulled on cobalt micro flex surgical gloves. Don looked at the cutters in her hand. "I'm waiting Don."

"Won't tell anybody." Don said in shaky voice.

Eva said gracefully. "I don't believe you Don." She then looked down between his legs saying. "Looks awful small. I make it smaller."

Eva grabbed his penis put it in the clippers and using both hands cut it off at the base. Took more effort than she thought. Don screamed wriggled trying to break loose, but it was no use. When he settled a bit, Eva said. "I want you to tell me again that you won't tell anybody."

"Won't tell anybody." Don screamed. Eva took his penis and put it to his lips. Don turned his head. A man grabbed his head and held it up. Eva put the penis on his lips saying. "Kiss your dick. Then I might believe you."

Don sweating struggling mentally kissed it. Eva and the men laughed. Then placing it on Don's stomach She said. "I still don't believe you."

Eva went to work on the remaining parts between his legs. Using both hands and grunting she finally cut them off. He yelled bucked wriggled to no use. She placed them on his stomach. "You look like a girl now," Eva said humorously. Everybody laughed. Don in extreme pain knew he'd never be the same. It's over.

Eva looking at him asked. "I want you to tell me again that you won't tell anybody." Don just wriggled saying nothing. Her voice in a distance place.

Eva grabbed his left-hand snipping off the thumb. She needed effort to break the bone but liked the sound. Don screamed and screamed. Eva snipped and snipped. Another finger; more screaming. She did this until left hand was empty of fingers. She had to flex her hands because the strength needed made the muscles hurt.

She then went on to his toes. Piling them up in a pile and her hands ached. When she got to his right hand something happened. Don's head turned to one side and his body fell limp. A man put a hand to Don's chest and then shook his head.

Eva sat on the floor and put down the clippers. Looking at dead Don she said. "Was going to let you go but you died."

Eva shook her head saying. "Shit happens," with a laugh. The men let go of Don's body and enjoyed a good laugh. She held a hand out and a man helped her up. She brushed off her bottom saying. "Get rid of him."

"Yes, Miss Eva. Boat's waiting and he's shark meal."

"Ivan, my bag."

Ivan left then came back with a briefcase. He placed it on the table and opened it. Inside was stacked with money. Eva walked over motioning for the men to come over saying. "A little bonus."

The men nodded and said thank you. Eva looked at all of them with a smile saying. "The Czarina thanks you."

To leave comment email:
ms@mikeseigler.com